I've left my common sense back in England.
Elizabeth hadn't meant to confide in Haverford, hadn't meant to disclose her past. The dratted man was like no kind of aristocrat Elizabeth had met—or kissed—before.

Haverford was trying to convince her he was a lazy kisser, but he was lazy like a prowling lion, bringing infinite patience and focus to his advances. His lips moved over Elizabeth's in gentle brushes, and she scooted closer, the better to grip him by the lapels.

He came closer as well, spreading his knees, and sliding a hand into Elizabeth's hair. *His kisses were lovely.* Tender, teasing, maddeningly undemanding.

"I want—" Elizabeth muttered against his mouth. She took a taste of him, and his every movement, from his breathing to the susurration of his clothing, to his slight shifts on the hassock, stilled.

"Again," he said. "Please."

Elizabeth liked the sound of that, liked the feel of the word *please* spoken against her mouth. And as the kiss deepened and became a frolic followed by a dare, punctuated by a challenge, she rejoiced.

I was wrong. I was so very, wonderfully wrong. All men weren't inconsiderate louts. They weren't all monuments to self-satisfaction. At least one man could kiss and kiss and kiss....

HIGH ACCLAIM FOR GRACE BURROWES

THE TROUBLE WITH DUKES

"The hero of *The Trouble with Dukes* reminds me of Mary Balogh's charming men, and the heroine brings to mind Sarah MacLean's intelligent, fiery women...This is a wonderfully funny, moving romance, not to be missed!"

—Eloisa James, *New York Times* bestselling author

"*The Trouble with Dukes* has everything Grace Burrowes's many fans have come to adore: a swoonworthy hero, a strong heroine, humor, and passion. Her characters not only know their own hearts, but share them with fearless joy. Grace Burrowes is a romance treasure."

—Tessa Dare, *New York Times* bestselling author

"*The Trouble with Dukes* is captivating! It has everything I love in a book—a sexy Scotsman, a charming heroine, witty banter, plenty of humor, and lots of heart."

—Jennifer Ashley, *New York Times* bestselling author

"Exquisite writing, outstanding characters, a gorgeous romance, and a nail-biter of an ending. *The Trouble with Dukes* is the definition of a perfect historical romance!"

—Fresh Fiction

"Readers who enjoy Tessa Dare will embrace...this affecting and clever tale."

—*Booklist*

ALSO BY GRACE BURROWES

The Windham Brides Series

Too Scot to Handle

The Trouble with Dukes

NO OTHER DUKE WILL DO

WINDHAM BRIDES #3

GRACE BURROWES

FOREVER
New York   Boston

Copyright © 2017 by Grace Burrowes
Preview of *A Rogue of Her Own* copyright © 2017 by Grace Burrowes
Cover design by Elizabeth Turner
Cover illustration by Chris Cocozza
Cover hand lettering by Jen Mussari

Forever
Hachette Book Group
1290 Avenue of the Americas, New York, NY 10104
forever-romance.com
twitter.com/foreverromance

First Edition: November 2017

Forever is an imprint of Grand Central Publishing. The Forever name and logo are trademarks of Hachette Book Group, Inc.

The publisher is not responsible for websites (or their content) that are not owned by the publisher.

The Hachette Speakers Bureau provides a wide range of authors for speaking events. To find out more, go to www.hachettespeakersbureau.com or call (866) 376-6591.

ISBNs: 978-1-4555-7001-0 (mass market), 978-1-4555-7000-3 (ebook)

Printed in the United States of America

OPM

10 9 8 7 6 5 4 3 2 1

To the librarians!

ACKNOWLEDGMENTS

Some books do pretty much write themselves. This was not such a book. My dear readers have heard me muttering on social media for months about The Welsh Duke, and what an obstreperous, challenging fellow he could be, despite the size of his...library, *and* his vast stores of subtle charm. I am indebted to my editor, Leah Hultenschmidt, for inspiring me to persist in befriending this dragon of a hero, because his story was well worth telling. Turns out, he's my favorite duke so far, and not just because of all those wonderful books he has so fiercely protected behind his castle walls. Leah, your patience isn't always rewarded, but it is appreciated.

Readers, I commend Julian, Duke of Haverford, to your keeping now—yours and Elizabeth Windham's!

GEORGE WINDHAM *d.* m. **AGATHA DRYSDALE** *d.*
The Duke of Moreland   The Duchess of Moreland

EUSTACE *d.*

ANTHONY
m.
Gladys Holsopple

PETER *d.*
m.
Arabella

ELIZABETH
m.
JULIAN
featured in
No Other Duke Will Do
BOOK 3
WINDHAM BRIDES

CHARLOTTE
m.
LUCAS
featured in
A Rogue of Her Own
BOOK 4
WINDHAM BRIDES

MEGAN *m.*
featured in
The Trouble With Dukes
BOOK 1
WINDHAM BRIDES

Kathleen St. Just ·········· *affair* ·········· **PERCIVAL WINDHAM**
The Duke of Moreland
m.
ESTHER
The Duchess of Moreland

Their Graces: The Courtship
PREQUEL 1

BARTHOLOMEW *d.*

VICTOR *d.*
legal marriage?
Guinevere Hollister
m.
Douglas

**DEVLIN
ST. JUST**
m.
Emmaline
Farnum
featured in
The Soldier
BOOK 2
WINDHAM FAMILY

GAYLE
The Earl of Westhaven
m.
Anna Seaton
featured in
The Heir
BOOK 1
WINDHAM FAMILY

VALENTINE
m.
Ellen Markham
featured in
The Virtuoso
BOOK 3
WINDHAM FAMILY

WINDHAM *Family Tree*

JAMES MACHUGH *m.* SUSAN MALCOLM

HAMISH

ANWEN *m.* COLIN

featured in

Too Scot to Handle

BOOK 2
WINDHAM BRIDES

ALASDAIR

ANGUS

MAGNUS

RHONA

EDANA

.... *affair* .... Cecily O'Donnell

The Duke And His Duchess

PREQUEL 2

MAGGIE
m.
Benjamin Portmaine
featured in
Lady Maggie's Secret Scandal
BOOK 5
WINDHAM FAMILY

SOPHIE
m.
Vim Charpentier
featured in
Lady Sophie's Christmas Wish
BOOK 4
WINDHAM FAMILY

EVE
m.
Lucas Denning
featured in
Lady Eve's Indescretion
BOOK 7
WINDHAM FAMILY

LOUISA
m.
Jos. Carrington
featured in
Lady Louisa's Christmas Knight
BOOK 6
WINDHAM FAMILY

JENNY
m.
Elijah Harrison
featured in
Lady Jenny's Christmas Portrait
BOOK 8
WINDHAM FAMILY

AUTHOR'S NOTE

In my literary wanderings, I happened upon the illustrious doings of Arthur Annesley (Angelsey in some spellings) who had the good fortune to participate in the Restoration of the English monarchy under Charles II. Arthur, who'd been a mere viscount previously, was granted an earldom by a grateful king. What did Arthur do to remark his improved circumstances? He bought books, of course! At the time of his death in 1686, he owned some 30,000 volumes, which his heirs—who must have been daft—subsequently sold. There is much more to the family tale (Arthur had 21 siblings), but that number—a personal collection of 30,000 books—caught my eye.

That is some To Be Read pile, readin' buddies. That is, in fact, a TBR collection worthy of a duke...and thus did our Welsh dragon—I mean duke—seize upon books as the object his family chose to hoard.

Happy reading!

Chapter One

"STOP TRYING TO CHEER me up, or I'll call you out."
Julian Andreas Cynan Evan St. David, twelfth Duke of
Haverford, wanted to blast away at *something*, though the
Marquess of Radnor, being both a dead shot and Julian's
dearest friend, made a poor choice of target.

"Are you upset with your sister for the expense this
house party will cause," Radnor asked, "or for the number
of eligible young ladies you'll have to partner at whist?"

"Dukes do not become upset. If you continue nattering,
you'll frighten the fish away."

Radnor made an elegant cast into the middle of the
stream. "Haverford, if it's a matter of coin—?"

"Do you *want* me to blow out your brains, Radnor, assuming even I could hit a target that small?"

Radnor's line dipped, then bowed down. Julian gathered
up his rod and maintained a respectful silence while the
marquess did battle with a trout intent on putting a presuming aristocrat in his place.

The morning was lovely as only Wales in spring could be lovely, the hills Eden-green, the sky full of fluffy white clouds—lamb clouds, Glenys used to call them—and the breeze scented with freshly scythed hay.

The valley was coming into its most impressive verdure, and of course, Glenys had timed her house party ambush to show off the estate as well as her older brother.

Radnor swung his line from the water, and Julian took up a net. He snagged the thrashing trout and held it up for the marquess to admire.

"Fine specimen," Radnor said, setting his pole aside. "Though I'm sure we have larger fish in my ponds at Radnor Hall."

"Larger perhaps, but not with more fight." Julian gripped the trout about the back and eased the hook free. The fish wiggled in his grasp, fighting to the last, its mouth moving in a desperate effort to sustain life.

"He'll make a lovely addition to the table—what the deuce, Haverford! That is my fish."

Julian tossed the trout back into the water, and it was off downstream with an indignant swish of its tail.

"We have enough," Julian said, nudging a wicker basket with his toe. "That one earned his freedom, while I have tarried here as long as I dare. Glenys expects me for the midday meal, and then I must meet with my land steward."

"I accept your invitation to dine," Radnor said, reeling in his line. "To do otherwise would leave Lady Glenys to endure a tongue-lashing at table, which thought my gallant nature shudders to contemplate."

"Your gallant nature wants to brag about your success as an angler."

Radnor was being kind, ensuring Julian would have an ally when Glenys maundered on regarding her plan to end

Julian's bachelorhood. Radnor meant well, Glenys meant well, the damned trout had probably meant well, drat the lot of them.

Julian had his own plan for ensuring the succession, and according to that plan, hunting for a duchess would begin in approximately eight years and seven months, assuming no radical fluctuations in market conditions occurred.

A costly, pointless house party did not figure into his plans *at all*.

He and Radnor walked in silence toward Haverford Castle's back terrace. The prospect across the gardens was lovely and should have been soothing. Unlike many titled landholders, Julian had not ripped up his ancestors' formal parterres to replace them with an artificial—and astronomically expensive—wilderness landscape. His gardens were old-fashioned, and a duchess would consider redesigning them just one of the exorbitant projects she was entitled to undertake.

The indignant trout came to mind, thrashing his heart out to preserve his freedom.

"The young ladies invited to this house party will exhaust themselves trying to gain my notice," Julian said. So would their mamas, if the gathering ran true to tiresome form. "Glenys will also have to invite a suitable number of bachelors. That suggests I can turn the gathering to a more worthy purpose."

"Where young ladies gather, there are also chaperones, widowed mamas, and other delights. Is that the more worthy purpose you refer to?"

"Your imagination suffers a sad want of variety, my friend."

"A sad want of variety characterizes your social life," Radnor countered. "You're suggesting that Lady Glenys's attempt to find you a duchess will end in her ladyship's own engagement?"

Radnor was a quick study, for all his cheerfulness. "Precisely. Glenys should have chosen a husband five years ago." Though how much more bleak would the past five years have been, without her company and good humor?

"Lady Glenys will doubtless have a score of offers by the end of the first week," Radnor said. "No man with any sense tarries in London during the heat of summer, and the daughters of dukes—much less lovely, sensible, gracious daughters of dukes—are rare marital prizes."

Julian ignored the wistful quality of Radnor's compliment, just as Glenys ignored every flirtation and lure Radnor pitched at her.

"My sister will have offers, and I shall ensure one of them is the right offer. The solution is clear: We must make a list."

The marquess stopped and set the end of his pole on the ground. "Not another list."

"Organization and determination have bested many a challenge," Julian retorted, without breaking stride. "Glenys has sent out her invitations. I'll simply send out a few of my own."

On the remaining half-mile hike to the castle, Julian suggested names, all of which Radnor took exception to. This man was a gambler, though handsome. That one had a solid fortune, but no sense of humor.

"Why don't you offer for her?" Julian asked, as they approached the back of the castle.

"You are hopeless, Haverford. One doesn't offer unless the lady has expressed a desire for one's company. I'm Lady Glenys's spare project. When she tires of managing you and Griffin, she manages me. It's…sweet and vexing as hell."

"Rather like marriage, I suppose."

The sweet part was tempting. Julian was thirty-six years old, and yet the dukedom could not at present afford a duchess. She loomed in Julian's future as a reward for years of hard work and self-discipline, and by God, he would choose carefully and well when finances permitted him that indulgence.

Across the back terrace, a table had been set for the midday meal. Lady Glenys occupied one of three chairs beneath the white canopy, and busied herself arranging a pot of daisies in the center of the table.

"If you think to distract me with a picnic, Glenys, think again," Julian said, brushing a kiss to her cheek. "We are not through discussing this house party of yours."

She shared the height, dark hair, and swooping eyebrows that had been a hallmark of the St. Davids for generations. Her eyes were hazel, while Julian's were green, and this for some reason made her jealous.

At present those hazel eyes were turned on him in a transparent facsimile of innocence. "Dock my pin money, if you must, Haverford. I am determined to have my way in this, and nobody is more determined than a St. David. Radnor, apologies for mentioning finances before a guest."

Nobody was more determined than a St. David *duke*, but even he couldn't put on a respectable house party with mere pin money.

"Now I'm a guest," Radnor said, bowing over Glenys's proffered hand, "after having run tame in this castle since I was in dresses. I'm onto your tricks, my lady. You're summoning half the unmarried women in England to fawn over your brother, when in fact, it's my matrimonial prospects that will be imperiled. Not well done of you."

Glenys snatched her hand back, pink staining her cheeks. "Haverford, please dispense with those fish. Elfryd, see to the sporting accoutrements."

The footman stationed by the buffet stepped forward to take the rods and the wicker basket holding the morning's catch. Julian washed his hands in the basin provided, and Radnor did likewise.

As Julian reached for a towel, Radnor flicked water at his face, a taunt they'd been exchanging since childhood. Julian passed Radnor the towel rather than retaliate.

They weren't boys, and would never be boys again.

Over beef pastry and mashed potatoes, Glenys launched into a discourse on the best preparation of estate trout for a buffet. The topic left Julian bilious. If Glenys had her way, he'd be hooked, landed, and filleted by the conclusion of her infernal party.

He complimented her ideas, and mentally refined the list of bachelors he'd recruit to distract her ladyship from her matchmaking. He also created a sub-list of young ladies who might suit Radnor, who had depths beyond his charm.

Lists, plans, budgets, and unwavering attention to detail were slowly but surely bringing the Haverford finances to rights, and they would see Julian through this farce of a house party as well.

He would make sure of it.

* * *

"Shoot me," Charlotte Windham moaned. "Please, if you have any love for me at all, take out the coach pistol and end my torment."

"I could read to you, Charl," Elizabeth Windham replied from the coach's backward-facing seat. "Everybody is taxed by long journeys."

Charlotte sprawled on the opposite seat, one foot braced on the floor, one hand on her middle. "I am not taxed, I am dying. Why did nobody warn me that the roads in Wales are instruments of torture?"

Elizabeth put her copy of *Childe Harold* aside. "It's not the roads making you ill, it's probably the ale you had at the last inn."

Charlotte was pale, dyspeptic, and had stopped to visit the bushes three times in the last five miles. Thank goodness, bushes were in generous supply in this part of Wales. Aunt Arabella had chosen to ride in the second coach with the ladies' maids, so that "poor Charlotte" had room to stretch out on the bench.

"I look a fright," Charlotte said, "and I feel worse than I look. A lady isn't supposed to perspire, much less cast up her accounts, much less—dear God, have we arrived?"

The coach had turned up a long drive shaded on both sides by towering oaks. In deference to Charlotte's condition, progress was stately.

Haverford Castle was—unlike many buildings referred to as castles—splendidly regal. Crenellated turrets stood at either end of a golden façade five stories tall, and the circular drive curved around a fountain that sprayed water twenty feet into the air. Potted salvia adorned a raised front terrace and circled the fountain, creating red, white, and green splashes of color against the stonework.

"Haverford owns all this?" Charlotte asked, sitting up to peer out the window. "Moreland isn't half so grand."

"Moreland is probably two centuries more modern. You're at death's door, so what do you care?"

"I feel a miraculous revival coming on," Charlotte said, straightening her skirts. "Or I might presently. Ye gods, I shall never drink another drop of ale."

The coach lurched forward, and Charlotte's pallor became more marked.

"Lie back down," Elizabeth said. "The bushes are disobligingly sparse along this drive."

Charlotte subsided to the bench. "I'm to be humiliated before all of society, dragged from the coach in a state of obvious ill health. Perhaps I will die in Mama's homeland, and out of guilt, Papa will grant you the spinsterdom you long for."

"Spinsterdom is not a word. If you die, may I have your mare?" Perhaps teasing might hurry along Charlotte's miraculous recovery.

"Cousin Devlin has prior claim on my horse. You may have my jewels."

"You have the same pearls and pins I do."

Charlotte put her wrist to her brow. "I yield my entire treasure to you. Please have the coach circle around to the back of the castle. I cannot appear before the most eligible bachelors in the realm looking like some cupshot chamber maid."

Vanity was a reassuring sign when a sister professed to be expiring. "I'll get you up to a bedroom, and nobody will think you're anything but travel weary."

"I must write to Mama of the foul brew served to the unsuspecting in her homeland. Rest assured the Welsh bachelors have lost ground in the race to offer for my hand. Such misery would never befall me in England."

As the coach lumbered along the drive, Elizabeth made out a sculpture of a rampant gryphon at the center of the fountain. Bright afternoon sunshine combined with the fountain's mist to create a shimmering rainbow over the creature.

Maybe Mama was right when she claimed that Wales was enchanted.

"We're almost there, Charlotte." Despite the magical fountain, Elizabeth felt nearly as dyspeptic as Charlotte appeared. House parties were the consolation rounds for debutantes who'd failed to secure a marriage proposal during the season. For Elizabeth, house parties were a special purgatory.

A woman who remained unmarried despite a decade of seasons wasn't quite a spinster, but she was so far from a debutante as to be a different species of female altogether.

The coach swayed to a halt, and Charlotte pressed a wrinkled handkerchief to her lips. The vehicle rocked as footmen climbed down, then the door opened and the steps were unfolded.

"I suppose I must move," Charlotte muttered.

"I can have the footmen carry you," Elizabeth replied. Charlotte was nearly gray about the mouth.

"Oh, the ignominy. Dragged to the door like some hapless sparrow in the clutches of a tomcat—"

"Our hostess approaches," Elizabeth said, rising to accept a footman's hand. "I'll explain, and you'll produce a ladylike swoon."

Technically, Lady Glenys was their host's unmarried sister, though thank a benevolent providence, nobody had to explain Charlotte's malady to Haverford himself. Dukes, in Elizabeth's experience, did not deal well with life's most unglamorous realities.

A delicate bunch, dukes. Marquesses and earls weren't much sturdier.

"Miss Windham." Lady Glenys bobbed a curtsy. "I've

been anticipating the pleasure of your company in particular. Are Lady Pembroke and Miss Charlotte with you?"

"Charlotte is somewhat the worse for the journey," Elizabeth said. "Her digestion has grown tentative over these last few miles. Our aunt is traveling in the second coach."

Charlotte peeked out, gripping both sides of the coach door. A hapless sparrow would have been more attractive than the pale, bedraggled creature blinking in the bright sunlight.

"My heavenly stars," Lady Glenys said. "You poor dear. I am so sorry you're feeling not quite the thing. We'll have you up to your rooms in no time."

Charlotte tottered from the coach, a footman assisting on one side, Elizabeth on the other. "I'd curtsy, but I've no desire to end up face down on your cobbles."

"Hush, dear," Elizabeth murmured, as Lady Glenys took a step back. "We'll simply follow her ladyship into the castle, and find you a nice, soft, *private* place to settle yourself."

The footmen stepped away, hands behind their backs. Lady Glenys looked torn between distress and sympathy, and Charlotte hung heavily on Elizabeth's arm.

"Can you walk to the door?" Elizabeth asked.

Charlotte glanced up at the crenellated façade, her expression grim. "If I must."

Why would nobody offer aid? Grooms held teams for two coaches and a landau behind the Windham coach, while Lady Glenys wrung her hands.

"Come along," Elizabeth said, tucking an arm around Charlotte's waist. "It's not far, and you're a Windham."

Bootsteps crunched to Elizabeth's left, and then Charlotte's weight was plucked away.

"Allow me to aid the lady," said a tall gentleman in

riding attire. "I apologize for presuming, but I'm guessing a bad batch of Merlin Jones's summer ale is to blame. Lady Glenys, which bedroom?"

He smelled of horses and hayfields, his boots were dusty, and his dark hair was less than tidy. Charlotte's rescuer had the steady gaze of a man who solved problems with common sense and hard work. He held her as if striding about with a full grown woman in his arms was part of his daily routine.

"Take her to the east tower," Lady Glenys replied. "Both Miss Windham and Miss Charlotte are in the Dovecote."

Charlotte looked to be enjoying her first convincing ladylike swoon.

"Miss Windham," the man said. "If you'll join us?"

He had green eyes framed with dramatic dark brows, and his expression held no flirtation, no suggestion of humor at Charlotte's expense. Sober and steady when sober and steady were desperately needed.

"My thanks," Elizabeth said, falling in step beside him. "Who is this Merlin Jones?" *And who are you?*

"He's the innkeeper at the nearest coaching inn, and known to occasionally mix up a bad batch of summer ale. Because he serves the suspect brew only to those traveling on, he's not held accountable for his mistakes."

Charlotte's rescuer spoke with the lilting diction of the educated Welshman, and even carrying Charlotte up a grand curved staircase, his strength was not taxed. Something about the angle of the gentleman's jaw suggested Mr. Jones would be held accountable this time.

"The Dovecote is one of the tower suites," he said. "The views are lovely, and you're close to both the family wing and the guest wing. If the apartment is not to your liking, I'm sure Lady Glenys can see to other arrangements."

He was local, then, a neighbor, cousin, or close friend of the family. Was he a guest at the house party?

"I'm sure the accommodations will be fine. Charlotte, how are you feeling?"

"A little better," she said, lashes fluttering. "What a lovely castle."

"Haverford Castle can be cold as the devil's root cellar in winter," the gentleman replied. "This is your suite."

He carried Charlotte straight into a circular chamber graced with three windows. The walls were more than two feet thick, the plaster a mellow cream. A lone red rose stood in a crystal vase on the sideboard.

The gentleman set Charlotte on a tufted sofa and regarded her, his hands on his hips. In his dusty boots and with a streak of dirt on one sleeve of his riding jacket, he might have been a steward assessing a heifer gone off her feed.

"Fresh air, I think," he said, wrestling two of the windows open. The latches screeched in protest, but the breeze was heavenly. He knelt before the sideboard and opened a cupboard. "At the risk of being indelicate, you might also need this."

He rose, holding a porcelain basin painted with daffodils.

"At the risk of being pathetic," Elizabeth replied, taking the basin, "we thank you. You are very kind, sir."

Though not exactly proper. Why didn't the fellow introduce himself?

"Haverford is known for its hospitality as well as its library," he said. "Shall I send the housekeeper to have a look at you, Miss Charlotte? I must warn you that some of her remedies bear results that make Merlin's bad ale look like meadow tea."

"I've brought a few tisanes," Elizabeth said. "Charlotte will come right with time, quiet, and rest."

Charlotte's ailment also provided the perfect excuse for missing the first night's buffet, a cheering thought when *Childe Harold* was the alternative.

The gentleman bowed. "I'll leave you then, ladies. A footman is on duty at all times at the top of the main staircase, and will alert the kitchen should you need anything. Welcome to Haverford."

Elizabeth dipped a curtsy, and then took the place beside Charlotte when the gentleman had quietly closed the door on his way out. He was a handsome specimen, in a mature, un-fancy way.

A bit short on charm though. "Shall you live, Charl?"

"I've been carried to my boudoir in the arms of a duke," Charlotte said, flopping against the back of the sofa. "I'm not sure I can bear the strain such an honor has put on my maidenly nerves."

"*That* was His Grace of Haverford?"

Charlotte began unbuttoning her cuffs. "I stood up with him for a minuet three years ago. Doubtless, he'd be pining for me still if he'd bother to recall the occasion."

Elizabeth set the basin on the low table. "I am certain you've been his elusive dream all this time. What sort of duke fails to introduce himself?"

"One focused on aiding a damsel in distress. I was truly having a bad moment. Did you bring any peppermint tea with you?"

Alas for His Grace, if Charlotte was more interested in peppermint tea than the duke's manly attributes.

"Mama sent along practically everything but henbane and eye of newt. I'll find a footman to fetch us hot water and a tray. Do you suppose the bedroom is up those stairs?"

Steps curved along the portion of the wall that lacked a window. Like the furniture, chandelier, sconces, and upholstery, the bannister was in the elegant, refined style of the last century.

"I'll have a look," Charlotte said, "but unhook me and unlace me before you go, lest I expire for want of air."

Elizabeth obliged, then went in search of a footman. Upon inspection, Haverford Castle was all of a piece, its decorative scheme reminiscent of the grander styles and more elaborate flourishes of a bygone era.

Plaster cherubs smiled down from intricate molding, old-fashioned Sèvres vases held single blooms in the occasional windowsill. The floors were polished wood, which was fine for keeping down the dust, but doubtless contributed to the castle's winter chill.

All very orderly and understated, of which Elizabeth approved. She was orderly and understated herself, on her good days. Though when she considered what she'd seen of the castle and what she'd seen of its owner, she admitted that this house party hadn't started off like any of the others she'd endured.

No bowing, fortune-hunting bachelors, no effusive greetings from women who secretly wished Elizabeth to the Antipodes merely because Papa was titled.

But one handsome, healthy duke with green eyes and a practical streak. What a pity Elizabeth hadn't met him ten years earlier, when she'd still believed fairy tales could come true somewhere other than the pages of a storybook.

Chapter Two

"THE WOMEN ARE MULTIPLYING like spring lambs in Dorset," Julian said, scowling down at the guests assembled in the courtyard. "I vow Glenys showed me only half the guest list."

Radnor sauntered over to the window. "Ladies bring their maids, chaperones, sisters, and companions, so one lady turns into three, like the loaves and the fishes. To some fellows, that's one of the nicer aspects of these gatherings."

"This has become a refrain with you. We both know that I will not be marrying any of these women."

Julian was in the ducal sitting room, enjoying the last few moments of privacy before joining the crowd on the back terrace. The terrace and the central court connected through an arch in the castle's southern wall, and guests were strolling about like so many sheep waiting for somebody to bring them fresh fodder.

A shriek went up as two young women charged each

other, arms flung wide. This display was followed by synchronized air kisses and more public effusions.

"In all of Papa's lectures and exhortations," Julian said, "he never once warned me about the ladies of polite society. I received endless admonitions about drink, gambling, the crown, the church, the tenants, and even our dear neighbors, the Sherbournes, but never did he instruct me regarding the ladies."

Julian spoke in Welsh, which he'd not do with even Radnor if other titles were within earshot.

Radnor turned him by the shoulders and fluffed his cravat. "And how does the abundance of feminine pulchritude below challenge a man of your consequence?" he asked in the same language.

"I haven't sufficient *charm*," Julian said. "Not enough for the demands of that entire platoon of females."

Radnor held up a gold cravat pin tipped with an emerald. The gem was not of the first quality, but nobody would notice unless they were examining Julian's attire from very close range and in good light.

"Hold still lest I stab you through the heart before Cupid has a chance." Radnor situated the emerald near the center of Julian's lacy cravat.

"Cupid had best aim his arrows elsewhere." Julian examined Radnor's efforts in the vanity mirror. "You always get it off center."

"And you always fix it," Radnor replied, as Julian moved the pin a quarter inch to the right. "So you aren't charming. You're a duke. Being a duke beats being charming any day or night. Even I have trouble being charming to Delphine St. David, though. How on earth did she get onto the guest list?"

Julian gave himself a final inspection. His sartorial

tastes were considered old-fashioned, tending toward heavily embroidered waistcoats, and cravats and cuffs on the lacey side. Tonight's waistcoat had begun life as one of Grandpapa's formal court coats, back before the late king had lost his wits. At Julian's instruction, the castle seamstress had salvaged the exquisite embroidery, thus saving money while providing a touch of financial revenge on a profligate ancestor.

"Delphine is family," Julian said, returning to the window, "and she's dangerously bored. I could no more keep her away from a gathering like this than I could...I forgot to introduce myself."

"Have you been at the brandy already?"

In the courtyard below, Miss Elizabeth Windham and an older lady had joined the guests enjoying the walkways.

"I cannot afford to be at the brandy," Julian said. "I forgot to introduce myself to the Misses Windham earlier today."

He'd nearly forgotten what it was like to be around a lady who didn't simper and flutter at everything in breeches. Elizabeth Windham wasn't a classic English beauty—red hair prevented that cliché from befalling her—but in her quiet composure, she was attractive.

"It's not like you to forget who you are," Radnor observed. "Which one is she?"

"Miss Elizabeth Windham is the redhead near the dragon." The redhead with the tidy figure and calm blue eyes.

"You'll have the next three weeks to remedy your oversight. She's not a debutante."

Miss Windham hadn't been a debutante for some time, another point in her favor. She'd also been genuinely concerned for her sister, which was impressive considering the behavior of many young women when making the acquaintance of a bachelor duke.

"She and Glenys might be of an age," Julian said. "And there's a younger sibling along, Miss Charlotte Windham, also red-haired and beyond the silliest years."

"Lady Glenys was never silly." Radnor produced a silver flask. "Care for a nip?"

"I'll be meeting most of my guests for the first time, bowing over countless hands, and running the gauntlet of chaperones and companions, and yet you suggest I have strong spirits on my breath."

"You never know," Radnor said, tipping the flask to his lips. "If you display a fondness for drink, you might have fewer debutantes popping out of linen closets at you."

Julian swiped the flask and took a sip. Excellent brandy produced a quiet warmth that would fade all too quickly. "My thanks. What do you know of the Windham ladies?"

"The two young women are Moreland's nieces." Radnor pushed the curtain aside and peered down at the courtyard. "Lord Anthony Windham, the duke's brother, has four daughters. One daughter recently married a Scottish duke, another daughter married the duke's heir. Miss Elizabeth and Miss Charlotte are the older two and nearly on the shelf."

"If Elizabeth Windham is on the shelf, why will my window bear the imprint of your nose when you quit this room, Radnor?"

"Because Sir Windy is standing too close to her," Radnor said. "One must not turn one's back on Nigel Windstruther when a pretty lady is about."

"All the ladies deserve respect and protection. Pretty ought not to matter."

Though honor did not require that a man ignore feminine beauty. The words that came to Julian's mind where Miss Windham was concerned didn't relate to physical attributes, though, but rather to the intangibles.

She was gracious, sensible, steady, *settled.* Julian's first impression of her had been that she would have taken half the day to escort her ailing sister abovestairs if necessary, no hurry, no self-consciousness about their progress.

Elizabeth Windham was a woman who'd stick to her plans, and sensible plans they'd be, too.

"Good God," Radnor said, taking another sip of brandy. "Now Hound Dog is on the scent."

Viscount Haldale—Hound Dog being his *nom de guerre*—spent his fortune mostly on soiled doves and hunters, or as the wags said, on mounts and being mounted. Haldale joined Miss Windham, Sir Nigel, and the older lady, bowing elaborately over the hands of both women.

"We'd best get down there." Radnor put his flask away. "What were you thinking when you invited those two, Haverford? If Lady Glenys allows either of them so much as a dance, then her judgment is not to be trusted."

"Lady Glenys will dance with all of the bachelors, just as I will stand up with all of the debutantes. Haldale and Sir Nigel came with sisters, with whom I will also dance."

"I daresay you'd sound more enthusiastic about having a tooth drawn," Radnor muttered, leading the way toward the door. "You'll frighten all the poor little dears, and I'll have to charm them out of returning to London by post."

"You must not exert yourself on my behalf," Julian said, taking Radnor down the footmen's stairs, which saved time and offered privacy. "It does occur to me—merely in passing—that you are in want of a wife, and one of my lovely guests might willingly fulfill that office."

"If you start matchmaking, Haverford, our friendship is quits."

Julian paused before opening the ground-floor door.

"Likewise, I'm sure. However, when you are overtaxed by the ladies' demands, then you shall remove to Radnor Hall, claiming the press of business calls you away."

Tuck tail and run. The best plans were often that simple, though Julian's plan—be a gracious duke and endure the next three weeks—struck him as a bit too simple.

"Thank God for the press of business," Radnor said, pushing the door open. "You will please introduce me to Miss Windham."

"You aren't already acquainted?"

"I was probably introduced to her ages ago, but a woman with blood that blue can forget even a handsome, witty, charming, single marquess when it suits her."

"Modesty, however, makes a lasting impression. You should give it a try. Is Miss Windham an heiress?"

Not that her financial circumstances mattered, of course.

"I'm sure her settlements are respectable." Radnor gave Julian's cravat a flick, so the emerald was clearly visible amid the lace. "But her dowry should be a matter of utter indifference to a duke who took a vow of chastity when he turned thirty."

"I took a vow of prudence when Helena Mulbridge claimed I'd trifled with her when I was a mere lad of nineteen." The memory still gave Julian nightmares, while his father had laughed uproariously. "Miss Windham's enviable connections and her poise will doubtless result in the bachelors bothering her without mercy."

While Julian would admire her from afar.

Radnor paused before a pier-glass and smiled at himself.

"Too bold," Julian said. "Try for more élan."

"Élan? What the devil has élan—? Like this?" Radnor put some eyebrow into it, and a hint of humor in his gaze.

"Much better. You'll frighten every woman under the age of fifty. About Miss Windham?"

"Rumor has it that Lord Anthony is mad to fire her off, especially now that two younger sisters have scampered up the church aisle. I fancy a bit of maturity in a woman."

"Opposites attract, I suppose."

Radnor was damned good-looking. His dark hair had a Byronic curl, and his eyes were a warm brown. He was kind, funny, tolerant of human foibles, and no fool. When the right woman came along and made an honest marquess of Radnor, Julian would miss his friend.

His lordship set off at a more decorous pace. "Scoff all you like, Haverford, but if the object of this exercise in extravagant hospitality is to find a husband for Lady Glenys, then the sooner Miss Windham is spoken for, the more chance you have of seeing your sister married off."

"So when you drool all over Miss Windham's bodice, you'll be doing me a favor?" Julian asked, as they stepped out onto the terrace.

The image of Radnor fawning over Elizabeth Windham had no appeal. None at all.

"Just so. I'm a marquess. The other fellows will retire from the lists when they see that the lady has earned my favor. No need to thank me. What are friends for, after all?"

* * *

"I counted forty-two carriages," Griffin St. David said. "That's a lot of carriages."

Biddy kept kneading the bread. Biddy liked to knead bread, and that was good, because Griffin loved to eat it, especially with butter and jam.

"Forty-two is a lot," she said. "Hadn't you better be at

your studies, Master Griffin? His Grace will come around again, asking what you've learned, and you won't want to disappoint him."

His Grace was Julian, though Biddy never called Griffin's older brother anything except "His Grace," or "the duke," or "his worship." Griffin did not want to disappoint Julian, ever, but Biddy was wrong. With all those carriages up at the castle, Julian would be too busy to visit anytime soon.

"Why did so many carriages go up the drive, Biddy?"

She smacked the dough hard, which was to make certain the bread baked up without holes. Griffin used to help her make bread—he was very good at smacking the dough—until Abner had explained that making bread was women's work.

Women grew vexed if men stole their work and left the ladies feeling less than useful, according to Abner. Griffin suspected Biddy had different views on the matter.

"I couldn't say what all those carriages are about, Master Griffin. Can you tell me any new stars?"

Griffin knew the stars well enough, and liked to lie on his back in the garden and talk to them. "You know all the ones I know. I've never seen forty-two carriages before."

"That is a lot, though why they're at the castle, I could not say."

Biddy didn't want to talk to him. She was seldom cross, but when she said the same things over and over, she didn't want to talk anymore.

"I'm going for a walk," Griffin said.

She left off punching the bread dough. "This evening might not be a good time for a walk, Griffin. Looks like rain to me."

The evening sun shone brightly, and the clouds weren't the kind that brought rain. Biddy was telling a fib.

"This *is* a good evening for a walk. I didn't take a walk this morning, because I hoped Julian would visit, even though he hadn't sent his card. Then he paid a call on me. Now I want to take a walk."

Biddy wiped her hands on her apron, which got flour all over it. "You can't go up to the castle now. They have company there."

Griffin took a pinch of dough. Soon the kitchen would smell wonderful, and then the fresh bread would taste wonderful. "They have lots and lots of company. I counted forty-two carriages."

"If there were two people in each carriage, how many people would that be?"

Biddy was trying to distract him from taking a walk, and for a moment, that would work. Griffin could not do large sums in his head, but he loved sums on paper.

"I will solve that riddle, then take a walk," he said. "I want to see the carriages, Biddy. I won't pay a call. I know a gentleman doesn't pay a call without sending a card first. Besides, I'm not dressed for visiting."

Biddy had to tie his cravat when he went out socializing, because he could never get the fancy knot right. Julian was very good at fancy knots. When Glenys tied them, they were always too tight, but Griffin would never hurt his sister's feelings by complaining.

"If you walk up the hill, you can see the carriages, but promise me you won't visit at the castle, Griffin. Your word on that as a gentleman."

A gentleman never broke his word. Griffin took another bite of dough while he considered whether he could make this promise. Biddy got *very* disappointed when he broke promises, and Julian paced about and lectured and looked worried.

Griffin hated when Julian worried. "I will not stop in at the castle this evening."

"Take King Henry, then. Come home before dark, and don't leave the property."

This time of year, the sun set very late, meaning Griffin would have a good, long ramble. "I love you, Biddy Bowen."

"Go on with you, Master Griffin, and be careful."

She always told him to be careful, but he wasn't a little boy anymore. He had his own house, his own servants, and his own dog, after all.

Griffin took a final pinch of dough and left the kitchen, then stopped by his room for his telescope, and called for King Henry. He went into the study to work out the two-people-in-each-carriage question with a pencil and paper. The vehicles were lined up behind the Haverford carriage house, so he could count them again from Tudor Hill.

He would not pay a call, though. A gentleman always kept his word, and a gentleman told the truth, but a gentleman also formed his own plans and made his own decisions too.

Julian always said so.

* * *

"Now will you allow me to return to Charlotte's bedside?" Elizabeth muttered.

"Don't be ridiculous," Arabella Windham, Lady Pembroke, scoffed. Her scoffs were more effective for being amused. "This buffet is like the organizational gathering before the race meet begins, when you draw lots for your position at the starting line. If you retire abovestairs, the ladies will label you standoffish, and the gentlemen will become more persistent."

Elizabeth and her aunt strolled past a topiary wolf that was a bit too lifelike in the courtyard's evening shadows.

"Those fellows are the same gentlemen who considered a quadrille with me a penance earlier this year," Elizabeth retorted. "They are hardly likely to turn up persistent now."

"You have yet to dance a quadrille with Haverford," Aunt replied, coming to a halt.

Two men had joined the group on the terrace. Both were dark-haired, tall, good-looking specimens, but one was dressed with subtle touches of individuality. His cuffs were edged with lace, his cravat was exquisitely knotted, his hair longish and devoid of fashionable curls.

And he could carry a woman the length of the house as if she weighed no more than a pampered house cat.

"Which one is Haverford?" Elizabeth asked. She knew which one, though his companion was also a fine-looking fellow.

"The one who bears a resemblance to Lady Glenys, of course. You must pay attention, Elizabeth. I'm to report to your parents that you're the toast of the house party, have smitten swains slobbering over your hand by the score, and have passed a few gallants Charlotte's way too."

"Before we've had our first meal?"

Sir Nigel and Lord Haldale had been Aunt's first meal. She'd disentangled Elizabeth from their fawning after the longest five minutes of Elizabeth's life.

"Don't be daft, my dear. Before the end of the week will serve. Haverford and Radnor are both maturing nicely. I have heard talk of an unnatural relationship between them, but you mustn't heed it. Radnor in particular did his bit for the petticoat regiment when he came down from university, much like his father and uncles did."

"Aunt, we are in public."

On the journey to Wales, Elizabeth had come to appreciate that Arabella Windham was an ally, for all her outspokenness. Aunt had been widowed relatively young, before her daughters had made their come outs, and in all these years, she hadn't remarried.

Her literary salons were lively and well attended, her reputation spotless, and her store of social intelligence an endless marvel.

"Young men are lonely," Aunt said, taking Elizabeth by the arm and moving her past the wolf. "They hardly know it, they're so busy with their cockfights, mistresses, and stupid wagers. Drink excuses their rare flights of honesty and allows them to forget when they turn up a bit too human. Your Uncle Peter came up with that theory."

Aunt never referred to him as Elizabeth's "late" Uncle Peter, though Elizabeth had only vague memories of the man. He'd been tall, quiet, pale, and kind. Most of Elizabeth's recollections of Uncle Peter were of him sitting in a Bath chair or shuffling about on the arms of two stout footmen.

A bad heart, according to the physicians. A very good, bad heart, according to Aunt.

"Now that's an interesting addition to the gathering." Aunt paused near a pot of salvia that looked in need of a drink. "Delphine St. David is a cat among the pigeons, and there go the pigeons."

Both Sir Nigel and Lord Haldale had left the punch bowl to bow over Mrs. St. David's hand.

"She's fast?"

Aunt opened a fan sporting a pair of painted doves, and used it to shield her words. "Despite being married to the duke's second cousin, she's a comet streaking across the firmament of willing young men," Aunt said quietly.

"Whoever invited her knew what they were about, because she'll separate the gentlemen from the hounds. Shall we sit?"

"Of course. I hope you were able to rest before changing for dinner."

"Elizabeth, if you attempt to nanny me, I'll see you compromised with Haldale. I would not have made this journey had I thought it would tax me unduly."

Haverford was working his way about the courtyard, while Radnor had joined the group greeting Mrs. St. David.

"You cannot be nannied," Elizabeth murmured, pouring her glass of water into the salvia, "but I'm to be treated like a dimwitted schoolgirl?"

Aunt patted her hand. "No need to sulk, Bethan. You've more titles hanging from your family tree than the rest of the guests put together."

Because of those titles, the prospect of the next three weeks left Elizabeth feeling as wilted as the salvia beside the bench. For the past ten years, she'd vacillated between being the charming, pretty-ish schoolgirl who diligently flattered every man to whom she wasn't related, and the bluestocking who'd given up on matrimony and men for unassailably sound reasons.

Contorting oneself into what potential suitors wanted was tiring and hadn't borne results worth repeating. Why were men unconcerned about what women wanted?

"How did you do it, Aunt? How did you endure being a titled widow with means? Sometimes I think I'd have been better off marrying the first fool to try to steal a kiss under the rose arbor."

Aunt snapped her fan closed. "Elizabeth, this is not the time to indulge in a case of the mollygrubs. You might be

surprised to know I'm as determined to keep you from settling for the wrong man as I am to see you give the right
man his due."

His due being everything Elizabeth owned, intimate
rights, and the rest of her life.

"Excuse me, ladies. I've yet to properly welcome you."
His Grace of Haverford accepted Arabella's hand and
bowed. "Lady Pembroke, if you'd do the honors?"

As Aunt trotted through the introductions, Haverford
bowed over Elizabeth's hand, his grasp neither protracted
nor familiar, more's the pity. Nothing in his demeanor suggested he'd passed Elizabeth a porcelain basin not two
hours earlier.

"Could that be Benedict Andover?" Aunt remarked,
when the topic of the lovely weather had been suitably
flogged. "I haven't seen dear Benny for an age. Your
Grace, Elizabeth, please do excuse me. One must not miss
an opportunity to catch up with old friends."

She swanned off, waving her fan in the direction of a
lean elderly gentleman with snow-white hair clubbed back
in the old style.

"I'm sorry," Elizabeth said, rising. "Aunt Arabella was
about as subtle as an artillery barrage. Don't feel compelled to keep me company, Your Grace. I've imposed on
your kind nature enough for one day."

Haverford stood out from the other gentlemen, in part
because of his height, but also because he was sub-
tly…*splendiferous*. Other men wore embroidered waistcoats, but not in such bold colors. Other men sported lace
on the edges of their cravats, but not in such elegant abundance. The duke made an impression without trying, and
how Elizabeth envied him his self-possession.

"Don't do that," he said, his expression remaining cordial despite his terse words. "Don't make yourself an object of pity. I'm simply greeting guests and saving myself a scold from my sister, at whose feet the blame for this entire gathering must lie."

He hadn't meant to say that, based on the intensity with which he studied the topiary swan at the end of the walk.

"I thought the purpose of the party was to parade eligible bachelors before Lady Glenys." Elizabeth's parents had promised her that this house party would feature only the most well-bred, handsome, well-heeled bachelors, gentlemen worthy of the notice of a duke's sister—or a duke's niece.

Haverford leaned two inches closer. "Lady Glenys conceived of this party as a means to remedy my bachelor status. I mitigated the damage as best I could. I trust you'll keep that in confidence."

He smelled of cedar, a simple, lovely scent. Now that Elizabeth wasn't pouting over her own fate, she noticed a surfeit of fetchingly attired, desperately vivacious young ladies amid the crowd.

"You poor lamb," she said. "You will be pleased to know that I have no intention of pestering you for a proposal."

He nodded to some prancing dandy over at the punch bowl. "Nor have I any intention of offering any proposals. I'll keep your secret if you'll keep mine."

What a lovely smile he had. A little off center, a bit conspiratorial, and—who would have thought?—a touch dashing.

"We have a bargain, Your Grace. Please do not take my aunt into your confidence or even my sister Charlotte."

"My lips are sealed, et cetera and so on, Miss Windham.

Let me introduce you to Lord Radnor, if you've not had the pleasure. He'll appreciate a woman of sense."

Within a few minutes, Elizabeth was being escorted to the buffet on the Marquess of Radnor's arm. He was charming, witty, handsome, and *boring*. Haverford, by contrast, had been more genuine than Elizabeth had anticipated, and standing close to him, she'd seen the determination lurking beneath the satin and lace.

Haverford truly didn't intend to propose to anybody—a refreshingly honest sentiment.

Also—for no reason Elizabeth could discern—a trifle disappointing.

Chapter Three

"Forty-odd carriages, sir." Canford delivered this fact with a sad shake of his head, as if French spies had been spotted in the Welsh countryside. "Haverford is having a house party."

"An astute deduction," Lucas Sherbourne replied, without looking up from the column of figures on the page before him. He delighted in his ledgers, and Canford's conclusion wasn't exactly the work of a genius. "You're blocking the light, my good fellow."

Canford hopped to the left. "Beg pardon, Sherbourne. Not extending an invitation to you is the height of bad form. The very height, and there's not a man in the shire who'd say differently."

Of course there wasn't, at least not among the lot who owed Sherbourne money, including Jeptha Canford. The unfortunate squire had three daughters, each of whom had required at least one London season. The youngest, a plain-faced lisper whose laugh brought to mind a donkey *in extremis*, had required three seasons.

The young ladies were well situated now, but Canford's finances had fallen into dire straits before the first grandchild had come along.

Sherbourne rose, his back pleasantly stiff from sitting too long among his accounts. "We can't expect our local duke to socialize with mere neighbors when he can instead get drunk of an evening with half the peerage. Perhaps the neighbors will be asked to fill up the ballroom before the festivities are concluded."

"Mrs. Canford would like that."

Mrs. Canford was doubtless quivering for a chance to flounce about in the ballroom at Haverford Castle. His Grace, like his predecessors from time immemorial, opened the castle to all and sundry on Boxing Day, and did a fine little punch and cakes drill for the locals. At planting and harvest Haverford Castle hosted picnics that left many a yeoman with a very sore head, and St. David's day was another occasion for ducal largesse.

If a grand ball figured on the house party schedule, the surrounding gentry would be invited. Sherbourne might have admired all this hospitality, except Haverford could afford none of it. Such a pity, when a fine old family ran afoul of financial realities.

Such an opportunity too.

"Let's away to the dining room, Canford, and you can tell me how the grandchildren fare. You must be up to a dozen by now."

"Only five, with a sixth on the way." Bashful pride colored Canford's words, though all of those children would require feeding, clothing, and educating. What manner of stupidity failed to grasp that the consequence of being fruitful and multiplying was an increase in expenses? Surely the old fellow who'd penned that bit of Scripture had known he was writing a recipe for penury where the gentry were concerned?

"You're blessed in your family," Sherbourne said, leading his guest down a carpeted corridor. Landscapes graced the walls, interspersed with brightly burning sconces and antique Sèvres porcelain. Sherbourne liked to look at these exquisite treasures, but he liked even better the effect they had on guests, servants, and all who beheld them.

"I do envy you those children and grandchildren," Sherbourne went on, which was only a small lie. He had yet to acquire even a wife, an oversight he'd soon remedy. Wives cost money—that couldn't be helped—but they could also add cachet to a man's name that opened all manner of doors.

Canford paused to let Sherbourne precede him into the dining room, an elegant chamber that sat thirty when all the leaves were added to the table. The staff had set two places, one at the head with another to the immediate right.

"I always begin my meals with a toast to dear Grandpapa," Sherbourne said, taking his place at the head and gesturing to the footman stationed by the sideboard. "I have him to thank for so much."

When jilted by his St. David bride nearly at the altar, Grandpapa had accepted his fate with calm practicality and flattered his way into the good graces of the loneliest heiress London had to offer. She'd been a brewer's granddaughter and a banker's daughter—also keenly astute in business matters—and her money had launched a financial empire that would allow Sherbourne to redress the wrong done his family.

The first step in that process had been to fit out

Sherbourne Hall in a style worthy of a duchess, which Grandpapa had considerately seen to. The second had been to ensure that the St. David family was deeply indebted to the Sherbournes. That honor had fallen to Papa. The final step toward establishing the Sherbournes as one of the foremost dynasties in the realm required that blue blood be added to their venerable and hardworking lineage.

That happy task fell to Lucas, and the Haverford house party might well see him achieve his goal.

* * *

"I'll lay you odds that Mrs. St. David is already abed with somebody other than her husband," Radnor said. "Possibly more than one somebody."

"One doesn't speak ill of a lady," Julian replied. "Shall I pour you a drink?" He could still offer good brandy to a guest, though he'd take none for himself.

"I'm attempting some moderation. Three weeks from now, I'll doubtless be in a state of constant inebriation, and you're right, I ought not to castigate Delphine for doing at a house party exactly what bored, married persons discreetly do at a well-run house party."

The ledgers sat on Julian's desk. He moved them aside, when he'd rather have pitched them down the nearest garderobe. Alas, the Haverford moat had been drained two centuries ago.

"The gathering is off to a pleasant start," he said, "which is the apex of my ambitions at this point." That, and scraping together more funds to dower Glenys.

Radnor wandered to the study's antique telescope and peered into the eyepiece. "You truly have no intention of choosing a bride from among the ladies?"

"I'm not that old, and I have cousins. There's no need to be precipitous about starting a family."

There was every need.

"Beautiful night," Radnor said, adjusting the focus. "You're not that young either, and if you want to be on hand to raise your own offspring, time is flying."

Julian took the seat behind the estate desk, though the last thing he wanted to do was *sit*. When people referred to Parliament sitting, they spoke literally. A man who voted his seat sat for hours listening to speeches, sat in committee meetings, sat at political dinners, and sat yet more through interminable lunches intended to sway his vote.

At Haverford, the sitting shifted to meetings with stewards, secretaries, men of business, factors, tenants, and socially inclined neighbors.

"My nature is temperate," Julian said. "Unlike my father and grandfather, who were plagued by immoderation in many regards, I plan to be available to my children for a good long while after they arrive. Will you be offended if I go up to bed? The day has been long, and you're entirely right that the next three weeks will be challenging."

Radnor left off pretending to peer at the stars. He was no sort of astronomer, though his botany was encyclopedic and he was a fine amateur architect.

"Miss Windham made you smile, Julian. The duration of your smile was less than two seconds, but I know what I saw. I also know you haven't truly smiled since I came off my horse in Hyde Park last March."

Even the memory amused—Radnor cursing virtuosically in Welsh, while a fractious gelding cursed right back at him in equine. Just when Radnor had been congratulating himself on gaining the upper hand, the horse had tossed him to the ground like a load of wrinkled cravats.

"Anybody would have come off that beast," Julian said, "and you soon had him going like a gentleman."

"Soon is a relative term. You need to marry soon."

Julian needed to get up to bed much sooner. "I have Glenys to provide lectures on that topic, thank you very much. She's far more proficient at it than you could ever be."

Radnor propped a hip on the corner of Julian's desk. He didn't even look fatigued. He looked handsome, exquisitely attired, and in need of a stout blow to his middle. Radnor had so far refrained from pointing out that Griffin was Julian's heir, and saddling the boy with a dukedom would be the outside of cruel.

Should Griffin inherit the title, the ducal finances would teeter from precarious to ruined. Radnor would mitigate the damage as best he could, but the Chancery court would get involved, scandal would ensue, and creditors would pick the bones of the St. David fortune clean within a year.

"Miss Elizabeth Windham made you smile," Radnor said. "What's more, you made her smile. I'm tempted to ask the young lady's sister how frequently that miracle occurs."

Julian rose. The padding on his chair needed restuffing, but he'd had it restuffed five years ago, and the damned thing had been lumpy since.

"I suspect," Julian retorted, "that Miss Windham, being a well-bred lady of sensible years, even smiled at *you*. Besides, I'm the host. I'm supposed to make the ladies smile."

"Except you rarely do, not like that. They smile *at* you, not with you. They simper, they wave their fans, they smooth out their gloves ever so gently, which is supposed to mean something, but I can never recall exactly what. They aim the same weaponry at me. I'm telling you, Haverford, you and Elizabeth Windham had a *moment*."

I wish I were with you. That's what a slow smoothing out of the gloves meant.

"I'm for bed," Julian said. "It's far too early in the house party for *moments*, and when they occur, I will be nowhere in their vicinity, unless they are awkward moments. Then I will ease them away as a conscientious host is required to—"

The door opened.

"I beg your pardon." Elizabeth Windham stood in the doorway, clad in a high-waisted brown day dress, a sky-blue shawl about her shoulders. "I was in search of the library, and my aunt. She's not abed yet, and the hour grows late."

"Well, I can assure you she's not—" Julian began.

"Do come in," Radnor said. "I saw Lady Pembroke in the library with Mr. Benedict Andover. They were playing piquet and reminiscing about the late king. Or something. One can't tell with the elders when they get to gossiping."

"I'm afraid I've misplaced the library." Miss Windham did not budge from the doorway, much less join two single gentlemen behind a closed door late at night.

Sensible to her toes. Not a simper in sight.

"I can show you to the library," Julian replied. "We have two, not counting the documents stored belowstairs. Your aunt would be in the main library, which will be kept warm and well-lit for my guests."

Miss Windham's hair was caught back in a simple bun, accentuating the elegant line of her jaw. Had she chosen that shawl to match the azure hue of her eyes?

"I wouldn't want to put you to any trouble," she replied. "If you give me directions, I can find my way. Haverford isn't like some castles, all twisted about inside, with narrow passages and unexpected stairways."

"You should give the lady a tour, Haverford," Radnor

so helpfully suggested. "This castle has its share of priest holes, secret stairways, and hidden passages. As boys, we delighted in exploring them."

"Until we got lost." Julian wanted to stuff the Marquess of Matchmaking into a priest hole. "If you proceed along this corridor until the next turning, then go right, the first stairway you come to will take you down to the library corridor. Third door on the left. Has the Welsh dragon carved on the door."

"Half your doors have that deuced dragon on them," Radnor said. "You should offer the lady your escort."

Miss Windham was smiling again, or trying not to. Her smile was more of the eyes than any other feature, a softening of her gaze that enjoyed without mocking. Her mouth was on the full side, but she pursed her lips as if to hold in her amusement. A few strands of hair had come down from her bun, and in shadows cast by the sconces, they put Julian in mind of fairy lights or—

"Excuse me, ma'am." Abner Jones stood in the corridor behind Miss Windham, hat in hand. He was hopelessly out of place in his yeoman's attire, and his rheumy eyes held worry.

The lady stepped into the room, allowing Abner to join them as well.

"Good evening, Abner. What's amiss?"

"It's Master Griffin, Your Grace. He went out for a ramble earlier this evening and hasn't come back. He always comes back before dark, but it's been hours and we've seen no sign of him."

"The moon will soon be up," Radnor said. "We can rouse the gentlemen and organize a search."

"What of the dog?" Julian asked. "Has the dog come home without him?" King Henry was ferociously loyal to his owner. If Griffin had been waylaid, the dog would have returned to the cottage—assuming the dog was alive. Every tenant farmer and dairy maid knew that beast, and anybody intent on harming Griffin would dispatch the dog first.

"King Henry's still out as well," Abner said. "The young master noticed all the coaches here at the castle and wanted a closer look."

"Would he have been walking up the hill behind the stables?" Miss Windham asked.

"Aye," Abner said, circling his hat in his hands. "That he were. He was keen to count the carriages again."

Damn Griffin's infernal curiosity. "Did you see him, Miss Windham?" Julian asked.

"I saw a fellow striding up the hill with something shiny in his hand, and an enormous dog at his heels. The dog was brindle or brown—I couldn't be certain in the fading light. The owner was wearing a hat and from what I could discern, country attire. I concluded he was a neighbor or employed on the estate, because he seemed to know where he was going."

"That hill is crisscrossed with paths," Radnor muttered. "Can you draw us a map of his location?"

"Better still," Julian said, "can you take us to where you saw him?"

Radnor cleared his throat.

The lady was not dressed to hike about the Welsh hills by moonlight, which was just too damned bad. One night in early spring, Griffin had sneaked out with two flasks of brandy. Julian had found him an hour before dawn, snoring peacefully not three yards from the lip of a quarry, King Henry keeping watch at his side. Lung fever had followed within days.

That was merely Griffin's most recent misadventure.

"I'll be happy to show you where I saw him," Miss Windham replied, "though I'll need to put on my boots."

"And you'll need a cloak," Julian said. "Abner, if you'll fetch some lanterns, we'll meet you at the laundry."

Radnor followed Abner, then stopped two steps into the corridor. "Shall I alert—?"

"Not yet," Julian said. "We'll probably find Griffin has nodded off against the wishing oak, none the worse for his wandering. Come along, Miss Windham."

He took the lady by the arm, intent on escorting her up to her room. She shook free and set a spanking pace for the stairs.

No questions, no sidelong looks, just quick and uncomplaining compliance with what was asked of her. She had the makings of a duke, did Miss Windham.

And she'd keep her mouth shut about this night's work, which suggested she might also have the makings of a friend.

* * *

Some men tried to protect women from life's harsher realities.

Many men were more interested in protecting themselves from a woman's reactions to life's challenges. Haverford was worried about the missing young man, and Elizabeth suspected His Grace did not worry easily. His manner was that of a man contemplating a mere constitutional about the grounds, except that he'd run his hand through his hair three times as he and Elizabeth had traversed the corridors.

"I'll be only a moment," she said, when they reached the door to the bedroom she shared with Charlotte. Aunt

Arabella occupied a chamber across the corridor, when she wasn't indulging in a piquet marathon with some old friend or other.

"Where have you been?" Charlotte murmured from the depths of the bed.

"Searching for Aunt, who has apparently developed a fondness for midnight card games. Go back to sleep." Elizabeth fetched her cloak and boots and returned to the corridor rather than give Charlotte an opportunity for further questions.

"That was fast," Haverford said, taking the cloak and swirling it about Elizabeth's shoulders. "I apologize for imposing on you this way, but the hills can be treacherous at night and time is of the essence."

He fastened the frogs with the competence of a man used to dressing—and perhaps undressing—women. His fingers brushed Elizabeth's chin, fleeting warmth to accompany the sense of capability.

"Boots next," he said, leading Elizabeth to a window seat in an alcove down the corridor.

"I can put on my own boots, Your Grace."

And stockings.

The duke turned his back rather than observe Elizabeth donning her footwear. The gesture was gentlemanly, also ridiculous. Feet were feet, and hers were not likely to drive any man mad with desire.

"I'm ready," she said, rising. "Let's be off."

"This way." He turned the opposite direction Elizabeth had thought they'd go, and stopped a few yards farther on beside a door designed to blend in with the paneling. "The stairwell will be dark," he said, taking Elizabeth by the hand. "Ten steps, a landing, then ten more. We don't keep the sconces lit, so be careful."

That was her only warning, before she had nothing but the grasp of Haverford's hand to orient her.

"We regularly dust the stairwells," he said, as they were enclosed by stygian darkness. "Don't envision yourself surrounded by mice, cobwebs, or bats. The steps are immediately before us."

The sound of their footsteps echoed, indicating that the passage traversed several floors. The duke didn't hurry Elizabeth, and his grip on her hand was secure.

"The landing," he said, "and now we go to the left, then ten more steps."

They passed a window that let in light from torches on some terrace or balcony. The duke was momentarily silhouetted against the panes, then he led Elizabeth down the last four steps.

She bumped into him at the foot of the stairs, a warm, solid wall of cedar-scented man.

"Beg pardon, Your Grace."

"Finding the latch always takes a moment. The fairies move it, or—ah, here we are."

They emerged on the outer side of the castle wall, the scent of the breeze placing them downwind of the stables. Lanterns bobbed near the outline of a small building that might be the summer kitchen or the laundry.

"Take a moment," Haverford said, turning Elizabeth by the shoulders. "That's Tudor Hill, where you would have spied Griffin earlier if he was intent on counting the coaches. On which path did you see him?"

Chapter Four

IN THE DARK, NOTHING was the same. Vision dimmed, while other senses became more acute. Haverford stood at Elizabeth's back, still in his evening attire, no more appropriately dressed for a hill trek than she was. He stood close enough that she could feel his heat and sense how their bodies would fit together in an embrace.

Perhaps the fairies were trifling with Elizabeth's imagination.

"The man I saw looked to be aiming for the large tree about halfway up the hill," she said. "He took that path to the left."

"Then Griffin's headed for the wishing oak. He loves that damned thing. The views from its branches are breathtaking, and at least four different paths lead to it. Come."

Elizabeth let herself be tugged along, even as she marveled that His Grace of Haverford had climbed that tree and treasured the views.

Radnor and the man called Abner joined them at the laundry, and the party started up the path Elizabeth had indicated.

"If the way is too challenging," Radnor said, "I can return you to the house, Miss Windham."

"It's merely a hill, my lord." Without stays to confine her breathing, keeping pace with the men was easy.

As they ascended, the moon rose, and the way became less difficult to navigate. Elizabeth held on to Haverford's hand nonetheless.

She hadn't held hands with a man before. Had Haverford held hands with many women?

The path crisscrossed the hill, growing more rugged as the trail ascended.

"My goodness," Elizabeth said. "I hadn't realized we're so close to the sea." Off in the distance, the ocean was a flat silver mirror peeking between two hills.

Abner and Radnor continued to climb, and for a moment, Elizabeth was holding hands with Haverford under a moonlit sky, the splendor of a wild nightscape before her.

"I'd forgotten what the view up here is like at moonrise," Haverford said. "No wonder Griffin was disinclined to turn for home."

The breeze rustled through the oaks higher on the trail, but other than the fading sounds of the other men's footsteps, quiet descended.

"We'll find him," Elizabeth said. "The night is mild, he's on familiar ground, and you won't rest until he's safe."

Whoever this Griffin was, he meant a great deal to the duke.

"I believe you are reassuring me," His Grace said, resuming their progress. "The experience is novel and appreciated."

Odd comment. Elizabeth toiled on beside him in silence for another few minutes before Radnor's shout broke the night's quiet.

"Found him! Bugger's fast asleep beneath the tree, just as you predicted, and damned if the dog wasn't napping as well."

The duke's relief was evident in the relaxation of his shoulders and the easing of his grip on Elizabeth's hand.

Radnor came bounding down the path a moment later, his lantern bobbing in the shadows.

"The lad's fine. A bit sheepish and hungry, but none the worse for his outing. Did you know you have forty-two coaches ranged around behind your stables and carriage house?"

"Griffin is well?" Haverford asked.

Something passed between the two men, more than a simple question. Radnor touched Haverford's shoulder.

"Absolutely safe and sound. Peckish and fretting that Biddy will tear a strip off him for getting his coat dirty. Abner and I will walk him home, and I'll see you at breakfast. Miss Windham, good evening, and mind your step on the way down. Many an ankle has turned on this descent."

Radnor waited, as if anticipating an argument from Haverford.

"My thanks, Radnor. Until breakfast. Miss Windham, shall we?" The duke dropped Elizabeth's hand to gesture back the way they'd come.

Well, drat. Elizabeth started down the path, disappointed that the closest thing she'd had to an adventure was so soon over.

"I should precede you," Haverford said. "A gentleman should precede a lady, so he can break her fall."

"A lady should wear her boots, so she's surefooted enough not to land on her face. Besides, if you're in front of me, and you lose your footing, I'll trip over you."

"Now you scold me. The novelties of this evening multiply apace."

Elizabeth slowed, because Radnor had been right. Descending could be more treacherous than climbing. "Nobody scolds you? Ever?"

"Not as effectively as you just did. Lady Glenys remonstrates with me, my valet chides, Radnor takes me to task, but you have a way with a scold." He sounded intrigued rather than put off by Elizabeth's way with a scold.

"I have three younger sisters and many younger cousins. My older cousins are most in need of scolding, though. They meddle." They also foiled would-be kidnappers. Elizabeth shied away from that thought.

"I cannot abide meddlers. They are busybodies who cloak their attempts to manipulate under false solicitude. I was surrounded by such concern upon my father's death, and in each instance, somebody stood to profit by taking an interest in my situation. Misplaced trust can exact a fearful cost."

Elizabeth was sure His Grace would not have made that admission in the light of a summer sun. Perhaps he'd been figuratively waylaid, as Lord Allermain had waylaid Elizabeth.

"The next time somebody tries to cozen your trust, sir, try a cold silence. Dukes have a knack for an arctic reproof that conveys itself without a single word."

Haverford had drawn even with her as the path had grown more level. "I like that. A cold silence. Radnor has one, though he uses it so seldom, one forgets he's capable of it." For the third time, the duke glanced over his shoulder, toward two lanterns bobbing across the hill, traveling away from the castle.

"You can scold Griffin in the morning," Elizabeth said, taking Haverford's hand. "Some scolds are better for a bit of rehearsal, and sometimes, not scolding a miscreant works magic on his guilty conscience."

"You are full of helpful suggestions. Griffin would never trouble anybody on purpose. He'll be apologizing to me before I'm off my horse."

At this conclusion, Haverford's stride opened up, and he shifted his grip on Elizabeth's hand so their fingers linked.

Maybe gloves were worn on most social occasions because the grip of a man's hand said a lot about his confidence and his character. Haverford held hands easily, his grasp warm and secure without being presuming.

"You would have found Griffin," Elizabeth said, "no matter how far he rambled, no matter which hill he climbed. He's under your protection, and you'd not fail him."

"That's the theory. I hope Griffin never tests it to the point of proving it false."

Elizabeth walked along, wrestling with the most extraordinary urge to hug the duke. Not steal a kiss, insinuate herself into his affections, or flirt. To offer him the comfort of an embrace, and perhaps steal some comfort for herself too.

She liked him. If she should ever come under his protection, he'd move heaven and earth to find her when she wandered, and he'd neglect all else until he'd assured himself she was safe.

Not that Elizabeth would inconvenience him like that— he had enough to look after without a prodigal party guest adding to his burdens.

Besides, she wasn't lost.

* * *

"My appetite has returned," Charlotte said. "My appetite for food, that is. You were up early, sister mine."

Elizabeth smiled in greeting and Viscount Haldale bestirred himself to hold Charlotte's chair at the breakfast table. He was blond, tall, and blue-eyed, and Charlotte had learned years ago not to waste her waltzes on him. His conversation was sadly predictable, dealing invariably with one topic and one topic alone: himself.

"Thank you, my lord. Might I prevail upon you to fetch me some eggs?"

"Of course, Miss Charlotte. Miss Windham, anything for you?"

"No, thank you."

He sidled down the length of the breakfast table, which was full of chattering guests organized into the usual groups: Chaperones and mamas clustered near the head, debutantes and other hopefuls near the foot, with bachelors and husbands sprinkled about as manners or empty chairs dictated.

His Grace and Lady Glenys had yet to join the group.

"You look well rested," Charlotte said, giving Elizabeth a sororal inspection. "Much better rested than when you stay up until all hours reading. This puzzles me, for His Grace's book collection is among the largest in the realm, and I'd expect you to have hidden yourself among its shelves."

Where a gentleman's library was concerned, size mattered to Elizabeth, and Haverford's library was enormous.

Elizabeth speared a strawberry from her plate. "As Lord Byron put it, 'If I could always read, I should never feel the want of company.' I am well rested, though. The lovely Welsh air agrees with me."

Something agreed with Elizabeth. She had resisted this house party vehemently, and then for reasons Charlotte had yet to winkle out of her, abruptly changed her mind.

"Your eggs, Miss Charlotte." Haldale set the plate down, leaning too near and doubtless ogling Charlotte's décolletage. He smelled of neroli, a heavy scent for the early hour.

"My thanks, your lordship. And I'll have that rack of toast, if you don't mind."

He sat and passed Charlotte the toast. His lordship was a tribulation in breeches, for she had to pluck the butter from the middle of the table herself, and that meant nudging up against his arm.

Why must house parties be so predictable, and why must Elizabeth radiate such serene contentment, nonetheless?

"Elizabeth, did I dream that you took a pair of boots from the wardrobe last night?"

She set the teapot before Charlotte's plate. "You must have, another symptom of that awful ale. Sugar?"

Charlotte had not dreamed it, nor had she dreamed Elizabeth taking her cloak from the hook on the wall, *nor* was she dreaming that her sister's smile this morning held a hint of mischief.

"The sugar typically goes into the tea," Elizabeth said. "One uses a spoon, but takes care not to stir *noisily*."

Charlotte helped herself to two lumps. Elizabeth was right—one did not discuss late-night outings over breakfast, particularly not when Mrs. Delphine St. David was disdaining a place among the mamas and chaperones and plunking herself down directly across from Haldale.

He rose and bowed. "Mrs. St. David, you're looking radiant, as usual."

She shot him a look, part exasperation, part threat. Her expression suggested they'd been lovers in the past, but Mrs. St. David wasn't inclined to renew those festivities.

"Some toast?" Charlotte asked, moving the rack close to Mrs. St. David's plate. "And help yourself to the butter. Will Mr. St. David be joining us this morning?"

Hugh St. David appeared older than his wife by a decade or so, and he was aging handsomely. He bore a resemblance to Haverford, though Mr. St. David's features were more weathered. Charlotte had bested him at piquet the previous evening, and then he'd excused himself claiming his day would start early.

"Hugh is off hunting for fossils," Mrs. St. David replied. "He's mad for his antiquities and very knowledgeable about where the best ones can be found."

Her mouth was smiling, while her eyes told a different story. Mr. St. David's absence let the entire company know that fossils interested him more than sharing breakfast with his wife, and thus Charlotte didn't blame the lady for her mood.

"Would you care for some preserves?" Elizabeth asked, passing over a jam pot. "I admire a man who pursues his passions."

"Do you refer to Haverford's libraries?" Haldale asked. "I'd heard about the St. David family penchant for collecting books, but thirty thousand volumes goes beyond a mere passion."

"Thirty thousand is nothing more than a number," Elizabeth said. "The St. David collection is as well-known for its quality as for its quantity. I hope to become much better acquainted with it during my visit. The family has been collecting literature since well before the invention of the printing press, and I'd be a fool…"

Her diatribe trailed off as Lady Glenys and her brother joined the guests. Haverford cut a handsome dash in morning attire, while her ladyship looked composed and gracious.

She and Elizabeth had that in common—an ability to bear up serenely despite all vexation to the contrary. Charlotte, by contrast, was ready to elbow Haldale in the ribs if his leg casually brushed against hers even once more.

"Greetings, all," Haverford said, holding his sister's chair. "I hope you appreciate the fine weather I've ordered for you this morning. Blink, and the sky will be pouring torrents."

He spoke with the various guests seated at his end of the table, made Aunt Arabella laugh over some quip concerning a hedgehog, and poured out for his sister as only a man of innate gentlemanly sensibilities would.

Charlotte had *not* dreamed that Elizabeth had snatched a cloak and boots late last evening, and disappeared into the night with them. She also hadn't dreamed the sound of Haverford's voice from the corridor.

Which raised a question: Had Elizabeth agreed to come to this house party because she was impressed with the Haverford libraries, or with the man who owned them?

* * *

The Haverford maids had apparently been too busy to open the windows in the library. The smell from last night's gathering thus nearly overpowered Elizabeth.

The gentlemen would have waited until the ladies had retired to get out the port and cigars, but she had a theory that cigar smoke was no better for books than coal smoke.

She opened the French doors, then started on the windows, letting both morning sun and fresh air into the room. This being a newer part of the castle, the windowsills were merely a foot and a half deep, though the hinges were still stubborn. One gave a great squeak—were the footmen too busy to oil hinges in this castle?—and from the depths of the sofa near the fireplace came a snort.

Or a snore?

Elizabeth could not recall seeing any hounds in the castle. She crossed the library to investigate and came upon His Grace of Haverford fast asleep, a ledger book on his chest. He put her in mind of the deceased at a wake, with a Bible placed over his heart, though no deceased had ever sprawled in such casual splendor.

His tall boots were neatly positioned at the foot of the sofa, and a pair of gold-rimmed glasses sat upon his nose. Those two items—the boots and the glasses—spoke volumes about the man and his station.

Though gracious saints, what if some scheming debutante should come upon the duke? She'd take down her hair, curl up near him in a wanton pose, and wait to be discovered in a compromising situation.

"Your Grace."

Another snore. He wasn't a loud snorer, but he was far gone in slumber.

"Haverford. Wake up."

"Not at the moment, thank you." He shifted to his side, and the ledger book slid to the carpet.

Elizabeth picked up the ledger. This had to be a book for tallying the expenses, for every entry was a deduction. "Sir, you must rouse yourself."

He scooted around, scratched his chest, and sighed.

The poor man was exhausted. Shaking his shoulder was like trying to shake one of the marble lions couchant atop the castle's gateposts. "You must wake up, Your Grace. The castle's on fire."

Two sets of dark lashes swept up. "Haverford Castle is made of good Welsh stone. It cannot burn."

"No," Elizabeth said, removing his glasses. "But your reputation can go up in flames along with mine if you don't bestir yourself. How can you see anything with all these smudges?"

She used a handkerchief to polish the duke's spectacles.

He sat up and reached for his boots. "Miss Windham. Good morning. I should beg your pardon."

His hair stood up on one side. Elizabeth combed her fingers through it enough to set it to rights. The texture was silky, despite its thickness, like a healthy cat in winter plumage.

"You're a bit disarranged." She positioned his glasses back on his nose, then gave his hair an extra smoothing. "I should be begging your pardon. This is the famous St. David library, and you haven't given me permission to borrow from it."

He sat through her fussing, tugged on his boots, and stood. New boots were the devil to put on, because they were made to allow for the leather stretching to the wearer's exact conformation. Haverford's boots hadn't been new for some time, though they'd been lovingly maintained.

"You come upon me, dead asleep in the middle of my own house party, and your objective is to become better acquainted with my books."

He was amused, or appalled. Elizabeth wasn't sure which.

"I am devoted to lending libraries, Your Grace, for they make knowledge available to everybody. Books are wonderful, but if you can't afford them, then they are only one more privilege that God in his infinite wisdom has granted only to others. Did you know the Welsh are among the most literate people on earth?"

"Because of the circulating schools that sprang up in the

last century," Haverford said, "thanks to dear old Griffith Jones."

Elizabeth was to be denied the pleasure of reciting the rest of the tale, for apparently Haverford knew it. Griffith Jones had been a shepherd turned Anglican priest, and in the 1730s, he'd got onto the notion of opening a school for a period of months, long enough to teach an entire village to read. When basic literacy had been achieved, the school moved to another village, and the brightest pupils took on the teaching of neighboring settlements.

Over the next fifty years, half of Wales had learned to read, and very likely had also been predisposed to Methodism, for the Bible was the most reliably available printed text in any village.

"We're also literate because of the Welsh spirit of inquiry," Elizabeth said. "We are a curious people, interested in taking charge of our surroundings, else we'd never have become such a center of industry."

Haverford removed his glasses and pinched the bridge of his nose. "That industry is creating some of the worst slums in Europe, Miss Windham, and our literacy has not spared us one iota of misery. The poverty and filth in the mining villages are unimaginable, and the surrounding countryside has been ruined for farming."

Mama often sang the same lament. "This matters to you."

He tucked his glasses into a pocket. "Reading is a luxury, but people must eat. We can ship steel and copper all over the world, but if we ruin our countryside in the process, will John Bull give us butter and wheat for free? I suspect not. The Irish live in penury as bad as ours, and the Scots have learned from long habit to look after their own."

"You are *Welsh*," Elizabeth said, beaming at him. She'd considered him a duke, an aristocrat, a member of the

House of Lords, and a few other things—splendiferous in evening attire, for example—but she hadn't attributed *Welshness* to him.

"I have that honor, though should any inquire, I am simply a peer of the realm with a perishing lot of books cluttering up my castle."

"My mother is Welsh. As a child, I visited here frequently. Mama says that's why I'm passionate about books and reading. My father says I love books because Windhams must always go their own way, though that doesn't explain why I am the only Windham so fond of books. You have a lovely library, Your Grace."

And Elizabeth was babbling—about books, of course.

"I have an enormous library," Haverford said, "and I do not love books, not these books. Nonetheless, the loan of a few volumes to a guest will be a gesture in the direction of their intended use. Come, I'll give you the tour, and you may choose whatever you please."

He'd taken her hand again, though they weren't on a darkened hillside. Surely his comments about the books were ducal grumbling? Uncle Percival complained about the expense of maintaining a stable, but knew every pony and pensioner in his paddocks.

"We should open the door, Your Grace. The appearances could result in unpleasant talk."

Haverford looked down at their joined hands, his expression for an instant uncomprehending, then he slipped his fingers free of Elizabeth's grasp.

"You are absolutely correct, Miss Windham." He opened the library door and drew back the last set of drapes. "You probably noticed that my cousin, Mrs. St. David, has a mischievous streak. She would delight in coming upon us in a compromising position."

Elizabeth would have said vexatious rather than mischievous. "You're family to her. Why should she make trouble for you?"

"Because she can. She and Hugh have no children, and that's always worrisome in a ducal family without an abundance of spares. Do you favor poetry?"

He gestured for Elizabeth to join him before the tall shelves marching down an interior wall.

"I favor good poetry, and am reading Byron at present." Elizabeth dearly, dearly wanted to linger over the volumes surrounding her, but His Grace wasn't thinking clearly where his cousin was concerned. "Mrs. St. David doesn't strike me as bored, so much as she is hurt."

The duke eyed the shelf before him as if the books were recruits unprepared for parade inspection.

"You will think me ungentlemanly when I tell you that Delphine St. David's sentiments revolve around her next pleasure and the inadequacies of her last pleasure. Let's find you a book, shall we?"

"Three books, at least, and how would you feel if your spouse thought of nothing but rocks, fossils, ancient mud, and long-dead sea creatures?"

Or if your lot in life were to be regularly overlooked—or worse, pitied—and invited to social functions only to make up the numbers when your cousins weren't available?

The duke drew a volume down from the shelves. "I might be relieved to be left to my own devices, provided my duchess otherwise attended to her responsibilities. Do you read French?"

"Of course. You must not reply so bluntly should another of your guests raise a similar question, Your Grace. You'll crush the ambitions of nearly every young lady in the castle."

He peered at her over the top of the book. "Miss Windham, some of these women will not be deterred by Greek fire or lunatic St. David uncles wandering out of dungeons. Nothing short of true scandal would render me ineligible in their eyes, and most of them met me only yesterday."

Elizabeth plucked the poetry from his grasp. "Your cousin apparently neglects his wife shamefully. As head of the family, it's your place to take him to task. He has, by his actions, let all and sundry know his wife's behavior matters to him not at all, and a day getting sunburned and ruining his boots holds more appeal than a meal by her side." .

Haverford held his ground, so he and Elizabeth stood very close. Elizabeth was torn between an urge to shake her finger in the duke's face—Mrs. St. David's situation was not of her own making—and the compulsion to scamper off with the book he'd chosen for her.

He stared over Elizabeth's right shoulder. "Your hypothesis is that Delphine strays in an effort to gain her husband's notice?"

"And to shame him, as he shames her with his indifference."

"You've deduced this over a single plate of eggs?"

Elizabeth resolutely ignored the French verse she'd likely never have another opportunity to read. "'Man's love is of man's life a thing apart/'Tis Woman's whole existence...,'" Elizabeth quoted. "One could deduce Mrs. St. David's discontent over a single cup of tea, did one *pay attention.*"

Chapter Five

Haverford turned back to the shelves, giving Elizabeth an opportunity to note the breadth of his shoulders. He truly was a splendid specimen, and he was *listening*.

"I am coming to enjoy your scolds, madam. They have about them the ring of common sense. I will consider your theory and perhaps have a word with Hugh."

Consider and *perhaps* would do Mrs. St. David no good. "Do better than that. Move Hugh into his wife's room because the chimney must be cleaned in his. Ask them to lead a team for the scavenger hunt. Invite them to visit when an entire house party isn't underfoot."

His Grace passed her a second book. "You are a font of ingenuity, or matchmaking, depending on one's perspective. I hadn't realized Lady Glenys was inflicting a scavenger hunt on us. You will insinuate yourself onto my team, Miss Windham."

A third book joined the two in Elizabeth's grasp. "You will not tell me what to do, Your Grace."

His lips twitched. "Do forgive my imperiousness, Miss Windham. If you would condescend to join my team for the scavenger hunt, I would be eternally in your debt."

Haverford's word choice brought to mind all the expenses marching down the ledger page, entry after entry. He was a duke. He need not tarry with her in the library, much less choose books for her, much less compliment her scolds.

Or tolerate her *imperiousness*. Elizabeth might not owe him an outright apology for her meddling where Mrs. St. David was concerned, but she owed him an explanation.

"Griffith Jones had a wealthy sponsor," Elizabeth said. "All his dreams, his great plans, would have had little impact, but for Madam Bevans. She financed his schools, took Jones in when he was an aged widower, continued his work after his death, and left a substantial grant in her will for the support of the circulating schools."

His Grace braced a shoulder against the shelves and crossed his arms. He was a good-sized man, along the lines of Elizabeth's male cousins. He wasn't a great hulking brute; by her standards he was simply man-sized.

Perfectly man-sized.

"You are about to make a point," he said. "I would like to hear it."

"I have only modest settlements," Elizabeth said. "But I am a Windham, and well connected. Between what funds I can command and what donations I could inspire, I can make a difference. Few women have that privilege. I cannot imagine the depth of Mrs. David's frustration, to be invisible to the one person who ought always to see her."

The duke regarded her, nothing casual or coy in his gaze. He not only listened, *he saw*.

"Lending libraries are worth supporting," Elizabeth went on, lest she lose her nerve. "They bring the wider world, the most learned prose, the most exciting ages, within reach of any village curate, any milkmaid who's been to the local dame school." Any young woman facing yet another lonely London season. "I want to support lending libraries."

"A worthy cause."

Haverford turned, so he stood in profile to Elizabeth. Regret washed through her, for she liked looking at him, and hoped her maunderings hadn't created awkwardness.

Though how could they not?

His Grace used the lip of the shelf to scratch his back, which was extraordinarily informal behavior. Elizabeth was about to reprove him for it, when she recalled the duke telling her that nobody scolded him.

Nobody scratched his back either.

"For gracious sake, let me." Elizabeth set her books aside and pushed Haverford around to face away from her. She used her nails and gave him a solid scratching, for he wore a coat, waistcoat, and shirt.

He stood still for a moment, then braced himself against the shelves.

She finished with a pat to the middle of his back. "Better?" she asked, picking up the books.

"Has anybody told you that you have tendency to manage whoever and whatever is at hand?"

Elizabeth had not been merely *told* she had managing tendencies, she'd been admonished at length on the topic, and yet, the duke's assessment was inaccurate.

"I did not manage Lord Allermain." Elizabeth's admission surprised even her. "I'm ruralizing in Wales because I attracted his less than respectful notice."

Though of all people, Haverford would know how it felt

to be pursued as a prize rather than as a person, and he'd respect a lady's confidences.

The duke wandered away from the bookshelves. "I don't care for him, but then, I'm considered pernickety in the company I keep. I assume he bungled badly."

Elizabeth's parents had implied that *she* was the bungler, frittering away season after season without choosing a husband, while every last ducal cousin pelted up the church aisle.

"Allermain put a soporific in my wine and nearly waltzed me into his waiting coach. My cousins intervened, and his lordship is now kicking his heels on the Continent. At my parents' insistence, I am kicking my heels among the largest concentration of titled bachelors in the realm. I am also being somewhat…managing. I apologize for that."

Elizabeth was also kicking her heels amid all these lovely books, which she would inspect when she'd finished burdening Haverford with her woes—assuming he didn't have her escorted from the property first.

The duke stood before the open French doors. Having turned his back to Elizabeth once—at her insistence—he was apparently willing to do so again.

"Your cousins allowed this varlet to decamp for parts unknown?"

"They did. Scandal must never be linked to a woman's name and so forth, but now my parents demand that I marry. Allermain sought to ally himself with a large, influential ducal family, and there I was, all unmarried and female, tempting him to rash measures."

Haverford stalked toward her, his boots thumping so hard against the floor Elizabeth felt the impact where she stood.

"*That* is utter balderdash, madam. That is the rankest

tripe, do you hear me? A gentleman owes his protection to all who are weaker than he—children, the elderly, the infirm, and women especially. No matter the advantages a woman's family connections or fortune might offer, or the invitation in her smile, or the effects of drink—no matter anything—Allermain's behavior was inexcusable."

Haverford's indignation washed across Elizabeth like a scouring wind, though rather than upsetting all in its path, this gale set a few things to rights.

"You are correct, of course." *And Papa was wrong.* Haverford had no doubt about who had bungled, and who should have been held accountable.

"Now you turn up agreeable. I am not deceived, Miss Windham. When I commit the least transgression, you will correct me. But I am in your debt, and I came in here to find a book for you."

"You've found three." The titles of which Elizabeth hadn't bothered to glance at.

"I meant a book to give you. You rendered assistance last night when it was much needed. A book struck me as a suitable token of my appreciation. You must choose one for yourself."

He looked both determined and uncomfortable, as if giving away even one volume of his precious collection pitted generosity against the ire of the St. David ancestors who'd amassed this treasure. Elizabeth approved of both sentiments—the magnanimity of bestowing a book on her, and the reluctance to reduce his family's library by even a single title.

The room was lined on three sides with shelves, and those shelves ringed a second story. His Grace had also mentioned a *second* library, and a document collection in the bowels of the castle.

"I'm to choose one book, from all of these?"

"Choose wisely and take your time. This room holds more than thirty thousand titles. The bawdy tales are up there," he said, gesturing across the room. "That corner is all French and Italian. There are a few Bibles, the usual medical treatises. Take whichever one you please." He fixed his gaze in the direction of the bawdy tales. "The last time Griffin wandered, I found him mere yards from a precipice."

"That had to be upsetting."

"I raised my voice to the boy for the first time in years. *That* upset him. Years ago, he fell into an abandoned mine shaft, and when we found him the next day, he was already suffering fevers and a badly sprained wrist. If I make haste, I'll have time to discuss last night with the prodigal himself. I bid you good day, and again, you have my thanks. For everything. And Lord Allermain is ruined. Your cousins have likely already put matters in train, but I'll add my discreet efforts, and you won't see him in a proper ballroom again. That much remains within my power."

He kissed Elizabeth's cheek, a soft brush of cedary warmth, and then he strode off.

The room contained more literature than Elizabeth had ever beheld in a private home, and three weeks wouldn't be enough for even a cursory perusal. As the duke's steps faded down the corridor, Elizabeth couldn't give a tinker's curse for the books.

The Duke of Haverford had *listened to her*, taken the situation with Allermain in hand, thanked her for everything, and kissed her. What was *everything*, and when might she kiss him back?

* * *

"You're disappointed in me." Griffin skipped a rock across the river, flicking the stone so hard that it bounced six times before sinking.

"I am." Julian was also worried as hell. Griffin had not come bounding from the cottage, spouting apologies and looking chagrinned.

"You didn't send a card," Griffin said, striding along the bank. "When a gentleman comes calling, he's supposed to send a card. If you send your card, I can ask Biddy to make tea, but you didn't send your card."

"We'd look a bit silly taking our tea along the river here."

"We could have a picnic. I wasn't lost, Julian. Last night, I wasn't lost at all."

Julian wanted to change the subject, to ask the names of the plants growing on the path, to listen for the bird calls Griffin knew by heart. Papa had taught him those bird calls, and taught them to Julian too.

The lad remembered everything, except his older brother's lectures.

"I don't get lost," Griffin said, rounding on Julian. "*Never, never, never.* I have never been lost. Why do you keep thinking I'm lost when I'm only having a ramble on our land? The sheep and horses and cows sleep outside *all the time*, and you never worry about them. Am I more stupid than a sheep?"

What the hell? "You're far more intelligent than a sheep."

"So why did you and Radnor and Abner and that lady come looking for me? I would have awoken when I was rested and come straight home like I always do."

God save me. Griffin could fixate on details—Why did clouds have the shapes they did? Why did Monday follow

Sunday every week? Why hadn't Marged Pryce's breasts been exactly the same shape?—and worry over them for days.

Griffin had apparently seen Elizabeth Windham on the path below the oak and would doubtless remark her presence at the worst possible time in the worst possible company.

"We came looking for you because we were worried about you."

Griffin resumed walking. "Because you think I'm stupid. I am stupid, but I don't get lost. If you let me go to London, I might get lost, because London is very, very, very far away. You never let me go to London."

As a small boy, Griffin had had frequent tantrums. Then his disposition had calmed as his studies had progressed. Julian had breathed a sigh of relief, telling himself Griffin had acquired what maturity one of his nature could.

Marged Pryce's meddling was an aberration, a rough patch Julian ought to have foreseen.

"I've explained this to you, Griffin. In London, nobody speaks Welsh. You could not order a pint at the tavern or ask directions."

"You could do those things for me. You go to London *all the time*. Glenys goes to London. Abner went once, when he was a boy. I'm not a boy."

Oh, yes, you are. "We are very far afield from the topic of your misadventure, Griffin. You owe me, Biddy, Radnor, and Abner an apology for making us worry."

Griffin was on the path beside Julian one moment, and up in the branches of an oak the next. He'd grabbed onto the limb that hung over the path and swung upward in one lithe arc. For all his intellectual limitations, Griffin was strong, fit, and hale.

Seizures notwithstanding.

"What about the lady, Julian? Should I apologize to her?"

"I will not address myself to a tree."

"I talk to the trees *all the time*. They don't think I'm stupid."

Nothing for it. Julian climbed into the tree, though with far less grace than Griffin had.

"You were thoughtless, Griffin, and that's not like you. You're usually kind, but to go off and leave us to wonder if you'd turned your ankle, taken a fall, or been bitten by an adder was inconsiderate."

Mention of the snake dimmed the grin Julian's clambering into the tree had inspired. "I don't like serpents. I don't understand how they move without legs. You said they are shy."

"On summer evenings, they like to go out for rambles too, and right next to you would have been a nice, warm place to take a nap."

Griffin looked entirely at home lounging on a branch, his back propped against the trunk. "Then I'll climb the wishing oak, next time."

"There won't *be* a next time, Griffin. You must give me your word on that. No more rambling until all hours. You come home when it's dark."

"You don't come home when it's dark. You were out with that lady, looking for me, and it was well past sunset."

Time to fire off the fraternal artillery. "I am disappointed in you."

"You said that already. Radnor walked me home, when I never get lost."

Julian watched the water babble by beneath the tree. This was a peaceful spot, probably one of dozens Griffin knew that Julian had walked by for years. Griffin's mood was unrepentant, which was most unusual for him.

"Radnor is a good friend," Julian said.

Griffin twisted off a leaf and cast it down to the river, to be immediately carried away. "Radnor said Charity is learning her letters."

Damn Radnor, though he'd probably been making conversation as best one could with Griffin. "She thrives in his care."

"Is she learning *English* letters?"

The question was oh so diffidently offered, but it explained everything about Griffin's mood.

"Welsh and English use the same letters, Griffin, though each language puts them together to make different sounds."

Griffin pushed his hair out of his eyes, perfectly capable of balancing on the branch without using his hands.

"So I already know all the English letters?"

That pleased him. "You do, while Charity is just beginning her study of them."

Griffin skewered Julian with a direct look. "Will she be smart, Julian, or will she be like me?"

In Griffin's gaze was as much pride, determination, and self-awareness as Julian had seen in the eyes of any duke. That gaze demanded honesty, when whatever answer Julian gave would likely hurt Griffin's feelings.

"She appears to be quite bright. She's learning her letters at the same age Glenys did."

Griffin closed his eyes and hunched up his shoulders, his face transfigured by joy. "Glenys is wicked smart."

"She seems to think so."

"I want to visit Charity. I want her to show me her letters."

A normal longing. Julian wished he could spend more

time with the girl himself. "After the house party, I'll take you to Radnor's for a visit, but you must promise you'll not wander about the hillside after dark again, Griffin."

"I didn't do it on purpose," Griffin said, swinging to the ground as nimbly as a monkey, "but there are forty-two coaches behind the carriage house. I counted them twice, and then I fell asleep. If each coach had two people inside, that would have been eighty-four people. Do you have eighty-four guests, Julian?"

Julian's descent was more decorous, also somewhat reluctant. Long, long ago, he'd napped in the occasional tree.

"It feels like eighty-four hundred. I can't keep their names straight, and they eat like a regiment of dragoons and drink like sailors on shore leave. Thank God, most of the people who came in those carriages are not guests, but maids, footmen, valets, and grooms."

"All those people cost a lot of money to feed, don't they?"

Why couldn't Glenys grasp what Griffin saw easily? "A fortune. You're not to worry over it."

"I'll have my Biddy send you some bread."

Julian slung an arm around his brother's shoulders. "That is very generous of you, but let's not put Biddy to any extra trouble. She has her hands full looking after you and Abner."

"Who was the lady, Julian? You held her hand."

Oh, that lady. "I was being gentlemanly, ensuring she didn't take a fall on an unfamiliar path." *And for once, I'd forgotten to worry that a woman would get ideas about becoming my duchess.*

Holding hands with a pretty houseguest hadn't been part of Julian's plans, but it hadn't upset his plans either. Not enough to trouble over.

He and Griffin ambled in the direction of Griffin's cottage, when Julian would rather have walked another mile or two along the river. He hadn't spent much time with his brother lately, which was an attempt to respect the independence of Griffin's household.

And perhaps, just a little neglectful on Julian's part.

"But what was the lady's name, Julian?"

"Miss Windham. She's a friend of Glenys's."

Griffin gave him a hard shove, which nearly sent him into the river. "You don't hold hands with Glenys's other friends. Does Miss Windham make your tallywags ache?" Griffin's smile was sly, masculine, and naughty.

"You and your damned tallywags," Julian countered, shoving back. "Gentlemen don't ask such questions."

"I'm your brother. My tallywags ache every time I see Nan Pritchard, down at the Boar and Barrel. She's almost as pretty as Biddy."

Marged Pryce had been pretty. Nan Pritchard could be trusted, however, and Biddy's perceived beauty was likely a result of her abilities in the kitchen.

"You know what to do about aching tallywags, Griffin." He'd figured out the joys of self-gratification by himself, St. David blood running true when it came to animal spirits. Learning to keep such behaviors and discussion of them private had taken the better part of several years.

"Does Miss Windham make your—"

Julian shoved him again. "Hush. Apologize to Biddy for worrying her last night, and to Radnor."

"I could write a note to Radnor. I could write a note to Charity too."

"You have a beautiful hand." Griffin could copy anything, including Julian's copperplate script. "I'm sure a note would suffice."

"I'll write Radnor a note. And Charity."

That exercise would take the remainder of the day at least. Griffin was a perfectionist when it came to his penmanship.

"I'm off, then," Julian said as they approached the cottage.

"Give Miss Windham my love."

"I'll do no such thing, you scamp."

Griffin accompanied Julian to the barn to fetch his horse, just as a polite host would with a caller. Nothing would serve but Julian must also have his hand shaken, and then be given a stout hug and a kiss to the cheek before he was allowed to mount up on Rhodri.

"Visit again soon," Griffin said. "If you send a card, I'll have Biddy make tea and shortbread."

"Next time, I'll send a card," Julian said, saluting with his riding crop. "Biddy's shortbread is not to be missed."

"And bring Miss Windham!" Griffin called as Julian sent Rhodri cantering down the drive.

Oh, right. Bring Miss Windham, and introduce her to the ducal heir, who would sharpen eight quills before he began to write a short note. Who would spout off about his aching tallywags before any company, and who spoke barely twelve words of English.

And yet, Julian wished he could introduce Elizabeth Windham to Griffin. She would be kind without being condescending. She'd brook no nonsense, and even in her rebukes, she'd charm and soothe.

And damned if the woman didn't, indeed, make Julian's tallywags ache.

Chapter Six

"The targets are set up, the prizes arranged," Radnor said. "The servants are putting out the punch bowls on the terrace, and the outdoor staff has been warned to stay away from the west park for the duration of the afternoon. What else might I do for you, Lady Glenys?"

He'd like to kiss her silly, which would probably get him escorted from the property on the business end of her fowling piece.

She put down her pen. "I'm forgetting something. I know I'm forgetting something."

Lady Glenys was forgetting how to laugh, how to enjoy herself. This chamber in the south turret was her private parlor, despite looking like an estate office. She kept lists and ledgers, much like the duke did, and the furniture was a hodgepodge of castoffs that should have been relegated to the attics.

Her ladyship claimed the sofa, chairs, and chaise had

sentimental value, but what each piece truly possessed were scratches, faded upholstery, and worn cushions.

"I told Abner not to let Griffin ramble on the hill today," Radnor said. "One never knows where a stray arrow might land."

Particularly an arrow shot by that master of mischief, Cupid.

Lady Glenys shifted from the escritoire to her mother's rocking chair. "I've been neglecting my younger brother. Not well done of me. I had to learn about last night's escapade from the undercook, who heard it from the boot boy, who got it from one of the stable lads, who visited with Abner while bringing in the yearlings after a night at grass."

From long acquaintance, Radnor did not wait to be invited to sit. "Griffin came to no harm, my lady. Haverford will lecture him sternly, Biddy and Abner will keep a closer eye on him, and the incident will soon be forgotten."

Lady Glenys closed her eyes and leaned her head back against the rocker. "Griffin never forgets anything. Never, never, never."

"While you're certain you've overlooked some vital detail. Shall I order you a pot of tea?"

She treated him to a hazel-eyed glower. "Don't presume to cosset me."

"Somebody must. This is your first house party, and keeping the whole business organized is more complicated than you realized."

Her glower faded to a pensive frown. "I hadn't grasped the cost. Haverford will kill me."

"I'll call him out if he's the least bit ungentlemanly toward you, and His Grace makes a sizeable target. Send to Radnor for what you need, be it wine, extra stable hands, parlor maids, or kitchen help. I have more than I need, and you'd do the same for me."

Haverford might kill Radnor outright—*Code Duello* be damned—for that presumption, but the staff at the castle would be run ragged over the next three weeks if something wasn't done to augment their ranks.

"I like you better when you're being obnoxiously witty, Cedric."

"No, love. You *dislike* me better when I'm being obnoxiously witty."

He'd *almost* made her smile.

"Order me a pot of tea and some biscuits on your way out, your lordship. I'm so busy being charming and gracious at meals, I'm not eating enough."

Radnor would tear a strip from Haverford's ducal consequence for leaving his sister to fret like this.

"The house party is off to a wonderful start, and the gods of weather are smiling on your archery tournament. As long as the sun shines and the breeze remains soft—"

"The weather," she said, pushing to her feet. "I have nothing planned if the weather should turn fickle, which is all the weather does in Wales. Between the sea and mountains—what am I to do if it rains, Radnor? I know it will rain. It always rains here when nobody needs rain. I'd forgotten about the rain."

She'd forgotten about *him*. Radnor caught up with her on her second circuit of the room.

"If it rains, then we will enjoy an impromptu musicale. I'm always good for a Welsh ballad or two, and the Windham sisters come from a musical family. Delphine and Hugh can play a duet at the pianoforte, and Haverford still has a guitar around here somewhere."

Glenys studied him, and Radnor braced himself for the

first compliment from her in years. A musicale was a brilliant suggestion, if he did say so himself.

"You look tired, Cedric. Have you been getting enough sleep?"

He'd been going very much short of bedsport—for years. "I confess I was up past my bedtime last night. I saw Griffin home, and then walked back to the castle by the lanes. The moon was lovely." *And I should have been sharing it with you.*

"The moon was too bright. I couldn't sleep."

Radnor hadn't been this close to Glenys in ages, and her lemon verbena perfume ambushed him. The urge to take her in his arms and kiss the daylights out of her was a physical yearning beyond the merely sexual.

Protectiveness and affection colored Radnor's sentiments, as well as plain old possessiveness.

And yet, Glenys was tired. Behind the usual hauteur in the angle of her chin and the relentless dignity of her bearing, she was tired and overwhelmed.

"Take a nap," he said. "I'll explain to Haverford that you're seeing to the last-minute preparations for the tournament, and he and I will manage at luncheon. I'll warn him to tune his guitar, and I'll have a word with the Windham sisters. Sir Nigel has a fine baritone, and I can accompany him if the tournament must be postponed due to weather."

Glenys freed a fold of his cravat from his waistcoat, a single finger's worth of familiarity that made Radnor's heart beat erratically.

"I cannot take a nap, you gudgeon. I should have prepared two scavenger hunts. One for indoors, one for outdoors, and somebody must make copies of the lists of items to retrieve."

A knock sounded on the door. Radnor answered it, and accepted the luncheon tray from a startled maid.

"I took the liberty," he said, setting the tray on the sideboard. "I'll also have a maid fetch you in ninety minutes, leaving you time for a short respite. There are sandwiches on this tray, and you will please partake of them. I'm happy to copy lists, shoot arrows, or flirt with Lady Pembroke, but Glenys, you must not try to do all of this by yourself."

She crossed to the sideboard and peered at the tray. "I have dozens of servants to help me, Haverford is being the perfect host, and—these are ham and cheese sandwiches on rye bread. I adore rye bread, but you know that." She sniffed the bread, much as Griffin might have, then took a bite. "Away with you, Cedric, and if you let me sleep through my own archery tournament, I will never forgive you."

Just don't forget me. "I have my orders. Your servant, my dear."

Radnor kissed the hand that wasn't holding a sandwich and withdrew, only to find the Duke of Haverford coming up the corridor.

"Is Glenys hiding in there?"

"She's planning your wedding to Miss Windham. It only *looks* like she's fretting over an archery tournament, a riding party, a musicale, two scavenger hunts, a country dance, a regiment of feuding housemaids, and your errant brother."

Haverford regarded the door to Glenys's *sanctum sanctorum* as if it were inscribed with the warning, *Hic sunt dracones.* A single dragoness, rather.

"Please spare Miss Windham your jests, Radnor. She has good cause to loathe all bachelors. Lady Glenys can make no such claim. Were you canoodling with my sister?"

How I wish. "If I had attempted the smallest gesture in the direction of canoodling with Lady Glenys in her present mood, you'd be measuring me for a shroud."

Haverford retreated across the corridor, and took a wilting rose from a vase on the windowsill. He wrestled the window open, tossed the flower to the garden below, then closed the latch with more squeaking and scraping of old metal.

"I sought my sister out to suggest she steal a nap during luncheon. I can certainly preside over a midday meal without Glenys. I do fear this gathering constitutes biting off more than her ladyship can chew."

"And you," Radnor said, taking Haverford by the elbow before some guest caught His Grace impersonating a footman, "who can be a pontificating, humorless prig, are tempted to leave her hoist on her own petard, because the poor darling failed to adequately *plan, schedule, and budget* for this gathering."

Haverford twisted free of his grasp. "Have I given offense, Cedric?"

Why was everybody determined to use familiar address today? "You have not. Lady Glenys's foul humor is contagious. Let us prepare to be charming at the luncheon table while her ladyship puts the finishing touches on the afternoon's diversion. You will ignore my ill-chosen remarks."

"Don't tell me what to do."

"Like you, I intended merely to *suggest*. Shall we have a bout of fisticuffs here in the corridor or cry friends and shake hands?"

Haverford glanced up and down the corridor, then leaned closer. "A bout of fisticuffs might be just the thing. Griffin has developed a *tendresse* for Nan Pritchard."

"God save us, and have mercy on your account at the tavern." The lad fell violently in love, and tended to be constant in his attentions to the point of obsession.

"I'm convinced this house party has put the very stars out of alignment. Clouds have gathered to the south. Do you know if Glenys has anything planned for the afternoon in case of rain? I could always lead a tour of the damned library."

"Glenys is ten steps ahead of you," Radnor said. "If it rains, we're to have an impromptu musicale. I'm to trot out my ballads, and you're to play the guitar. Sir Nigel and the Windham sisters are on the program, and I suspect Hugh and Delphine might favor us with a duet."

Haverford cast a look over his shoulder in the direction of Glenys's turret. "Perhaps I've underestimated my sister."

"It wouldn't be the first time. She really does have all in hand."

"Do you suppose she'd send me to the pillory if I asked you for the loan of a few stable hands or chamber maids? A spare footman or three wouldn't go amiss either."

"You may rely on my discretion and on my staff. Far better that they lend a hand here, than expect me to host one of these grand operas. A country house party is enough to drive even one of my singular fortitude barking mad."

"My mother always said you had delicate nerves."

Radnor was on the point of tripping his best friend when he realized that Haverford was smiling—truly, broadly smiling—and that his remark had been meant as a jest.

While Radnor had spoken in complete earnest.

* * *

"Miss Windham, excuse me."

"Your Grace, good evening."

Haverford was silhouetted in the doorway of this odd, round, parlor-cum-office, looking severely handsome in his evening attire. The sconces flickered with the draft from the corridor, sending shadows across the page Elizabeth had just sanded.

The walls of Lady Glenys's tower chamber were not plastered smooth or covered with silk. Rough stone climbed to exposed timbers that marked this as an older part of the castle.

"If you'd please close the door, sir, I won't have to re-light my candles."

His Grace complied, and crossed the room to peer over Elizabeth's shoulder. "Has Lady Glenys set you to copying her scavenger hunt lists?"

Cedar blended with the scents of candles and peat as Haverford's shadow fell over the list Elizabeth had copied: Three acorns, one rosebud, a sprig of lavender, one white feather, a four-leaf clover...

My dignity. Since Haverford's courtly gesture in the library—his *kiss*—Elizabeth had thought of little else. She would bet her personal copy of Boswell's *Life of Samuel Johnson* that Haverford hadn't kissed any other guests.

"I volunteered to help," Elizabeth said. "I got turned around seeking my apartment after lunch and came upon her ladyship hard at work here when she ought to have been napping. She promised to have a lie down if I'd make six copies of each of her lists before tomorrow."

Haverford settled into the rocking chair near the hearth. "You are kind, Miss Windham, but you dissemble. Here's the truth: You plucked the lists from Lady Glenys over her protests, told her to seek her bed, and assured her you'd make the copies. Your sister is quite the markswoman."

He would notice that. Elizabeth had noticed that Haverford had partnered Helen Windstruther, a shy young lady rumored to have only modest settlements.

"Charlotte was showing off, Your Grace. She has decided to torment Viscount Haldale."

"She missed her target, if she was aiming for his lordship."

In a sense, Charlotte had been aiming for Haldale, and she hadn't missed. She had barely nocked her figurative arrow. Haldale had been dragged away by Delphine St. David, and had spent the rest of the afternoon admiring Charlotte from the vicinity of the punch bowl.

"I was sent to this house party to find a spouse, Your Grace. Charlotte accompanied me out of loyalty, not a desire to find a husband."

Haverford rocked slowly, the chair creaking in counterpoint to the crackling of the fire. His legs were crossed at the knee—an informal pose—but then, the hour was late, and the day had been long. By firelight, Elizabeth could see the man he would become—features a bit craggy, visage tending to sternness. He'd age well and slowly, like his castle.

"If your sister prefers tormenting Haldale to winning my notice, I'll be the last to complain of her choice of pastimes. Have you selected a book from my library yet?"

Elizabeth had sat amid a hoard of literary treasures, contemplating Haverford's casual kiss until Aunt had dragooned her into serving on a pall mall team.

"Choosing a book from among thirty thousand tomes will take some consideration. While I'm delighting in your library, I suspect Charlotte might sample the charms of a discreet bachelor if the opportunity presents itself. She could view this party as her last chance for... adventure."

Elizabeth had no interest in adventure, though another kiss from Haverford would be lovely.

The duke rose and began rummaging in the sideboard. "Care for a drink?"

A lady never partook of strong spirits, save for medicinal purposes. She also did not permit herself to linger in a compromising situation with a handsome duke.

At least, not more than twice a day. "A drink of what, Your Grace?"

"Let's be a bit wicked, shall we? Glenys's medicinal stores include madeira, brandy"—he opened a plain brown bottle, sniffed, and winced—"whiskey, if I'm not mistaken. My, my, my. Glenys has latent heathen tendencies. A pear cordial, a cherry cordial—my sister is quite the connoisseur."

"Pear cordial sounds interesting." As did a nightcap with the duke.

"I'll have a nip of the same. Radnor predicts I'll be a raving sot by the end of this house party. He's promised to join me in that folly, and I suspect a *tendresse* for Lady Glenys might explain the source of his torment."

"Thank you," Elizabeth said, accepting a serving of pear cordial. "To a house party happily concluded for all."

"A fine notion," the duke replied, resuming his seat before the fire, a glass of amber liquid cradled in his palm. "Shall I warn Haldale off where Lady Charlotte's concerned? On the roster of duties assigned to a conscientious host, preserving the innocence of maidens likely sits near the top."

He made preserving the innocence of maidens sound as if it belonged on a list between meeting with the steward and inspecting the tenant cottages.

"Charlotte is a woman grown, sir. Who am I to meddle in her decisions?"

"You are one of the most forthright, sensible females it has been my pleasure to know. Why hesitate to save your sister from folly?"

Forthright and sensible. Elizabeth would rather *kissable* figured among His Grace's compliments, but then, he was complimenting her with his time, his honesty, and his company late at night.

Haverford wasn't the first man to kiss Elizabeth, though he was the first to share a pear cordial with her, the first to offer her a book of her choosing, the first to hold her hand under a moonlit summer sky.

The pear cordial was pleasant and surprisingly complicated. Such a drink too often became like so much jam in a glass—mostly sweet, a bit of fruit, a hint of spirits. Nothing remarkable. A touch of spice lurked in this version, an unexpected elegance.

"I have said nothing to Charlotte thus far because I'm not sure I should," Elizabeth replied. "She typically takes no notice of bachelors, other than to skewer their presumptions."

Haverford saluted with his cordial. "A fine use of the typical bachelor, and it begs the question: Is she merely amusing herself with Haldale, or setting him up to be skewered at dinner Tuesday next? I might like to see that."

So would I.

His Grace was out of the chair and back at the sideboard, and this time, he produced a handkerchief, and took Lady Glenys's collection of spirits from the cupboard bottle by bottle.

"What are you doing, sir?"

"Leaving my sister a warning," he said, dusting each bottle in turn. "Lord Haldale fancies himself a buccaneer of the bedroom, if I may speak bluntly. Miss Charlotte might appreciate a word of caution too."

Haldale's rutting made him dashing, while Charlotte would be called fast if she shared two consecutive dances with the same man.

"What is your pleasure, Miss Windham?" the duke asked, replacing the bottles in the same arrangement he'd found them in. "Shall I say something to Haldale? Perhaps have a chat with Lady Pembroke?"

Haverford was trying to be helpful—drat him—and Elizabeth was trying to be agreeable, but pleasantries and platitudes eluded her.

"I will speak bluntly as well," Elizabeth replied. "If Charlotte accepts what Haldale offers, she'll not view the whole business of marriage as some great secret worth sacrificing her entire future for. Men approach their vows without the ignorance women are supposed to guard so carefully, and as a rule, the groom is far more deliberate about the business than the bride is. This is true, even when for many husbands, the vows are a formality they have no intention of honoring."

Perhaps pear cordial made one loquacious—or pugnacious—for Elizabeth hadn't expressed that thinking even to her sisters.

Haverford tucked his handkerchief away, folding it to hide streaks of dust. "Miss Windham, the subject of why a person marries, or does not marry, particularly in the case of a man who regards himself as the sole support of his family, is a more nuanced undertaking than you might grasp at first glance."

Elizabeth knew that patient tone, that measured cadence. His Grace was warming up for a diatribe on a topic about which Elizabeth had been lectured past endurance. Though why were they discussing Charlotte, marriage, and perishing randy bachelors *at all* when they might have been discussing poetry or great literature?

Or kisses?

"Please do not explain marriage to me, Your Grace. I am blessed with two sisters and eight cousins who delight in regaling me with the joys of the wedded state. You have no comparable source of perspective."

And those joys were beyond Elizabeth's reach. Her sisters and cousins were radiant with marital glee, while Elizabeth had searched in vain for a bachelor who inspired even a small glow of contentment.

Nor, apparently, would she find such a man at Haverford Castle. She rose and passed the duke her unfinished drink.

"I ask you to excuse my impertinence, Your Grace. I am tired, and out of sorts. I will copy the rest of her ladyship's lists in the morning."

The duke stood between Elizabeth and the door, which would not serve when tears were so inconveniently threatening.

"You are angry with me, Miss Windham."

Elizabeth was merely disappointed in Haverford. She was furious with a society that preferred a woman marry— marry anybody, no matter how brutish or self-absorbed— rather than live out her life in contented solitude. She was enraged with men who were willing to *tolerate* her literary interests because she was a means of establishing a connection with a ducal family.

She was angry with—and hurt by—that same family because they saw her only as a spinster-in-waiting.

And she was angry with herself, for being so easily intrigued with a simple kiss and the loan of a few books.

Elizabeth offered the duke a shallow curtsy. "I apologize for expressing myself so strongly, Your Grace. I know my views of marriage are unconventional. I'll bid you good night, if you'd stand aside."

"That, I cannot do."

Chapter Seven

Elizabeth Windham was a quiet presence at any meal, a polite conversationalist while waiting to take her turn with a bow and arrow, a dutiful companion to her aunt—and she was a walking, talking, smiling liar.

Were all women this good at dissembling? For the gracious, unassuming Miss Windham hid volumes worth of indignation and passion beneath her quiet exterior. If Julian were a betting man, he'd put money on lending libraries appearing in every village in the realm within ten years.

She had intrigued him with her demure composure, while this hidden ferocity fascinated him.

Miss Windham occupied the center of the room, dignity and ire crackling about her. Julian had offended a lady, and that was not an acceptable way to end his day—or hers.

"Madam, you place before me an impossibility. How can I have a pleasant evening, when I have so clearly upset you? At least finish your cordial."

She likely wanted to dash her drink in Julian's face, but faultless manners were part of her duplicity.

Miss Windham retrieved her glass from him and tossed back the contents in one gulp, then began coughing. Julian dared not laugh, but he did presume to lead her to the rocking chair.

"That was foolishness," he said. "That was rank, reckless foolishness and a waste of Lady Glenys's favorite recipe. If you wish to become inebriated, then you keep a patent remedy in good supply, and when nobody is about, tipple to your—"

"Haverford, cease instructing me, or I will strike a blow where you will never forget it."

She apparently referred—in deadly earnest and at close quarters—to his tallywags, or possibly to his pride.

Julian took a step back. "I apologize." A safe place to start, though inadequate. "Whatever fellow or fellows led you to have such a dim view of marriage, or its intimate joys, or of life in general, did you a disservice."

He passed her his handkerchief and realized too late it was less than pristine.

"I've considered that," Miss Windham said, finding a clean corner and dabbing at her eyes. "I've considered that I chose poorly when deciding to cross the bounds of strict propriety—though how is a woman to develop a sense for such matters? All men adopt fine manners, charm, and good humor when they're in the ballroom. That apparently means nothing in the bedroom."

Welsh curses came to mind in quantity.

"Maybe I chose poorly," she went on more softly, "both times."

Julian drew up the hassock and planted himself upon it, lest her revelations lay him out on the carpet. "You should not be telling me these things, but I beg you, if you have a scintilla of mercy in your soul, do not mention names."

"Why not? Surely you don't care if some baron—"

He put two fingers to her lips, and glowered as old Offa must have glowered at the barbarians to the east of his dyke, then he withdrew his hand before the texture of her mouth became too intriguing.

"—you cannot care who among your peers is a bad kisser," Miss Windham said, "or doesn't bother with kissing at all."

St. David, pray for me. "If I know their names, I'd have to call them out. Two duels would be hard to keep quiet. Allermain might get word I've neglected him, and three duels is the outside of too much."

"Allermain will spend at least the next year in Paris. Why would you call out men who'd merely accommodated my wishes?"

The hour was late, Julian was tired, and his mind refused to sort through the demands of honor when Miss Windham's hurt feelings obscured all logic from his view. No plan he might have concocted, no list or ledger, would have prepared him to have the conversation he was having with her now.

"Those men disappointed you. I'd call them out for disappointing you. Let's leave it at that. A gentleman might dally discreetly, as might a lady under very limited circumstances, but even a dalliance should be undertaken with a certain respect for one's lover."

"I suspected I'd chosen a pair of rotters. What foul luck. Might I have a bit more cordial?"

Julian poured her a generous portion and resumed his place on the hassock. "Did either of these varlets offer marriage?" And had they broken her heart or merely disappointed her?

"I had an understanding with Theodore, but then his mother's god-daughter turned up in immediate need of a husband. She was pretty, four years younger than I, and her settlements included a lovely estate in Hampshire. He was very sorry, but duty compelled him to aid a damsel in distress."

He was sorry, all right. Snippets of gossip connected in Haverford's head. Teddy Morningside was the younger son of an earl, a bad card player, and a good dancer. He'd dropped out of the social scene about five years ago, though he was rumored to be filling his nursery in Hampshire.

"You're better off without a man whose honor is so easily obliterated by coin."

"I am, and he couldn't kiss worth a bent farthing."

"Always a consideration."

Miss Windham took another sip of her cordial. "With the baron, I yielded to impulse. He said he had as well, but he'd neglected to tell me of a fiancée kicking her heels in County Mayo. He didn't kiss at all."

"Irish barons are always a risky bet. You can't let those two encounters color your whole perception of the male gender, or of marriage."

"They were experienced men, Your Grace. I chose them knowing they'd bring at least that asset to the proceedings."

Her logic was faultless, and her lips had been very soft against Julian's fingertips.

"I have years of experience being a duke. That doesn't mean I have any talent for it. I wish you the joy of your lending library scheme, and I'm sure you'll benefit many a village with it. On behalf of my gender, however, I'd like to offer one gesture by way of apology, or perhaps as a counterexample to your theories regarding marital pleasures."

Julian took her drink from her hand and ignored the voice in his head that sounded like Radnor delivering a lecture.

"A counterexample sounds promising, Your Grace."

"Julian. If we're to be sharing counterexamples, you must call me Julian."

He cradled Miss Windham's jaw against his palm, lest she mistake his intent. When he was confident that he had her consent, *and her attention*, he kissed her.

* * *

I've left my common sense back in England.

Elizabeth hadn't meant to rant at Haverford much less confide in him, hadn't meant to disclose her past, or even discuss Charlotte's inchoate schemes with him. The dratted man listened, though, most of the time. He was a duke, and yet he was also like no kind of aristocrat Elizabeth had met—or kissed—before.

Haverford was trying to convince her he was a lazy kisser, but he was lazy like a prowling lion, bringing infinite patience and focus to his advances. His lips moved over Elizabeth's in gentle brushes, and she scooted closer, the better to grip him by the lapels.

He came closer as well, spreading his knees, and sliding a hand into Elizabeth's hair.

His kisses were lovely. Tender, teasing, maddeningly undemanding.

"I want—" Elizabeth muttered against his mouth.

His tongue danced across her lips. She braced herself for an invasion, for a crude imitation of coitus, but Haverford surprised her by pausing to caress the nape of her neck.

"If you don't like it," he said, "you show me what I'm doing wrong. You are gifted at chiding and correcting. Chide me."

Oh, my. Oh, gracious. Oh, yes. Elizabeth explored

the shape and texture of his mouth, the contours of his lips, the arch of his eyebrows. His jaw was only slightly bristly—he must have shaved before dinner—while his eyebrows were soft.

Elizabeth took a taste of him, and his every movement, from his breathing to the susurration of his clothing, to his slight shifts on the hassock, stilled.

"Again," he said. "Please."

Elizabeth liked the sound of that, liked the feel of the word *please* whispered against her mouth.

And as the kiss deepened and became a frolic followed by a dare, punctuated by a challenge, she rejoiced.

I was wrong. I was so very, wonderfully wrong. Every man wasn't an inconsiderate lout. They weren't all monuments to self-satisfaction. At least one bachelor could kiss and kiss and kiss.... Elizabeth took one more taste of pleasure, then drew back enough to rest her forehead on Haverford's shoulder.

"I need a moment, Your—Julian."

He stroked her hair, his cheek resting against her temple. "Take all the time you need. I'm in rather a state myself."

Elizabeth hugged his admission to her heart. He'd restored her faith in something—perhaps in herself. The fault had lain not with her, but with the men she'd chosen, and if she could be wrong in this, she might be wrong about the joys of marriage, about her own dreams, about anything.

Elizabeth sat back and smoothed the duke's cravat. "My thanks. You deliver an impressive counterexample. You've given me something to consider."

One mink-dark eyebrow quirked. "Such effusive praise will surely turn my head, Miss Windham."

"Elizabeth. If I'm turning your head, you may address me as Elizabeth when private."

They shared a smile, conspiratorial, sweet, and a bit dazed. This was how it was supposed to be between a man and a woman, both comfortable and daring, a private adventure.

Haverford rose and tossed a square of peat onto the fire, then poked it to the back of the flames, so the fire could both breathe and consume the fresh fuel.

"Shall I say something to Haldale regarding your sister?" he asked, giving the peat one last nudge.

"With the subtlety common to all dukes, you should let him know that if he pursues what Charlotte offers, he must do so with utmost discretion and care. Charlotte is merely bored, not desperate, and I suspect Haldale will regret any impertinence."

"As you wish. A warning rather than a threat. I'm loath to leave you here alone at such a late hour. Might I escort you to your room?"

He was back to being the polite host, and yet, Elizabeth knew better. Haverford was a superb kisser, one who had probably made a few poor choices of his own, late at night in crowded, lonely ballrooms. The knowledge warmed her from within, like the subtle spices of the pear cordial.

"Yes, please, provide me your escort, Your Grace. I might get turned around again, and spend eternity trying to find the right tower."

The duke repositioned the screen in front of the fire, set his glass on the sideboard next to Elizabeth's, and went to the door. He first peered into the corridor, then gestured for Elizabeth to join him. The chill was bracing—this was a castle, after all. And yet, Elizabeth's heart was warmed too.

Haverford had made sure nobody would see them leaving Lady Glenys's parlor. He might kiss Elizabeth witless, but he'd protect her reputation from even a hint of gossip.

What was that old saying about the third time being a charm?

* * *

One institution in all of England was above what Lucas Sherbourne's father had called "persuasion by coin." Almack's assembly rooms were managed by a board of patronesses, a coven of well-born females who might trade in influence and favors, but never in cash.

Sherbourne's father had tried to bribe his way to vouchers and been unsuccessful. The only worse social disaster would have been a voucher granted and subsequently revoked.

"Perhaps next season, I'll hold my annual ball on some evening other than Wednesday," Sherbourne informed his grandmama's portrait. Almack's held its gatherings on Wednesdays. If Sherbourne couldn't attend, the least revenge he could take was to ensure half of polite society was in absentia with him.

The half who owed him or his bank money.

"Next year will be different," he assured his powdered, smiling granddame.

He rose from the table where he'd dined in lordly solitude. One did not become an aristocrat by swilling ale from pewter tankards or setting the table with Sheffield plate instead of silver.

When Sherbourne acquired a wife, she'd find herself in a household worthy of a duchess.

His path took him back to his estate office, where he kept the best Armagnac. The guest list from Haverford's house party sat in the center of the morocco blotter on his desk. The family names marching down the page had all been admitted to Almack's for at least the past quarter-century. Those people knew one another, they socialized with one another, they *married* one another.

"They are the aristocratic equivalent of an English infantry square, unrelentingly loyal to the regiment, closing ranks against all threats."

Battles took a toll on those squares, though, and new recruits were necessary to keep Britain's aristocracy funded. Sherbourne controlled fourteen seats in the House of Commons, and depending on market conditions, at least that many in the House of Lords.

"Still not enough," he said, passing a glass of fine French brandy beneath his nose. "But more than many an earl can command."

Haverford didn't control seats in the House of Lords, he *voted* his seat. Ever the conscientious nobleman, was Julian, Duke of Indebtedness.

Sherbourne settled into the chair behind his desk, studying the list. Lady Glenys was the only ducal daughter amid the females, and she was, of course, his marital objective. Approaching her would be easier if he knew how much she comprehended about Haverford's financial situation.

Only a fool antagonized the woman who might bear his children.

The list was incomplete, because it hadn't been stolen from Haverford Castle. Such larceny would have been unsporting, given how little attention the St. Davids paid to the security of their domicile.

Sherbourne's list was a compilation of servants' gossip reported by Sherbourne's housekeeper, observations offered by Squire Canford, rumors gleaned by Sherbourne's land steward from forays into the local tavern, and a final few items from Sherbourne's vast correspondence.

Never had so many single, wealthy, aristocratic bachelors gathered in one place, excepting perhaps Ascot during the race meets. Haverford was determined to parade his sister before every eligible of note.

That would not do. Lady Glenys was the highest-ranking female for several counties in any direction, and Sherbourne had all but decided she'd become his wife. He'd been patient long enough, and in the manner of good families down through the centuries, theirs would be an advantageous match for all concerned.

Sherbourne wasn't a barbarian, and the St. Davids couldn't afford to be choosy.

"A proposal from me would flatter any young lady of sense," Sherbourne muttered, giving the list a final perusal.

A name near the bottom caught his eye: Windham, Miss Elizabeth and Miss Charlotte, accompanied by their elderly aunt, Lady Pembroke. The Windhams held a ducal title. In fact, they were the only other ducal family represented at the gathering besides the St. Davids.

Interesting.

Sherbourne consulted Debrett's as he finished his drink, and then took himself off to bed. As his valet got him changed into a nightshirt and dressing gown, Sherbourne considered Haverford's house party.

Lady Glenys remained the most desirable objective, though she'd never been anything more than cordial to Sherbourne. Ladies were like that, though. They could hide rage, affection, resentment, and attraction with equal skill.

"Her ladyship is no great beauty either." Sherbourne knew who the great beauties were, because their papas needed great fortunes to clothe and dower them.

Sherbourne's valet paused on his way to the door, a day's worth of wrinkled linen in his arms. "Beg your pardon, sir?"

"Nothing of any moment. Has my trunk been packed for tomorrow?"

Turnbull had been wooed away from the household of a Scottish marquess who'd served in the Caribbean. Not by a twitch of an eyebrow did he betray surprise.

"All is in readiness for tomorrow, sir. Good night." Turnbull's voice bore the lyrical cadence of the islands, a counterpoint to the brisk dignity with which he went about his duties.

He withdrew silently, and Sherbourne settled into bed with a report from his London solicitors on the progress of various bills to regulate child labor. The aristocracy made polite noises about ensuring no children younger than nine were apprenticed in the textile factories and that such children never spent more than twelve hours a day at their work.

Of course, the same tender-hearted lords did nothing to make the laws enforceable, and most children in the factories weren't apprenticed. Many were younger than nine, and they worked as much as sixteen hours a day for perhaps one-sixth the wages paid their fathers.

Sherbourne spent thirty minutes skimming the report, finding nothing more than the usual posturing by the usual titled nincompoops. Great lords giving great orations that ignored the great profits reaped by the same aristocrats using the very child labor they decried.

Parasitical hypocrites, the lot of them. Sherbourne blew out the bedside candles, and a thought occurred to him in the darkness.

No competent general went into battle without a contingency plan, and a mature, un-married niece of a duke, a woman of advancing years and no particular beauty, was probably a sensible creature.

Miss Elizabeth Windham would see the wisdom in an advantageous alliance, if Haverford and his sister proved difficult. The more Sherbourne considered his contingency plan, the more he liked it.

Having Haverford for a brother-in-law when Sherbourne was poised to ruin His Grace of Inherited Disaster would be awkward, after all.

Chapter Eight

Confiding in a handsome duke, late at night, behind a closed door, was not wise. Elizabeth longed to repeat the experience soon and often.

Haverford's kisses followed her into slumber and provoked restless dreams that had her rising early. She made her way to the breakfast parlor while the servants were still arranging the buffet on the sideboard. Elizabeth slathered butter and jam on three scones, cut herself a slice of cheddar, grabbed a small orange, and wrapped the lot in a linen serviette.

She was new at confiding, and to best savor the folly of the previous evening—if folly it had been—she wanted fresh air and solitude. Charlotte, by contrast, had demanded to be left in peace amid her pillows.

Haverford Castle sat on a rise, and beyond the back terrace, the formal gardens merged with a park that gave way to wilderness and countryside. Tudor Hill rose to the east, and a river bisected the park. Elizabeth struck out for the river, which she intended to follow along the base of the hill.

The scythed grass sparkled with dew, the air was brisk, and the sunshine benevolent. No wonder Mama was often homesick, and no wonder she and Papa journeyed to Wales frequently. Something about the light put Elizabeth in mind of fairy tales and legends, magic caves, and....

Midnight kisses.

The river was a swath of silvery brilliance in the morning sun, at variance with the geometric gardens closer to the house. A river, unlike an almost-spinster, had some say in its direction.

Elizabeth's objective was to find a place to settle with a sketch pad. While admiring the view, she'd enjoy a solitary picnic, pretend to draw, and consider developments with Haverford. He'd kissed her of his own free will, no flirting or prodding on her part required, and that...that gratified some undignified girlish fancy Elizabeth had denied for years.

"Good gracious!"

One moment, the path before her had been empty, the next it was filled with the most gorgeous young man Elizabeth had ever beheld. A rustling of the oak branches overhead was her only clue that the fellow hadn't sprung up from some fairy mound.

"Good morning." His greeting was in careful English, and his smile both bashful and merry.

"Good morning," Elizabeth replied in Welsh.

This exquisite creature was dark-haired, neatly attired, and possessed of the finest brown eyes ever bestowed on an adult male. His countenance conveyed no guile, arrogance, or caution. Angels gazed on the world with this much benevolence, though what angel had the St. David eyebrows?

He was attired not as a farm lad or yeoman, but as a country gentleman out for a morning constitutional. Everything, from his field boots, to his shooting jacket, to his neckcloth, was clean and well made.

Whoever he was, he came from means.

"Griffin St. David, at your service." His bow was punctilious, despite the rustic surrounds, and he'd spoken in cheerful Welsh. "You're supposed to curtsy now, and you should tell me your name. If we were at church, somebody would introduce us, but if we were at church, we'd be neighbors. I know all of my neighbors, and I've never been introduced to you. Did you know there are forty-two coaches behind the castle's coach house?"

His earnestness was childlike, though he looked in every way whole and adult. This was very likely the "Griffin" who'd gone missing two nights ago, and no wonder his disappearance had caused the duke worry.

"I had not counted the coaches," Elizabeth said. "Are you related to Haverford and Lady Glenys, Mr. St. David?" He had to be, given those eyebrows, the dark hair, the height, and his complete ease on Haverford land.

"I have my own household," he said, obviously quite pleased about this. "You're supposed to curtsy."

Elizabeth remedied the oversight, because Mr. St. David was absolutely correct, though by rights a mutual acquaintance really should have introduced them.

"I've come outside to sketch," Elizabeth said. "I suspect the views from the hill are spectacular."

"I can show you the way. I'm a gentleman. I won't let you stumble or get lost." Mr. St. David spoke in all seriousness, and if he was a St. David cousin or by-blow, he probably did know every path and pasture on the estate.

"I would appreciate your escort, but you mustn't expect too fast a pace. I want to enjoy the scenery."

"I won't run," he said, setting off along the river path. "Do I take your arm or not? I could hold your hand. Biddy says I'm to take her arm, but sometimes we hold hands too. Biddy makes the best shortbread."

If only all men were so willing to inquire about a lady's preferences. "I can manage on my own, provided you'll show me the way. Perhaps you'd be willing to carry my haversack?" Elizabeth passed him the leather bag holding her breakfast picnic and her sketching supplies.

Griffin looped the sack over a sturdy shoulder. "You didn't tell me your name. I won't forget if you tell me, but I must not presume-an-acquaintance until we've been introduced, even if you are a friend to Lady Glenys or Biddy or Julian."

Elizabeth chose the least formal and most Welsh version of her name. "I'm Bethan. Do you live nearby?"

"At my own house, with Biddy and Abner. Oscar comes to help sometimes, and Emry Davis helps Biddy on laundry days. Are you tired yet? If you're tired, we can rest."

He was very dear. "I'm managing."

Griffin shot her a furtive, puzzled look, and Elizabeth realized she'd spoken in English.

"My apologies," she said, switching back to Welsh. "I'm fine for now, though I doubt I'd be able to keep up if you weren't making allowances for my shorter legs. You have a dog, don't you?"

Griffin waxed enthusiastic about King Henry, who was talented at flushing hares and named for the Welsh-born sovereign. Next came a monologue on the flora and fauna of the area, about which Elizabeth's escort was astonishingly knowledgeable.

"We can see the coaches from here," he said when they were about halfway up the hill. "Yesterday everybody shot arrows. Radnor and Glenys argued, but they always argue. You mustn't think anything of it."

Where had Griffin been, that he'd overheard the marquess and Lady Glenys having a tiff?

"House parties can be demanding for the hostess," Elizabeth said. "I'm sure Lord Radnor was only trying to help."

"Glenys makes his tallywags ache. I like to sit on that rock there. King Henry does too."

Tallywags? The term was English, more or less, and it had no place in a lady's conversation in any language. Though…poor Radnor. Poor Lady Glenys, if she provoked such a response from her neighbor and didn't realize it. Aching tallywags went well beyond a genteel *tendresse*.

"Let's rest our feet," Elizabeth suggested. "This would be a lovely place to start sketching."

The countryside unfolded across the valley in a patchwork of pastures, hayfields, cultivated land, and woods. Far off to the west, mist drifted from the underside of a rain cloud, but in every other direction, the landscape was drenched in sun.

"Radnor is my friend," Griffin said, sitting down right next to Elizabeth on the smooth flat stone.

He was as guileless as a boy, and even less self-consciousness. The combination of handsome adult male appearance and innocent male mind was disconcerting, and yet, Elizabeth would have said Griffin was a good man.

A gentleman, as he'd said, and a gentle man.

"Will you sketch me?" he asked. "I'm handsome. That is not my fault. Biddy says my hair needs a trim."

"You are quite handsome. If you can sit still for a few moments, I will happily sketch you."

He remained utterly unmoving for about five minutes, until Elizabeth passed him a scone. "I took more than I needed from the breakfast offerings. Tell me more about Biddy."

"She's very pretty. Her real name is Bridget and she's Abner's niece." His manners were careful, though the scone soon disappeared. "Nan Pritchard is pretty too, but I like Biddy better. Who do you like?"

Interesting question. Elizabeth liked what she knew of Julian, Duke of Haverford, and what a relief that was. Beyond her family, she liked very few men, particularly very few single young men. Haverford wasn't exactly young, though.

He'd probably never been young, while Griffin would always be youthful.

"My sister has traveled here with me," Elizabeth said, "and so has my aunt. I like them both. I like Lady Glenys. Would you care for another scone?"

"Yes, please. Julian says if we eat outside, we don't have to say grace out loud, but we should still be grateful. I'm very grateful because today I made a new friend."

The second scone absorbed him for a few minutes, as Elizabeth tried to sketch both Griffin and the rural surrounds that made such a fitting setting for him. He was not quick in the sense of being socially sophisticated, but his lecture on plants and animals suggested he took keen notice of everything in his environment.

"You spoke English," Griffin said, gazing at the ocean sparkling in the distance. "I speak only Welsh."

"You greeted me in English," Elizabeth replied, shading in his left eyebrow. Haverford's eyebrows were thicker, but then, Haverford was probably ten years Griffin's senior.

"When we go to services, I listen, and sometimes, I learn a word, and try it out on Biddy, but she says I don't need the English. Julian speaks English *all the time*, unless he's calling on me. Julian is smart."

Such carefully guarded pain lay beneath Griffin's words.

"Does Julian know every bird and bush on this hillside?"

Griffin shook his head vigorously. "Julian is busy. He's the duke. He goes to London."

A stout defense, though laced with genuine bewilderment. Who would waste time in stinking London when he could instead be here, admiring the sea and conversing with the birds?

"Shall I teach you some English, Mr. St. David?"

"Everybody calls me Griffin. I want to learn English. I want Julian to be proud of me, but I'm not smart."

I'm not pretty, I'm not well dowered, I'm not clever, I'm not witty.... Why were one's failings so often the sum of one's self-awareness?

"We will educate each other," Elizabeth said. "For every word or phrase I teach you, you will instruct me regarding a plant, a bird, a feature of the geography, or the local lore. Have we a bargain, Griffin?"

"I never forget anything," he said, nodding so enthusiastically, he bobbed up and down on his rock seat. "I can teach you everything Abner has taught me, and Abner knows *a lot*. He's old. He helped find me when I wasn't lost. Teach me something."

Elizabeth took up her sketch pad and turned over a clean sheet. "What would you like to know how to say?"

Griffin resumed studying the sea, presenting Elizabeth with a profile that would have eclipsed Byron's beauty on his most striking day.

"I want to learn how to say 'I love you.'"

"A good place to start and a simple sentence."

Though saying those words took courage, if they were meant honestly. If they weren't meant honestly, then they should not be said at all.

* * *

"I am ready to take vows," Julian said, guiding Rhodri down the path through the park. The fresh air was invigorating, and old Rhodri was eager to stretch his legs.

Radnor rode a mare, an unusual choice. He claimed mares had better self-preservation instincts than geldings, and weren't as easily distracted as stallions.

"Who's the lucky woman?" Radnor asked.

"Not those kind of vows. Is there some unwritten law that house parties turn everyone associated with them daft? I'm ready to swear a vow never to host a gathering like this one again." Witness, Julian had risen at the crack of doom for his daily ride and had had to bring Radnor along for safety in numbers.

Julian hadn't slept well for years, but last night's dreams had been uncharacteristically erotic. He was accustomed to dreaming of unpaid bills, crumbling turrets, and reproachful ancestors. Another frequent torment involved books turning into winged banknotes and fluttering into the blue Welsh sky. On his better nights, he dreamed of schedules and budgets, declining balances, and rising market prices.

The ancestors couldn't begin to compare to Elizabeth Windham for troubling his sleep.

"Lady Glenys would be hurt to hear you grumbling," Radnor said. "She's needed a project."

"Glenys needs a husband." And Julian needed a long swim in the river's coldest currents. "You will not allow Lady Inglesby onto my team for the scavenger hunt, Radnor."

"I was about to make the same demand of you. If I take on Lady Inglesby, you should have Delphine."

"Delphine should be *having* her husband, and I'm to remind him of that."

As head of the family, that was a task Julian should have undertaken several years ago. He'd been too busy fretting over finances, Griffin, Glenys, a subsiding wall in the gate house, a river determined to create water meadows out of pastures, and passage of a bill to prohibit the labor of young children in the mines.

Among other things.

"I'd say your house party is off to a good start," Radnor observed as they turned down between two hedges. "Intrigues are hatching, the elders are off in corners getting tipsy, and nobody was struck by any stray arrows yesterday."

Julian had been struck in the heart—and perhaps a bit lower. "Must you be so optimistic? I have no patience with optimism when careful planning and hard work are much more likely to produce a positive outcome."

Radnor drew up his mare. They were out of sight of the castle, and mist rose from the distant hills in the morning sun. Julian brought Rhodri to a halt too, though he shared his horse's longing to gallop hellbent across the fields.

Never a good idea when the grass was still slick with dew.

"Today, Haverford, you have no patience at all. What's amiss?"

Everything. "I tarried with Miss Windham for a short while last evening in Glenys's parlor."

"Miss Windham seems like a sensible creature, and she comes from very good family."

Julian nudged Rhodri forward. "She is *not* a sensible creature, and in her presence, I am tempted to toss sense straight over the parapets myself. She has hidden depths, Radnor, and a determined streak that somebody has been badly underestimating for years."

"Any somebody in particular?"

"Men."

"That narrows it down. Bad girl, Buddug." Radnor's mare had snatched at the reins, apparently intent on grazing despite the bit in her mouth.

"Miss Windham has red hair," Julian went on. "I should have known she wasn't as demure and tame as she looked."

"Tame? I know a certain duke whose hair might be described as darkish red."

"She's about as tame as a lioness, Radnor. Miss Windham is enthralled with lending libraries." And kisses. Protracted, passionate kisses. How would she respond to more adventurous overtures?

"Lending libraries are a heady topic. Would I be expecting too much to hope you'll make a coherent point anytime soon?"

"The point is, Elizabeth Windham is kind, passionate, independent, well read . . . and *I cannot court her.*"

"The passionate part," Radnor said. "I don't suppose . . . ? You are a gentleman, Haverford. I wouldn't want to have to call you out."

"Don't be tedious. She'd call me out herself if I gave offense, but I didn't." Pride, frustration, glee, and sorrow shadowed that admission. Elizabeth Windham had liked Julian's kisses, and he'd liked hers.

A lot. She was enthusiastic, articulate, alluring, and *utterly unavailable*.

"So she won't call you out. That's a relief. The prospect of arming irate women is disquieting in the extreme. If you didn't give offense, then why did this encounter trouble you?"

Trouble him and delight him. When was the last time Julian had been delighted with anything other than a good harvest?

"I finally find a woman who doesn't bore me, and whom I don't bore. A woman who's not dangling after my dukedom, a woman to whom I'm attracted, and I can do nothing to further my acquaintance with her."

Except stand aside while she contemplated spending her pin money on the likes of Robinson Crusoe and Robert Burns. She would have got on famously with Papa and Grandpapa, which should not be possible when she also got on famously with Julian.

"What do you mean, you can do nothing to further your acquaintance with her, Haverford? Vows of chastity taken when you're *non compos mentis* don't count."

The day was so achingly pretty, the sky brimming with sunshine that distilled all the beauty of the landscape, the same way a glass of champagne embodied the essence of the grape more intensely than did the fruit itself. Nowhere on earth stirred Julian's heart as did these verdant vistas of his own property, and yet, today, the brilliant light hurt.

"Glenys's plot to marry me off is doomed, Radnor. You know the state of my finances. I have made progress in recent years, but not nearly enough. I refuse to tear up the earth searching for copper or coal, blight the sky with foul smoke, exploit children—you've heard my speech enough times."

Radnor patted his mare, who was wringing her tail at some imaginary fly. "Half the Lords has it memorized. It's a fine speech."

"Which they applaud as cheerfully as they ignore. Someday, I might be in a position to offer for a viscount's daughter, if her papa is well off enough to be content with minimal settlements. I can't marry into another ducal family. Such a woman has no need of my title, and she would expect generous contributions to her settlements. A widowed duchess should live in a style appropriate to her station."

Not in a tower plagued with damp, mice, and subsiding walls.

"So this is about pride?"

"It's about money. Infernal, benighted money, and the lack thereof resulting from my forefathers' obsession with books, manuscripts, and all things literary."

"One little coal mine—"

"*Children die* in those mines, Radnor. Slums spring up where pretty villages used to be. The foremen and the owners grow wealthy, while half of Wales turns into a wasteland. People need to eat, and Welsh livestock is the best in all of Britain. I'll content myself with slow progress farming, and leave exploiting children and pillaging the land to those with the stomach for it."

Radnor's mare took a mouthful of leaves from the hedge along the bridle path. Her chewing punctuated an otherwise awkward silence.

Julian had overstated his position—there were responsible mine owners among his acquaintance. Sober fellows whose ambition was tempered by concern for those in their employ. Alas for Wales, such men were rarer than true copies of the Magna Carta.

"So don't marry Miss Windham," Radnor said. "You've spent five minutes with her in private, and been smitten by her red hair—or something. I know your grasp of courting subtleties is nonexistent, but even you couldn't get into too much trouble in five minutes. Take the next few weeks to enjoy the lady's company, see where things lead, and when the house party ends, morale will have improved all around."

"She's a gently bred unmarried woman, and you suggest I offer her a dalliance?" Though Elizabeth wasn't entirely innocent, and she wasn't on the hunt for a husband.

"Aren't dalliances what house parties are for?"

"Not in Lady Glenys's opinion." Glenys appeared to be in the minority. "Do you think the grass is dry enough for a gallop?"

"No."

"Then we'll gallop on the damned lane. Why is your mare doing that with her tail?" The beast was in a taking over something.

"The poor dear is probably coming in season. House parties are no respecter of species."

"And you are no comfort to a man in house party hell, Radnor." Julian pressed his heels to Rhodri's sides and the gelding took off at a pounding gallop. Radnor's mare gave chase, and for the length of a mile, Julian lost himself in the sheer pleasure of equestrian exertion.

As the path joined the course of the river, though, he spotted a familiar figure trundling down the hill, a haversack in her hand, and the morning sunlight turning her red hair into a beacon he saw no earthly reason to resist.

Chapter Nine

Elizabeth had agreed to meet Griffin again tomorrow morning, weather permitting. He was a gifted mime, and delighted in the acquisition of each new word or phrase. He also had a larger English vocabulary than Elizabeth had initially suspected, having heard the language for much of his life. He'd simply been hesitant to test what he knew before others.

The St. Davids doubtless had as much pride as the Windhams.

Elizabeth looked forward to tomorrow's outing. Griffin was joyous company, albeit not in the common way, and—

A subtle concussion reverberated beneath her feet. Her first reaction, even before her mind assigned a source to the sensations, was panic.

Damn Lord Allermain for a scoundrel. There was no need to be fearful of a pair of fellows having an impromptu steeplechase along the river's edge. As the horsemen drew closer, Elizabeth's momentary upset turned to pleasurable anticipation.

Haverford and Radnor drew rein ten yards in front of her, their horses' sides heaving, the duke's hair wind-blown.

"Your Grace," Elizabeth said, dipping a curtsy. "Lord Radnor. Good morning."

Radnor's mare danced sideways, as if she wanted to re-sume the race. She'd been a good length behind the duke's gelding.

"Miss Windham, good day," Haverford replied. "Shall we walk with you?"

What would it be like, to welcome him with a kiss after his morning ride? To ride out with him, galloping neck and neck across the countryside?

"I would enjoy the company."

"You must forgive me," Radnor said, touching his riding crop to the brim of his hat, "but I'm promised at the break-fast table to a certain lady. Haverford, I can take your horse if you'd like me to walk him to the stables."

Lord Radnor was matchmaking, and for the first time in memory, Elizabeth approved of the activity.

"My thanks," the duke said, swinging down and passing his reins to the marquess. "Good job, Rhodri." He gave his horse a resounding pat. "There's a carrot for you if you be-have on the way home."

"I'll explain to Lady Glenys that she's not to worry over either of you," Radnor said, turning the horses in the direc-tion of the castle. "Nor will *I* worry about you."

On that cryptic remark, he trotted off, his mare pinning her ears and swishing her tail, to which the stolid Rhodri paid no mind.

"Radnor is my dearest friend in the entire world," the

duke said, taking Elizabeth's haversack, "but sometimes, I don't understand him."

"That's the essence of friendship, isn't it? To accept somebody even when you don't entirely grasp their reasons?" Also the essence of being a sister or a cousin, sometimes.

"One hesitates to extrapolate from Radnor to an entire class of relationships, but I will take your word on the subject."

Elizabeth was beamishly happy to see Haverford, a sentiment His Grace apparently did not reciprocate, if his clipped diction was any indication.

"Should you be gathering your nerve to apologize for kissing me," she said, taking her haversack back, "let me spare you the bother. I am not about to apologize for kissing you."

She did her best to flounce away toward the formal gardens, though flouncing in half boots came off rather like stomping. The duke ruined her dignified exit by falling in step beside her and easily keeping pace with her.

"You did kiss me," he said. "Made a proper job of it."

"I make a proper job of most undertakings. Before I could read, I was trying to keep up with five male cousins. Charlotte had the sense to turn up her nose at the lot of us, but that only left me more determined to keep up with the boys."

A doomed undertaking, of course.

"Lady Glenys followed your sister Charlotte's example and left Radnor and me to our boyish nonsense, though as a very young child, she was our shadow. I have wondered if my sister wasn't lonely, for all she disdained our company."

Elizabeth's steps slowed. "Have you asked her?"

"It's too late," Haverford said, pausing beneath the oak Griffin had dropped from earlier. His Grace peered up into the branches. "Glenys would not give me a truthful answer, lest she add to my burdens. This is a good climbing tree."

To blazes with the oak, though it was a lovely, enormous specimen. "Are you sorry you kissed me or not?"

He wrested the blasted haversack from her, laid it on the ground beneath a hawthorn bush, and cupped his hands before him, as if he were offering to boost Elizabeth into the saddle.

"Let's discuss last night's encounter somewhere more private, Miss Windham." His eyes held a dare, or maybe a wish.

One never forgot how to climb a tree. Before Elizabeth had exchanged trailing behind heedless boy cousins for the reliable companionship of books, she'd climbed hundreds of trees and got stuck in a few.

She put her booted foot into Haverford's hands, and grabbed a sturdy branch as he hoisted her upward. The oak was huge—no sign of dry rot, lightning strikes, or disease anywhere—and Elizabeth was soon twelve feet above the ground, her back braced against the enormous trunk.

"I have met your cousins," Haverford said, making the branches shake as he found a perch several feet away. "I cannot imagine either Lord Westhaven or Lord Valentine climbing a tree."

"Because you were never one of five brothers," Elizabeth said, closing her eyes and enjoying the peace of a leafy hideaway. "The oldest boy, Devlin—Rosecroft now—would climb anything, and then pride demanded that the younger boys and I clamber after. Devlin's mischief was good for us and still is. I could not keep up with the boys, but for years, I did try."

More tree branches shook. "I want to kiss you again."

"Must you sound so disenchanted with that prospect? I won't tolerate advances from a man who resents an attraction to me." Five years ago, five days ago, Elizabeth would have been less blunt—and less sure of herself.

The rustling from His Grace's vicinity stopped. "I do not resent an attraction to you."

"Be still my heart." Elizabeth managed a bored tone, while inwardly she rejoiced. His Grace *was* attracted to her, and she doubted he'd invited any other woman to climb a tree with him, ever.

"Miss Windham . . . Elizabeth, last night you took me by surprise. I haven't been surprised for many a year."

She opened her eyes to behold a man in the grip of bewilderment. "Neither have I. The last time I was surprised, it was to find myself being hurried from a ballroom by Lord Allermain."

Haverford studied her, the entire tree seeming to go still with him, save for a soft rustling many feet above them.

"That presuming bounder frightened you."

"Worse than I realized. The fear steals over me when I think how differently that night might have turned out, and then I need to find a very good book in which to bury my imagination. I had no inkling a man with whom I'd waltzed would serve me so ill."

Haverford stretched up to grab the branch over his head. "He frightened you, and your confidence was kidnapped, even if your person came to no harm. Kissing you abducts my . . . makes off with all the tidy, sensible, dignified plans I'd made for myself, and I had made many. A prudent duke is a creature of forethought."

While an unmarried woman was a creature of frustration. "Isn't that what kisses should do? Make the rest of the world fade to insignificance and imbue a few moments with sheer wonder? I'm not an expert on the subject, but that's how your kisses made me feel."

What an odd, lovely conversation. The river rippled by beneath the tree, and the castle grounds spread out in green, summer abundance in every direction. The breeze held a whiff of clover, a soft counterpoint to the gleaming stone of the castle against the perfect clouds in the perfect sky.

"Parts one doesn't mention before a lady are growing uncomfortable," Haverford said. "Do you prefer to precede me from the tree, or shall I go first and catch you?"

"I prefer to finish this discussion." Elizabeth would also like to climb higher into the tree, to gain more distance from the troubles awaiting her on the ground. "I'll not trap you into matrimony, Your Grace. If your papa contracted a match for you when you were eight years old, and the lady is only now coming of age, you needn't explain. You betrayed no one with that kiss."

He plucked a green leaf and sent it twirling to the water babbling by below. "I told you that I would not be offering for anybody as a result of this house party. The reality is, I *cannot* take a wife, not now. I need heirs, as much as or more than any other titled man, but my circumstances are sorely embarrassed. My father and grandfather both spent profligately on books, maps, manuscripts, and the like. Matrimony will have to wait, possibly for some time."

Sorely embarrassed. Not merely embarrassed or a trifle constrained for the nonce.

When a man and woman of consequence became engaged, negotiation of the marriage settlements ensued. The groom's family was expected to contribute to the funds established, for much of that money could be inherited by the couple's children, or by the groom himself.

No wonder His Grace hadn't any affection for his library, if funds that might have gone to marriage settlements had instead gone to Chaucer and Boccaccio.

His Grace of Haverford was up a tree, so to speak.

"You might be surprised to learn that the Windham fortunes have not always enjoyed robust health, Your Grace, and I do not seek a marriage proposal from you." That pronouncement sounded convincingly assured, though a corner of Elizabeth's heart lamented. Haverford was a good man and a wonderful kisser. "I might need assistance getting to the ground."

Haverford dropped nimbly from the tree and turned, arms extended upward. "Down you go."

Getting out of the oak was awkward. Elizabeth hung suspended from the lower branch, and Haverford caught her about the hips, then let her slide down the length of his body. When her feet touched solid earth, he continued to hold her.

Elizabeth wrapped her arms around him. "If you could marry, would you take a bride?"

"Of course. A duke without his duchess is a lonely fellow."

Young men are lonely, Elizabeth. Aunt Arabella's words rang in memory. Young men might be lonely—young women certainly were—but they didn't admit it. Haverford was no longer young, and Elizabeth liked that about him.

"I am in want of friends," she said, stepping back. "For the duration of this gathering, you could remedy that lack."

Haverford gathered up Elizabeth's haversack and looped it over his shoulder, his movements putting Elizabeth in mind of Griffin.

"I still want to kiss you, Elizabeth. Rather a lot."

"That sentiment is mutual," she said, setting off at a

brisk pace. "But where is it written that friends can never kiss, or otherwise express their attraction to each other?"

"It ought to be written somewhere," Haverford said, "in great bold copperplate. Kissing leads to—"

"I know where it leads, Your Grace, in the general case. The destination has been sadly unimpressive on past visits. I'd like to explore where kissing leads with you."

"You are—"

"I am lonely too." And doubtless bound for marriage to some charming, boring viscount with clammy hands and a tiny library.

"—quite fierce about this friendship business." His gaze was on the castle, and Elizabeth suspected he was trying not to smile.

"I'm quite fierce about everything." And only now coming to admit it.

"We shall be fierce friends, then, for the duration of a house party. One shudders to think what mischief—what the devil is *he* doing here?"

A coach and four was rattling up the drive a quarter of a mile away. The horses were all white, exactly matched for gait and height, and pulling a black coach with red wheels. A single trunk was affixed to the back, though no crest adorned the door.

"It appears you've a late-arriving guest." Or a bad fairy calling on the party, based on Haverford's expression.

"Not a guest, a problem. A most unwelcome problem."

* * *

Radnor was nearly knocked on his arse by Lady Glenys as she stormed forth from the east tower's servants' stairs.

"My lady, good morning."

"It is not a good morning, Radnor. Was it your idea to take Haverford out riding?"

Radnor fell in step beside her, which put him in mind of escorting a tempest. "If I say yes, you'll berate me for seeing to it that His Grace got some fresh air. If I say no, then you'll be wroth with your brother, which makes me a poor friend to him. Your archery contest came off flawlessly, so what has you in a pet today?"

"You are dodging my question."

Not nimbly enough. "Haverford will be back soon, but he came upon a guest out walking and did what a polite host ought to do, else he would have returned with me."

They came to a door all but hidden by the wallpaper and wainscoting. Radnor opened it, and Glenys swept through.

"I ought not to be using these staircases with you, Radnor."

"We've been using the stairways and passages since we were old enough to elude our governesses and tutors. What have you planned for today?"

"A boat race. The weather is fine, the guests have had a day to rest from their travels, and no self-respecting hostess puts on a summer house party without a boat race. The gentlemen can show off their athletic skills, and the ladies can wager on their favorites."

She barreled across the landing, then tripped and would have gone sprawling down the steps had Radnor not caught her about the waist.

"Steady, Glennie. You'll make a very fine picture at the table with two black eyes and a chipped tooth."

Had she lost weight? Glenys was a substantial woman, but she hung against Radnor for an instant, and he gained an impression of frailty and nervous exhaustion.

"I'm fine," she said, straightening. "Which guest did Haverford come upon walking at such an early hour?"

Radnor put her hand on his arm and set a decorous pace down the steps. "Miss Elizabeth Windham. She looked to be enjoying a constitutional along the river. I suspect she was up early enough to enjoy the sunrise."

Glenys unwound herself from his arm on the next landing and peered out a window that had probably begun life as an arrow slit.

"Griffin likes to walk along the river. That must be Haverford and Miss Windham in the park."

Two figures, a man and woman, were cutting across the grass toward the castle. Radnor studied them from immediately behind Glenys, though mostly, he was sneaking a chance to inhale her perfume.

"Why do you always smell good, milady?"

She brushed a finger over the glass, getting a smudged fingertip for her efforts. "Because it perplexes you."

"As good a reason as any, but that's not what I meant. Other women wear perfume, and it's pleasant enough at the start of the evening, but by the supper waltz, the scent has faded to resemble a clove compress or some other medicinal. You smell as good in the evening as you do in the morning."

"I wear simple fragrances for that reason. They hold up. Haverford is walking rather close to Miss Windham."

Not as close as Radnor was standing to Glenys. "He's being a proper escort. They're in plain view of the castle, I don't think his virtue is at risk." Being a loyal friend to the duke, Radnor hoped those words were in error, meaning no disrespect to the lady.

Glenys turned, arms folded. "I have a theory. You will please tell me it's a ridiculous theory."

What was ridiculous was the urge to kiss a woman who'd slap him for his presumption. Why, oh why, had he ever called her a pestilential plague of a pint-sized female?

"I have to hear this theory before I can discredit it."

"I am concerned that Haverford has remained unmarried because he knows his duchess will depose me as lady of the house. He's unwilling to see me become the spinster auntie, and thus, he hesitates, and hopes some bachelor will come along and take me off his hands."

Glenys tried for a smile, and broke Radnor's heart.

"This is not ridiculous," he said, drawing her into his embrace. She kept her arms crossed for a moment, then relented and pressed her forehead to his shoulder.

"I knew it, Cedric. This entire house party, this enormous, inexcusable expense—"

"Your theory so far surpasses the bounds of ridiculousness, I must conclude the fairies have invaded your dreams. Haverford would never, ever put his duty to the succession in second place behind anything so insubstantial as fraternal regard for you. If he hasn't married, he simply hasn't found the right duchess."

Radnor stroked Glenys's hair, and for a moment, she allowed the comfort. He'd never held her like this before, never let himself pay attention to the brush of her breasts against his chest, or the fit of her contours to his body. She wasn't as tall or as substantial as she seemed.

"This should feel awkward," Glenys said, making no move to step back. "You're Radnor, and I'm about to be late for breakfast."

He stole another caress to her hair. "You wear simple fragrances because you can make them here at Haverford rather than put your brother to the expense of buying them in London."

"That feels good. Are you seducing me, Cedric?"

No, actually, he wasn't. "Should I be?"

Glenys moved away, down the stairs. "Julian would kill you."

"Does that prospect please you?"

Radnor bickered with her all the way to the breakfast parlor, which seemed to restore her spirits as much as it ruined his. Nonetheless, as he seated Glenys at the head of the table, and took a place across from Lady Pembroke, some of his natural optimism reasserted itself.

He and Lady Glenys had had a *moment*. Not a passionate moment, not even an amorous moment, but a moment.

A precious moment, and that was progress in the very direction he longed to travel with her.

* * *

Offering to walk with Elizabeth Windham had been folly, for she was radiant in the morning. Then she'd called Julian's bluff and climbed the oak, compelling him to do likewise. Ensconced against the sturdy trunk, she'd looked entirely comfortable and entirely too kissable.

The path across the park was visible from two sides of the castle, and worse, from the drive where Lucas Sherbourne was now sauntering forth from his coach. He'd taken that conveyance as payment for a debt from an impecunious baron and showed it off at every opportunity. Cursory examination revealed the barely painted-over crest on both doors and the boot.

"You should greet your guest," Elizabeth said. "Perhaps he hasn't realized you have a house party in progress."

She was so naturally poised—and such a passionate kisser.

Sherbourne always behaved himself around the ladies, but Julian didn't want his neighbor within four counties of Elizabeth Windham.

"He brought luggage with him," Julian said, as two footmen lowered a large black trunk from the boot. "And yet, I can assure you, he was sent no invitation."

"Perhaps Lady Glenys extended the invitation in person, if he dwells close by."

That was... possible. Sherbourne attended Sunday services and greeted both Julian and Glenys with unfailing cordiality in the churchyard. Glenys wasn't privy to the details of Julian's dealings with Sherbourne and offered him polite replies on every occasion.

"Glenys labors under the misperception that a duke's sister is to be gracious at all times," Julian said. "She might have invited him and neglected to tell me. The vicar will join us for dinner some evening, as will most of the dames and squires in the neighborhood. Glenys has spared me a recitation of that list, and she might have consigned Sherbourne to the same category."

Neighbors at the table meant more expense. More inane socializing when there was work to be done.

"You should greet him civilly. Haverford is known for its hospitality."

Julian's own words thrown back at him, as Elizabeth marched him smartly in the direction of the drive.

Sherbourne actually patted his coach, then stood beside it, smacking his pristine gloves against his exquisitely tailored breeches. The breakfast parlor was at the back of the castle, directly over the kitchens. This display—for Sherbourne did nothing without premeditation—was likely without much audience other than servants.

"You're right, I should goddamned greet him civilly."

Elizabeth wound her arm through Julian's and smiled sweetly. "You can goddamned introduce us too."

Her foul language was offered in such friendly, polite tones, she provoked Julian to smiling. "Yes, ma'am. At once."

For no reason Julian could bear to examine, having Elizabeth at his side fortified him for the ordeal of welcoming Sherbourne. He did not hate Sherbourne, any more than he hated adders. Adders behaved according to the laws of nature. Those laws dictated that Griffin might be bitten while out rambling some evening and made very ill as a result.

When fevered, Griffin tended to seizures, and seizures could be fatal. Julian might kill an adder frequenting paths Griffin favored, but he would not hate the adder for being true to its nature.

"Sherbourne, good day," Julian said, "and welcome to Haverford Castle." *To what do we owe the pleasure of this invasion?*

"Your Grace, good morning," Sherbourne replied, bowing nominally. "May I congratulate you on holding a house party when the weather is so fine? Won't you introduce me to your companion?"

Julian put his hands behind his back when he wanted to slip an arm around Elizabeth's waist. "Miss Elizabeth Windham, may I make known to you my neighbor, Mr. Lucas Sherbourne. Sherbourne, Miss Windham is a friend of the family, and our guest for the duration of the gathering."

She dipped a graceful curtsy while Sherbourne took her bare hand in his.

"Mr. Sherbourne, a pleasure," she said. "You will be desolated to learn that you've missed yesterday's archery tournament, where my sister Charlotte quite distinguished herself."

"Perhaps you'll introduce me to your sister at breakfast? I am something of a marksman with my bow, and would have enjoyed the tournament."

Sherbourne was a predator, and his arrow of choice was a bank draft, aimed where it would buy him the most influence and create the most misery. Even he should have known that introductions were the province of the host and hostess, though.

"Oh, my gracious," Elizabeth called to the footmen wrestling the trunk. "You fellows can't mean to haul that right through the front door, can you?"

They set the trunk down and shot Sherbourne an uncertain look.

"You heard the lady," Sherbourne said, waving his gloves. "Not through the front door."

The next look was exchanged between the footmen, both of whom wore Sherbourne's livery. Clearly, neither they nor Sherbourne grasped exactly how the luggage was to get into the castle. A small slip, but made before a lady, and inordinately gratifying to Julian.

"Around to the side," Elizabeth said. "The service entrance faces the stables, though if Mr. Sherbourne has a small valise, one of you may hand it to the first footman or butler once His Grace has escorted his guest from the drive. The house staff will see that the valise is brought up to Mr. Sherbourne's room immediately."

The footmen tugged a forelock in Elizabeth's direction before heaving the trunk onto the back of the carriage.

"One must be patient with staff," Elizabeth said. "House parties are a challenge all around, don't you agree, Mr. Sherbourne?" She sent him a good-natured smile, and Julian wanted to howl.

Sherbourne smiled back. Glenys referred to him as a

handsome devil, though she knew not how literal her description was.

"You have the right of it, ma'am," Sherbourne said. "House parties can be an endless challenge, but a great diversion as well. Might I escort you into the house?"

Another blunder, for the host was on hand to perform that office.

"Haverford has kindly extended me his escort for my morning constitutional," Elizabeth said, tucking her hand around Julian's arm, "but perhaps you'd carry my haversack, Mr. Sherbourne? I'm sure the other guests are still at breakfast, and Lady Glenys will be relieved to know the last of the company has arrived."

Julian passed over the haversack, and by exercise of monumental self-discipline, refrained from sticking his tongue out at Sherbourne. Elizabeth was simply being a lady, the niece and granddaughter of dukes, and her manner was honestly friendly.

Sherbourne took the proffered haversack and idled along on Elizabeth's other side as Julian led her into the house. She made small talk with the effortless charm of one to the manor born, charm Julian had misplaced twenty thousand pounds ago where Sherbourne was concerned.

When Elizabeth led Sherbourne into the breakfast parlor, every guest in attendance looked to be seated at the table, even Cousin Hugh. Conversation drifted to a halt, and Sherbourne's slight smile said he enjoyed disrupting his social superiors at their leisure.

"Sherbourne," Radnor said. "Good day. Have you come by for tea and toast?"

All eyes turned to Glenys whose expression would have done credit to a hind pursued by a pack in full cry.

"You are mistaken, my lord," Elizabeth said. "The last

of Haverford's guests has arrived, and I had the great good fortune to be introduced to Mr. Sherbourne the moment he alighted in the drive. He accounts himself something of a marksman, but I wonder how well he'll acquit himself at the oars."

"Is the boat race today?" Haldale asked. "Lovely weather for it."

"Lovely day for a drubbing, you mean," Windstruther retorted. "I was captain of my team for three years at university."

Good-natured taunts and wagers soon joined the clatter of porcelain and requests for more tea. Elizabeth asked Sherbourne to sit beside her, and was drawing him into the general conversation, while Julian took his place beside Glenys.

"Did you invite him?" Julian murmured as Glenys poured him a cup of tea.

"I would never—I would never have done so on purpose," she said, dropping in a lump of sugar and stirring. A slosh of tea spilled over onto the saucer.

Julian added cream, a luxury he usually denied himself. "Did you invite him by accident, perhaps?"

"Perhaps. The topic of the house party came up after services one week. I'd forgotten the conversation, but Mr. Sherbourne apparently took it for an invitation. I haven't a bedroom made up."

"Put him down the corridor from my quarters in the family wing. The rooms are comfortable, and I'd prefer that Sherbourne be where I can keep an eye on him if I must have him underfoot."

Halfway up the table, Charlotte Windham was challenging Sherbourne to an archery contest, and Cousin Delphine's eyes had acquired an avaricious gleam.

Sherbourne, though, was bent close to Elizabeth, his expression entirely, genuinely charmed.

Julian took a sip of his tea, scalded his tongue, and nearly hurled his teacup at Sherbourne's handsome head.

* * *

Elizabeth had left Mr. Sherbourne in Charlotte's care—her gunsights, more like—and was intent on changing into a day dress when Lady Glenys overtook her on the stairs.

"Thank you," her ladyship said. "I was completely taken aback by Sherbourne's arrival. Haverford is unhappy with me, but I might well have left Mr. Sherbourne with the impression that he was welcome. I was at a loss, and I'm in your debt."

Her ladyship was slightly out of breath, and the watch pinned to her bodice was at an odd angle. Watches kept time best if they hung straight, but nobody thought to provide women a watch pocket for that purpose.

"You are not in my debt," Elizabeth said. "I was simply being polite and reciprocating the hospitality you and His Grace have shown me. Come help me choose suitable attire for admiring the company's oarsmen."

Lady Glenys peered at the watch. "I really ought to confer with my cook. She's growing temperamental, and I can't—"

"Do not indulge the tantrums of your senior staff," Elizabeth said, linking arms with Lady Glenys. "My mama and my aunt swear that only encourages more dramatics. You pay the woman a handsome salary, she's had weeks to prepare for this gathering, and nobody expects more than typical fare in larger quantities. Tell me about Sherbourne."

For that was the real reason Elizabeth wanted a moment

with her hostess. Haverford loathed the man, and to loathe a neighbor was never convenient.

"Lucas Sherbourne is wealthy," Lady Glenys said. "His family bought our original dower house back in German George's day, and there was some talk of great-grandparents marrying, or grandparents. Haverford would know."

They rounded the turn in the stairs, the sounds from the lower floors fading. "The dower house must be quite close to the castle."

"Two miles or so across the fields. When did this wing acquire so many stairs?"

"Probably three hundred years ago." Haverford's circumstances were sorely embarrassed and Sherbourne was wealthy. Elizabeth didn't think that alone would cause Haverford's antipathy toward his neighbor.

They reached Elizabeth's room, which had a good view of the lake.

"If you set up the tents on the far side of the lake," Elizabeth said, "the breeze will carry the stable flies away from the party rather than straight to it. Then too, we'll have shade over there."

Glenys wrinkled her nose. "Flies?"

"Nasty creatures. Remind the ladies to take their fans."

"Have you managed a house party before?"

"My mother certainly has, my aunt has, and as the eldest daughter in my family, I've been their right hand. Which do you prefer, the blue or the green?"

Elizabeth had opened the wardrobe, where a rainbow of dresses hung on a series of hooks. The whole smelled of lavender, and beneath each dress sat a pair of matching slippers.

"For you, the green, though it would look less attractive on me. Do you think Mr. Sherbourne is handsome?"

Elizabeth laid the green dress, one of her favorites, on the bed. "He's attractive, if a lady favors a fair countenance."

Mr. Sherbourne was a tall, broad-shouldered exponent of good Saxon breeding, with blond hair brushed back from a high forehead, even features, keen blue eyes, and good teeth. Despite his size, he dressed in the latest fashion, had fine table manners, and smelled faintly of bay rum.

All in all, he was a little too perfect, a little too much the picture of a fine gentleman.

"You should have a seat, Lady Glenys. My mama claims that during a house party, the hostess should sit and use the necessary every chance she gets. Half boots today, I think."

Her ladyship subsided onto the bed. "Your mama sounds very sensible. I barely recall mine. Haverford says she liked to laugh and was mad for my papa. They were second cousins, and she was a St. David even before he married her."

Such wistfulness. "My parents are like that, mad for each other." Elizabeth sat on the bed, and gave Lady Glenys her back. "If you'd oblige?"

When Elizabeth's hooks had been undone, she took the green dress with her behind the privacy screen.

"Will you bet on Lord Radnor's boat to win today?" she asked.

"Radnor? Half the ladies present will bet on him. Radnor has charm, Haverford has gravitas, and I have aching feet."

Elizabeth shimmied and the dress settled around her like a benediction. Everything about this frock was just right—the drape, the cut, the weight and swish of the fabric, the color. She was pretty in this outfit, confident, comfortable, and a bit out of the common mode. The lines were simple and the neckline was low for daytime, but a cream fichu made an illusion of daring out of a modest ensemble.

"I have wondered where your companion is," Elizabeth said, emerging from behind the screen. "You do have one?"

"That is a luscious dress."

"One of my favorites." She resumed her seat on the bed as Lady Glenys did up her hooks. This exchange—women's small talk over a change of dresses—was so familiar Elizabeth had taken it for granted. With her mother, her sisters, her cousins, and cousins-in-law, she often had a private moment to compare notes, share gossip, or rest her feet.

While Lady Glenys had a brother much occupied with the business of his dukedom.

"I have a companion," her ladyship said, finishing the last hook. "Have had one for years, but she spends much of the summer with her family. She's a cousin to the Archbishop of Canterbury, or second cousin. You are truly wearing half boots with that dress?"

"We're hiking around the lake, unless you intend to assemble a parade of conveyances in addition to the kitchen carts."

"I'd planned to set up closer to the house until you mentioned the flies."

"It's a pretty day for a walk, and the gentlemen will enjoy a chance to escort the ladies. Keep a pony cart on hand for transporting the elders or those fatigued by their exertions."

Some would be fatigued by their over-imbibing. One needn't belabor the obvious.

Lady Glenys leaned back and braced herself on both

hands. "I was daft to hold this house party. I had no idea of the expense, but the practical considerations are beyond me as well. You really must stay close to me at all times, Miss Windham, lest I have my guests picnicking downwind of the muck heap."

She'd apparently planned for them to do exactly that.

Elizabeth rose to examine her reflection in the vanity mirror. Her bun was still tidy, despite her morning rambles. She approached the bed and unpinned her ladyship's watch.

The watch had already lost a quarter of an hour against the clock on the mantel. "You chose to have the house party now so your companion would not be in the way, didn't you?"

"She's quite set in her ways, and while I love her dearly, I feel increasingly like it's my job to attend to her wants and wishes, and to afford her my company, not the other way around."

Elizabeth adjusted the watch and repinned it, as a sister or friend might have. "Do you have a room for Mr. Sherbourne?"

"The maids are seeing to that now. Haverford said to use a bedroom in the family wing, where he and Radnor can keep an eye on him."

Why would they need to keep an eye on a neighbor of long standing? "Mr. Sherbourne strikes me as in need of guidance. For example, if you did extend a personal invitation to him to attend this gathering, he still should have sent his acceptance in writing."

Glenys peered down at the watch, a lovely little gold article. "I might have misplaced his note. I'm not exactly current with my correspondence."

Oh, dear. "You will give me your correspondence, my lady, and Charlotte and I will sort through it for you. The house party will last another nineteen days, more or less, and if you lack a personal secretary, you'll have to make do with the resources at hand."

"A secretary costs money. Even Haverford eschews that expense."

Sorely embarrassed. His Grace had not exaggerated.

"One more handsome bachelor can hardly be a problem, can he?" Lady Glenys asked.

One more handsome, *wealthy*, good-looking bachelor. "I suppose not. You'll give me your correspondence?"

Chagrin assailed Elizabeth once more. She'd been so resentful of her family's meddling, so heedless of their concern for her. How did anybody manage without sisters? Or cousins, in-laws, and a doting uncle and aunt?

Lady Glenys rose. "I will surrender my correspondence to you, purely because I'm desperate and you're the closest thing I have to an ally."

"I do believe Lord Radnor is your ally, as is Haverford, but you must leave them no doubt as to when and how their support is needed."

Lady Glenys marched to the door, chin high. "Radnor sees me as a younger sibling, one in need of his constant supervision, or something. He's handsome, though, I'll grant you that, and charming."

He was also Haverford's dearest friend, and of a lofty enough station to offer for the daughter of a duke—unlike Mr. Sherbourne, who was a bit rag-mannered, and disliked by her ladyship's brother.

Nineteen days was no time at all when Elizabeth contemplated her friendship with Haverford, but an eternity from other perspectives.

"You'll have the tents set up on the far side of the lake?" she asked.

"Just as soon as I stop by my own apartment and heed your mama's advice."

They parted at the top of the main staircase. The encounter, however brief, had given Elizabeth much to think about. If Lady Glenys felt a lack of allies, how must Haverford feel? Payment for all the house party expenses was his responsibility, not her ladyship's, and he'd been exceedingly unhappy to see Sherbourne's coach tooling up the drive.

Goddamned unhappy.

Charlotte came up the steps, munching a triangle of toast. "You left Mr. Sherbourne desolated for want of your company. I took pity on him." Her grin was feline rather than coquettish.

"You did not add him to the breakfast menu, I trust?"

"I'm saving him for dessert, once I'm through with Haldale and Windstruther. They are the most self-important pair of ninnyhammers I've met in ages. I do love that dress."

And yet, Charlotte had never asked to borrow it. "I love it too. Would you bring my parasol when you come down?"

"Of course, and Aunt's too. Where are you off to?"

"Mr. Sherbourne has piqued my interest. I'm off to get to know him better, before one of your famous stray arrows puts a period to his dignity."

Chapter Ten

"I love you, Biddy Bowen." Griffin had waited years to say that phrase in English, and had repeated it the whole way to the oak so he wouldn't forget how. Then he'd sat high, high up in the oak practicing silently, until Julian and Miss Elizabeth had come along.

Biddy went on taking the laundry down from the clothesline. "Sir, you mustn't tease me like that."

She was smiling, though. Biddy had the prettiest smile.

"I love you, Biddy Bowen." Clearly, he'd got it right, so he tried a bit of decoration on what Miss Elizabeth had taught him. "I very, very love you."

Her smile was beautiful, like the oak leafing out in spring. All soft edges and full of light. "You're practicing English again, are you?"

She'd answered in Welsh.

"Yes," Griffin said, wishing he knew more English. "I

want Julian and Charity to be proud of me. I can learn. I'm not smart, but I can learn."

Biddy's smile dimmed and she snatched the next pillowcase from the clothesline. "Stop saying you aren't smart. You're very good with the animals, you know all the bird songs, you get around in the kitchen better than any man I know."

I very, very love you, Biddy. "I'm not smart like Julian. He goes to London, and he can say anything he wants to in English and French and Latin." Griffin had tried Latin, but it was unkind to the ear. Welsh was very kind to the ear, and English was somewhere in the middle.

"What matters smart," Biddy snapped, jerking another pillowcase from the line, "when a titled man can barely pay his debts? What matters smart, when a lady shut up in a castle grows so lonely her brother must lure bachelors to her side with parties he can't afford? You're smart, Griffin St. David, too smart to think that only Latin and London make a man worth loving. There's not a yeoman for thirty miles who'd have a wife and family if that were the case."

Biddy sometimes got cross, like when Abner had too many pints in the village and Griffin had to fetch him home in the rain, but she was seldom angry.

"I'm not a yeoman. My brother is a duke. I'm not smart."

Biddy flung the last of the pillowcases into the basket. "I must not speak ill of my betters, but your brother is no smarter than you are, he's only smart in a different way. You visit with the tenants more than he does. You notice when Mrs. Cransberry's limp is worse and bring her a tisane from Mrs. Hanscomb. You carry acorns in your pockets so every child you meet can plant a tree for themselves. You sing in church like all the joy in heaven fills you, you don't just move your lips."

Griffin picked up the laundry basket. "I love to sing." And he loved Biddy in both Welsh and English.

She regarded Griffin for a moment, her expression complicated. She looked angry, but not with him. He and Julian were smart *in different ways*, she'd said, and that was worth thinking about in the oak tree, where Griffin had peace and privacy—usually.

Biddy took one handle of the laundry basket, Griffin kept the other, and they walked into the house together.

"I learned something today," Griffin said.

"You learned some English," Biddy said. "Very clever of you, but please don't be telling all the women at the pub that you love them, Griffin." She took the laundry basket from him and set it on the kitchen table with a thump.

"I don't love them. They just make my tallywags ache. I love you."

The smile came again, along with a blush. "You awful man, the things you say."

Whatever he'd said, she wasn't angry anymore. "I learned something from Julian and Miss Elizabeth. She's a guest at the house party, and very nice. She's Julian's friend. He should have more friends."

Biddy shook out the last pillowcase to come down from the line. A whiff of sunshine and lavender filled the kitchen, happy scents.

"Were you eavesdropping again, Griffin? You know you're not supposed to do that."

"I was not eavesdropping. I was overhearing, because nobody looked up. Why doesn't anybody ever look up, unless a bird flies by?"

"You look up, you look everywhere, and you see what you behold."

Griffin took the next pillowcase. Biddy had shown him

exactly how to fold a pillowcase. He liked folding sheets better, because it took two people to do it right.

"Julian and Miss Elizabeth did not look up, but they are friends. They decided that. You're my friend, Biddy."

Saying those words felt good, because it was true. A gentleman was always honest.

"I am that," she said, taking up another pillowcase. "I will always be your friend. So what did you learn, Griffin?"

Not sir, not Mr. St. David.

"I learned that friends sometimes kiss each other, and I would dearly like to kiss you, Biddy Bowen."

* * *

"Miss Windham, good morning."

Julian must restore her to the status of Miss Windham, not his companion of the towering oak and summer sunshine, not the charming phantasm of his dreams.

Though of course he wanted to kiss her again. She wore a simple green frock that hinted at the curves beneath, especially as she strode across the library and began wrestling with a window.

"Good morning, Your Grace. Lady Glenys should instruct the footmen to open these windows each evening after the card parties break up. The cigar smoke isn't good for the books or the portraiture."

Neither of which mattered to Julian the way they should.

"The footmen also need to oil the window latches," Julian replied, reaching past her to shove the sash up. Cool air bearing a hint of the sea wafted into the room and blended with the scent of lily of the valley on Miss Windham's person.

Julian moved away, lest he stand about like a fool, his nose pressed to the lady's neck—and his tallywags aching.

"I've come to find a book to take with me across the lake," she said, surveying the rows and rows of literature arrayed around them. "I finished the three you lent me."

"You'd rather spend this afternoon here with the books than socializing on the lakeshore. You love books."

Once upon a time, as a small boy, Julian had been enthralled with books too. In the general case, he still respected literature, but the collection for which too much coin had been paid by too many former dukes of Haverford merited only his disgust.

"I love what books can do," Miss Windham replied, moving to another window. "Milton said, 'Who kills a man kills a reasonable creature, God's image, but thee who destroys a good book destroys reason itself.' Books can preserve wisdom."

Julian let Elizabeth struggle with the window, because he liked the lines of the dress from the back almost as much as he did from the front.

Almost. The window gave and she moved to the next.

In defense of his dignity, he opened the two windows on the far side of the fireplace rather than again assist the lady.

"Books," she went on, dusting her hands, "can reach from beyond the grave and provide comfort and knowledge from somebody long dead. Books can instruct and entertain, they can—well, you must value them as I do, for you've amassed a treasury of books."

Julian had no treasure whatsoever, unless acres of Welsh countryside counted. "The first marquess of Haverford was a bibliophile, and his descendants have maintained and added to his collection as a family tradition, whether we could afford the expense or not. Books, in addition to the many fine qualities you name, can beggar an entire dukedom."

And drive a young man to Bedlam. How Julian had worried, every time Papa had brought home some precious new tome, delighted with his acquisition, oblivious to its cost. Julian had come to dread Papa's sojourns to London, for they always meant new books and more unpaid bills.

Elizabeth would read these books, though. If she were Julian's duchess, winter by winter, shelf by shelf, she'd learn the depth and breadth of all three of the collections. Julian would learn too, for she'd read to him, and he to her.

By the time he was reading to his children, he might possibly have begun to forgive his father.

"You do not behold your library with any joy," Elizabeth said, when all the windows were open. "Or perhaps the prospect of the afternoon's activities dims your pleasure in the day."

She had a vocabulary of walks. Outdoors she moved quite freely, and inside the house, she could set a good pace too. She also had a ladylike saunter suitable for strolling the gardens or accompanying another guest into the breakfast parlor.

"I'd rather be lounging about on the lakeshore than shut up in this library," Julian said. He'd rather be almost anywhere other than the library.

Elizabeth studied him from beneath the previous duke's portrait. "Truly? You don't like this room?"

Julian pointed to the northwest corner of the second tier. "Up there...that whole area. Papa risked traveling to France in wartime to bid on those blasted books at an exclusive auction, and he sold off one of our best tenant farms to pay for them. Fortunately, he sold the land to Radnor's father."

"He bought an *entire farm's* worth of French novels?"

That Elizabeth was dismayed by Papa's folly was reassuring—and maddening all over again.

"A small farm," Julian said, "but a beautiful property. The Haverford dower house was also a very attractive domicile. My great-grandfather sold it to a Sherbourne ancestor to finance an interest in illuminated manuscripts, many of which turned out to be forgeries."

This was not the tour of the library Julian so often gave, not one he was proud of, but half the public collection was associated with liquidation of some asset that could never be regained.

Elizabeth glanced around, her expression suggesting Julian had dimmed her delight in the books. "So you truly hate this library?"

Julian should dissemble, put a polite face on the truth, and pretend these damned books hadn't caused him to wonder if the St. Davids suffered from a peculiar strain of lunacy.

"I resent the library bitterly."

She stepped closer, as if she didn't want her next words to be overheard. "You could sell the books. They have value in the eyes of many, Your Grace."

The specious claim of every bookseller was that books had tangible value. Julian's solicitors had been at pains to advise him otherwise.

"If the collection has monetary value at all, that's in the eyes of only a select few, Miss Windham. To me, the whole collection is one, enormous cautionary tale. When I consider buying a new horse or purchasing a pretty bracelet for Lady Glenys, I have thirty thousand reasons to keep my coin in my pocket."

The books gave Julian the discipline to adhere to his budgets, plans, and schedules. Thirty thousand times, generation after generation, a St. David had yielded to impulse; thirty thousand times, they'd put more faith in providence than prudence.

Which was thirty thousand times too many.

"Sometimes, I want to burn the lot," Julian went on, taking Elizabeth's hand and kissing her fingers. "But that would be as irresponsible as buying them in the first place. When the solicitors explained to me the extent of my inherited debts, I dreamed of setting fire to these books, and that fantasy wasn't a nightmare."

Though the first few years after Papa's death had been nightmarish. Grief and betrayal had been subsumed into a determination that Julian carried with him still, determination to protect the honor of the family name, and to leave future generations of St. Davids more to be proud of than a pile of bloody books.

Elizabeth covered his hand with her own. "I am sorry, Julian. When family serves us a bad turn, it's doubly painful."

He let go of her hand, because the door was open, and the pleasure of touching her too tempting.

"You speak from experience."

"Nothing so dramatic as the debts you've been saddled with, but yes. I've mentioned my cousins." She began tidying the nearest shelf of books—plays, which the house party guests had already cast into disorder.

"The eight obnoxiously blissful cousins?"

"There were ten when I was growing up, four boys, all in a row, and I was the only girl. Charlotte was a mere babe, and so I was special without even realizing it. Then His Grace took an illegitimate daughter into his home and an illegitimate son. I love them both dearly, but they were novel, and I was..."

The shelf was quite in order.

"You were jealous."

"Oh, very, and my tribulation was only beginning. Her

Grace had the audacity to start producing daughters, and somewhere between daughter number two and daughter number four, I just...gave up. I was very much an older sister by then, and required to set an example. Telling you this now, I must seem petty and self-centered, but to a small girl..."

Julian drew her between the botany texts and German medical treatises and took her in his arms.

"You were lonely, as Glenys must have been lonely while Radnor and I conquered the Andean jungle and sailed to the Orient without her."

Elizabeth rested her forehead against his chest. "I was lonely, but I also became *invisible*. I do not care for the status of non-entity, Julian. I'm not good at it. Then one Christmas before I'd even put up my hair, the whole family was assembled for a meal, and at some point in the conversation—one of those unpredictable lulls—I replied to my uncle with a quote from Shakespeare. 'Our doubts are traitors...'"

"'And make us lose the good we might oft win by fearing the attempt,'" Julian said. "*Hamlet*?"

She gave him a smile such as pirates turned upon undefended treasure. "*Measure for Measure*. The duke laughed and said that was the perfect quotation for a speech he was to deliver in Parliament. My cousins looked at me as if a tiara had appeared on my head, and in a sense, it had."

"They saw you."

She stepped back, and again, Julian let her go. "They saw me, they heard me, they respected who and what they beheld. In my books, I'd found something better than being invisible."

But had she found herself, or merely a means of garnering notice in a large, busy family with a surfeit of self-important lordlings?

Elizabeth started on another set of shelves, opera libretti in various languages.

"Do they see you now?"

"I'm one of only two unmarried cousins remaining. Now I feel as if my family sees me rather too well. Tell me about Mr. Sherbourne. He was intent on making an entrance in the breakfast parlor this morning, and your sister says he might not even have been invited."

In a sense, Elizabeth's query was not a change of subject—Sherbourne was part and parcel of the challenges Julian faced—though her question certainly changed the mood.

"I can guarantee you Sherbourne wasn't invited, for no acceptance of an invitation has shown up in my correspondence, and he'd best not be directing mail to my unmarried sister. If she invited him personally, he still has no excuse for showing up a day late."

Elizabeth took a window seat, sunshine slanting over her shoulder and making the simple green gown shimmer like spring grass in a morning breeze.

"I broached the topic of his presumption with Lady Glenys," she said, "but I gather she's been too overwhelmed with planning this event to keep track of every detail. How old was she when your mother died?"

"Five." Julian's niece, Charity, was five, and all over again, he was struck with how tender and vulnerable that age was. He would ask Elizabeth to choose some children's books for her, and send them...

No, he would not.

"Five is far too young for a child to lose her mama," Elizabeth said. "No wonder her ladyship is struggling so with this undertaking. You must be sure to commend her on every detail, Haverford. Praise her for what goes smoothly, and for managing all the little moments she handles that refuse to go smoothly."

When was the last time Julian had praised his sister for anything? "Who praises you, Elizabeth?" *Who sees that you are more than a walking collection of learned quotes?*

She scooted about on her pillow and smoothed her skirts. "You said you like my kisses."

Didn't see that coming. "I adore your kisses. Let's find you another a book, shall we?"

The library door stood wide open, and from down the corridor, Julian heard the last of his guests finishing their breakfasts. He held out a hand to Elizabeth and she rejoined him between the bookshelves.

Twice he'd let her slip away. This time, he kissed her, or she kissed him. The undertaking was gratifyingly mutual.

Julian's dreams and recollections had not matched the reality of Elizabeth Windham stealing kisses. She was both sweet and fierce, attractive in her soft curves and tender overtures, and compelling in the sheer determination of her grip on his arse.

She hauled him closer and her tongue danced across Julian's mouth. He reciprocated, and a stolen kiss became an utter rout of his self-restraint. He backed Elizabeth up against the shelves—biographies, the last rational corner of his mind noted—and drew her as close as a man could hold a woman.

She held him even closer and wrapped her leg around his thigh. Elizabeth would delight in pleasures taken amid the scent of books, and forever after, Julian would look less bitterly on his collection of biographies.

The lady eased her mouth away and rested against him.

"The door is open," she whispered.

He and Elizabeth were not visible from the door, of

course, but one of them really ought to move. Julian was a duke, the host of the gathering, and responsible for protecting her reputation. All of that was very true, though what inspired him to prudence was a nascent erection that needed only a hint of inspiration to become obvious arousal.

Julian stepped back, even as he stole a parting kiss. Elizabeth looked as tidy as a dowager's sewing box, while Julian felt as if he had fallen headfirst from the mighty oak. Rather than stare into her eyes—or at her mouth—his gaze landed on the books behind her.

"We've upset the biographies," he said, taking another step back. "Some of those volumes recount the illustrious doings of my ancestors."

She turned, presenting the elegant line of her shoulders and back, and began setting the books to rights.

Saved by the books, Julian thought, forcing himself to put more distance between himself and the nape of Elizabeth Windham's neck.

* * *

Elizabeth let Haverford wander away to the windows, while she pretended to fuss with the biographies. In truth, she struggled not to tackle him where he stood, hands behind his back, breathing deeply.

He'd breathe like that in bed. So would she, *with him*. She'd not gaze over her lover's shoulder, noting the cobwebs in the molding, or wondering what was wrong with her, that lovemaking—the great, illicit, necessary, central activity of the human species—should strike her as tedious and undignified.

Elizabeth focused on the books, which were shelved

in no discernible order. She let His Grace have a moment of fresh air by the windows, while she regained her composure amid old friends.

An enormous volume, titled *Mr. William Shakespeare's Comedies, Histories, and Tragedies*, had strayed among the biographies. Elizabeth opened the book, and was greeted by the lovely scent of old paper, along with a familiar portrait of the Bard.

He'd known a thing or two about passion. The date beneath the portrait was 1622, and yet, people still quoted Shakespeare when their own gift for expression failed. Elizabeth was just starting on the elaborate letter from the publishers "to the Great Variety of readers," when footsteps sounded on the library carpets.

"Sherbourne, good day." Haverford's tone was polite.

Oh, dear. Oh, drat.

"Your Grace. Enjoying the family book treasury?"

"Some do treasure books, Sherbourne, and learning. I treasure civility, among other attributes. If you wanted to attend this house party, you had only to ask and I'd have sent you an invitation."

Why would Haverford have been so accommodating with a man he disapproved of?

"That's the very point, Haverford. I don't like asking. I prefer being asked." Sherbourne's voice sounded closer. "Some of these dusty old relics might have a bit of value. Shouldn't you keep the air from them?"

Dusty old relics? Elizabeth hugged the Shakespeare as if to cover the Bard's ears.

"Actually you're wrong." Haverford moved away from the window, not so much as glancing in Elizabeth's direction. "Smoke is bad for the books and for the portraiture. Coal smoke, peat smoke, cigar smoke...they all take a toll.

Damp doesn't do the books any favors either, but on fine days, the room should be aired."

"You really are impressive," Sherbourne said, taking up a position at the window Haverford had vacated. "You have the knack of shaming others with your graciousness, making them feel they ought to be grateful for your pontifications. Is the object of this gathering to fire off Lady Glenys?"

Haverford took a seat in the reading chair before the hearth. The stacks of books obscured most of him from view, so Elizabeth could see only a lacy cuff, one unadorned hand, one thigh, a knee, and a field boot. Even that visual excerpt suggested the man occupying the chair was an aristocrat at his leisure.

"The object of this gathering," Haverford said, "is to enjoy congenial company during Wales's loveliest weather. Any hostess knows the numbers ought to at least match, and better if the eligible men outnumber the single ladies."

"Oh, right. And what's old Benedict Andover doing among the pigeons?"

"I like him," Haverford said. "I *respect* him, and he's widowed. He and my father used to talk about books by the hour. He's been a friend to the St. Davids since before I was born, and he has other friends among the older guests."

Did that mean Sherbourne was disliked, disrespected, and had not a single friend at the gathering?

"As long as you're not considering the old boy for Lady Glenys," Sherbourne said. "In your determination to keep her from my foul clutches, you might be tempted to desperate measures. I have no wish to see your sister consigned to such a fate when better options are right at hand."

Haverford rose. "At the risk of inflicting more of my graciousness on you, Sherbourne, allow me to point out that if you seek to court my sister, protocols apply. Those protocols do not start with you threatening to call in my notes. If Glenys is amenable to receiving your addresses, and if she looks on your suit with favor, I would not gainsay her choice, providing the settlements could be worked out."

Sherbourne abandoned his post by the window. "You'd approve a match between Glenys and me?"

He sounded honestly curious. Did he harbor a *tendresse* for his hostess? Was that what his uninvited presence was about?

"I would hate to see my sister shackled to any man she could not esteem," Haverford said. "Let's leave it at that, shall we? And you will address her as Lady Glenys or risk embarrassing yourself before the other guests."

"Of course. *Lady* Glenys," Sherbourne said, "because her papa happened to be a duke rather than a brewer or a banker. My mistake. Enjoy your petty displays, Haverford. Unless you want your guests and half of London learning exactly where the metes and bounds lie between us, you'll comport yourself as mine most gracious host."

"Exactly what I am, a most gracious host," Haverford said. "I'd best see if my sister has any orders for me."

"Host" had social meaning, of course, but Elizabeth wanted to remind Sherbourne that a host could be a mighty army too.

Another set of footsteps thumped into the library at a brisk pace. "Ah, Haverford, there you are," Lord Radnor said. "Sherbourne, good day. The ladies have decided we'll process to the tents in another half hour, and all good gentlemen are to present themselves below for escort assignments. Come along, both of you."

"After you, Sherbourne," Haverford said with grave politesse.

The duke was taunting his guest, for that's how men were. Three sets of bootsteps moved toward the door, and Elizabeth gently reshelved the Bard among the biographies. She gave him a final pat—what a contribution he'd made to literature and language—and took the chair by the hearth, where she'd be in full view of the door.

The seat was well padded, the dimensions commodious, the whole sturdy and comfortable. A couple could cuddle in this chair, amid all these books.

Or a lady could take a moment to reflect on what had transpired in the past quarter hour.

What on earth was afoot between Haverford and Sherbourne? Lady Glenys had to marry somebody, and many a titled family sent their daughters into the arms of wealthy commoners.

Very wealthy commoners, with impeccable pedigrees, excellent manners, and spotless reputations.

Elizabeth resolved to further acquaint herself with Mr. Sherbourne, should the opportunity arise. Lady Glenys had awarded her the status of a friend, and friends didn't let friends contract a mésalliance.

Of more significant interest was Elizabeth's next question: Which of these many, many books should she take along to help her endure an afternoon of flies and flirtation?

And when might she and Haverford find another moment to trade confidences and stolen kisses?

Chapter Eleven

"Can you ride out with me tomorrow?" Julian asked, taking a seat uninvited beside Elizabeth Windham.

She occupied a blanket, a book in her lap. She'd chosen a spot in the shade, leaving the sunny bank of the lake to the younger ladies who were apparently desperate to remain in view of the bachelors at every moment.

In Julian's opinion, the great Haverford house party regatta was proceeding amid more jollity than the occasion warranted.

Not quite more than was proper. The gentlemen had rowed across the lake in groups of four boats, and a respite had been declared for tea and sandwiches, so that all might restore their athletic powers before the championship race.

"I would like to ride out with you," Elizabeth replied, using a stem of grass as her bookmark. "But my time is promised to another tomorrow morning. Perhaps Charlotte or Miss Trelawny might accompany you."

Miss Trelawny would cheerfully have accompanied

Julian right into his bedroom, did he allow it. She was rumored to have twenty thousand a year thanks to her uncle, the widowed banker. Her father was a viscount, and she was exactly the sort of female Julian ought to pursue.

"What are you reading?" he asked. *And why must you look so lovely where any of these prancing nincompoops might realize what a gem hides in their midst?*

"*Cecilia*. Mrs. Burney's second novel, which for some reason, is twice the length of her first, and half as interesting, but it's a favorite at the lending library I frequent in London."

"You criticize a book, Miss Windham? I thought books were sacred." Julian's forbearers had certainly been of that daft persuasion.

She set Mrs. Burney aside. "You have a first folio of Shakespeare tucked among your biographies. Books might not be sacred, but mis-shelving the Bard surely constitutes blasphemy."

"So that's where it got off to. We have some of his quartos in the family library. Who claims your time tomorrow?"

None of Julian's business, that's who, but for the next eighteen days, he could comport himself like a callow swain where Elizabeth Windham was concerned.

"I'm enjoying my constitutional with a relation of yours—Mr. Griffin St. David. He shares many of your handsome features. We met as I began my walk this morning."

Part of Julian's mind seized on the thought *Elizabeth thinks I'm handsome* even as the rest of him grasped the substance of her words.

"How did you and Griffin meet?"

"You needn't look so severe, Your Grace. Griffin chanced upon me strolling by the river. He's very friendly."

Unlike me? "What you call friendliness has landed him

in a great deal of trouble. I'll see that he doesn't bother you again."

Elizabeth turned such a look upon Julian that he was reminded of Sherbourne's words, about shaming others with graciousness. Elizabeth's gaze held great kindness and even greater disappointment.

"Griffin's situation is complicated, Elizabeth."

"Fortunately, I am possessed of sufficient intelligence that even complicated matters, when explained, are within my grasp. Who is Griffin St. David to you?"

Julian shredded a handful of clover and considered dissembling, but Griffin wasn't a secret. Lady Pembroke probably knew of him, as did any of the guests of her generation. Debrett's had eventually, for a sum certain, seen fit to forget about him.

"Griffin is my brother."

"Your full brother?"

"My full, legitimate brother, and Lady Glenys's too. He lives in his own household on a former Haverford tenancy, and I do not want to have this conversation where anybody can interrupt." *Or eavesdrop.*

Elizabeth passed him the book. "You do not want to have this conversation at all. Pretend you're reading to me, and we won't be disturbed."

He wanted to read to her, preferably late at night as they prepared for bed. "I'll be called upon to referee the championship race at any moment."

"The competitors are still very much concerned with besting one another at the buffet. Are you ashamed of your brother?"

Not even Radnor would have posed that question, but Julian was pleased to answer honestly.

"Of course I'm not ashamed. Griffin St. David has more

decency in his smallest finger on his worst day than most people can claim on Easter morning. He's brave, he's determined, he's kind, and in every way resembles a gentlemanly paragon more than I ever will. He wanted his own household, and Glenys supported him."

"Open the book, Julian. You opposed this notion?"

Julian. "I cannot protect him as effectively if he's living on his own. He's been taken advantage of in the past, with serious consequences to him and to others. I trusted the wrong people once before, and Griffin paid a high price."

The book felt heavy in his hands, as weighty as a brick, not quite as useful a weapon as a brick would be.

"He's Lord Griffin," Elizabeth said.

"You must not address him as such, for he has it in his head that all lords, even courtesy lords, go to London to sit in Parliament. I cannot take him to London. He'd be made a laughingstock, and—lest you think I haven't considered it—Lady Glenys's prospects will be diminished when people learn that she has an impaired younger brother."

That silenced her, while ten yards away, Miss Trelawny was clambering into a boat and getting her hems wet. Sir Nigel splashed about in the shallows, probably ruining his boots while the lady shrieked about not having any oars.

"Society can be vicious," Elizabeth said. "That much is true, but would Lady Glenys want a husband who couldn't accept her brother?"

"In my experience, trusting to the compassion of human nature is folly, at least among my peers. My father's outlook regarding his fellow man was more sanguine, or more foolish. I shall have to rescue that damned woman. Didn't Mrs. Burney have something to say about a lady's reputation?"

" 'Nothing is so delicate as the reputation of a woman,' "

Elizabeth quoted quietly. "'It is at once the most beautiful and most brittle of all human things.'"

The little boat was drifting out into the lake. Spectators on shore shouted suggestions, Sir Nigel trudged to the bank in his wet boots, and Miss Trelawny sat in her boat, slipping farther from dry land.

"We haven't finished this discussion," Elizabeth said. "Come by your sister's parlor after supper, and if the hour is not too late, I'll be there."

Julian pulled off his boots and set them on the grass. "Until tonight."

He kept walking, right out into the lake, which was surprisingly pleasant in temperature. The crowd on shore took to calling encouragement, though all that was wanted was to get behind the boat and give it a shove toward land. The water was little more than waist deep, and the boat soon bumped solidly into the bank.

"Well done, Your Grace," Haldale called, applauding. "You showed Sir Nigel how to deal with a damsel in distress!"

The damsel was sitting prettily in the boat, waiting for a handsome swain to get her to shore.

"Some worthy gentleman needs to carry the lady to the bank," Julian replied. "I'd oblige, but then Miss Trelawny would be as soaked as I am."

Haldale had no witty rejoinder, and Sir Nigel was staring morosely at his wet boots.

Sherbourne waded into the water and lifted Miss Trelawny from her perch. "My pleasure, madam. Perhaps if you're that eager to be on the water, we should have a lady's regatta at next year's house party."

He aimed that remark at Julian, though Sherbourne knew damned good and well there would be no Haverford house party next year or any other year.

"If the company will excuse me," Julian said, splashing to the bank, "I'll see to my attire and join you all at supper." He assayed a bow at Glenys, who looked torn between laughter and mortification.

"I'll drive you back to the castle," Radnor said, signaling to the groom who held the dogcart five yards off.

"My thanks." Julian left his boots right where they were, twelve inches to the left of Elizabeth Windham's book, and climbed into the cart.

"What was Sherbourne about," Radnor asked as they rattled off at a trot, "stepping forth to rescue Miss Trelawny? He has no need of her money, and she has no need of his."

"He was doubtless trying to impress us with his manners, and I admit, he surprised me. Sherbourne might be preparing to ask for permission to pay Glenys his addresses."

The bench beneath Julian's wet backside was hard and warm, and in truth, he was glad to be spared the rest of the afternoon by the lake.

Not glad to have abandoned Elizabeth, though.

"If Sherbourne presumes to court Lady Glenys, will you laugh in his face and have him tossed out the door?" Radnor asked.

"You know I can't."

Radnor drove along in silence for a quarter mile, while the sounds of the boating party grew mercifully quieter. "Will Lady Glenys look with favor on Sherbourne's suit?"

"I honestly don't know. I suspect she'd consider Sherbourne in the hope that her marriage would ease my financial situation." Which it would not, though it might prevent Sherbourne from causing the outright ruin of his wife's family.

Radnor tried to steer the cart around a pothole, but the way was narrow, and jostling inevitable.

"Lady Glenys would martyr herself to the St. David

debt, as you have. I'd lend you my last groat, Haverford, you know that."

"You'd give me your last groat without a thought of repayment, for which I do love you, but you've done enough. Besides, the St. David debt would eliminate all your reserves and still not be half repaid."

Not that Radnor's reserves were vast. He was comfortable, but like Julian had not turned to exploiting mineral resources to augment his fortune.

"So you'd allow a match between Sherbourne and Glenys?"

Was Radnor's question too careful? He pulled the dogcart up at the back entrance to the castle, where the baggage and tradesmen's deliveries were accepted.

"Sherbourne himself asked the same question, and all I could say was that I'd hate to see my sister shackled to any man she could not esteem. I hesitate to antagonize Sherbourne, and yet, neither can I allow him to ride roughshod over me."

A groom jogged out from the stables, and Julian hopped down from the cart. The grass was cool and soft beneath his feet, another summer pleasure he'd forgotten.

"Will you return to the revels by the lake?" Julian asked, for Radnor had remained on the bench, his expression oddly severe.

"Haverford, Lady Glenys will marry that well-dressed barbarian for your sake. Do you want that on your conscience?"

"Of course not, but what if he's her only choice? I don't care for Sherbourne, but he'll keep her in far better style than I can, and he knows her financial situation as well as I do. I don't want her spinsterhood or a life lived in unrelenting penury on my conscience, much as I detest the man."

Radnor sprang down, landing directly in front of Julian. "He'd treat her like a prize of war, parade her around London before his banker friends, and *get children on her*. How can you consider Sherbourne a suitable match for Glenys? He'd make her miserable."

Julian waited until the groom had turned the cart around and led the horse some distance away.

"Radnor, for the daughter of a duke to remain unmarried is probably the definition of misery. You don't have a sister, you can't know how much store young women set on their come out, who is marrying whom, and who has been brought to bed with a child. Glenys is not happy, and she will never be happy without a family of her own. If I marry, her situation becomes even more pathetic."

Radnor stuck his nose in Julian's face. "Sherbourne is not her only option, you dolt."

Good God. Radnor was not in a temper, he was *lovesick.* Julian took a step back and bruised his heel against a rock hidden by the grass.

"Have you told this to Glenys?"

"That you're a dolt?"

"That you are in love with her." Not merely fond of the lady, not in the grip of a passing sentiment, but hopelessly, wonderfully far gone.

Radnor turned away, his gaze fixed on the tents gleaming white across the lake. "I'm waiting for the right moment."

House parties made the wisest people daft. "Cedric, one suspects you've been waiting for years. Sherbourne is probably right now bowing over her hand and fetching her another glass of punch. There will never be a right moment, and if you want to be seen as a suitor, you'd best start comporting yourself like one."

"I've your permission to court her, then?"

"If you were anybody else, I'd tell you that Glenys's wishes will be controlling, but you're you, so I'll simply wish you the best of luck and warn you not to muck this up."

"Any worse than I already have, I know," Radnor said, striding off in the direction of the dogcart. "Timing is everything, Haverford, and it's time for a bit of courtship."

He jaunted off, leaving Julian damp and slightly chilled outside the castle walls, his foot throbbing.

Sherbourne would have a royal tantrum if Glenys married Radnor, though Glenys would be safe and happy, which mattered a very great deal.

"I hate house parties," Julian informed nobody in particular.

But he loved the idea of ending his day with Miss Elizabeth Windham in the cozy informality of the lady of the castle's tower parlor.

* * *

The boat races had tired the other guests sufficiently that Elizabeth had to wait only until eleven o'clock to make her way to the tower parlor. She lit a fire for warmth and arranged a few candles, then occupied herself reviewing the stack of correspondence Lady Glenys had set out for her.

This meeting with Haverford was not a seduction, but rather a discussion between new friends. Elizabeth had no intention of drawing out the conversation, for she must keep her appointment with Griffin early in the morning.

"You waited for me," Haverford said, slipping through the door. "Thank you."

"And you brought sustenance," Elizabeth replied, rising and taking the tray from him. Another man—another duke—would have summoned a footman to bear the tray, thus jeopardizing the privacy of this assignation.

This conversation, rather.

"Our orangery was built on an ambitious scale, and we have fruit in abundance as a result." The tray held a tea service for one, shortbread, and an orange. "A modest feast, but the scullery maid nearly had an apoplexy when I dared trespass belowstairs to request a tray."

Given the single teacup, not even the scullery maid would suspect the duke intended to share his tray.

"You probably interrupted her flirtation with the boot boy." Elizabeth set the tray on the table before the sofa and lifted the lid of the teapot. Clove and citrus wafted up. "What manner of tea is this? The scent is delightful."

"Glenys blends it, probably to stretch our stores of China black. Did you lay that fire?"

Elizabeth settled on the sofa and began peeling the orange. "I did, and I lit it from the sconce in the hallway. I gather her ladyship does try to practice economies, some of the time."

His Grace prowled the room, tidying the desk—for which his sister might kill him—and moving the candles on the mantel so they were exactly symmetric.

"Tell me about Griffin, Haverford."

"Perhaps you'd prefer cordial to tea?"

"I'd prefer you tell me about your brother." Elizabeth suspected His Grace had no one with whom to discuss Griffin's situation, much less Lady Glenys's marital aspirations, or the problems with the estate. The right duchess would halve his sorrows....

Elizabeth set the orange down half-peeled.

"My mother's labor with Griffin was difficult," Haverford said, his back to Elizabeth. He appeared to study the landscape over the mantel, but the art was so old and so poorly preserved, that in the dim light, he was staring into shadows. "The midwife said the cord had wrapped about his neck, and unlike most children, he didn't come squalling into the world. He had to be encouraged to draw breath, and his early days gave us all great anxiety. To this day, he can't stand anything tight around his neck."

"He looks to be at least ten years your junior."

"Twelve, and Mama was not young when I came along. Papa was overjoyed at first, for he'd given up hoping for a spare. Then we began to notice problems. Griffin was a clumsy baby, slow to gain strength, and even after he learned to walk, he'd have awful tantrums. The nurse said he was frustrated by a lack of words, because those too were slow to come along."

And all of this would have been unfolding as Haverford navigated the rocky shoals of adolescence.

"Griffin speaks well now," Elizabeth said, "and he's nimble as a goat."

"For years, he lagged behind other boys his age in terms of speech, and he's learned to compensate for what he doesn't grasp. Most metaphors are beyond him, though he won't confess his confusion. He nods politely, as a gentleman should at various points in a conversation. May I sit with you?"

Both St. David brothers were gentlemen. "Of course. Griffin has a thorough grasp of facts, though."

"Some facts," Haverford said, settling in with a sigh. "Others he's parroting from memory, oblivious to their significance. He has artistic skills in the same vein. He can copy any text in beautiful copperplate, but has little sense of its meaning. He knows the words to every hymn and has a lovely voice, while I struggle to recall more than the first verse. In many ways, Griffin is the truest gentleman I will ever meet, and yet, he's vulnerable."

Elizabeth took Haverford's hand, because she could, and because somebody should. "As a child is vulnerable?"

"Worse. Griffin looks, recalls, and often acts like an adult, but he reasons as a child does. He raises no livestock for meat, because the notion of slaughtering a beast reduces him to weeks of despondency. They all become pets to him. That the chicken in the stew was raised in somebody's yard and fed by somebody's children seems to escape his notice. If he feeds that chicken himself, however, the bird will enjoy a lifetime of good care and be given a carefully chosen name."

"He sees the world through the eyes of a child." A child much loved and sheltered.

"Exactly." Haverford stroked his fingers over Elizabeth's knuckles, absently, as he might have petted a cat. "Griffin has befriended the occasional woman too."

"Oh, dear." *Taken advantage of* and *vulnerable* acquired dire significance.

Haverford leaned his head back and closed his eyes. "I had hoped that my brother would be spared a young man's usual zeal for the ladies, but a guest who'd come to visit Lady Glenys a few years ago realized that Griffin is my heir. She seduced him, which probably took about two seconds given Griffin's nature, and conceived a child—a daughter, as it turned out."

The wrong that had been done, to Griffin, to his family, and to the child was stunning, and yet, Elizabeth had heard not a hint of scandal regarding the St. Davids.

And clearly, Haverford blamed himself for what had befallen his brother. "What did you do?"

"I explained the situation to Griffin, who did not grasp

that he'd been played for a fool until the young lady laughed at him before others. She'd found a way to marry a ducal heir, acquire a courtesy title, and escape all the strictures husbands can legally put on wives. Her plan was to live out the rest of her life fashionably estranged from her spouse, a portion of St. David wealth and consequence hers to command for her silence regarding Griffin's limitations."

Uncle Percy, in all his shrewdness, assisted by Aunt Esther, with her vast stores of sense, would have been hard put to untangle such a muddle.

"I gather Griffin is not married to this disgrace." Though Griffin hadn't mentioned a daughter either.

"I put the choice to him. He could marry this woman, knowing exactly how badly he'd misjudged her and what sort of person she was. His daughter would be legitimate, the lady would become a member of the St. David family, and Griffin would have his one and only wife until the woman's demise. In the alternative, he could remain unwed and we would raise the child as a by-blow."

Elizabeth took a nibble of shortbread, and held the remainder of the biscuit to Haverford's mouth. He took a bite, and she brushed the crumbs from his cravat.

"Which did Griffin choose?"

"He asked me if I would promise to love the child, and be as good an uncle to her as Abner was to Biddy. I gave my word, as did Glenys as the girl's aunt. Radnor and I are Charity's guardians. She bides with Radnor, though the poor mite has the St. David eyebrows."

Elizabeth rather liked those eyebrows. "She's assumed to be your child?"

"I don't care what's assumed about her. I care that she's loved, protected, and raised with the privileges of her station. When Glenys is married, I'll bring Charity here, where she belongs."

"She doesn't belong with her father?"

Haverford opened his eyes and gestured for more short-bread. "I can't ask Biddy and Abner to care for half my family, Elizabeth. We're letting the tea get cold."

The teapot was swaddled in toweling, which would hold in the warmth. One-handed, Elizabeth poured out a cup and added two lumps of sugar. "Milk?"

"Please."

They drank three cups of tea between them and finished the orange and half the shortbread. The modest fare was comforting, as was Haverford's willingness to share the single cup.

"What happened to the young lady, if one can call her a lady?" Elizabeth asked.

"By agreement with her father, she married another man after Charity's birth, a fellow her father could trust to overlook the entire situation. I conveyed to the groom a life estate in a sizeable farm in Gloucestershire, one I'd intended to include in Glenys's settlements. If I hear a whisper of a rumor regarding Charity, I will revoke the life estate. Until then, the rents go to the couple or their oldest son."

"Neatly done." Charity's mother was motivated to keep her mouth shut, and her husband and family were moti-vated to keep the lady away from polite society. Haverford, however, was out income and property in exchange for their silence.

And the child.

"This is not a cheering topic," Haverford said, his head resting on Elizabeth's shoulder. "I apologize for burdening you with family problems, but you've met Griffin. If you failed to keep your appointment with him tomorrow, he'd worry for you, or worse, worry that you didn't like him because, in his words, he isn't smart."

Elizabeth slipped an arm around the duke, who fit nicely in the circle of her embrace. "I'll keep my appointment with Griffin. He's a pleasant change from the company at the breakfast table, excluding mine host, of course."

She would also put off until another time a discussion of the bills piled neatly on the desk across the room.

Bills that Lady Glenys had doubtless forgotten to separate from her social correspondence, for Elizabeth shuddered at the amounts she'd seen. Surely her ladyship wouldn't want anybody but family to see those figures.

Haverford kissed Elizabeth's cheek. "Your host is the soul of graciousness, of course. I should see you safely to your rooms."

Elizabeth knew the way now. Very likely, Charlotte would still be awake and full of questions.

"Let's bide a while here and enjoy the quiet."

"Can you swim?" Haverford asked.

"Quite well, though I haven't since girlhood."

"We'll remedy that oversight." He was soon breathing regularly, an exhausted, warm weight against Elizabeth's side. Perhaps his explanation of Griffin's situation had tired him, or perhaps the duke sensed that in this tower, in Elizabeth's arms, he was free to rest from his many labors.

The moment wasn't lover-ly, but it was intimate. Elizabeth remained with Haverford for another quarter hour, and when the clock from the hall below struck midnight, she eased away. A shawl purloined from the back of the chair at the desk was the best she could do to keep him warm.

She kissed his cheek, checked the corridor for stray footmen or straying debutantes, then made her way alone through the darkness to her room.

Chapter Twelve

"And when the fair young maid required a pair of strong arms to convey her to shore, I obliged," Sherbourne said. "Take that dratted cap away, for God's sake. I'm little more than thirty years old and in possession of a full head of hair."

"My apologies, sir." Turnbull put the nightcap back in the chest beneath the window. "Will there be anything else?"

"What do you hear about the Windham ladies?"

Socializing belowstairs, swilling ale in the servants' hall, and befriending everybody from the housekeeper to the boot boy also numbered among Turnbull's duties.

"The two younger Windham sisters are recently wed to a Scottish duke and his heir, respectively, and both are off to Scotland. The older sisters are highly regarded."

Of course a pair of *ducal* spinsters would be highly regarded. "I'll take the green dressing gown," Sherbourne said. Miss Windham had worn green today, and looked quite fetching. Miss Charlotte hadn't cut the same elegant, relaxed dash, though her walking dress of brown and cream muslin had been pretty.

Fashion mattered to the titled set. Sherbourne had learned that before he'd gone up to university.

Turnbull held out the desired dressing gown, which was velvet lined with lighter green silk, and worth a year of the valet's wages for the embroidery alone. Even a practical man was allowed the occasional touch of vanity.

"Miss Charlotte has a tart tongue," Turnbull went on, "but is kind to the maids. The bachelors seem to regard her with a mixture of awe and dread. Miss Elizabeth is a champion of lending libraries and literacy and is left mostly to her own devices by the aunt."

No news there. "The aunt being Arabella Windham, Lady Pembroke, who is probably the pattern card for Miss Charlotte in later life. As for Miss Elizabeth Windham, what sort of woman likes lending libraries? She even confessed this predilection to me. Books just sit there, collecting dust and making one feel guilty for not having read them."

"Sherbourne Hall has a fine library, sir," Turnbull said, turning down the sheets.

"I have a library full of books bought by the box from estate sales to fill the shelves, as you well know. Is there talk concerning my intended?"

Turnbull came around the four-poster bed, a lovely old specimen that would comfortably hold six people. Sherbourne couldn't fault Haverford's hospitality—yet.

"Lady Glenys is said to be bearing up well."

"What does that mean? She's frolicking the entire day away with a bunch of handsome idlers." While Sherbourne endured more tittering, fan-waving, and simpering than sanity allowed. No wonder Haverford had a reputation for lurking among his books.

Turnbull left off fussing the bed. "Frolics, as you call them, do not happen spontaneously. Somebody must decide where to place the tent, what recipe to use for the punch, how many cakes to make, and how to get them all under the tents. Somebody must ensure the boats have a fresh coat of paint and are seaworthy. Her ladyship has managed the whole and will have far more to do than her guests."

This was why Sherbourne paid Turnbull exorbitant wages. The valet was more astute than a royal finishing governess, and knew when to be blunt—seldom—and when to be deferential—always.

"Then I can ingratiate myself into her ladyship's good books by being useful?"

"A gentleman never ignores a lady in need, sir."

"Is there a lady whom Haverford finds difficult to ignore?" The Trelawny creature, perhaps. Haverford had got a good soaking pushing her boat to shore, then inquired after her well-being solicitously at supper. He'd taken off his boots before wading into the lake, though, suggesting—delightful thought—even the cost of a pair of new boots would pain him.

Miss Trelawny was exactly the sort of featherbrain His Grace ought to marry. She'd make him miserable, but bring him closer to solvency. To trade personal happiness for financial health was the best bargain Haverford would make with life and better than he deserved.

"His Grace is cordial to all of his guests, sir."

All save Sherbourne. "Off to bed with you, Turnbull. There's more to be learned tomorrow, I'm sure. Keep a lookout for how I might be of service to her ladyship or to the Windhams. Miss Elizabeth is not hard on the eye, for all she's getting long in the tooth."

"Of course, sir. Good night, sir."

Perhaps Haverford fancied one of the Windhams. Miss Charlotte's vinegar would suit his dour nature, and Miss Elizabeth would get on well with Lady Glenys.

Regardless, Haverford could have neither of the Windhams. Sherbourne would see to that. When His Grace married, he'd be in such financial difficulties, he'd be grateful to wed an American banker's lisping, giggling daughter.

* * *

"Chocolate." The word was distinguishable amid other mumblings coming from Lady Glenys's bed. Radnor made out "toast," "damn," and "mustn't tell Haverford."

Radnor's beloved talked in her sleep. Did anybody else know that about her?

He lifted the covers and joined her in the bed. "Glennie?"

"Please not yet."

"We must talk."

She flopped onto her side, giving him her back. "Go away."

Then she sat up straight. "What in the illuminated holy scriptures are you doing in my bed, Radnor?" Her hair was a thick dark braid going frazzled near the end. She whipped it over her shoulder, lashing Radnor's cheek.

"You're awake."

"I'm not awake. I'm having a nightmare if you're paying a call at this hour, especially if you somehow got turned around and intended to end up in somebody else's bed."

The pillow had creased her cheek, and her nightgown had pink rosebuds embroidered on the décolletage. Radnor hoarded those details and folded his hands beneath his head lest he touch her.

"I'm in the right bed, at the only hour when we're likely to have privacy. I love you."

She drew the covers up under her arms. "You've been drinking."

Not the most encouraging response. "I haven't had a drop since dinner, and may I compliment you on the merlot."

"That wine was from your cellar, and you need to get out of my bed."

Radnor needed to kiss her. He didn't dare touch her. "I love you, I have for years, and I'm determined to court you."

She ceased fussing with the covers. "That's very sweet of you, also insulting. I can inspire somebody to offer for me without you pretending an interest, Radnor."

"We're in bed. The least you can do is call me Cedric." He caught her braid and tugged her down, so she rested against his side.

"You bathed," she said, sniffing his shoulder. "You don't smell of those awful cigars. I need to find another location for the evening card parties, or the library will stink for the next twenty years."

God rot all card parties and all ducal libraries. "Glenys, I want to marry you."

Her sigh fanned across his chest. "No, you don't. You're being noble, or gallant, or a good friend—I know not what. You have to marry somebody, I want to marry somebody, and you perceive what I should have known all along: Haverford can assemble as many titled bachelors as England has pubs, and none of them will offer for me. I'm not... I'm not attractive in the way women attract eligible men."

Radnor laced his arm around her shoulders and kissed her temple. "I agree. You are entirely lacking in silliness, vanity, stratagems, flirtation, chatter, and jealousies."

"I am not winsome," Glenys said, gravely, as if this mattered.

"I'll be winsome enough for the pair of us," Radnor replied. "You worry over both of your brothers, which few would have sense enough to do, though Haverford and Griffin are equally worth worrying over. You never complain, you manage this household with too little help, you are kind and sensible, and you will never expect me to be something I'm not."

"I expect you to be out of this bed immediately."

"Glenys, there's not another woman whom I esteem half so much as I do you. I'm baring my soul to you. Please be serious."

She raised herself up on one elbow and peered down at him. The hearth held some coals, but the room was dark. Fortunately.

"You've bared your chest to me too." She ran a hand over Radnor's belly, then over his heart, and across his collarbones.

He endured that torture, but refused to allow the moment to turn into a dalliance.

"I used to spy on you," Glenys said, pillowing her cheek on his chest. "You and Haverford. You'd go swimming in the river, and I'd hide in the oak to watch you. I was very naughty."

"Very resourceful. I need a resourceful marchioness."

She kissed him, a quick press of lips, as if tasting a glass of wine to see if the vintage went with the dessert.

"Haverford would kill me if I let you court me. I've incurred such expenses with this damned house party, Cedric.... You have no idea what extravagance I'm guilty of. I had no idea. I can't be seen to engage your affections, or the bachelors will one by one find excuses to leave early. The young ladies will join them, and my house party will be the realm's costliest failure."

To Radnor, whose mental processes were admittedly suffering a momentary inefficiency, calling off the whole house party seemed a capital notion. He was reminded of Haverford's warning, though: Women set store by a social agenda that men treated far more casually. A failed house party would follow Glenys's reputation for decades.

"Tell me the truth," he said. "Do you object to my attentions because they will discourage all the other bachelors and ruin your house party, or because you cannot esteem me as a woman esteems her intended?"

Delicately put, if he did say so himself.

"I've been esteeming you as a woman esteems a handsome, charming, bothersome specimen since I was fifteen years old, Radnor. You came home from university and I wanted to gobble you whole. I was years away from making my bow, though, and you never lacked for female attention."

She *esteemed* him—she esteemed *him*!

"Many of those women were simply trying to gain your brother's notice." Radnor hadn't figured that out. One of the ladies had told him, straight to his face, even as she'd asked him to lace her up. In some ways, he'd been as naïve as dear Griffin.

"Everybody wants Julian's notice, but that's another reason why you must not be seen to court me. He needs a wife, Cedric. I hadn't seen it before, but he's lonely. I think he regrets letting Griffin establish a separate household, though Griffin's happy, and Julian would never impose on anybody."

Haverford was showing signs of imposing on Miss Elizabeth Windham, and she on him. Now was not the time to distract Glenys with that development.

"I will be just another gallant swain for the duration of this blasted house party, then," Radnor said. "But the day those coaches disappear down your drive, expect to be besieged, Glennie. I'll sing ballads beneath your window, recite poetry while I climb your trellises, and swim naked for you in the river."

"The next seventeen days will be an eternity," Glenys said. "Do gallant swains ever steal kisses?"

Radnor shifted over her. "All the time, my dear. All the time."

* * *

"A word with you after breakfast, if you please." Julian kept his voice down, because other guests were finding places at the breakfast table, Sherbourne among them.

"Of course," Glenys replied.

In the sunshine slanting through the tall windows, she looked tired, but also relaxed. Perhaps she'd realized that a house party wasn't quite as complicated as moving an army across Spain, though it was to cost Julian nearly as much.

He held her chair, he greeted his guests, and he nodded cordially to Sherbourne, who was turned out in the first stare of fashion. Julian's neighbor was clearly pleased to be strutting among a crowd of titles, and if Sherbourne was pleased, somebody else was bound to be suffering soon.

"Tea, Haverford?" Glenys held one of the six matching Meissen teapots that graced the table, a fortune in antique porcelain.

Julian didn't want any damned tea. "Thank you. May I fetch you some eggs?" He didn't want to fetch anybody any damned eggs either.

"I'd like some eggs," Cousin Delphine said from Glenys's left. Cousin Hugh was nowhere to be seen, but then, the day was fair.

"Your servant, ladies." Julian rose and bowed.

"Haverford, good day," Sherbourne said, helping himself to the strawberries at the sideboard. "I'm surprised to see you joining us at the breakfast table."

"Do you think I subsist without the same sustenance other mortals require?" Julian ought not to have said that. Nobody had overheard, but Sherbourne's smile went from smug to gloating.

"I'm sure your consequence alone keeps you warm at night, but did you know your walking partner has left the premises without you?"

"I have a walking partner now? How fortunate for me. Will you leave a few strawberries for anybody else? I hadn't taken you for a glutton."

A petty victory, but Sherbourne had heaped a bowl nearly to the brim with fresh fruit.

"I'm sure your larders can supply an endless bounty, you being a duke and all, and we wouldn't want such luscious fruit to go to waste, would we? I refer to Miss Elizabeth Windham, whom I saw walking up Tudor Hill on the arm of some other swain."

The innuendo—luscious fruit—had Julian slapping eggs onto a plate. "You saw Miss Windham walking out with my brother, whom she has pronounced better company than many at this very table. Would you care for some eggs?"

Julian held the serving spoon, heaped full of eggs, and measured the angle necessary to splatter those eggs all over Sherbourne's intricate cravat.

Sherbourne's smile faltered. "She's walking out with your brother?"

"He's teaching her the Welsh words for our local flora and fauna. Miss Windham's mother is Welsh, and she will enjoy surprising her mama with an expanded vocabulary."

The moment turned *lovely*. Griffin in the role of teacher was something Sherbourne clearly could not fathom, and that Elizabeth preferred Griffin's company was a source of further confusion to Julian's neighbor.

"Miss Windham is a lady," Julian said. "A true, genuine lady, and Griffin is a gentleman. I do hope all those strawberries won't make you ill."

He dumped the spoonful of eggs onto Sherbourne's plate so they half-covered the toast, which would have driven Griffin wild, then served more eggs onto plates for Delphine and Glenys.

Sherbourne scraped most of the strawberries back into the serving bowl and marched off to take a place between Haldale and Lady Pembroke.

Bad form, that, putting food back into a serving dish.

Julian endured breakfast, though he was pleased to think of Griffin and Elizabeth up on the hill, trading words and phrases as the sun rose. Griffin loved to expound, though he sometimes had no grasp of the facts he recited—much like half the House of Lords when delivering their speeches.

"I've had enough tea to float a royal barge," Glenys said as the meal wound down. "If you're to deliver a verbal flogging, let's go to my tower."

"Excellent suggestion."

Julian loved his sister dearly, but what he'd found in the tower upon rising came perilously close to a betrayal, and from the one person whose loyalty he'd felt entitled to rely on.

Glenys was stopped twice on the way upstairs, once by the housekeeper asking if twenty kites would be enough for the afternoon's activity, and another time by the butler asking if storing the excess wine in the root cellar was acceptable until room could be made for it in the wine cellar.

"We're flying kites this afternoon?" Julian asked.

"You have a better suggestion?"

Griffin was wicked good at flying kites. "I would approve the activity as involving singularly little expense, except I know you'll put out punch, sandwiches, and cake in great quantity, kite flying being a strenuous endeavor."

"You're angry."

Julian held the door to her parlor. "Furious, and not a little bewildered." Glenys scuttled past him, and he felt like a bully, though he'd simply been honest.

"You snooped through my correspondence," Glenys said when the door was firmly closed.

"I did no such thing. I came up here last night in search of privacy. Your shawl was on the back of the chair, and I thought to use it as a makeshift blanket while I enjoyed some solitude. When I rose to replace your shawl where I found it, the stack of bills sat in plain sight."

The shawl was neatly folded across the back of the chair, a supporting witness to Julian's edited recitation.

"I haven't been through them yet," Glenys said, retrieving the shawl and draping it around her shoulders. "Are they very bad?"

Julian dropped onto the sofa where he'd found such comfort the previous night. "They are awful, Glenys. An ice sculpture of a swan in the heat of summer? What possessed you?"

She took the place beside him. "Ignorance possessed me. I've never purchased an ice sculpture before, you see. Nor pineapples, nor kites. I had no idea. . . . Haverford, I'm sorry. This is my fault, and if you must reduce my settlements to pay for the party, then reduce them."

"Your settlements involve very little funds anymore," Julian said, though he'd reviewed the situation with her at the turn of the new year, as he did every year. "I'd have to sell land, which means reducing rental income, and land prices aren't what they were."

She worried the hem of her shawl with her forefinger against her thumb, a habit left over from infancy. "Are we rolled up, Julian? Have I spent our last groat?"

He was her brother, the head of her family, and in some regard responsible for her ignorance. He should have given her a budget, should have asked her for estimates—but then, he'd never purchased pineapples or ice swans either.

His parents and grandparents had done rather too much of both, and more than too much of purchasing books.

"In a detailed sense, I don't know where we stand, Glenys. I'll have to tally the sums due, see what assets I might be able to discreetly liquidate, prevail on Radnor for a spot of cash, and hope it tides us over to harvest and fall markets."

"You'll hate asking Radnor for help."

"And Radnor will hate that I'm reduced to needing his aid, but there's nothing else for it." The exposed stone walls surrounding Julian for the first time felt not like a testament to long family history and sturdy defenses, but like a prison. His grandfather and father had decorated their prison with books, and borrowed from Sherbourne's antecedents to do so.

Julian had never decided if borrowing under those circumstances had been sheer stupidity or arrogance.

Probably both. "How do you fancy having Miss Trelawny for a sister-in-law?" he asked.

Glenys left off worrying the edge of her shawl. "She's silly, vapid, and half your age. I'd say she might mature out of it, but her own mother put her up to that stunt with the boat yesterday."

"She's very likely my best prospect for surviving our current penury." The notion of marrying for money, theoretical for years, loomed as all too real—and awful—now. "Consider how the vaunted St. David book collection will fare in her hands, what sort of mother she'll be to your nieces and nephews, and how she'll take to having Griffin for a brother-in-law."

Glenys rose. "Haverford, you can't. There has to be another way."

"She's a viscount's daughter—a mere third viscount—and she's an heiress, Glenys. I can't afford to ignore her, and you invited her here exactly because I must consider her, and women like her for my duchess."

Glenys began to pace in a circle, for that was all the chamber allowed. "I hate this. I hate that you can't have any joy, nothing but duty, nothing but drudgery, and there's Sherbourne, happy as a spring lamb, very likely scheming to snatch Miss Trelawny from under your nose."

"She'd bore him silly in a week. I suspect it's you he wants."

Glenys dropped into the chair at the desk. "I had that thought, but it was a cobwebby notion—I brushed it aside and pretended it wasn't there. What makes him think I'd entertain his suit? He's not awful, and he's not bad-looking despite his Viking dimensions, but he's . . . he's not warm."

Julian suspected the same criticism could be leveled in his direction. "He is exceedingly well fixed, Glenys, and there were debts between his father and our late papa that I haven't been able to pay off."

Ten years after Papa's death, more than three hundred monthly payments already made, and a substantial sum—probably the exact value of Julian's soul—was still owing to Sherbourne. The promissory note that had most recently come due only added to that misery.

"And then I order ice sculptures."

Plural? "You can un-order them. The ball isn't for two weeks. We have flowers aplenty this time of year, and they will have to do for centerpieces. The pineapples can be un-ordered, and you can limit the afternoon offerings to punch and dry cake. Add a bottle of wine to the punch and no-body will complain about the lack of sandwiches."

Glenys leafed through the stack of bills. "Radnor might have some ideas about how to economize."

She'd saved Julian from making the suggestion. "Once the kite flying is over," he said, "I'll go through those bills and see what else might be done to reduce expenses. Put aside your animosity toward Radnor long enough to gain the benefit of his cleverness, but do not, under any circum-stances, accept a loan or a gift of money from him, Glenys. I'll handle that discussion if it becomes necessary."

"Radnor will assist any way he can. You might consider consulting with Miss Windham too, Haverford. She's been to many a house party and has already made useful sugges-tions. I like her."

I love her. The thought flew into Julian's mind softly, the way a dove landing on an open windowsill brought sun-shine and joy into a whole room.

"Then we will also consult with Miss Windham, but please do not think to matchmake in that direction, Glenys."

Glenys set the letters and bills on the far corner of the desk. "Why not? She's of suitable family, she's sensible. She'd *do*, Haverford, and she is about as well connected as an unmarried woman can be."

"While I am a ruralizing, penniless duke. Imagine how that will look, when our solicitors approach the Duke of Moreland, hat in hand. My family seat is decades overdue for repairs, my heir has the wits of a ten-year-old, and I'm rumored to have a by-blow in my best friend's nursery. Add to that, I struggle to pay even the trades, and no sane duke should allow his niece within three counties of me."

Glenys hugged the shawl more closely about her,

though the room wasn't particularly cold for a woman used to living in a castle. "The debts are worse than I thought, then."

"And the talk is worse too. I vote my seat, in part because a conscientious record in the Lords is one way to repair the damage gossip does to our standing season by season."

He and Glenys should have had this talk five years ago, or even ten, and regularly thereafter. He hadn't wanted to burden her with their misfortunes, and now pineapples and ice sculptures had been heaped on the damage done by Papa and Grandpapa.

"I should never have arranged this house party," Glenys said, moving to the window. The frame still bore the contours of an arrow slit, the windowsill forming a wedge that narrowed to a small aperture fitted with mullioned glass.

"You were determined to find me a bride. I was determined to find you a husband, and it appears Sherbourne, of all people, intends to offer for you. He's the last man I'd like to see you marry, though, so you're not to consider him seriously. We'll get through this, Glenys."

"Right," she said, arms crossed. "Dry cakes, no sandwiches, and cancel the flourishes. I can do that. You should still consider Miss Windham."

"Not if I esteem her, which I do. See what ideas Radnor has, and I'll look forward to flying kites in the park after lunch."

Glenys's eyes bore banked panic, and Julian was tempted to offer her some token comfort—a single ornamental pineapple, one modest ice sculpture—but that way lay yet more bills he could not pay, more years without a duchess, while Sherbourne perched like a raptor on the castle parapets.

Julian would keep to his budgets and plans, despite all temptation to the contrary, even if affording a duchess took another ten years.

And he would spend his afternoon flying bedamned useless kites and pretending to enjoy it.

Chapter Thirteen

"I don't believe Mr. Sherbourne did it intentionally," Elizabeth said, "but the kite bearing the red dragon is up there somewhere, nonetheless. Two years from now, somebody will see it wafting among the parapets, and you'll have a proper ghostly legend for your castle."

She'd kept her distance from Haverford for most of the day, resisting the urge to recount for him the pleasure of her morning walk with Griffin. The younger St. David brother was spontaneous, cheerful, and guileless, probably very like the duke had been, long, long ago. She and Griffin had agreed to meet tomorrow, weather permitting, though Elizabeth had wondered—idly—if Griffin would have enjoyed the kite flying.

He'd certainly not have got his kite stuck up among the castle's crenellations. He'd have been absorbed with flying the kite, not flirting with the young ladies. The other bachelors would have been dumbstruck to see how the ladies flocked to Griffin's side as a result.

"We have legends enough already," Haverford said, leading Elizabeth down a gravel walk. "Come with me." He'd appeared at her side as the party had left the park to return to the castle, then tarried with her behind the larger group in the formal garden.

"Where are we going, Your Grace?"

"To retrieve your damned kite."

He was in a temper over something, though he'd flown the St. Andrew's cross for Miss Trelawny with cordial competence. Elizabeth had ignored them as best she could with Mr. Sherbourne affixed to her elbow.

"It's only a kite, Haverford, and I'm sure you have better things to do—"

He opened a gate in the garden wall. "The view I'd like to show you is even better than the view from the oak, as grand as the view from the hill."

The wall ran into the castle itself three yards to the right. The duke opened a low door in the arch of the gateway between the garden and the park, and Elizabeth spied a passage.

"You want me to follow you into there?" she said.

"We'll leave the door open at the bottom, and soon find ourselves in a servants' stair. This wing of the castle has no ghosts, I assure you."

He held out his hand. The other guests were strolling toward the house, probably intent on resting before changing for dinner. Miss Trelawny was draped about Mr. Sherbourne's arm like seaweed wrapped about a floating spar.

Elizabeth took Haverford's hand and bent low to follow him into the passage.

"The castle is full of hidden rooms, extra staircases, and even tunnels," he said. "We managed to dance our way through the Civil Wars, the Protectorate, the Restoration, the Jacobites, all of it, in part because the castle was designed with escape routes and hiding places. Our plan was to be hard to find and hard to follow in our own sanctuary. The old dower house has a few of the same features."

They reached a spiral staircase, dimly lit from above. Elizabeth dropped the duke's hand. "Will Lady Glenys set up housekeeping in the dower house anytime soon?"

"I certainly hope not. I think I've mentioned that Sherbourne owns it. I hear he's turned his home into a temple to modern conveniences. Watch your step."

The boards of the landing creaked beneath Elizabeth's feet. Unlike the other stairwell she'd traversed with Haverford, this one was neglected, and smelled of old stone and damp. The next segment of steps was straight, though, with proper landings, and went up for three floors.

"Sherbourne watches Lady Glenys," Elizabeth said. "He was distracted the whole time he kept me company, stealing glances at her and Sir Nigel."

Even Aunt Arabella had participated in the kite flying, though Mr. Andover had got her kite—a shamrock—aloft for her.

"Sherbourne will probably offer for Glenys, for which presumption, I'd like to toss him into an oubliette, though ours was filled in when we drained the moat."

The duke unlatched another low door, one made of a single board carved with an arching top. The door was likely centuries old, suggesting they were in the most ancient part of the castle.

Sunlight, painfully brilliant, assailed Elizabeth. Haverford took her hand again, though they were surrounded by the castle's highest defenses. Crenellation was expensive, and could only have been undertaken with the permission of the sovereign, for it made a castle easier to defend and harder to besiege.

This entire section of roof was lined with crenellations, stone walkways running beneath them about three feet above Elizabeth's head. The stonework was so old and worn that wild roses had taken root in crevices and crannies, the blossoms small and profuse. Two ancient cannon sat at diagonal corners of the whole, the nearest one serving as a perch for a seagull.

"They nest up here in spring," Haverford said, "and there's the kite."

The red dragon on a silk field of white and green was wedged beside the other cannon. Haverford trotted up stone steps gone uneven with age, and tossed the kite down to Elizabeth.

"May I come up?" she asked.

"Be careful. This is one of many parts of the castle needing attention."

She set the kite by the old door, tucked up her skirts, and ascended the steps. The feel was wrong, the height of the risers and width of the steps conforming to the dictates of earlier centuries, and no handrail protected the unwary from overbalancing.

"Gracious angels, the view..."

Wales in all her green and gold glory lay at their feet. The sea shimmered blue off to the south, and dark patches of forest alternated with land in cultivation and pastures. The river wound like a skein of silver toward the sea, and the breeze bore the scents of grass and goodness.

"What does it feel like, to own this?" she asked.

Haverford stood at her back, as solid as the castle's stonework.

"I personally own very little other than a lot of old books," he said. "The dukedom is entrusted to me, and I steward those resources for those who come after me. I should spend more time up here."

Elizabeth turned, struck by an odd note in his voice—sadness, perhaps. "I feel the same way about literature. Books are entrusted to us, to be shared with those in need of the learning and the comfort, so future generations won't have to discover all over again the wisdom we've already accumulated."

The breeze whipped at Haverford's dark hair. "Or the wisdom we've lost, because somebody shelved the Bard among the biographies?"

Elizabeth kissed him, for they likely had more privacy here than anywhere else on the estate. "I found the Bard. He's safe for now."

Haverford shifted her, so a massive expanse of stone was at her back, and the duke was wrapped around the rest of her. The stone was warmed by the sun, but the breeze was brisk, and his embrace protected her from its bite.

"I could kiss you all day," he murmured. "I could make love with you all day." He pressed nearer, and Elizabeth felt the arousal a mere few kisses had inspired.

"So why don't you?"

Haverford ceased his kisses and stared down at her.

The seagull left its perch on the cannon, and desolation swamped Elizabeth. "Forget I said that." She tried to slip from his embrace, but he drew her closer, which was just as well, for then he couldn't see her face. "I have no notion how to conduct a liaison," she went on, "and if you're having second thoughts, or interested in pursuing other directions, you need not be delicate about it."

Haverford's embrace was secure, and yet, Elizabeth sensed he was holding on to her as much as holding her.

"One gift I can offer you is my time," he said. "For the next two weeks, I would like to show you a glimpse of what it is to be courted, rather than merely dallied with. I would like to be your swain, not the polite host or bachelor duke. Of coin I have little, but my time is mine to spend. May I give you that boon?"

"I don't understand the question." Elizabeth understood that Julian was dear to her, and embroiled in a situation generations in the making, and yet, he hesitated to share intimacies with her. "Your version of respect, if that's what this is, feels like rejection."

Their bodies fit together so wonderfully. That didn't feel like rejection at all.

"We have a short span of days," he said. "Not enough time, not nearly enough, and then you'll get into your coach, wave farewell, and be about your life. When you leave here…"

"Yes?"

"Don't settle, Elizabeth. Don't compromise, don't accept less than your due. Keep to your plans and dreams, and let nothing wrest them from you."

He kissed her then, still trying to make some obscure point. Elizabeth would have devoured him whole, while Haverford was intent on enjoying her like a rare delicacy— niece of duke with a sauce of intellect, desire, and determination, garnished with a subtle loneliness and a sprinkling of insecurity.

Gradually, she quieted and became absorbed in his caresses. She and Haverford had *some* time, time enough to kiss, to touch, to share a lovely view. She had time to learn the contour of his shoulders and the musculature of his back, to absorb the rhythm of his breathing and the feel of his heartbeat beneath her cheek.

Gently, slowly, he laid her back on the flat expanse of warm stone between two crenellations. The sky was brilliant blue above her, the ground many feet below, the castle solidly beneath her.

As hard as the stone was, her skirts were that soft, whispering up over her knees as Haverford rearranged her clothing.

What an odd place to make love, both beautiful and lonely. Appropriate, considering their circumstances.

Haverford tossed his jacket to the stones and knelt between her knees. He lifted her skirts higher, petticoats and all, so she was bared to the bright afternoon sunshine. No other man had seen her thus—none had bothered to look, and she wouldn't have allowed it in any case.

"Your hair is lighter here," he said, ruffling her curls. "More fiery."

What followed had no precedent in Elizabeth's experience. Haverford touched her—intimately, expertly. Not a few fumbling strokes to locate an objective, but caresses that turned desire into an affliction.

"When will you—?"

"I wish I could peel this dress right off you."

So did Elizabeth, to the extent her wishes were still coherent. Haverford knew things about her body she didn't, about how to build desire so it retained only a tenuous connection to pleasure. Elizabeth shifted into his touch, even knowing he watched her.

His caresses became demanding, and she demanded right back, with her hips, with her grip on his wrist.

When the pleasure came, she cried out in surprise, for the sensations were new and overwhelming. She was left panting and dizzy, the sky a great blue bowl above her, her heart beating wildly, and her insides a wonderful muddle.

"I hadn't known," she said. The duke rested his cheek on her belly, his arms around her. "Haverford, I hadn't known."

He shifted, and Elizabeth's skirts dropped over her knees. She resented the fabric between them, but had no energy to move. She wanted to remain where she was, in a never-ending moment of wonder, as the seasons changed and the castle endured.

Haverford scooped her up and carried her to a stone bench near the cannon. "I need to hold you."

"I need to be held." Forever and ever and ever.

Elizabeth's joy faded with that thought, despite the delights she'd shared with Haverford. He and she didn't have forever, they had only days. A handful of days, and then they'd part.

"Don't be sad, Elizabeth."

"How can you tell?"

"It's like that sometimes, afterward."

So much she didn't know, so much she'd never learn from books. The realization was sobering and a relief. Books were precious, but they weren't *everything*.

For another span of silent minutes, Elizabeth remained in the arms of her lover—Haverford was her lover, already—and contemplated nothing much at all. Sensations preoccupied her—the heat between her legs that felt as if it could easily blossom into an echo of the pleasure she'd just experienced, the blonde lace of Haverford's cravat soft against her chin.

Somewhere on the castle's battlements, a pennant snapped in the wind.

"Sleep if you like," Haverford said.

"I'm too amazed to sleep." He kissed her for that, then Elizabeth shifted to sit beside him. "I will never be the same, you know."

His smile put her in mind of Griffin—mischievous and beautiful. "Neither will I."

They held hands until Elizabeth rose and retrieved Haverford's coat. She shook it out, though it didn't look much the worse for its ordeal, and passed it to him.

They made their way back to the ancient door, and Haverford escorted Elizabeth through a warren of back stairs and passages, so she emerged not far from her own tower rooms. He remained within the castle walls, and was gone from sight before Elizabeth could remind him that they'd left the kite up on the parapets, a ghost legend waiting for the right breeze on the right moonlit night.

* * *

"I love you, Biddy Bowen." The words were as great a pleasure to say now as they had been when Griffin had first offered them to her.

"You must stop saying that," Biddy replied in Welsh, though she sounded happy.

They moved down the row of boxes, the hens watching them with bright little eyes. Griffin slid the egg out from beneath old Princess, a grand lady with soft red feathers, and passed the egg to Biddy.

"Why should I stop saying it? It's the truth. A gentleman tells the truth."

"You should not say it, because people could get the wrong idea."

"Chickens are not people." Julian said things like that. "They are chickens," Griffin added, because that also sounded like something Julian would say. Julian made grand pronouncements out of things anybody could notice, and he always sounded impressive when he did.

Griffin found two more eggs. The hens hardly ever tried to peck him anymore. When he'd first learned how to find the eggs, they'd made him work for each one.

"If Abner overheard you," Biddy said, "he'd have to tell His Grace."

"I love Abner too, but not the same way." Miss Elizabeth had helped Griffin figure that out. She'd explained that in English, one word often had more than one task, just as Griffin had many chores to do around the farm. "I don't want to kiss Abner."

Biddy smacked him a good one in the belly. "Don't you start with the kissing again, Griffin St. David."

Griffin wanted to kiss Biddy very much. Telling her he loved her had only made that longing worse.

"I know all about kissing," he said. "I could show you."

"No, you could not. Kissing can lead to babies, and His Grace would see me on a ship for the colonies if I let that happen."

They finished collecting eggs, and Griffin went back down the row, giving each hen a pat to say thank you. Eggs were wonderful food, especially when Biddy made cake with them.

"Babies do not come from kissing, Biddy." This Griffin knew from experience, and also from Julian's lectures.

"I know very well where babies come from, and we shouldn't be talking about this." She set the basket of eggs down by the pump, and Griffin worked the handle, as he had every day they'd collected eggs.

"Why shouldn't we talk about babies?" he asked over the squeak and thump of the pump. "I like babies. Charity is my baby, though she's already five. Don't you want babies, Biddy? They're ever so dear."

Biddy sat on the plank bench where she always sat when they washed the eggs. "Of course I want babies, and of course babies are dear, but His Grace has it in his head that one daughter is enough for you, and even if I wanted to . . . Damn, I've cracked this egg."

Biddy never used bad language.

"Henry loves to eat the cracked eggs," Griffin said, taking the egg from her and sitting beside her. "Are you angry, Biddy?" With Biddy, he didn't have to pretend to understand, he could simply ask.

She studied the cracked egg in Griffin's hand. The insides of the egg weren't broken, only the shell, so there was no mess.

"Yes, Griffin, I am angry, but not at you."

He set the cracked egg in the grass and washed two eggs in the bucket beneath the pump, though they weren't very dirty. Washing eggs was a waste of time, because the dirt didn't get inside the eggs, where the food part was, but Biddy said eggs had to be washed, and Griffin liked to help her.

"Are you angry at Julian?"

She handed him another egg, a brown one, still warm from being tucked beneath Princess in the straw. "I believe I am, Griffin. He doesn't see you."

"He came to call a few days ago. He sees quite well."

"It's like the cracked egg. To me, the cracked egg is proof that I handled my basket carelessly. King Henry sees that egg as the best snack, the loveliest part of his doggy day. Haverford only looks for the cracks in the eggs, he doesn't see that they'll make Henry happy and fill up his belly."

This was complicated and important. "I'm not an egg, Biddy." Maybe she meant Griffin's shell had cracks? Or maybe...

Maybe she meant *Julian* was the cracked egg? The idea filled Griffin with equal parts protectiveness toward his brother and hope.

"You're not an egg, but you're not a fool either, Griffin, or a small boy, or less than any other man who's willing to work hard, try his best, and keep his word. His Grace should be proud of you, for I certainly am."

"Thank you, Biddy." Griffin wasn't sure exactly what Biddy was saying, but she was complimenting him. He knew that much from her tone.

She passed him a white egg. "Most of running this farm is about hard work and paying attention. You do that better than many who were born farming. His Grace loves you, but he's so busy being a duke, sometimes he forgets to be your brother. That egg is clean enough."

"Julian is always my brother. I love Julian."

"When he came chasing after you the last time you fell asleep on the hillside, were you angry with him?"

For two more eggs, Griffin considered the question. "I was disappointed in him. I never get lost, and he thinks he must always find me. He's sometimes not as bright as I wish he were, but he's always my brother."

Biddy had a lovely, lovely smile. "Exactly. Sometimes, His Grace isn't as bright as we wish he were. You never disappoint me, Griffin. You are always your good, dear, trustworthy self."

"So you'll let me kiss you?"

Biddy sorted through the basket for another egg, though they were all the same, and would all be washed before she took them into the kitchen. She wanted time to think, maybe. Biddy had gone only to the dame school, though she always seemed to understand what was important and she was quick with sums.

"I want to let you kiss me, Griffin, but you'll tell everybody, and then I'll be sent away. I couldn't bear that."

"Why would you be sent away for kissing? Julian kisses Miss Elizabeth, and nobody sends him away." Griffin liked Miss Elizabeth, and hoped Julian found a way to keep her at Haverford. Julian was lonely, and Miss Elizabeth was nice.

"His Grace is protective of you. He can't imagine

that I might be kissing you because I've longed to for years."

Griffin wanted to squawk and flap about as the hens did when they were surprised. Instead he moved Biddy's egg basket aside. "One year is a long time." Three-hundred-sixty-five days, most years.

"Don't I know it, but I'd miss you for the rest of my life if His Grace sent me away, and Uncle Abner would be disappointed, and have nobody to do for him, and it won't serve, Griffin. If I want to stay with you here, then we can't be kissing."

Griffin washed the rest of the eggs, and thought and thought and thought, and wished he could talk this puzzle over with Julian. Biddy was missing something, something important, though Griffin couldn't quite name it. Something to do with...

"Biddy, may I kiss you if I *promise* to tell no one? A gentleman keeps his word. If I promised you I'd tell no one, then Julian would not learn of it, and neither would Abner. Nobody would learn of it, if I gave you my word."

Biddy looked right at him for a long time. She had the most wonderful eyes, all soft brown and serious and sweet.

"Give me your word you'll tell nobody, Griffin. Not King Henry, not His Grace, not Miss Elizabeth. You can't tell. Not ever."

Griffin took her hand, and for a moment was too pleased to say anything. Biddy trusted him to keep his word, and *she* wanted to kiss *him*.

"I won't tell anybody ever, Biddy." And then he kissed her.

Chapter Fourteen

"Too many of these airs are gloomy," Julian said. "Sing something optimistic."

Radnor sat beside him on the piano bench and leafed through more music, for they were rehearsing in case of rain. The weather thus far had been as accommodating of the house party as Welsh weather could be. Julian was preparing for the afternoon his guests were shut up indoors, with nothing to do but eat him out of house and happiness.

"The gloomy songs show off my voice to best advantage," Radnor said. "Besides, you can't abide an optimist. Said so yourself."

Well, yes, Julian had made some such proclamation, but that was *before*. Before Miss Elizabeth Windham had shown him the view from the parapets, so to speak. Yesterday afternoon, Julian's world had undergone a fundamental shift.

Radnor set a piece of sheet music on the pianoforte's rack. "This one's in a minor-ish key, but not gloomy."

"Ca' the Yowes," a Scottish tune that celebrated the joys of herding ewes by the full moon with a lover.

"As if shepherding is a nocturnal activity in Scotland," Julian said, placing his hands on the keyboard. He began the introduction, and Radnor did justice to the tune. By the second chorus, a feminine voice had joined in.

Glenys stood in the doorway to the music room, her contralto finding nuances in the music that Radnor's baritone had left hidden. They sang every verse and chorus, their duet growing in beauty and complexity with each phrase.

As the final notes died away—*Fair and lovely as thou art/thou hast stolen my very heart/I can die, but canna part/My bonnie dearie*—insight smacked Julian.

Glenys returned Radnor's esteem in full measure. Julian's best friend and his sister were in love, did they but know it. Radnor had only to find his courage, and the right moment, and Glenys would see that the happiness she deserved had been right next door all along.

Elizabeth would be pleased for them and for Julian.

And yet, true love had chosen an inconvenient moment to bloom: The bachelors at the house party would take on mightily should Radnor win the fair maid too soon, and the debutantes would go into a decline en masse if Radnor were spoken for.

"You should play a repeat of the chorus, Haverford," Glenys said. "More softly, and end on a *tierce de Picardie*."

She referred to ending a minor song with a major chord, a metaphor for the possibilities this house party presented.

"I'll do exactly that," Julian said. "You two must rehearse more duets. Your voices blend well, probably from long practice."

Radnor and Glenys exchanged a look Julian couldn't

fathom. They were either preparing for a verbal duel, or united in their consternation at his encouragement.

"I haven't time," Glenys said. "Have either of you seen Elizabeth Windham? Her sister was looking for her to form a fourth at whist after supper."

"I'll stop by the Windham sitting room on my way to the estate office," Julian said, rising. "I can leave a note, if nothing else. Radnor, you're in good voice. Perhaps Glenys can accompany your next selection."

"First you've grown tolerant of optimism, and now I'm in good voice," Radnor said. "Yesterday's expedition with the kites must have agreed with you."

"Exceedingly." Julian bowed and withdrew, leaving Glenys and Radnor to their bickering. Perhaps for them, flirtation required an acrimonious edge. He had yet to see Elizabeth, and the afternoon was advancing.

"Do you have a moment?" he asked, coming upon the lady alone in her sitting room. "I'd like to show you something."

She wore a cream dress with pink and green flowers embroidered about the bodice, hem, and cuffs. The look on her was youthful and demure, though the roses reminded Julian of the wild blossoms on the parapets. The effect of those memories was to accelerate his breathing and make his hands itch.

"Your Grace, good day." She set aside a letter and stood, remaining by the escritoire. "I'm free at the moment."

And she was uncertain. Julian glanced up and down the corridor, saw not a soul, and stepped into the parlor.

"I am not free," he said, closing the door all but a crack. "I am followed everywhere by thoughts of you. You, striding across the park to meet Griffin by the oak. You, marching up Tudor Hill in the middle of the night because I asked you to. You, cast away with passion, cradled in my arms, sweet with repletion. I would love to take you up to the rooftop again, but I am determined to honor the promise I made yesterday."

She tidied correspondence that already sat in a neat stack. "What promise is that, Your Grace?"

"To treat you to every evidence of my esteem, to cherish you, and *dote* on you."

That earned him a smile. "Never has doting sounded like such a fierce undertaking, sir." Still she remained on her side of the room.

"Elizabeth, are you well?"

She shook her head. "I'm fine."

Julian closed the door—bedamned to propriety if he'd made Elizabeth cry—and crossed the tower. "Tell me. If I've upset you, I'm sorry. If I can make it right, I will."

"It's Griffin," she said, going to the window and turning her back. "We talk of many things when we converse, and I try to focus on words that will be useful to him. He has his own agenda, though, and he's determined that we address it."

The St. David menfolk were creatures of planning and organization. "Griffin upset you." Except, Griffin was also the soul of consideration.

"He asked me today how to say, 'I miss you,' and 'I will miss you.' He wants to say those words to you, Julian, and I ought not to share his confidences, but *I* will miss you. Yesterday was a revelation, and I cannot bear the thought—"

Julian had hurried her too quickly down from the parapets yesterday. "My doting is out of practice," he said, taking Elizabeth in his arms. "Is this revelation unhappy, Elizabeth?"

His capacity for doting was as newly discovered as her capacity for erotic pleasure, in all likelihood, an unexpected talent that bewildered even as it pleased.

She laid her head on his chest as if weary to her soul. "I have spent the day considering my feelings, and I conclude that in my ignorance of the pleasure a woman can share with a man, I was safe. Disappointment kept me from giving my heart away, or even thinking of—I'm making a muddle of this."

A thought clamored for expression: *You're lovely when you're muddled*—which blather would comfort the lady not at all.

"You and I have little tolerance for being muddled," he said, "and yet we're far beyond where the rules of deportment apply. Perhaps you are saying that what passed between us yesterday was more intimate than your previous encounters, despite the nature of my participation."

She gave him a measuring look he'd occasionally seen from Griffin. "Possibly. The others…I could not lose a sense of self-consciousness with them, and with you…I would like to become very lost, indeed."

She was unhappy about that, but Julian delighted in her honesty, for he shared her sense of having stumbled upon far more than he'd bargained for.

"I would like to become lost with you, too, Elizabeth, but not in this parlor, where anybody might chance upon us. Will you come with me?" He stepped back and offered his hand.

She linked her fingers with his, then stole a kiss to his cheek. Julian reciprocated by kissing her on the mouth, then preceded her to the door. The corridor was still empty, so he bowed her through the door, and prepared to share with her what many regarded as the Haverford ducal treasures.

* * *

Elizabeth felt an echo of the pleasure she'd experienced yesterday. The physical sensations weren't there, but her mind was almost as overwhelmed with delight—almost.

"I cannot believe you have all of this, just sitting up here, gathering dust."

The room was small, but it was crammed floor to ceiling with books. Old, rare, precious books, each one of which could have absorbed her for days.

"They are dusted regularly," Haverford said. "If the book has a red string tied about it, then it's fragile. A white string means it was acquired in my father's lifetime, a purple string means my grandfather was the purchaser."

The white strings outnumbered the purple by a wide margin, but the most plentiful color was red. "And the blue strings?"

"My great-grandfather. They could not resist an interesting book, regardless of cost. I have not added to the collection, but I do make certain it's adequately cared for."

Elizabeth turned in a slow circle, admiring another tower room, this one on the castle's highest story. The walls were lined with shelves, and in the center of the room sat an enormous desk dark with age. The panels were carved with fantastical flowers and leaves, and the leather of the blotter looked as old as the desk.

A wide daybed took up the only wall not lined with books, and the sole source of heat was a small fireplace into which a parlor stove had been fitted.

"Do you spend time here?" she asked.

"Not much anymore. As a child, I often found my father in this room, and I have memories of his father reading to me at that desk. They were never happier than when among their books, or sharing their collections with other enthusiasts. This is the personal ducal library, and I offer it to you for your enjoyment while you bide at Haverford."

He produced a heavy iron key nearly six inches long.

"You are giving me the keys to your family's private collection?"

"Who better to enjoy these books?" he asked. "You'll find the Shakespeare quartos here somewhere, two of the Welsh Bibles, a pair of King James Bibles, one inscribed by the sovereign. My father was very proud of these books."

A sentiment that clearly puzzled the present duke.

Elizabeth gripped the key, wrapping her fingers around not only the cold iron, but also his hand. "I will disappear up here for hours. May I tell Charlotte and Aunt Arabella where I am?"

"Of course, but please keep the door locked when you're elsewhere. I can vouch for my staff, but I would not want to put temptation before somebody else's footman or abigail."

The duke was temptation incarnate. "Thank you, Your Grace. I will allow no harm to come to your heirlooms." She plucked the key from his grasp and tucked it into a skirt pocket. "Do you regret what transpired between us yesterday?"

Elizabeth hadn't meant to ask that, hadn't meant to further betray the extent to which a half hour on the parapets had completely upended her concept of herself. Her only consolation was the suspicion that Haverford was at sea as well.

"In a sense," he replied, "I do have regrets. Shall we sit?"

Which meant, in a sense he did not. Neither did Elizabeth. "You sit at the desk, and I'll take the chaise." She wanted to have an image in her memory of him sitting where his grandfather had read to him, where one day, Haverford might read to a grandson.

He went so far as to prop a hip on the desk. "I'll not ravish you uninvited, Elizabeth, much as I might long to."

Haverford was back to being fierce, which Elizabeth

found reassuring. "You'll only ravish me if I invite you to?"

"Exactly, and with respect to the reciprocal pleasure, you have a standing invitation, despite that offer embodying a certain novel spontaneity on my part."

"You are quite on your dignity, or possibly shy. I'm invited to ravish you?"

His reply was a look so...pleased, that Elizabeth subsided onto the chaise lest her knees fail her.

"We are in the presence of at least four Bibles, Your Grace."

He sat upon the desk. "Do you know how much fornication takes place in the Old Testament?"

Rather a lot. "We did not fornicate." Even saying the word caused Elizabeth to blush.

"I'd like to. I'd like to fornicate, swive, tumble, and copulate with you, Elizabeth. Mostly, I'd like to make love with you, and beyond even that, I want you to be happy."

There were apparently degrees of carnality about intimate encounters. Two weeks would not be long enough to learn them all. As for being happy...

"I am determined," Haverford went on, "that your wishes and wants, not mine, shall guide us. I will leave you to the books, but please don't deprive me of your company at dinner tonight." He pushed away from the desk and bowed over Elizabeth's hand.

The books called to her with the insistent lure of rare jewels, but they would have to wait. Elizabeth rose and wrapped her arms around Haverford, then kissed him as if he'd offered not only his personal collection of books, but the right to share them with him for all time.

He was *shy.* What a delightful insight.

"I want it to be here," she said. "When we make love. I

want the first encounter to be here, and I want it to be soon, Haverford. We have such a short time."

"If I kiss you the way I long to, soon will become now, and no less personage than your aunt has commanded my company on the hour for a cup of tea. I cannot arrive to her sitting room in a *state*, Elizabeth, nor will I allow intimacies with you to be rushed. I should have spent at least another hour with you yesterday afternoon, and instead I left you to fret. This is what comes of neglecting to plan a lady's pleasures. Not well done of me."

Elizabeth looped her arms around Haverford's neck and gloated. She was not the sort of woman who put a man in a *state*, and yet, Haverford was aroused.

"Aunt is looking you over," Elizabeth said. "She'll report back to my parents, and to my aunt and uncle, and I daresay she'll admit to approving of you."

"No duke worth his strawberry leaves would allow his niece to marry me," Haverford replied. "My financial situation is not sound."

"But mine is," Elizabeth retorted. "I have decent settlements, and I'm in a position to choose a spouse based on factors other than worldly riches."

He took her hand, his grip warm. "You could have anybody you pleased, and we haven't spent nearly enough time together for you to be throwing caution into the moat. Marriage is a decision that should involve planning, forethought, consideration, and written agreements."

She'd expected arguments, not entire lectures in miniature. "Haverford, you can't admonish a woman to choose for herself, to not settle or compromise, then take issue with her choice."

"Elizabeth Windham, I brought you up here to admire

my library, not to start an altercation. Enjoy the books, madam." He kissed her lingeringly. "If you can."

He was out the door before Elizabeth had stopped laughing.

She'd enjoy his books, and she'd enjoy arguing with him again soon too. His Grace was determined to be honorable and gentlemanly and a lot of other codswallop, but he was Elizabeth's choice. She had two weeks to explain to him that he was worth more to her with empty pockets than any other man would be, despite commanding a duke's ransom in riches.

* * *

"Bother the tea, Your Grace." Arabella Windham, Lady Pembroke, waved a hand that bore a single diamond ring. "At my age, you come to detest tea. Let's have a restorative tot. I daresay you could use one."

One didn't argue with a lady. "As you please, your ladyship."

She poured two glasses half-full of amber liquid and passed one to Julian. "To my health."

"Your health." The Armagnac was brisk and confident with a gracious suggestion of spice and wisdom—like the lady.

The marchioness downed a portion of her drink, and set the glass on the table with a solid thump. Julian mentally braced himself for a dowager's version of arm wrestling.

"You've caught Elizabeth's notice, Haverford. What are your intentions?"

Not arm wrestling—outright pugilism. "If I have found favor with Miss Windham, I can assure you that I esteem her in equal measure. This is very good potation, my lady. May I inquire as to its origins?"

"Haverford, I am twice your age. I haven't time for dithering. Inquire of Andover regarding the spirits, for this bottle is a gift from him. *About your intentions.*"

This parlor, like much of the castle, was genteelly out of date. A week ago, Julian would have ignored its faded elegance, though it bothered him now and doubtless made an impression on her ladyship as well.

"I am not in a position to have intentions, such as your ladyship intimates. Miss Windham deserves a man who can offer her every comfort and security, and I am not that man."

Her ladyship snorted. "A fine speech, very gentlemanly, and you even mean what you say, you daft boy. My Peter died when he wasn't much older than you."

"Peter" had to have been the late Marquess of Pembroke, the husband who had left her ladyship widowed decades ago.

"I'm sorry for your loss, ma'am."

She finished her drink in one swallow. "You have no idea of my loss, no idea what it feels like to surrender your entire heart into the keeping of somebody who wants nothing more than to treasure you for the rest of his life. Then he's taken from you, day by day, fading into a shadow of the handsome specimen you married. Your sorrow is vast, but most of it is for him, who must live knowing he'll not see his daughters make their bows. Peter wasn't in much physical pain, but he suffered greatly."

As had her ladyship. "Did he die of a wasting disease, my lady?"

"A bad heart, or so the quacks claimed, but do you know, as handsome, charming, and utterly irresistible as he was when we became engaged, his illness showed me exactly what a fine choice of husband I'd made."

Was this how Griffin felt when Julian got to prosing on

about a point of protocol? For her ladyship had a point of some sort, and Julian was at a loss to fathom it.

"Your husband was heir to the Moreland dukedom, was he not?"

"He was, which mattered a very great deal to my parents. What mattered to me was that Peter could make me laugh. He made me feel special. When he proposed, he made me feel as if he was getting the better of the bargain, though I wasn't the wife his parents had in mind for him. My papa was a mere ruralizing viscount, and not even wealthy."

Did Elizabeth know this story? For all that Lady Pembroke was widowed, Julian suspected she would have chosen the same man and the same marriage, given the chance.

"Yours was a love match, then."

She tipped up her empty glass, examining the dregs. "Pour me another tot. Ancient history leaves one with a thirst."

Julian obliged.

"Peter told me after our younger daughter was born that before we married, he was already tiring more easily, and the social season had become drudgery. He attributed his symptoms to advancing age—he was in his twenties, for God's sake—and then to his father's growing insistence that the heir take over the business of the dukedom. Even as Peter married me, he was dying. We simply didn't know it."

"You are sharing this unhappy story for a reason."

"This is *not* an unhappy story, you simpleton. Peter was the love of my life. I had more than fifteen years with him, and I treasure each and every memory of those years. He gave me two children, his family became my family, and he left me well provided for. By the time he was your age, he could no longer sit a horse for even an hour, and we'd danced our last waltz. *You are wasting time, Haverford.*"

Elizabeth would be this fierce on behalf of family, if she ever saw the need.

"Your husband left you well provided for, but I can't promise my duchess the same security. What sort of titled husband expects his bride to take that risk?"

Her ladyship sat back, her drink in her hand. "Half of polite society is living in dun territory at any given time. Your situation is neither unusual nor hard to discern for anybody who looks closely."

There was a cheering bit of news. "Not hard to discern, how?"

"Your castle needs repairs, your sister hasn't been in London for a full season in years. I don't know what you've done with your brother, but I doubt he's eating off gold plates."

Julian had been prepared to endure pointed questions from her ladyship—Elizabeth had warned him—but not a reckless invasion of his family's privacy.

"What do you know of my brother?"

"Ah, now you take off the gloves. About time. Lord Griffin St. David appeared in Debrett's for the first five years of his life. Your papa was enormously pleased to have a spare, but then he became enormously quiet about his second son. Most people concluded the boy had died—these things happen. I had a cousin who ran off to the Continent with another man. Grandpapa paid Debrett's to misplace his entry too."

"I have not misplaced my only brother. Griffin has his own household nearby and he's in good health."

Her ladyship refreshed Julian's drink. "Is he the reason you've not found a duchess? I've heard he's not right in the brainbox."

Anger burned off the last of Julian's tolerance for this

inquisition. Had Sherbourne let that detail slip in her ladyship's company?

"Where did you hear that?"

"In the ladies' retiring room at some ball or other more than twenty years ago. The St. David spare was said to be daft. A rumor of bad blood or inherited weakness in a ducal family never dies. Peter knew that, and kept his situation quiet as long as he could."

Lady Pembroke slid Julian's drink closer to his side of the table, and he ignored it. "Who else have you told about my brother?"

"Nobody. Benedict Andover is well acquainted with your family history, but we're not your enemies, Haverford. I bring up his lordship—Lord Griffin, that is— because I'll not have Elizabeth making decisions without all the facts. Your brother attends services, I take it, so you haven't made a secret of him."

"You've made inquiries regarding my brother?"

"My niece's happiness is at stake, Haverford. Her parents aren't thinking clearly because two younger daughters have recently married, and Elizabeth is determined to be contrary. If Lord Anthony and his wife believe you're interested in Elizabeth, and she in you, they'll be eager to see a match made. Moreland will stick his oar in, his duchess will have to have her say . . . and priorities will be obscured."

In other words, nobody would *see* Elizabeth. Nobody would focus on her well-being, her security.

Julian rose, though the sitting room was tiny, probably a dressing closet in an earlier century, and he had nowhere to pace.

"I informed Miss Windham on the day she arrived that I'm not interested in matrimony. She assured me she wasn't looking for a husband."

Her ladyship worked at the label on the bottle with one thumbnail. "Young people."

"We were *trying* to be honest with each other, and our mutual lack of interest in matrimony formed the basis for an accord unique in my experience, and very likely in Miss Windham's as well."

Lady Pembroke gave him the same owlish look Elizabeth and Griffin did, as if his accent had become indecipherable, or nearly so.

"You fell arse over escutcheon in love," her ladyship said. "With the Windhams, it can happen like that. Strutting about full of their own consequence one day, and down on bended knee the next. They fall hard and fast, and are sometimes the last to know it."

Would Elizabeth know if she was in love with him?

"Be that as it may, your ladyship, my prospects are not sound, there is Griffin to consider, and in case it has escaped your notice, we're in the middle of the longest blasted house party ever to blight the Welsh countryside."

"Elizabeth's uncle Percival is a yeller," Lady Pembroke said, finishing her drink. "Her father, Lord Tony, is more the kind to quietly skewer those who transgress. I gather you're somewhere in between. What have you done with your brother?"

Julian resumed his seat. "I've tried to make him happy. Griffin lives on a tidy holding not a mile distant, with staff. His home is commodious—eight bedrooms, six hundred acres—and I see him frequently."

"He can't be that simple if he's on his own property."

"He's...for Griffin to inherit the title would be a hardship for him. He's aware that compared to others, he has limitations, and try though he might, being the duke is beyond him. I haven't had him declared incompetent because in many regards, he's quite capable."

To subject Griffin to an inquiry, strip him publicly of all authority over his own affairs, hold him up to ridicule and pity... Papa had wanted to for the sake of the title, and Julian had fought his father to a stalemate for the sake of his brother.

Lady Pembroke patted Julian's hand. "Many an idiot has sat in the Lords. Politics attracts the feebleminded, Peter used to say. Witness, dear Percival thrives on his legislative machinations."

"You just insulted one of the most respected dukes in the realm."

"His own children tire of his maunderings, and his daughters-in-law have written holiday poems mocking Moreland's political rantings. The Countess of Hazelton has threatened to collect her sisters' satires into a book and donate the proceeds to charity."

She was telling him this for another one of her unfathomable reasons. "This does not sound like any titled family of my acquaintance."

"And the lot of them are determined that Elizabeth should wed. Do you love her, Haverford?"

The window was open, and the only sound in the room was the Haverford pennant flapping in the wind atop the castle. The breeze was brisk today and scented with rain.

"I esteem Miss Windham very..."

Lady Pembroke folded her arms. She was an old woman who'd known much heartache and much love. She'd see through a lie, and through a man who told lies.

"I've fallen arse over escutcheon in love."

"Have you told her about your brother?"

"They meet in the morning for a constitutional, and he

plagues her with endless questions. She enjoys his company." Julian took another sip of spirits, for those words had given his throat an ache.

"So Lord Griffin won't be an issue. Now, what are we to do about your finances?"

The ache in Julian's throat grew worse. "I am making progress, your ladyship, but my father inherited debts from my grandfather, and my commercial ventures are not the kind that yield a quick return."

"So you're truly rolled up?"

"I have a plan to bring the finances around, though progress is slow. By the standards of polite society, I am barely solvent." For now, which was all the gossips cared about—*thank you once again, dear Papa.*

"That is a problem. Elizabeth can't marry a pauper."

"I'm not a pauper, and she can't marry a man who only esteems her settlements or aristocratic connections. I won't have it, but more to the point, neither will she."

Her ladyship smiled, and Julian grasped why a ducal heir would toss aside all other possibilities and risk parental excoriation to marry a mere ruralizing viscount's daughter.

"There's reason to hope, then," Lady Pembroke said. "Though I do despair of dear Charlotte. Don't suppose you have any suggestions on that score?"

"Not a one, my lady."

But there was *reason to hope*. Elizabeth's dragon of an auntie had pronounced the situation salvageable, and that was the best news Julian had heard since...since forever. He had a plan, and he had hope, and soon, he might have a duchess too.

Chapter Fifteen

Sherbourne liked pretty women, and he liked intelligent women. The former were a delight to look at, the latter were enjoyable conversationalists. A pretty, intelligent woman— as Charlotte Windham was pretty and intelligent—made him uneasy.

"Miss Charlotte," he said, bowing. "We never did schedule our archery exhibition."

She occupied a bench in the castle's inner courtyard, an odd place decorated with topiary beasts and the infernal red and white flowers favored by the St. Davids. The courtyard was sheltered from the wind, though the windows on all sides made it a public space.

"I challenged you to a contest, Mr. Sherbourne, not an exhibition."

She had yet to invite him to sit, and because the castle was crawling with *gentlemen*, or perhaps because Miss

Charlotte would skewer him for any presumption, Sherbourne stayed on his feet.

"Why insist on a winner and loser, when you know I'm likely to best you?"

"If you show yourself to be the better marksman, you'll lose."

Ducal families were prone to eccentricity, which was to be expected after so many generations of inbreeding.

"If I am the superior archer, I lose? Please do explain."

"You might as well have a seat," the lady said, moving aside a parasol, quiver, and arrows. "If you best me at archery before all the assembled guests, you reveal yourself to be lacking in gentlemanly refinement, for you have used your superior strength—an accident of biology—to cast a lady's talents in the shade. Then I win, because I will have warned all the young women of your true nature."

Win the battle, lose the war. An old concept, and Sherbourne should have seen the trap she'd set—the trap he'd set for himself, rather.

He took a seat nonetheless, because Charlotte Windham was an exponent of the social strata he expected to marry into. Ducal spinsters didn't wander into the wilds of Wales all that often.

"How would I win the challenge?" he asked. "If I display my marksmanship honestly, I'm castigated for using the strength God gave me. If I cheat and pretend to lose, I'll be castigated for humoring a woman who should have known better than to challenge me."

"That tears it. Come along." She snatched up her bow, shoved her parasol at him, and marched off.

Nobody told Lucas Sherbourne to *come along*, and yet he was on his feet, frilly parasol in hand, walking beside Miss Charlotte as she headed for the archway that led to the back terrace. She wore a russet walking dress, and such was the vigor of her stride that with every step, Sherbourne got a peek at cream-colored petticoats with bright red embroidery about the hems.

"Even I know that accompanying you somewhere private is not wise, Miss Charlotte."

"Don't flatter yourself. We're in full view of the castle, where we shall remain while I disabuse you of your manly arrogance. I ought not, in part because it's rag-mannered of me to correct a relative stranger, even if he is long overdue for a setdown. I also ought not because my aunt will lecture me for being a hoyden, and I do not relish her tirades. You'll want to remove your jacket."

"Women don't usually instruct me to disrobe." *Said the man toting a lacy parasol.*

"Which admission suggests you need to work on your flirtation as well as your manners, for you aren't all that bad-looking, despite your size, and you're known to be wealthy."

She'd escorted him to the formal garden, where an archery butt sat a significant distance away. For a man who knew what he was about, on a still day, the target was manageable. A woman would need considerable strength to match his performance.

A bow leaned against a stone bench, and a quiver had been slung on the back of the bench.

"Were you expecting me?" Or better still, waiting on his chance passing because he *wasn't all that bad-looking*?

"I prefer to entertain myself with a variety of equipment."

Good God, had Miss Charlotte's innuendo been sexual? Her expression said not, but like the bright artistry winking from beneath her skirts, her retort bore hidden meaning.

"Am I allowed a few practice shots?"

"As many as you need."

The bow was a solid, elegant weapon. Centuries ago, the Welsh longbowmen had trained for ten years before taking a place on the battlefield, where their arrows could pierce armor and chain mail.

"My middle name is Herne," Sherbourne said, unbuttoning his jacket. Bond Street tailors sewed a jacket to fit a man like a glove, and Miss Charlotte's assistance was necessary to get Sherbourne out of his.

"So you were named for a predator," she said, folding his jacket over the back of the bench.

"I was named for a Celtic god of hunting, also for a gouty great-uncle." And damned if it didn't feel good to get out of that jacket, the better to show off an equally exquisite waistcoat to the lady. Doubtless, he was breaking some rule by removing his jacket, but Miss Charlotte had given him an order.

Never argue with a lady.

Sherbourne tested the tension on the bow, found it adequate, and nocked an arrow. Miss Charlotte moved behind him as he took aim, and his first arrow sank into the target a few inches left of center.

"Not bad," he murmured, nocking a second arrow. "I can do better." This time, Shebourne concentrated, or tried to. Charlotte Windham's skirts swishing distracted him. His arrow hit the target, several inches right of center.

"Third time's the charm," he said, taking up another arrow. He focused, ignoring the lady's attempts to distract him. The Sherbournes prided themselves on setting goals and achieving those goals, and just as Sherbourne would right the injustices of his personal world by thoroughly ruining Haverford—a necessary antecedent to bringing modern industry to the valley—so too would he show Charlotte Windham—

He let the arrow fly, certain in his bones that it was headed for the dead center of the target.

Except the arrow never reached the butt. Something knocked it from its path, so it fell to the grass several yards short of the target.

Charlotte Windham was lowering her bow by the time Sherbourne realized what had happened.

"You can't do that again," he said. "That was a lucky shot. Nobody can deflect one arrow with another twice in succession."

"Surely, the gentleman always knows best. Nock your arrow, Mr. Sherbourne."

She did it again.

"You are a prodigy," he said, as impressed as he was intrigued. What drove a woman to perfect a huntsman's skills?

"I am merely a lady about one of my pastimes."

"Is Haldale one of your pastimes?" The question was ungentlemanly in the extreme, and Sherbourne didn't care.

"If I distract Haldale from sniffing about my sister's skirts, and amuse myself at the same time, who are you to say anything to it, besides an indifferent marksman who invites himself to parties on the strength of his riches?"

Her assessment was uncomfortably accurate. "I'm the man who'll warn you that Haldale has two children, each by a different woman, and like many of his ilk, he's a very indifferent father."

He'd surprised her. At last, he'd done something to penetrate Charlotte Windham's aristocratic self-possession.

"Thank you for the warning," she said, crossing the grass in the direction of the target. "Few men would have disclosed that much to a woman."

Sherbourne fell in step beside her. "Not gentlemanly of me, I suppose." He didn't give a hearty tallyho what the gentlemanly course was in this instance. Charlotte Windham was too rare a creature to be wasted on the likes of Haldale.

"To preserve a lady from serious peril is the act of a gentleman," she said, yanking the two arrows from the target and passing them to Sherbourne. "And Haldale's present mistress is rumored to be carrying."

No lady should have known that information, much less disclosed that she knew. Sherbourne began to like Charlotte Windham, despite her blue blood, handsome appearance, and intelligence—or maybe, because of them.

"Are you in serious peril where his lordship is concerned?" Sherbourne asked.

"No, but you couldn't know that. Haldale's not in serous peril either, if you were concerned for him. I suspect Haldale is all but invisible to Elizabeth."

Sherbourne knelt to slide his arrow free of the grass, and passed Miss Charlotte her arrow too. That observation regarding Elizabeth Windham bore the solid certainty of a lance flying to the mark.

Elizabeth Windham wasn't distracted by Haldale because her attention was riveted elsewhere. Haverford had been with Miss Windham when Sherbourne had arrived. The duke had escorted her in from the kite flying. He'd been sitting with her on the day of the regatta. Those moments and a dozen others proved the accuracy of Miss Charlotte's surmise.

Haverford, who needed desperately to marry for money, was *smitten* with Miss Elizabeth Windham, who doubtless had some money and endless familial connections to more money.

Sherbourne would have to do something about that situation. The duke was not to have his cake and eat it too.

The economic fortunes of the entire valley depended on Haverford's ruin, for like every other titled family, the St. Davids were stuck in the past. Some baseborn ancestor had attracted the notice of an impoverished king or prince, and now the common man went without coin so that the aristocracy could cling to its drafty castles.

"Do you concede that my skill is the equal of yours?" Miss Charlotte asked as they turned their steps for the castle.

"At the risk of disagreeing with a lady, I do not. Your skill far eclipses mine, and I thank you for sparing me a public humiliation."

Her smile was shy, which made her alarmingly attractive, not merely pretty. "I am a lady. Sometimes I wish I weren't, but ladies don't go about outshining others for the arrogance of it."

"Losing to you was my pleasure, Miss Charlotte."

Sherbourne meant the compliment sincerely, except he hadn't lost. Oh, no, no, no. This interlude with Miss Charlotte had yielded information that Sherbourne would use to ensure that Haverford lost, though—lost very badly indeed.

* * *

For three days and three nights, Elizabeth wallowed in ancient tomes and small considerations. The first time she used her key to enjoy the duke's private collection, she found a bouquet of roses waiting for her on the desk. Their fragrance filled the tower room, blending with the vanilla and leather scents of the books.

She'd fallen asleep with a Shakespeare quarto in her lap, unwilling to reshelve it when she might never hold its like again.

The next morning, a tea tray had awaited her complete with the best fresh, warm shortbread she'd ever sampled. That afternoon, a cashmere shawl had been draped over the chair behind the desk. The morning following—she slipped into the tower every chance she got—a merino afghan appeared on the chaise.

Pillows, a footstool, a lap desk, an old-fashioned painted fan, more flowers...hour by hour, Haverford wooed her with comforts and pleasures. The chamber transformed from a room full of old books to a bower of delights.

Elizabeth was engrossed in Milton's *Paradise Lost* as published by Samuel Simmons in 1667. The library also had a later version, one revised by the poet to more closely resemble Virgil's *Aeneid*, but Elizabeth was drawn to the earlier work.

Such excellent drama had been made of the tired tales of the Old Testament, and the archaic language served to render the story all the more compelling.

"I am intruding." Haverford stood inside the closed door, looking handsome and harried. His hair needed combing, and his watch chain had snagged on a thread of the embroidery of his blue and silver waistcoat. Those details were precious to Elizabeth, for she doubted others saw him as anything other than the duke, the cordial host, the title.

"Come sit with me," she said, swinging her feet to the floor. "How did Milton write this—*conceive this*—when he could not see to put words on a page? How did he create beauty, having lost both wife and child, his *second* wife?

How does terrible sorrow—I'm babbling, but Haverford, you have such treasures here."

And he'd given her the key to them all.

He took the place beside her, and all at once, Elizabeth realized she'd been missing him. He'd given her this time to cavort with the great minds of the past, to sniff pages, and caress old leather, but the longer she frolicked in the tower, the more she'd felt Haverford's absence and had no name for it.

"I watched you reading for a good five minutes, Elizabeth. You didn't even know I was in the room."

"Such is the power of a good story, or you're that good a spy. Has Miss Trelawny been awful?"

Haverford kissed her. "Yes. Some fool told her, over and over, that a woman who laughs at everything is sure to marry a duke, and she took the advice very much to heart. She's sprained her eyelids batting her lashes at me."

"You poor darling. Perhaps you've given her nervous affliction."

"I have an affliction." He slid to his knees and slipped his arms around Elizabeth's waist. "How can I miss you when you're a mere two floors above me, and I can envision exactly what you're about? I do spy on you, you know."

He laid his head in her lap, and Elizabeth's heart ached. "You can't spy on me. I've been shut in my tower, delighting in your collection."

"You keep your dawn appointments with Griffin. Is he in love with you, Elizabeth?"

She stroked Haverford's hair and traced the contour of his ear. "He's in love with his oak tree. Did you know he gives all the village children acorns to plant?"

"My grandfather started that tradition, or perhaps his

grandfather. Our neighborhood has a lot of respectable trees to show for it, though none rival Griffin's tree. His oak appears on the surveyor's maps of the estate from Good King Hal's day. That feels good."

This felt good, this idle chatter about family traditions in the middle of the afternoon, this privacy and affection.

"Did you come up here to nap, Haverford? I can leave you in peace if—"

He lifted his head, and the look in his eyes assured Elizabeth he had not come in search of a nap. In search of dreams, perhaps, but not sleep.

"You will leave me no peace," he said, kissing her on the mouth. "You will torment me for the rest of my days. I have commenced doting upon you to the best of my feeble ability, Elizabeth. Has it been enough?"

He wasn't asking about teapots or shawls, and the honest answer was that, no, a few days of stolen intimacy would never be enough. The kind answer lay in a different direction.

"Your efforts have been appreciated," Elizabeth said, "but now I want more. Is the door locked?"

"Yes."

Ah, well, then. Elizabeth set Milton on the table by the chaise, and scooted sideways, presenting Haverford with her back. She'd worn her green dress today, because it made her happy.

Haverford undid her hooks, then loosened her stays. He knew what he was about, and his attentions were aimed at getting her out of her clothes rather than initiating a seduction. This was fortunate, for Elizabeth very much wanted to *be* out of her clothes.

She untied his cravat, and undid the buttons of his shirt and waistcoat, taking care to free the watch chain from the embroidery. Haverford pushed to his feet and took the place beside her on the chaise.

"You're sure, Elizabeth?"

The house party would soon be half over, and yes, Elizabeth was sure. She'd appeared regularly for meals, played piquet with Charlotte and Aunt Arabella, and turned pages for Radnor at the pianoforte, but all along—*for all of her adult life*—a part of her had been waiting for this moment.

She was desperately sure of what she needed from Haverford in the next hour. "Give me your clothes."

He passed them over, article by article, and Elizabeth folded them on the desk. To move about the room with her hooks and stays undone felt decadent and delicious. She toed off her slippers and began a second pile of clothing on the desk—hers.

Her favorite dress would have a few wrinkles. Her petticoat came next, like a frothy icing folded over the dress. Wiggling free of her stays was an undignified undertaking, but she managed it while Haverford was yanking off his boots. When he looked up, his left boot in his hand, he went still.

"Turn around, please."

Elizabeth gave him a slow pivot, her chemise still molded to her middle and very much wrinkled. "I want to leave my stockings on."

Her garters were green satin, her stockings white silk.

"Because," Haverford said, setting his boot down and starting on the second one, "to be not quite naked is more wanton than to be entirely nude. We can test your theory in all its variations. Should I put my shirt back on?"

"Please don't."

He was not pale and soft, as Elizabeth's first two lovers had been. She'd never seen a man entirely naked, mostly because she hadn't wanted to.

She wanted to now.

Haverford set his boots beside the desk, then unbuttoned his falls, and shoved off his breeches. Elizabeth took them and folded them, mostly for something to do with her hands.

"I shouldn't be nervous," she said, matching the legs of his breeches seam for seam. "I know exactly what to expect, and I've longed to be with you in this way, but—"

"Expect pleasure, Elizabeth. Expect consideration, affection, intimate joining, and joy, for I certainly do."

He took her in his arms, so only the lawn of her chemise separated them. Haverford gave off heat, and his arousal rose between them, an unabashed testament to desire. Elizabeth tucked closer, and braced herself for the coming intimacy.

And for the sorrow, because this was stolen pleasure, and when the house party ended, the price for this indulgence would be one broken heart.

Or, more likely, two.

* * *

Julian marshalled his self-restraint as Elizabeth ran a silk-clad toe up his calf. He'd racked his brain for how to turn this dusty little room into her version of a pleasure dome, and his plan had apparently succeeded.

"You claim to know what to expect," he said. "Have you ever made love in daylight?"

"I have not," she said, doing that business with her toe again. "The first time was in an unused parlor at a soiree, and both chilly and dark. I was glad for the darkness, and I think he was too. The second time was at a ball. We found a settee in the conservatory. Somebody had recently fertilized the roses, so to speak. My imagination conjures the most inappropriate memories at the scent of a muck cart."

Good God. "A cold parlor and a stinking conservatory. On behalf of my gender, I apologize, Elizabeth. My first time was in a saddle room at Marvin Jones's coaching inn. We always stopped there, coming and going from London, and one of the maids decided to make a man of me when I came home on holiday from my first term at university. I got a splinter in my arse, which did my manly prowess no good whatsoever."

Elizabeth snorted. "You did not."

"I had to wait until I got home to find a mirror and tweezers, and could barely sit my horse for the rest of that week, though like the young fool that I was, I gloried in the wound passion had given me."

Her next salvo was a soft stroke over his fundament. "I wish I'd met you sooner."

"We have now, Elizabeth." Lest she detail for him how inadequate *now* was, Julian cradled her jaw against his palm and kissed her. He refused to hurry, and not only because her previous experiences had been far less than they should have been.

Elizabeth inspired him to patience, to cherishing and cosseting, all the indulgences his too busy, too responsible life usually denied him.

And even better, Elizabeth cosseted Julian right back. She fondled and caressed every inch of him, lingering in odd locations—the turn of his hip, the soft indentation of his elbow, the arch of his eyebrows. Her touch was inquisitive, gentle, and luscious.

"My chemise—"

"Can stay on." Or not. The material was so fine, leaving it on was as erotic as taking it off. Elizabeth couldn't know that, not yet. "The decision is yours, Elizabeth."

She graduated from running her toe up his calf to wrapping a leg around his hip. "I will think of you when I read Milton."

Paradise Regained or *Paradise Lost*? Copies of both lay somewhere among the surrounding volumes.

"I will be incapable of thinking at all in about two minutes."

She smiled against Julian's mouth and took a step back. He followed and realized she was leading him to the chaise. He used the small space between them to shape her breasts, and Elizabeth arched into his touch.

"Do you like that, Elizabeth?"

"Exceedingly."

He caught her up in his arms and laid her on the chaise, then knelt beside her and took a moment to admire the picture she made. Her hair was in a ladylike chignon, her chemise was hemmed with violets and greenery, and those damned silk stockings...

Julian retaliated for the stockings and the green garters by stroking Elizabeth's breasts. She closed her eyes, her arms above her head, and let him use his hands and his mouth to pleasure her.

"You're good at this," she said, when Julian had eased her chemise aside to bare both breasts. "You have a sense of what's almost unendurable. It isn't fair."

He wrapped her hand around his arousal. "You're good at this. You sigh and move and mutter snippets of poetry I can't decipher, and I'm in a state."

She propped herself on one elbow and ran a fingertip around the crown of his cock. "We're good at this."

"Again, as slowly as you please."

Julian wanted the moments to last, to organize themselves in a tidy, easily recalled order, like the books on the shelves. This touch, that sigh, the whiff of roses when he arranged himself over his lover, but all the impressions ran together in one long, slow crescendo of pleasure, the way a fire consumes old wood.

When he'd borne all the mutual treasuring he could, he positioned himself between her legs.

"Are you sure, Elizabeth?"

"I'm a living monument to certainty—and impatience."

That was a yes. Julian sank slowly into her heat, the bliss rolling through him as Elizabeth wrapped her legs around his flanks. He was starved for the closeness she offered, starved for the wonder. Tears threatened, of gratitude and frustration, because all he could have with her were moments and not enough of those.

Elizabeth moved, a teasing undulation that inspired Julian to move with her. She'd been right—they were good at this. Beyond good, though Julian held off his own gratification for the near-equivalent of pleasuring Elizabeth.

She caught fire in no time, lacing her fingers with his and holding on tight.

"Julian..."

"I have you." For her, he had reserves of restraint, enough to send her soaring above the parapets twice before giving her a moment to rest. Desire was enjoyable—nature had made it so—but so too was the sense of forming a two-person sanctuary against all the troubles and disappointments of the world.

"It's wonderful when you're with me," Elizabeth said, brushing her thumb over Julian's palm. "The other—on the battlements—was lovely too, but this... I have no words."

She had kisses, though, and requests made with her hands, and suggestions that Julian dared not heed. When he could trust his self-discipline no more, he withdrew, and spent in silence on Elizabeth's belly.

The physical sensations were stupendous in their intensity, shuddering through him until he was draped over Elizabeth, a blanket of replete masculinity.

"I am undone," he murmured, kissing her ear.

She stroked his hair, which he took for confirmation of her own undone-ness.

They lay together, breathing in a reciprocal rhythm, bodies cooling. Julian eventually found the strength to sit back—dukes were a self-disciplined lot—and use a dampened handkerchief to wipe his seed from Elizabeth's belly.

She watched him tending to her, and the moment became as intimate as any that had gone before. This too was cosseting.

He tossed the handkerchief to the floor, lay beside her, pulled her into his arms, and twitched the blanket over them.

"Sleep," he said, kissing Elizabeth's crown. "The door is locked, you've earned your rest, and we have time."

She closed her eyes, her lashes tickling his shoulder.

He'd lied to her, of course, because in truth, they had only a few days. As Elizabeth's breathing slowed, and quiet settled around them, Julian made a choice. He loved this woman, and while he hadn't much to offer her, he had to at least try to secure a future with her.

He'd make the overtures to Elizabeth's father and to the head of her family. He'd be honest about his situation, and if hard work and a sound plan could earn him Elizabeth's hand in marriage, he'd spend the rest of his life devoted to her happiness.

On that thought, he let sleep claim him.

Chapter Sixteen

"So this is where you've been hiding." Charlotte peered around at the books in the tower room. "I should have known. Who has abducted you this time? Shakespeare? Donne? *Byron?*"

Yesterday afternoon, Haverford had abducted Elizabeth on the same chaise she'd occupied all morning. The better part of her wits and her entire heart were still unaccounted for.

"Byron will not earn a place on these shelves for at least a century. Come in, Charlotte."

Charlotte was impatient with anything that required her to sit for long periods—books, needlepoint, cutwork, church services—though she was better read than most young women of her station, because her mind was as active as her body.

"You must be in transports," Charlotte said, drawing her cream wool shawl closer. "I have never seen so many books as this castle houses."

"And you haven't seen them all. There's a third collection

kept in the cellars under lock and key, the smallest and oldest. Haverford described it to me." As afternoon had drifted toward evening, and Elizabeth had needed a way to ease back from the intimacy of lovemaking, Haverford had offered the topic with which she was most comfortable—books. Old, old books, and even illuminated manuscripts.

He'd regaled Elizabeth with anecdotes from St. David history. The fifth duke had chosen for his duchess a woman whose settlements included a trove of ancient documents. The eighth duke had won several Shakespeare folios by prevailing in a horse race. The stories were humorous, and yet, beneath the duke's amused tone, Elizabeth had heard bewilderment.

"Some of these look like they were shelved on the Ark," Charlotte said, peering at a row of bound volumes tagged with white silk cords. "You should marry Haverford."

Elizabeth agreed. She'd written to her parents intimating as much, and to blazes with Haverford's lack of wealth. Coin did not sneak a kiss to her nape when her stays had been done up. Coin did not take the time to show her pleasure when others had thought only to take it from her. Coin did not—

"I have never seen you wear quite that expression," Charlotte said. "I suggest holy matrimony, and you look ready to start a holy war."

"Matrimony for a man of Haverford's standing is complicated." Love, however, was the simplest thing in the world. "What has held your interest these past few days while I've been cavorting with great literature?"

Charlotte took the seat at the desk. The roses were beginning to droop, a fitting complement to Charlotte's demeanor.

"I've been naughty. I am ashamed of myself, but mostly, I am disappointed."

Elizabeth knew that sentiment. "Haldale?" He was handsome, charming, and not worth the smudge on Charlotte's slipper.

"Gracious days, not Haldale. Did you know he has two children? Aunt Arabella made it a point to inform me of this."

"You did not come up here to regale me with Haldale's indiscretions."

Charlotte touched a fading rose, and three petals dropped to the blotter. "I challenged Sherbourne to an archery contest."

"Is the household to gather and watch Mr. Sherbourne's humiliation?"

"You don't like him?"

Haverford didn't like him, and that was enough for Elizabeth. "He invited himself to this party, Charlotte, and harbors some sort of grudge against the St. Davids. I don't like how he looks at Lady Glenys, and he apparently longs to develop a mine in this beautiful valley."

"We burn coal in every household we inhabit. Why hold the mines against him? Dukes own mines, up north."

"And men, women, and children work themselves to death in those mines. You've heard Mama's tirades."

In the last century, Wales had become—literally—Britain's gold mine. Also its copper mine, iron smelter, slate quarry, and coal mine. Mama focused on the resulting slums, the valleys rendered infertile because of the smoky skies and dirty rain. She saw the poverty that lay beneath the great wealth of the coal barons and their managers.

Haverford saw those blights too, while Sherbourne apparently focused only on the wealth to be gained.

"I did not come here to argue politics," Charlotte said, sweeping up the fallen petals and tossing them into the dust bin. "I don't particularly care if Sherbourne's wealth is earned in the same manner as the Duke of Northumberland's. We don't own any mines, do we?"

"No, Charlotte. Did you bed Sherbourne?" Elizabeth hoped not, for Charlotte's sake.

"I said I'd been naughty, not demented. I bested him at archery. Shot his arrows from their flights, stopped him from proving his marksmanship."

Charlotte had perfected that trick by the time she was fourteen. "Well, yes, that was terrible of you."

"Be serious."

"Charlotte, did you fire an arrow through his hat, knocking it from his head before half the debutantes in Mayfair?"

"That was years ago, and the toad deserved it. He'd got a chamber maid with child and was bragging about it at the men's punch bowl."

Charlotte was quite the angel of justice when men failed to take responsibility for their actions, though she always claimed her retribution was merely accident, a misstep, an oversight.

"So what provoked you to besting Sherbourne?"

"I wasn't besting him, Bethan. I was warning him. What is wrong with a man being proud of his accomplishments? Why is it expected that a duke will stride about, full of his consequence, admired for his condescension, but a mere banker—whose wealth supports the very crown—or a brewer, whose product in another sense supports the entire populace—must be humble and obsequious?"

"And you said you did not come here to argue politics. Mr. Sherbourne is quite capable of looking out for himself."

"No, he is not. He thinks he is, but he doesn't know the company he's found himself among. Why didn't Haverford toss him down the drive, if he's here uninvited?"

"Because Haverford is a gentleman, and Mr. Sherbourne likely finagled an invitation from Lady Glenys without her realizing it."

Charlotte rose. "Lady Glenys should be more mindful of her words. Sherbourne thinks to marry her, I'm guessing. He wants to marry his way into the aristocracy, and that seldom works."

Had Sherbourne turned his marital aspirations on *Charlotte*? "It can work," Elizabeth said, "after two or three generations, provided the one doing the marrying has means." Which Sherbourne did, according to Aunt Arabella. "I'll have a word with Lady Glenys."

"Perhaps I'll have a word with Sherbourne." Charlotte leafed through a stack of papers on the desk. "What are these?"

"Those are merchants' bills for goods and services ordered for this house party. Lady Glenys asked me to see what orders could be canceled."

Lady Glenys had done no such thing, but Elizabeth could not very well admit that Haverford had brought the bills into the room, and muttered dire oaths about each one.

"Remind me never to host a house party," Charlotte said. "These sums are exorbitant."

"I thought so. I mentioned the price of the pineapples and Aunt Arabella was shocked as well."

"Aunt does not shock easily. We aren't that large a party, nor is transporting goods here by sea that difficult. What could Lady Glenys have been thinking?"

"She was thinking to find her brother a duchess."

Charlotte paged through a few more of the bills. "I could buy an entire orchard of pineapple trees for what she's spending on a few dozen fruits. Write to Her Grace. If Aunt Esther doesn't know to the penny what a house party costs, then nobody does."

That was a sound suggestion. The Duchess of Moreland had managed dozens of house parties and balls over the years. She'd know if pineapples were particularly expensive this year, or ice sculptures all the rage.

"Do you like Sherbourne, Charlotte?"

She set the stack of bills back on the desk. "I do not, particularly, but he's intelligent and he accepted my setdown with good grace. I respect him for that, even if I cannot abide his calculating air. I dislike Haldale and Sir Nigel—they are indolent and vain. Sherbourne is neither."

"He's a bit of a peacock."

"No more than Haverford is," Charlotte rejoined, heading for the door. "Do you fancy His Grace, Elizabeth?"

"I do."

"Then he'd better fancy you too."

She slipped out the door, and Elizabeth took the seat at the desk. Three opinions—Charlotte's, Elizabeth's, and Aunt Arabella's—all put the house party expenses beyond the pale.

Haverford seemed well liked by his guests, and respected by his staff. His younger brother adored him, Radnor counted him a close friend, and Elizabeth had yet to see Haverford refuse his sister any request.

And yet, the entire shire and half the merchants in Swansea seemed intent on bilking the duke of his last groat.

* * *

The difficulty with being a duke—one of the many difficulties with being a duke—was that Julian rarely had to ask anybody for anything, much less ask somebody of his own station. He thus sat at the desk in his personal sitting room, trying to compose a letter to the Duke of Moreland, and failing.

Miserably. Moreland was the head of Elizabeth's family, and Julian was simply trying to start a dialogue, to test the waters.

"My Lord Duke," he recited to the empty foolscap. "Or do I dare greet you simply as Dear Duke of Moreland? In any case, greetings, from Haverford Castle, which is falling to pieces as I pen this epistle. I am desperate to court your niece, but I have not two coins to rub together, and my situation isn't likely to change for at least twelve years. I can spend her settlements handily and not scratch the surface of the debts my family and my estate have run up, not that I'd touch a farthing of Miss Windham's portion."

Elizabeth's settlements were hers, her security against a future as a widow.

"I am further mortified to inform you," Julian went on, "that my sister remains unwed, in part because her dowry has grown so modest, that only a man very much in love will consider marrying her. I have reason to hope she will secure such an offer soon."

Which made Glenys sound like the hag of the bog, rather than the dear, delightful lady that she was.

Onward. "Your Grace will have heard that my younger brother and heir is a simpleton," Julian went on, closing his eyes and pinching the bridge of his nose. "That characterization is unfair, but not without..."

Christ. First Glennie now Griffin, betrayed by correspondence.

A tap sounded on the door.

Only Glenys or Radnor would disturb Julian in his personal sitting room. "Come in."

Hugh St. David admitted himself and stood on the threshold. "Your Grace wanted to see me."

No, Julian had *not* wanted to see Hugh, or any of the

other guests crowding around his buffets like street urchins at a Christmas dinner. He rose, nonetheless, hand extended.

"Hugh, please have a seat. We haven't had a chance to catch up." Julian gestured not to the chair flanking the desk, but to the sofa.

Hugh had been the older cousin who'd taught Julian how to cast a fishing line, how to smoke, and how to tie his first cravat. When Julian had inherited the title, the cousinly mentoring had faded. When Hugh had taken Delphine to wife, the relationship had become perfunctory.

Why did I let that happen? And worse, *Has Hugh banished himself to the cliffs and beaches to avoid not his wife, but his host?*

"Good of you to invite us," Hugh said, looking anywhere but at Julian. "The castle's always a pleasure to behold."

"The castle's falling apart."

Hugh was family, he'd been visiting the castle for all of his two-score years, and he fancied himself a scientist. He'd see changes in the family seat others ignored, while he'd completely miss his wife's growing restlessness.

"Castles do that. They fall apart," Hugh said, flashing a rare smile, "but truly subduing them takes a lot. As long as we're being honest, you might want to keep that Windstruther puppy away from Lady Glenys."

Julian poured two portions of brandy from the decanter on the sideboard, and passed one to Hugh. "Any particular reason I should look askance at Windstruther as opposed to every other bachelor?"

"A fellow from the Geological Society says any vowels Sir Nigel owes tend to be misplaced for months at time, and he's a hothead. Averages two duels per season and lives for the day when we're at war with France again."

"Good to know." Sir Nigel was subsisting on a quarterly

allowance, then, and minding neither his budget nor his words.

"Should have told you sooner," Hugh said, taking a sip of his drink. "Saved you some bother."

Julian took an armchair and wished Elizabeth were with them. She'd know how to broach the topic of a straying wife without embarrassing anybody.

"Is Delphine a bother?"

"She's a terror." Hugh's words blended admiration and woe. "My terror, though. Has she been pestering you?"

Blessed St. David. "One hopes she'd know better."

Hugh rose, drink in hand. "She had a theory, you see. She thought I was your heir, and because I'm a healthy specimen, I was to outlive you. We were to have a few sons, while you remained a bachelor. Devonshire's not married. Quimbey held out until recently. Dukes don't always marry when they have heirs to tend to the succession."

Julian sipped his drink rather than mutter profanities. "She was to become the next Duchess of Haverford?"

"And be treated with the deference owed one of her soon-to-be lofty station." Hugh finished his brandy and set his glass down a bit too hard on the sideboard. "Instead she got the boring life of obscure gentry, a husband who dreams of dead ferns, and not a son to be seen."

Hugh would make a good duke. He was sensible, for all his geological passions, and he loved the land.

"Should I be concerned for Griffin's safety?"

"You have to ask that," Hugh said, "because the lad's vulnerable, but everybody loves our Griffin. Delphine's problem is her choice of spouse. I no more want your title than I want you bringing coal mines into this shire. If that damned Sherbourne had his way, half the neighborhood would be torn up."

"It's petty of me," Julian said, "but to hear somebody honestly malign Mr. Sherbourne is a relief. He might yet marry Glenys, though, so consider keeping your opinions of him to yourself."

Hugh poured himself another half-portion of brandy. "He's the most disliked man in the shire, Haverford. Those who don't owe him will barely acknowledge him, though they're few enough in number. He has every merchant in his pocket, and talks of nothing but how their custom would improve if only we brought a mine or two into the valley."

Just as brandy both soothed and burned, Hugh's words were part solution, part problem. "I'm in debt to him," Julian said. "I hadn't realized others suffered the same indignity."

"Your father, God bless him, was not the most sensible sort."

A charitable characterization. The dukedom had lost financial ground during Grandpapa's day, while Papa had all but shoved the family finances over a precipice formed of books and unthinkable self-indulgence.

"My father could not resist the lure of a bound tome, and there was a canal scheme...."

"And Sherbourne's papa was likely the chief swindler," Hugh said. "I'm sorry. I've a bit put by, if that will help. My land is good, and I take care of it. Delphie's imprudent in some ways, but she doesn't overspend her pin money."

The words were on the tip of Julian's tongue: *I'm touched at your generosity, but won't need to impose to that degree....* A ducal proclamation, and a falsehood. The empty sheet of foolscap lay on Julian's desk, a reproach and a sign of hope.

"Glenys and Radnor are circling each other like two cats in a barnyard," Julian said.

"And kittens have been known to come from a lot of

hissing and caterwauling," Hugh replied. "Radnor has coveted my timber for years. If twenty acres of mature oak will aid the course of true love, I'm happy to donate it to the settlements."

A queer feeling came over Julian, equal parts humility, gratitude, and relief. Twenty acres of mature oak was a significant asset, and one that would appreciate for generations without costing a penny. Over the past two centuries, the British Navy had requisitioned nearly every sizeable oak tree in some shires, though pockets of Wales had escaped that plundering.

Those trees were worth a great deal now.

"I will accept that offer, Hugh, with more thanks than you can know, but I suspect the course of true love, or at least marital concord, might also be aided by a trip to Paris for you and Delphine."

Hugh sank into the chair behind Julian's desk. "We were not a love match, and I know you mean well, but... Delphie's mostly bored. She'll settle down in another few years."

Hugh had apparently been telling himself that twaddle since the wedding. "So take her somewhere she can entertain herself with the company of the man she married," Julian said. "She thinks you love your fossils more than you care for her."

"What?"

"She's humiliated when you leave at first light, day after day, in search of the perfect rock. She misbehaves to get your attention, to prove to herself that you matter as little to her as she matters to you."

When another man might have called Julian out for meddling, Hugh looked intrigued. "I take myself off for hours each day so she needn't limit her diversions on my account. At home, we can go for days at a time without saying more to each other than, 'Pass the salt,' or, 'Wasn't that a dreadful sermon?' Delphie doesn't need or expect me to hover."

"Hovering is different from waiting until after breakfast to go on your rambles. You might cosset her a bit, where others will take notice."

Hugh studied his drink as if the glass held tea leaves instead of brandy. "*Cosset?* She's my wife, not some blushing virgin twiddling her bonnet ribbons in the churchyard."

Sympathy for Delphine St. David was a novel and welcome sentiment. "Offer to escort her to breakfast, Hugh. Invite her to come along on your next hike, pack a picnic, bring a book to read to her, and don't look at a single fossil."

"These surrounds don't offer any good fossils," Hugh said. "I always bring a book, there being no library to equal yours, and after enjoying a pint or two in the village, I find a quiet place to read and nap, if you must know the truth."

Elizabeth had known the truth. "Partner Delphine at whist and flirt with her across the table. Steal a kiss on one of the unused stairways. Bring her a rose some night, and tell her the chimney in your room is stopped up, so you'll need to share her bed."

"My chimney.... You know, Delphie said something this morning, about her room having a draft. Do you suppose she was casting a lure?"

Bless Elizabeth Windham. "If she is, you'd best catch it. Griffin won't marry, I'm without a duchess, and you're a man in your prime. The weight of the succession, at present, rests on your shoulders, Hugh."

Hugh rose and tugged down his waistcoat. "I've considered reminding Delphie of that."

"When you do remind her, have a bouquet of roses in your hand."

"Roses and ferns are a lovely combination," Hugh replied, marching for the door.

"And Paris in autumn is beautiful."

"One step at a time, Haverford. One step at a time."

Hugh left, and Julian sent up a prayer for marital concord. For now, the weight of the succession truly did rest on Hugh's shoulders. Delphine's frolics might well have landed a cuckoo in the St. David nest, which was probably half of her motivation for frolicking in the first place.

"At least that problem shows some promise of a solution."

Julian took his drink to his desk, and sharpened a quill pen already sporting a perfect point.

Lady Pembroke had pronounced half of polite society in dun territory half the time. The law of the land prohibited a peer from being jailed for debt, probably because the entire aristocracy would otherwise find itself, in one generation or another, behind bars.

Julian scrawled a few sentences and sealed and franked the missive before self-doubt stayed his hand. To act on impulse was contrary to his nature, but in this case, inaction was intolerable. He gave the letter to a footman in the corridor, along with directions to send the missive to Moreland by express.

Despite the expense.

After Julian had spent another hour at his desk dealing with ledgers and political epistles, the same footman brought in the afternoon post.

"My thanks, Elfryd," Julian said. "If you'd get word to Hayes that I'd like to see him in the estate office on the hour, I'd appreciate it." Hayes being the butler Julian had inherited from his father.

"Of course, sir." Elfryd withdrew, leaving Julian with a pile of correspondence that very likely contained more bills.

One epistle was sealed with a ducal crest. Julian started there, prepared for a harangue by letter on some parliamentary matter.

Haverford,

Greetings and so forth. You are privileged to include two of my beloved nieces among your guests. Allow a rake, rogue, or fortune hunter within twenty yards of either of them, and I will gut you where you stand. Elizabeth, as the eldest of four, especially must not be allowed to entertain romantic notions regarding impecunious bachelors who think to presume on her parents' desperation.

You are a duke with an unmarried sister, so I'm sure you'll appreciate the *utter* sincerity of my sentiments.

Best regards,
Moreland
PS: If Elizabeth or Charlotte should be compromised while under your roof, my duchess assures me she will ruin what's left of you after I've had my turn.
PPS: Lord Anthony is a dead shot. So am I. So are Elizabeth's cousins. And cousins-by-marriage.
PPPS: Forbid the ordering of any ice sculptures. They're frightfully expensive and the damned things just melt before midnight.

Chapter Seventeen

"Why must every house party include a visit to the village?" Charlotte grumbled.

She walked arm in arm with Elizabeth, both of them having declined to accompany Aunt Arabella in Haverford's enormous landau.

"Because the local merchants need the custom," Elizabeth replied, "and it is a truth universally acknowledged that ladies need to shop." Besides, the guests hadn't left Haverford Castle except to attend services, and the house party was well into its second week.

"I hate to shop."

Charlotte could be that honest because she and Elizabeth were walking ahead of the general multitude. Elizabeth had chosen to lead this charge so she wouldn't have to watch Haverford offering his arm to Miss Trelawny, or Miss Penhathaway, or Miss...

Any of the damned misses.

"I have an alternate assignment for you," Elizabeth said, "if you're determined to keep hold of your pin money. Please make sure Sherbourne stays away from me."

The road was rutted and dry. Charlotte kicked a stone out of one of the ruts, right up onto the verge.

"You truly don't care for Sherbourne? I like his waistcoats."

Perhaps Windham women had a weakness for men in colorful waistcoats. "That is the first thing you've liked about anybody since we arrived at this house party."

"He's not afraid to go his own way. Sherbourne isn't stupid either."

Elizabeth drew Charlotte off the road so the landau could clatter past. "But is he honorable? While you are hanging on his arm and admiring hair ribbons, I will be questioning the shopkeepers about their prices." After a proper inspection of the village lending library, of course.

"That is not fair, Bethan. If you get to meddle, I should get to meddle too."

"You are diverting the enemy, or at least thwarting his reconnaissance."

Charlotte dropped Elizabeth's arm and resumed walking. "Sherbourne likes money. It's all very well for the aristocracy to pretend money doesn't exist, because they have pots of it. The rest of the world starves without money, and I don't judge a man for being mindful of that fact."

Sherbourne had appointed himself Elizabeth's partner in the card room for the past three nights. He played with a calculated skill barely hidden behind party manners. Sherbourne did not like money, he *coveted* it—money from the pockets of Haverford's guests in any case.

Elizabeth wondered if he didn't also covet *her*.

He was properly attentive, and not without humor. He

was also not Haverford, and now this—Charlotte *liked* his waistcoats.

This entire house party was a nightmare, but for the hours Elizabeth had stolen with Haverford in the book room.

"Regardless of Mr. Sherbourne's affection for coin," Elizabeth said, "I'd rather do my shopping without his escort. Mrs. St. David would be an ideal partner for me, because she'll know many of the local merchants."

"She and Mr. St. David went off looking for fossils this morning."

The village came into view on the far side of an arched stone bridge. Tudor façades were interspersed with stone cottages and shops along a cobbled street. Potted flowers contrasted with the granite and whitewashed architecture, creating a cheerful, tidy air.

"Are you envious of Mr. and Mrs. St. David, Charlotte?"

"He's devoted to her. I hadn't expected that."

"I don't think she did either."

As it happened, Hugh and Delphine St. David ended up in the village tavern at noon, along with the rest of the party. Elizabeth had spent her morning on Sir Nigel Windstruther's arm, and had had to rebuke him only once for standing too close to her.

She took the seat next to Mrs. St. David when Windstruther and Haldale got to wagering about the number of windows in the inn.

"Good day," Elizabeth said, as Hugh St. David held her chair. "What a pretty village this is."

"Wales shows to best advantage in summer," Hugh St. David replied. "Some of the houses go back centuries, and the ale here won't give anybody a bad turn. May I fetch you ladies your pints?"

"Please," Delphine replied. "And some bread and butter. I vow this morning's exertions have given me an appetite."

Hugh positively strutted to the bar, and his wife followed his progress with an appreciative eye.

Well. "I have a few questions for you," Elizabeth said, "if you've time to indulge me."

"Ask," Delphine replied. "I know more about fossils than probably anybody here save my husband, but other than that, I'm not particularly knowledgeable."

"Why are the shopkeepers and merchants, to a man, overcharging the castle for everything from ale to lime to carpet tacks?"

* * *

"Why do you hate Haverford?" Charlotte asked, for she intended to do more than simply keep an eye on Mr. Sherbourne.

She wanted to take him apart as she'd once taken apart her papa's watch. All those springs and screws and tiny parts were more fascinating than the clock's face. Two hands traversed the same twelve numbers over and over, while the genius of timekeeping remained tucked out of sight.

"I don't hate Haverford," Sherbourne said, tipping his hat to Aunt and Mr. Andover as they ambled in the opposite direction around the green. "I hate injustice."

If he'd passed Charlotte a box of French chocolates, she could not have been more pleased. "So do I, but in what sense is Haverford an injustice?"

Charlotte had envied Hugh and Delphine St. David not their relapse into marital affection, but their morning hike. The walk to the village, by contrast, had been undertaken at the pace of a drunken tortoise burdened with an uncertain sense of direction.

"Haverford is a duke. At the risk of offending present company, a duke is a strutting, braying injustice."

The green was only a couple of acres of ground, just big enough to hold a village market.

"Let's wander along the river," Charlotte said, "because I'm sure your views on this subject are as well developed as my distaste for purchasing hair ribbons."

"You don't enjoy shopping, Miss Charlotte?"

Charlotte steered him to the path between the livery and the apothecary. "Can't abide it."

"I have never met a woman who doesn't enjoy spending coin."

The path wound down to the river, the same body of water that ran through Haverford's park, though it ran more slowly here.

"You've never met a woman who didn't *profess* to love shopping," Charlotte said, "who didn't manufacture a display of enthusiasm for it, and you took that for an honest expression of joy. You are preoccupied with coin, so any woman trying to curry your favor knows to display an affection for what coin can purchase."

"Miss Charlotte, you are a terror."

"And you are walking by a river. Patronize me at peril to your tailoring." Sherbourne was good-sized. She might not be able to push him into the water, now that she'd given up the element of surprise. "Please explain your enmity toward dukes."

"Not only dukes, the whole peerage. The lot of them sit on their rosy fundaments, running the country while they do nothing to contribute to its well-being. The sovereign is a bad and very expensive joke, while the likes of Haverford can hold back progress on a whim, or pass toothless laws which they themselves then ignore."

The water meandered by, dark but not stagnant. A soft breeze stirred the trees along the bank, and wood warblers chirped and whistled overhead. Wales was beautiful.

And Sherbourne was an angry man.

Charlotte was angry too, much of the time. "Has Haverford held back *your* progress?"

Sherbourne walked along, the picture of a gentleman at leisure taking the country air.

"He refuses to allow even a single mine into the district. His father and grandfather took the same position. No mines, not when this valley can grow crops, and dot its hillsides with a lot of bawling heifers and stupid sheep. My grandfather hired a surveyor to dig some exploratory shafts and we do have ore here, Miss Charlotte. We have a wealth of ore."

His frustration was apparently every bit as precious to him as an inherited title would be to a ducal heir.

"You don't care for milk, cheese, butter, beef, mutton, lamb, or wool?"

"You are the most contrary woman I have ever met."

"Thank you. Answer the question."

"Of course, I see the value in those goods, but compared to coal, they are barely profitable. Haverford's beautiful vistas and plump bovines are a sentimental attachment the rest of us cannot afford. As a peer, he will never be jailed for debt, so his lack of funds is a mere inconvenience. For everybody else, our very freedom depends on having adequate coin."

"One cannot eat coal, Mr. Sherbourne. One cannot wear coal. As somebody who adores butter on my toast, I'm glad Haverford isn't as greedy as some."

Charlotte ought not to have said that. A lady could make a point without being insulting, but really, Sherbourne hadn't thought his position through.

"I'm greedy for wanting to bring progress to this valley? For wanting our young men to have a choice besides tramping into London and hoping they'll see their families again before they die of overwork and homesickness?"

"You're probably not greedy, but you cannot abide that Haverford, supported by all of his tenants and titled neighbors, can stop your mining scheme. You simply want to have your way in all things."

He stopped, both hands resting on his walking stick. "You make me sound like a spoiled duke."

Charlotte knelt to look for a stone—smooth, round, not too big. "You think Haverford's title is why he can thwart your coal mine, but his title has little to do with it. He owns thousands of acres. You could own thousands of acres if you pleased to. His family goes back centuries in this shire. Someday, your family might too if it doesn't already. He's respected and trusted, however, and that, very likely, is why he can keep the mines out of the valley."

She skipped the rock, making four bounces before it hit the opposite bank.

"He's respected and trusted because he's a duke."

"He's respected because he is a *gentleman* in every sense of the word. You are almost as stubborn as my uncle Percival on the subject of the Irish question. He claims it will split the government before we just damned deal with it."

"Please do not use foul language, Miss Charlotte."

She picked up another rock. "I'm merely quoting my uncle." She took better aim, so the trajectory would fall more nearly up the middle of the river, and got five bounces this time.

"I've always wished I knew how to do that."

"Five male cousins," Charlotte said. "I watched them and watched them—spied on them endlessly—then practiced in private. It's not difficult. Shall I show you how?"

He studied the spot where her rock had dropped below the surface. "If you wouldn't mind."

"You'll think about what I said? About Haverford's title not being the issue?"

Sherbourne removed his gloves and set aside his walking stick. "I will, if you'll give some thought to the notion that progress ought to benefit more than the titled few. I'll also ponder at some length how you look whipping that rock exactly where you want it to go."

Charlotte peeled off her gloves and stuffed them in a pocket. "Was that a compliment?"

"More of a complaint."

She thought about that reply as she explained the qualities of a good skipping rock. Sherbourne's first three attempts merely splashed into the river, but by the fourth try, he got a couple of bounces.

By the time Mr. Sherbourne had achieved four bounces, Charlotte had concluded that for her to haunt his thoughts was acceptable. He needed something to dwell on besides the perceived injustice of being a wealthy, handsome, shrewd commoner who lived next door to a principled nobleman.

"One more," he said, tossing a small rock between his hands. "Then I must return you to the company of my betters."

He focused on the river, much as Charlotte focused when she nocked an arrow. Everything—breathing, gaze, thoughts—came together in support of a single objective. He let the stone go with a hard flick of his wrist, and it bounced six times before striking an exposed rock many yards upstream.

"That was excellent," Charlotte said. "Very well done, Mr. Sherbourne. You are educable after all."

His blue eyes filled with consternation, and Charlotte feared she'd insulted him *again*. That would not do. She leaned close and bussed his cheek.

"I'm proud of you, sir, and you've spared me a morning of tedium at the mercer's and the baker's."

His smile was unexpectedly bashful. "I'm in your debt as well, Miss Charlotte. For the lively conversation and the instruction."

He tugged his gloves on, offered his arm, and with every appearance of gentlemanly consideration, escorted her back to the green.

* * *

"Moreland, you can't call a man out for asking to court our niece."

Percival regarded his duchess, whose tones in the past ten minutes had progressed from amused, to patiently firm, to mule-stubborn.

"The damned man doesn't even bother with diplomacy, Esther. He intimates that he'd give a lot of dusty books for the privilege of asking for Elizabeth's hand, then bluntly informs me he has no coin."

Percival tossed Haverford's message—it didn't qualify as a letter—onto the blotter.

The duchess stalked across the private ducal sitting room, and after more than three decades of marriage, Percival could read her mood in the very swish of her skirts.

"Tony and Gladys are desperate to see Bethan married,"

Esther said. "Tony himself suggested Charlotte and Elizabeth attend this house party, and need I remind you, sir, that Bethan would be Haverford's *duchess*."

Esther had doubtless spotted a mention of Haverford's gathering in some tattler, and had passed along the information to Gladys. Tony had probably been consulted as a courtesy, nothing more. Tony, alas, was off with Gladys in Brighton while his daughters hunted bachelors in Wales.

"As if Bethan cares that"—Percival snapped his fingers—"for being a duchess."

Esther picked up the note, though she probably had it memorized. "Elizabeth would make a fine duchess, which I admit in all humility is not an easy task. One must learn to manage to a duke, and that can be a delicate undertaking. What does it mean, that Haverford's circumstances are sorely constrained?"

"He hasn't a farthing to his name, though his castle is not yet mortgaged. I suspect the bankers won't lend to him anymore, because they know the extent of his debts."

"I've seen Haverford Castle," Esther said, taking the note over to the window. "Lovely grounds, magnificent edifice with an enormous library. His handwriting puts me in mind of yours."

The sunlight found fiery highlights in Her Grace's blond hair. Percival pretended to peer over his wife's shoulder, but mostly, he wanted to be closer to her. They were having a difference of opinion—behind a firmly closed door, of course—and he must tread carefully.

"Magnificent edifices are expensive to maintain, Esther, as are beautiful grounds. You will notice, nobody is building castles these days, despite an abundance of fine British stone in nearly every shire."

"Castles are drafty." Her Grace patted her husband's cravat. "I say you should give Haverford a chance."

The duchess knew exactly when to turn up reasonable and charming, and Percival would capitulate to her wishes. For the sake of his pride—and her amusement—he'd put up a show of resistance first.

"Do you want Gladys and Tony's grandchildren living without comforts, madam? Without the coin to make a proper come out? Without dowries or means?"

The duchess returned the letter to the blotter and settled on the sofa. "Percival, when I married you, you'd sold your commission, your family finances were a disgrace, the ducal heir was ailing, and your parents' marriage was nothing short of a domestic feud."

Not even a polite domestic feud. Percival's own marriage had been guided in part by a desire to avoid emulating his parents' bad example.

He took the place beside his wife. "I wasn't much of a catch, was I?"

"I was assured that marrying a duke's son was very presuming of me, but viewed pragmatically, you were a bad risk."

"A lusty bad risk." The babies had arrived one right after another, Peter's health had deteriorated, and the old duke's muddled finances had become a quagmire of debt and mismanagement.

Esther linked her fingers with Percival's. "But we contrived, Moreland. We endured, we did not give up. A few challenging years weren't the worst that could befall our marriage."

Losing Victor and Bart was the worst that had befallen their marriage. Esther didn't have to say that out loud.

"Bethan and her duke might have hard decades, Esther,

not simply hard years. Once a man has no capital to invest, his financial progress can barely plod toward better health. Haverford has a long road before him, and his politics incline liberally on too many issues for my liking. The only other characteristic the St. Davids are known for is having a blessed lot of old books."

"What asset could Haverford possibly have—besides honor—that Elizabeth would value more than books?"

"A loving heart, of course."

Esther kissed his cheek. "And that is why I married you. For your loving heart."

"I know what you're about, madam. You hope that if Elizabeth brings Haverford up to scratch, then Charlotte will capitulate to the charms of some swain or other. I think you have it backward."

Percival did not have a favorite niece or a favorite daughter—or maybe they were all his favorites—but he had a greater instinctive understanding of Charlotte than of her sisters.

Charlotte was ferociously loyal, could not abide unfairness, and would sacrifice herself for her sisters without a murmur of regret.

"Charlotte will have to marry, once Elizabeth has spoken her vows," Esther said. "Her sisters will see to it. Megan and Anwen will matchmake more effectively than we ever could, and enlist the aid of our own offspring."

"Charlotte is immune to matchmaking. She'll choose for herself or not at all."

Esther sat up. "Percival, was that a challenge? You claim I cannot find a suitable fellow for my own niece?"

Nobody had found such a fellow yet, and not for want of trying. Percival kept that purely factual observation to himself.

"Might we focus on one spinster niece at a time, my love? Haverford implies that Elizabeth is unconcerned about his financial situation, but I'll not have him marrying her in hopes that her settlements will ease his burdens."

"Why not?"

"For his sake. A man has his pride, or he should have his pride if he's marrying a Windham."

"Valid point. So what will you do?"

What did a competent officer do when the territory was unpromising, but had to be crossed? "I'll conduct more reconnaissance, and bring Tony into the conversation."

"I wrote to Gladys this morning. You can tuck a note in with my letter."

"Esther, please. This is a serious matter. You can tuck your letter in with my ducal missive."

She cuddled closer. "You're right, of course. My mistake."

Ever gracious in victory, that was Her Grace, but Percival wasn't about to turn a blind eye to Haverford's lack of fortune. Polite society wouldn't either, and sooner or later, Elizabeth would hear it whispered that she'd all but bought her tiara.

Which wouldn't do. For a Windham bride, that wouldn't do at all.

Chapter Eighteen

To Julian's delight, Elizabeth was an enthusiastic lover. She liked to try different positions, and could appreciate a slow, tender joining as well as a mad gallop to completion. She approached lovemaking without a plan or agenda, other than to be intimate and to share passion.

Julian reveled in her spontaneity, in the trust and joy of being with her in the moment, though without fail, he withdrew rather than risk her future for the sake of pleasure.

Elizabeth insisted on cuddling afterward, despite the awkwardness of sharing a chaise, and she didn't begrudge a man a short nap following his exertions. Nor did she begrudge herself a respite, and for that Julian loved her. She fell asleep in his arms, warm and naked, and gave him long moments to study her and to consider their situation.

Which was...challenging.

"You're awake," Elizabeth murmured, kissing his chest. "I could sleep for a week."

"Did this morning's walk to the village tire you?" He'd

wanted to buy her a hair ribbon, which was ridiculous. She doubtless had all the hair ribbons she needed, and Julian's purchase would have been observed and remarked.

"Being agreeable tires me," Elizabeth said. "I don't know how you do it."

"I tell myself that every minute I spend admiring Miss Penhathaway's sketching or Miss Trelawny's needlepoint is another minute closer to being with you."

Julian had also counted the minutes until Elizabeth would leave Haverford Castle—approximately fourteen thousand. Never before had fourteen thousand seemed like a paltry number.

Elizabeth sat up, and because she was straddling him, this put her feminine attributes on display.

"I want to discuss something with you, Haverford."

"I'm all ears." Not *all* ears. Not when she stretched like that.

"The merchants and shopkeepers in the village are bilking you at every opportunity."

Julian cupped her breasts, which were the most perfectly formed breasts in the history of breasts. "I'm a duke. That's what shopkeepers do with a duke."

"Be serious. You are paying at least twice if not three times what you'd pay in London for many goods. London is hardly a cheap market, Julian."

"I'm well aware of London prices." He was more aware of the brush of Elizabeth's sex over his cock.

"I love how you touch me." Elizabeth closed her hands around his, showing him how firmly she wanted to be caressed.

I love you. Loved her mind, her body, her heart. "I love how you can conduct a serious conversation even when I'm worshipping your breasts."

"I'm angry on your behalf." Elizabeth repositioned

herself along Julian's side, which meant wedging herself between him and the wall. "Just because you are a duke doesn't mean you should be cheated. You own that village, and those people should take pride in your custom."

"A fine notion, but a minority view." Julian did own the village, literally, and in theory he was owed rent for every dwelling, shed, and cow byre within its limits. "The overcharging started about five years ago. Soldiers who'd fought against Napoleon returned home to find there was no work, and then we had a spectacularly rotten harvest. Everybody had a bad harvest that year, and prices were understandably higher."

"So you carried them through and have been carrying them ever since."

"I'm the primary reason they don't have mines to work, Elizabeth, and most of them believe even a single productive mine would solve all their problems."

"Don't they have cousins and brothers who've seen what mining does to a farming region?"

Julian stroked Elizabeth's hair and battled resentment. This topic should not be allowed to contaminate their sanctuary, and they deserved, at least once, to make love in a damned bed.

Though Elizabeth had made the book room cozy. A different carpet covered the floor, a green and white pattern of fleur-de-lis intertwined with strawberry leaves and strawberries. A vase of fresh roses sat on the windowsill, and sheaves of lavender hung from the highest shelves and perfumed the air.

Given enough time, Elizabeth would have the entire castle put to rights, and she wouldn't spend a fortune doing it.

"Our mines would be different," Julian said. "Sherbourne has assured anybody who will listen that our mines would be different. Our waterways would remain clean, our skies would never see the blight caused by an ironworks, our families would never subsist in filthy hovels, and our children would never die of avoidable lung ailments when they ought to be learning their first Latin conjugation. I don't want to talk about this. Not here. Not now."

Not ever, but somebody had to speak the truth, and eventually—certainly not in Julian's lifetime—change would come.

"Without coal, we'd freeze," Elizabeth said.

Julian got off the chaise, which was hardly an ideal bed for two, much less for two intent on an argument.

"Do we need coal so badly we'll send five-year-olds to dig it for us? Make them work in the dark for sixteen hours at a time? Give them only a Sabbath to recover from their labors, pay them a pittance, ruin the land for farming so the mines become the only option?"

He pulled his shirt over his head, then stepped into his breeches. "I'm sorry, Elizabeth. My father, grandfather, and great-grandfather fought against the mines, not because coal is evil in itself, but because modern mining is as much a problem as a solution."

He took the chair behind the desk, his mood very much gone to hell. "Wages are inadequate," he went on, "while the owners and foremen get rich. The men in the ironworks go blind after a few years, because they can't tell if the ore is ready unless they look right into the blazing heart of the furnace. The owners don't care, the foremen don't care, because ten men are waiting for the next job at the works."

Elizabeth crossed the room, not a stitch on her, and climbed into his lap. "I'm sorry. I'm sorry I brought this up when we've better ways to spend our time."

The weight and warmth of her in Julian's arms were

comforting, but again, why were they cuddling in a creaky old chair instead of Julian's enormous bed?

"There is no good time to bring up the subject of mining with me. As much as I worry for my family's finances, I also worry for Britain. The common man deserves a dignified wage for his labor, and decent housing for his family."

"You mentioned that Griffin came to harm in an abandoned mineshaft," Elizabeth said.

"An exploratory shaft sunk by the Sherbournes near our property line." Though what had that to do with anything? "You'll take a chill sporting about in the altogether, madam."

"You'll keep me warm."

For the next fourteen-thousand-odd minutes, Julian would try to keep Elizabeth happy. He rose with her in his arms, and sat on the chaise, his back propped against the wall.

"You're worried," Elizabeth said, tugging the blanket up around his shoulders.

"I'm a duke. Worry comes with the job. Sleep now."

"What do you suppose Sherbourne worries about?" Elizabeth murmured. "Surely he must worry about something, or he'd not invite himself to house parties, or bother to turn an entire village against you."

More than a village. Half the merchants in Swansea, and a few of Julian's peers in the Lords, though Sherbourne was not solely responsible for that.

Julian's watch lay on the desk across the room, and the dratted thing always lost time when it lay flat.

Maybe that was a good thing, when only fourteen thousand minutes remained before Elizabeth would leave. Julian kissed the top of her head, her question refusing to remain rhetorical. What *did* Sherbourne worry about?

The answer floated by just out of reach as sleep claimed

Julian's awareness. Regardless of what bothered Sherbourne, the presuming varlet had the coin to resolve his annoyances, while Julian had virtually no coin at all.

* * *

"They're gone," Benedict Andover said, peering over the railing of the library balcony. "Young people and their foolishness."

"Their stamina, you mean," Arabella replied. "We were young once too, Benny." And they weren't *that* old now.

"We weren't as foolish as Haldale and that Trelawny girl. Her mother ought to know better."

"Her mother's trying to fire her off before the expense of another season, and Haldale must marry somebody. Shall I read to you some more?"

Andover took the seat beside Arabella on a comfortably worn sofa. He'd shown her this refuge on the second day of the house party. The sheer number of books in the room was so impressive, that other details—like a cozy reading balcony, or two-hundred-year-old family Bible—went unnoticed.

"I love how you make a story come to life," he said. "You have thespian talent."

"Every parent learns to read a good yarn, or they should. What am I to do about my nieces, Benny? Charlotte has ignored the overtures of half the young men on the premises, and Elizabeth has attached the affections of the only unsuitable duke in the realm."

Andover patted her hand. "When a duke is young, handsome, in possession of a castle, and managing one of the finest private libraries ever assembled, he can't be unsuitable."

Oh, yes he could. "Is the collection fine, Benny, or

simply enormous? Any ambitious commoner can buy books by the cartload for the sake of appearances."

"This collection..." Andover stood and went to the railing, a captain admiring the view from his quarterdeck. "The late duke was a genius at acquisition. Julian's father heard about all the best sales and got the best bargains—I was endlessly jealous and lived for the days when I could outbid him at the auctions. He knew exactly which volumes would appreciate in value, though he'd never part with a book once he'd acquired it. He claimed the library was his legacy to future dukes."

The library was also a deuced lot of dusting for overworked footmen. "So the books are valuable?" Why hadn't Haverford mentioned that?

Andover turned, back to the railing. But for the thinning of his hair, his looks hadn't changed much over the years, and he made a fine, distinguished picture amid the library's vast treasures.

"The books are valuable, Bella, and they're not. In the entire realm, perhaps a half-dozen people are qualified to evaluate this collection. They could put any price they pleased on the books—Haverford has rare antiquities by the hundreds—but then, where does one find buyers? The bibliophile is usually an impecunious beast, frittering away his coin tome by tome."

While the late duke had hoarded his treasures. "Does Haverford know what this library is worth?" He'd spoken as if he hadn't a feather to fly with, the daft boy.

"Likely not, and it doesn't really matter. If Julian so much as hinted that he wanted an appraisal, the gossip would start. I'm sure his solicitors have warned him sternly not to open that Pandora's box. If Haverford attempted to liquidate the library, the dukedom would be bankrupted by unkind speculation before the creditors even arrived on his doorstep."

"And they would take the books?"

"Probably loot the castle like a horde of rioting pirates. Haverford might be able to sell off a portion of his library discreetly, if he'd allow me to alert a few wealthy buyers. I suspect he knows that."

Arabella suspected he did not. "Have a word with him, Benny. Offer to dispose of the more valuable titles that can't be traced directly to this collection. See what he says."

Andover returned to the sofa, sitting right at Arabella's side. "He'll offer me a choice of pistols or swords, my dear. The boy is frightfully proud, and I'm a guest under his roof. I can't very well intimate he's in need of coin, can I?"

"You men and your delicate sensibilities. Tell me about the brother." Lord Griffin was a problem, a vulnerability. Ducal families could not afford—literally—too many vulnerabilities.

"A fine lad, if you ask me. Not in the common way, but good-hearted and hard-working. I've known him since he was in dresses, and we have an appointment to go fishing tomorrow. Perhaps you'd like to join us?"

Arabella's first impulse was to reply with a scoff and a sniffy, "I'm too old to go mucking about after trout." But for the past two weeks, her joints had ached less, she'd laughed more, and she'd had somebody with whom to reminisce and socialize.

Benjamin Andover was good for her. Peter had always enjoyed Andover's company, and even in old age, Andover was a more vigorous specimen than Peter had been for much of his adult life.

Which was unfair and mattered not at all.

"I could bring a book and do some reading." Why wasn't Elizabeth a fixture among Haverford's French novels?

"Griffin can fish with nothing more than a net," Andover said, "but I'm too slow. He throws them all back, as if fishing were a game between him and the trout. I'll idle along the bank, enjoying a pretty day with a pretty lady."

"You needn't flirt with me, sir." Though Arabella liked that he did. He had a light, warm touch with a compliment or a tease.

He rose—no creaky limbs or awkward pushing and scooting for him. "Bella, would you think me a pathetic old hound if I asked to pay you my addresses? I would never try to compete with Peter's memory, but you and I rub along together well, and I'm lonely. I mostly ignore the loneliness, but then you stepped down from your coach, and I've asked myself: Why ignore it? Why not *do* something about it?"

Old people could be so blunt. "If that's your idea of a proposal, your technique is in want of polish."

"If that's your answer, I'll apologize for presuming. Your friendship is precious to me, Bella."

He could apologize without imperiling anybody's dignity, a skill only a mature man could command.

"The problem is my nieces," Arabella replied. "I know how they think: If Aunt Arabella can manage so handily without a husband, surely spinsterhood can't be that terrible a fate. With the younger two married off, Charlotte and Elizabeth have formed some sort of pact: They will remain unmarried, and eventually keep house together. It's noble and entirely wrong."

"Not every woman is bound for a husband and children, Bella. Neither of my sisters married, and they're a jolly pair."

Arabella loved his sisters. She also loved her nieces. "Charlotte and Elizabeth are lonely too, Benny. They are Windhams, and thus they are surrounded by marital bliss on every hand. Tony and Gladys are shockingly besotted, and Percival and Esther..."

"Moreland's devotion to his duchess is a reproach to every peer who ever strayed." Andover picked up the novel Arabella had been reading—*Candide*—and ran a finger down the page. "Are you determined to see your nieces married?"

"Not determined, but willing to aid the cause of true love when I can. Elizabeth disappears for at least two hours every afternoon, and she's not resting in her bedroom. By odd coincidence, Haverford is nowhere to be seen during those same two hours. If I can get Elizabeth matched, then Charlotte is more likely to admit she's curious about Mr. Sherbourne."

He closed the book. "There's enmity between Haverford and Sherbourne. Bad blood that goes back to our day. I don't think His Grace is in a position to offer for anybody and certainly not for the niece of a duke."

"Young people can be so foolish." So could old people—old women unwilling to admit they had sacrificed enough years out of loyalty to a departed husband. Peter's dying wish had been that Arabella be happy, that she not wear weeds for the rest of her life and bury her heart next to her spouse.

"I suspect the young ladies aren't aware of all the facts, Bella, but back to the matter at hand. Shall I court you?"

There was more than one way to be a good example to a pair of headstrong nieces. "I believe you shall, and to the extent you are able, you will do what you can to make a path to the altar for Elizabeth and her impoverished duke."

"From what I hear, the bulk of Haverford's debt is to Sherbourne, courtesy of His Grace's late father. Marriage for His Grace to a woman of Elizabeth's standing is thus all but impossible."

"Not impossible, Benny. Improbable, certainly, and yet

I have faith in true love. Miracles can befall us when we least expect them. Witness, I'm inviting you to court me."

* * *

"You were wise to schedule the grand ball for Friday evening," Elizabeth said. "Your guests will have two days to recover before they set out for home."

She was making small talk, because Haverford was silent. He grew quiet when he worried, and for the past few days, he'd been very quiet.

Also very passionate.

As Elizabeth walked along beside him, she admitted to being a fool. Haverford had been nothing but honest with her—he could not afford a ducal bride—and yet, she had started to hope. The ball was tomorrow. The following day would be for resting and packing. Sunday services would mean another morning in the village, and then Monday, the coaches would depart.

"I wrote to your uncle," Haverford said, offering Elizabeth his hand as they came to a stile that separated Lord Griffin's pastures from his barnyard. The duke assisted her over, took two steps back, then vaulted the boards in a single, clean stride.

"You wrote to Uncle Percival?" Hope fluttered anew, cautious and uncomfortable. "What did you write about?"

"Books. The perishing damned books."

Chickens strutted underfoot, pecking at the dirt. A brindle heifer curled in the grass chewing her cud, and a mastiff trotted out of the barn, tail held high and waving slowly.

For once in her life, Elizabeth did not care at all about books, perishing or otherwise. "Any particular perishing damned books, Haverford?"

"My books. The books that have nearly bankrupted my family."

"I gather Moreland has not replied?" Uncle Percival was nothing if not responsive to correspondence.

"I told him I would give every book I owned for permission to court you, and I own more books than all the rest of the dukes in the realm put together."

Hope crashed against consternation. Haverford had asked for permission to court her—more or less—and Uncle Percy had not replied. He was doubtless conferring with Mama and Papa, gathering intelligence, and consulting with Aunt Esther.

Or he was on his way to Wales, ready to create a scene that would make Allermain's attempted kidnapping a farce? Or perhaps, Haverford's epistle had been too delicately worded, too conditional?

"Where is my brother?" Haverford asked, gazing about the tidy farmyard.

Griffin's cottage—more of a fieldstone manor house—sat some forty yards away, up a gentle slope. The drive was lined with venerable oaks leafed out in mid-summer glory, and the front steps held pots of red salvia.

"I expect your brother is inside waiting for his callers because we're a bit early. You did send a card? I'm told Biddy Bowen's shortbread is not to be missed."

That earned her half a smile. "Griffin told you that a dozen times if he told you once, and yes, I sent a card."

"Julian, you needn't worry."

He was attired for a call among country neighbors, but very much the duke today. Top hat brushed, cravat in a fancy knot, a carved walking stick in his hand. Setting an example for his brother, no doubt.

As always.

"Worry? About this call?"

"About Uncle Percy. He's mostly bluster, and can be both discreet and discerning where his family is concerned. Aunt Arabella doubtless wrote to Aunt Esther, and they will ensure that Uncle's reply is civil."

Elizabeth didn't particularly care how Uncle Percy replied. Julian had expressed a wish to court her. She was happy to be courted, she'd be happier to become his duchess.

The chickens made those odd little contented poultry noises, the dog sat by Elizabeth's side. Haverford took off his hat, ran his hand through his hair, and finally, finally looked at her.

"I also informed Moreland that my means are worse than embarrassed, and you don't seem bothered by my relative penury."

"You told him that?"

"In so many words. Was I correct, Elizabeth?"

A couple emerged from the barn, holding hands and laughing. They were entirely absorbed with each other. The man gathered the lady close, pressed her up against the wall of the barn, and kissed her madly.

She wrapped one arm about him—the other held a basket of brown and white eggs—and kissed him back with equal fervor.

The gentleman pulled away enough to shout in perfect English, "I love you, Biddy Bowen!" before resuming his enthusiasms.

"Oh, dear," Elizabeth murmured, just as Haverford bellowed, "What the hell is going on here?"

The duke stalked over to the couple, who continued to hold hands. Lord Griffin was the fellow, and the lady—clearly—was Biddy Bowen, baker of the world's best shortbread.

And keeper of his lordship's heart.

Lord Griffin reached around to take the egg basket from Biddy. "Good day, Julian." He bowed stiffly. "You are supposed to bow to Biddy."

The duke offered the lady—who was blushing bright pink—the merest hint of a courtesy. "Miss Biddy, good day. Unhand my brother."

Griffin and Biddy kept hold of each other.

Haverford had never displayed an ungovernable temper before Elizabeth, not when Sherbourne had invited himself to the party, not when Lady Glenys had run up extravagant bills, not when admitting the local merchants overcharged him.

And he wasn't displaying a temper now. He was upset, though, probably with himself for not having seen this situation developing.

"Good morning," Elizabeth said, joining the other three. "Griffin, a pleasure to see you." She made him a proper curtsy. "Won't you introduce me to your friend?"

"Miss Elizabeth." Griffin bowed far more correctly than Haverford had bowed to Biddy. "Good day. May I make known to you Miss Biddy Bowen. Biddy, this is Miss Elizabeth. She teaches me English, and I teach her birds and flowers."

"Shall we go into the house?" Elizabeth suggested, twining her arm with Haverford's. "I hear Miss Biddy's shortbread is the best in the world."

The brothers were glowering at each other, as brothers tended to. In other species, the same sentiments were accompanied by pawing, snorting, and much swishing of tails.

"Griffin favors my shortbread," Biddy said. "My real name's Bridget."

"That is a lovely name." Elizabeth gave Haverford's arm a discreet tug. "I adore fresh, warm shortbread."

Biddy dropped Griffin's hand and took his arm. "Griffin helps me make it, though he steals half the batch before it's in the oven."

Haverford yielded to Elizabeth's silent suggestion and escorted her up the path to the house. The dog and a half-dozen chickens followed, strutting and clucking.

"Did you receive His Grace's card, Griffin?" Elizabeth asked.

"Yes. Julian said he would call at ten of the clock, and it's not ten of the clock yet."

"We took a shortcut," Elizabeth replied. "The pastures are so pretty this time of year, and the lanes are dusty. This is King Henry, isn't it?"

"Yes."

Haverford was concerned, while Griffin was furious and hurt. He'd been kissing a pretty lady, shouting his devotion to the heavens, and Haverford had come on the scene like the wrath of Moses.

The gentlemen bowed the ladies through the front door, and then greater awkwardness ensued, for no servant came to fetch the egg basket.

Biddy was the servant.

"Let's take the eggs to the kitchen," Elizabeth suggested. "I'll help prepare the tea. Haverford, you might entertain Griffin with tales of yesterday's scavenger hunt. Miss Biddy and I won't be but a moment."

"I don't like hunting," Griffin muttered.

"It's not that sort of hunt," Haverford said. "It's more of a treasure hunt."

"We don't have any treasure," Griffin replied, some of his truculence fading.

"You have each other," Elizabeth said, sending Haverford an admonitory glance. "Come, Biddy, and perhaps we'll steal a bite of shortbread before the gentlemen have a chance."

"I should take your hat and coat, Julian," Griffin observed, passing Biddy the egg basket. "And your walking stick. That is Grandpapa's walking stick, isn't it?"

"The very one." Julian handed it over, and Elizabeth took the moment to retreat with Biddy to the back of the house.

The premises were spotless, commodious, and decorated with the occasional bundle of dried herbs or fresh flowers.

"You keep this house?" Elizabeth asked.

Biddy set the eggs on a sturdy wooden table in the kitchen. "I do for Abner and Griffin. You needn't pretend, ma'am. I'll not be doing for them now that His Grace caught Griffin kissing me."

She collapsed onto a stool and stared at her basket of eggs. Biddy wasn't a great beauty. Her hands were red and roughened, she had freckles across her cheeks, and her apron bore a suspicious streak of brown near the hem.

"You love him," Elizabeth said.

"With all my heart. Griffin isn't quick like a lord is supposed to be, but he's smart in his own way, and he's as good-hearted as they come. I should not have let him kiss me, though what's the harm in a few kisses? We forgot to wash the eggs. That will bother Griffin."

"Would he be faithful to you, Biddy?"

"Yes. There was that business with that woman, all those years ago, but Griffin understands what's what. He has only the one child, and misses her terribly. He'd be a good papa, if anybody would give him the chance. Family shouldn't be kept apart."

A tea tray sat ready on the table, two plates of shortbread stacked three layers high. Elizabeth offered Biddy one of the plates.

"Ma'am, I couldn't."

Elizabeth passed Biddy the topmost slice. "Yes, you could. They are merely brothers having a disagreement. Haverford doesn't deal well with surprises, and he's had rather too many of them lately. Take off your apron, wash your hands, and we'll show them how a pair of adults behave on a social call."

Elizabeth sounded very like Aunt Esther, which was probably why Biddy complied. She smoothed a nervous hand over her hair, and would have taken the tray, except Elizabeth lifted it first.

"If you'd hold the door?"

"You love Haverford, don't you?" Biddy asked.

"Madly." And how wonderful, to be able to say that.

"Good. He needs somebody to love him madly and take his mind off his troubles. Griffin worries for him so."

"Brothers do that too."

Biddy presided over the tea tray, saying little, perching on the very, very edge of her chair. Elizabeth coaxed Griffin into telling her about his hens, each of whom had a name, personality, and preferred place to leave her eggs.

The St. David menfolk were an attentive and mannerly pair. The visit passed without either brother erupting into a temper, though Elizabeth could feel Haverford's consternation boiling up inside him. He and Elizabeth took their leave, and like a conscientious host, Griffin escorted them to the door.

"I want to marry Biddy, Julian. I love her and she loves me too."

"Love is precious," Elizabeth said, "but a decision to marry mustn't be undertaken lightly. Perhaps after the house party, you and His Grace might discuss the situation further."

Griffin passed Haverford his hat. "I could get a mortgage. For the settlements. For Biddy." He pronounced the word mortgage carefully, using the English term.

"A mortgage?" Haverford said slowly, as if Griffin had offered to contract a wasting disease. "Who explained mortgages to you?"

Griffin studied the head of the duke's walking stick. "A friend explained it to me. I could sell some of my acres instead. I have hundreds of acres, all mine."

Elizabeth heard a sound that might have been Haverford's molars grinding.

"Griffin, please don't sign any mortgages or sell your acres until we've had a chance to speak further," Haverford said. "After the house party, we can discuss the nuptials as much as you please, but I'd ask you not to make any decisions until then."

"Biddy said mortgages are bad."

"And Biddy," Haverford said, "is a woman of great good sense. Witness her devotion to you. You will please keep Grandpapa's walking stick."

The walking stick had been carved into the shape of a dragon, with an intricately scaled tail winding down its length.

"You want me to have Grandpapa's walking stick?"

"You are out tramping around far more than I am, and I've had it long enough."

Griffin held up the walking stick, grinning at the dragon, who appeared to smile back at him. "Thank you, Julian."

Elizabeth remained silent, as did Haverford. He was quivering to lecture, advise, exhort, and be the duke—she could feel that too—but he said nothing.

"We can talk about mortgages after your guests have left," Griffin said. "I won't sign anything or make any promises. Biddy said I have to be careful about promises too. I want to marry her, Julian. I love Biddy Bowen."

Griffin's smile was beatific.

"I love you," Haverford said, kissing his brother's cheek. "My thanks for your hospitality. Miss Windham, shall we be on our way?"

Heavenly days, she was proud of them both. "Of course, Your Grace. Griffin." She curtsied, he bowed, and before the door had closed behind them, Griffin was bellowing to Biddy about his grandfather's walking stick.

"I shall curse now," Haverford said. "I shall curse and rant and behave most unbecomingly."

"Good," Elizabeth replied, taking his hand. "You're entirely allowed, once we get past the barnyard."

When they had cleared the stile and gained the footpath behind the hedgerow, Haverford did not curse or rant, or even carry on unbecomingly. He took Elizabeth in his arms, kissed her passionately, and then gathered her close, all without shouting anything at all.

Chapter Nineteen

I love you, Elizabeth Windham.

Julian kept a grip on Elizabeth's hand when he wanted instead to wrap himself around her and hold her as the seasons changed and the years marched past. He'd awoken from a nap the previous day, and she'd been sitting at the desk in the tower room, wearing only his shirt and his spectacles, stitching down a loose thread on his favorite waistcoat.

He loved her, for letting a tired man sleep, for looking after a possession he treasured, for wearing his shirt.

The previous evening at cards, Elizabeth had discreetly distracted Haldale from leering down Miss Trelawny's bodice. Julian would have planted the varlet a facer, thus embarrassing the young lady, the guests, the servants, and himself.

And just now, when Julian had been on the point of remonstrating with his brother before the ladies, Elizabeth had taken the situation—and Julian—in hand, and saved the fraternal relationship from a very bad moment.

She'd accomplished all of this with nothing more than pleasantries and good manners.

"The qualities you think make you uninteresting to others," he said, "are why I love you."

Two plump red hens were perched on the top of the stile, Princess and Louise, a pair of feathered dowagers. The scent of the barnyard wafted on the breeze, and King Henry was trotting down the lane, tongue lolling.

Could there be a less auspicious setting for a romantic declaration?

Elizabeth peered up at him. "I beg your pardon?"

"I love you, Elizabeth Windham, and if saying so makes me a scoundrel, when I've little material security to offer you, I'm sorry. Nonetheless, without some indication from Moreland that our match would be acceptable, I must insist that on Monday, you get into your carriage and return to England. I didn't want to send you home without expressing my sentiments to you."

"You love me, so you're sending me packing?"

His sincere, heartfelt admission was meeting with less than warm approval. "I do love you. You have a quiet competence, a pragmatism that balances a kind heart with common sense. You don't expect cosseting, and thus cosseting you is that much more a privilege. You never call attention to yourself, and yet, you fascinate me. You're protective of your family, and with Griffin…I am in your debt, Elizabeth. All other matters between us aside, I am in your debt for this visit with Griffin."

"You are an idiot, but we'll get to that in a moment. You needn't worry so about Griffin. Others love him nearly as much as you do."

Julian looped his arms over her shoulders and held her loosely. The impulse wasn't sexual, wasn't even particularly affectionate. He felt calmer holding her, and being held by her.

"I did not foresee this development," he said. "Marriage was not in my plans for Griffin, much less marriage to his housekeeper. My first thought was that if my brother marries, there will be a dozen more mouths to feed."

"You are ashamed of yourself for thinking that?"

"I am. Biddy cares for him. I should have seen that long ago. She loves him as he is, not because he's a duke's son. He names his hens, helps in the kitchen, and looks after Abner when the old boy has been at the ale. I assumed my brother's progeny will be my responsibility, when, without my noticing it, Griffin has found a life that works without my meddling."

"You will meddle some. He's family, after all."

If you were my duchess . . . "I will meddle as little as possible, but I'll worry a great deal. I will worry about you as well, Elizabeth."

"And worry you should." She wiggled free and marched off down the path. "My family will dispatch me to some other house party, where—one supposes—the dukes will have more coin. I have enough money that my dotage will not be impoverished, you foolish man. Why must you be so proud?"

Julian followed more slowly, in no hurry to return to his castle. "Not proud, Elizabeth, honorable. That is your money, and I daresay you will need every penny of it should your husband predecease you." Arguing with Elizabeth was a waste of their dwindling supply of minutes, but she needed to know the facts. "I owe more than twenty thousand pounds to Sherbourne alone, and my best efforts barely keep up with the interest. A bad harvest, a soft market for wool, foot rot in the herds...I'm hanging on by a few threads, Elizabeth."

She came to a halt. "Twenty...*twenty thousand*, to Sherbourne alone? How did that happen?"

The same question Julian had asked the first time the family solicitors had reviewed the ledgers with him.

Now, he knew the answer. One illuminated manuscript, one auction, one Shakespeare folio at a time, the edifice that had been the wealthy Haverford dukedom had crumbled, leaving nothing but a pauper's extravagant library in its place.

"My father made poor investments, and Sherbourne's father lent money. I suspect that Sherbourne senior also handed out bad investment advice on purpose, but I can't blame him for the fact that my parents never once practiced economies."

"Oh, Julian."

They stood on the path, two yards and twenty thousand pounds separating them.

"If I don't pay regular wages, Elizabeth, my staff will leave and the castle will fall to ruins. If I can't make improvements, I won't have tenants for my farms. I refuse to shackle the people I'm supposed to care about—my wife, my siblings, my offspring, my tenants, and employees—with my failure to bring the finances right."

"And you refuse to give up."

"I also refuse to take your money when it's the only security you have."

"But with trusts, and my family to oversee my portion, that money would be secure."

He closed the distance between them. "Sherbourne is determined, and if he chose to accelerate my debts, he could bring lawsuits that entangled your funds in my problems."

Elizabeth began walking, more slowly, her head down as if a strong wind thwarted her progress. "We have laws. He can't just snap his fingers and call in an entire sum, can he?"

"In this case, he can. My father signed promissory notes, then failed to pay installments when due, and that means I'm making payments at Sherbourne's sufferance."

The day was so achingly pretty that to discuss debts and duties was a form of blasphemy, but at least Elizabeth wouldn't return to England thinking Julian had rejected her out of pride.

"So why doesn't Sherbourne ruin you?" she asked. "He can destroy you, and yet he doesn't. Why not?"

A question that had been robbing Julian of much sleep lately. "Do you understand the concept of interest?"

"The longer the principle is unpaid, the more expensive the debt becomes for the borrower. Sherbourne enjoys watching you struggle."

"Or he thinks I'll approve a match between him and Glenys if he stays his hand financially."

They came to a rill that separated two hay fields. Julian stepped across, then swung Elizabeth over the water. She stayed where she landed, watching the water trickle over the rocks.

"You're not about to approve a match between Lady Glenys and Sherbourne," she said. "She and Radnor are trying to be discreet, but I saw them in the orangery earlier this week. I suspect you'll have a brother-in-law very soon, and become an uncle by this time next year."

"Which means nothing will stop Sherbourne from toppling me into ruin once Glenys and Radnor announce their engagement."

"I could give you every penny of my settlements and it wouldn't make a difference, would it?"

"No difference at all."

Elizabeth slipped her arms around him. The water burbled merrily on toward the sea and a harrier circled lazily overhead, while Julian asked himself again: Was there anything Sherbourne could possibly want as much as Julian wanted to spend the rest of his life with Elizabeth Windham?

* * *

"Can you ladies spare me a moment?" Haverford asked, overtaking Elizabeth and Charlotte in the corridor. "The household is at sixes and sevens in preparation for the ball, and I need trustworthy assistance."

His Grace was not yet in evening attire, and Elizabeth was to blame. He'd tarried with her in the tower that afternoon, saying silent, passionate good-byes that had heaped heartache on top of pleasure in an excruciatingly precious intimacy.

"I'm always available to lend trustworthy assistance to my favorite Welsh duke." For the rest of her life, Elizabeth would like to be available to Haverford, to lend assistance, affection, laughter, friendship, and so much more.

"I can help too," Charlotte added. "Though if you need me to carry you to your quarters because of a bilious stomach, I might enlist several footmen as well."

Charlotte could not wait to leave on Monday, while Elizabeth dreaded the trip down the drive. She'd promised Griffin a farewell visit before their departure, and he had promised to write to her.

Elizabeth had promised Haverford nothing, and he'd returned the courtesy.

"Where are you taking us?" Elizabeth asked.

"To the strong room," Haverford said, opening yet another paneled door. "This being a proper castle, all the interesting parts—the siege well, the kitchens, the wine cellars, for example—are belowstairs."

This stairwell wasn't as dusty as some Elizabeth had traversed at Haverford, but neither did it have an air of frequent use.

"I would love to make a map of this castle," Charlotte said. "It's like a pocket watch, but on a grand scale."

"A very old pocket watch." Haverford held open a door of thick planks secured with iron bands. "After you, ladies."

The air was redolent with cooking scents. Onions, garlic, meat, fresh bread and subtler hints—oregano, thyme, and basil.

"It's warm," Charlotte said. "I wasn't expecting warmth one floor above the cellars."

"The kitchens are on the opposite side of this wall, which is part of the reason the strong room is here. Doesn't do for the family treasures to be ruined by the damp. You are sworn to secrecy, of course."

He wasn't joking. "Of course," Elizabeth said, elbowing Charlotte into concurring.

The duke produced a key very like the one that opened the tower room, and another heavy door creaked open on substantial iron hinges. He lifted a lamp from a sconce and held it high before hanging it from a hook on a rafter.

"Behold, the St. David family vault, such as it is. An eternal resting place for a lot of musty old words."

The room was small, square, and had the utter quiet of a space enclosed in very thick walls. A clothespress, or something like it, sat along one wall, and oak cabinets fitted with stout locks stood on the facing side of the chamber.

"This feels like a confessional," Charlotte said. "I wouldn't like to be locked in here."

"I'd find you," Haverford replied. "I stop by here at least once a day, and when I'm in London, my butler has that office."

"The day would be very long, dark, and quiet until you happened along," Charlotte said. "What's this?"

Haverford didn't answer immediately. He was sorting through a ring of keys taken from a drawer in the clothes-press.

Elizabeth crossed the room to join Charlotte before a framed glass nearly a yard square.

In the dim light, she could see only that the frame held a single large document, one covered in dense, black script, with a dark reddish blob of something that might once have been wax suspended from the bottom.

"That is a 1297 version of the Magna Carta Liberta-tum," Haverford said, opening one of the cabinets. "The text is abbreviated medieval law Latin, which was a crush-ing disappointment to me when I first saw it as a boy. I expected something legibly Shakespearean. I mastered the law Latin eventually, because there's a deal of it to study on the premises."

He withdrew a velvet pouch from the cabinet, took a flat wooden box from within, and opened it. "Haven't seen these for quite a while."

The little box held a parure, diamonds and emeralds, but Elizabeth could barely spare the jewels a glance.

"You have a five-hundred-year-old copy of one of the world's most significant documents, and you were *disap-pointed* in it?"

"These are very pretty," Charlotte said, peering more closely at the jewels. "Don't you agree, Elizabeth?"

"Julian? The Magna Carta?"

"One of the later versions," he said, passing Charlotte the jewelry box. "That chest is full of such documents. In more tumultuous times, both the Crown and its detractors used Haverford as a document repository, and the St. Davids were happy to oblige because that responsibility reinforced our position as statesmen. The times are no longer so fraught, and we thus have a lot of parchment and vellum nobody cares about anymore."

"Did you intend for these jewels to go to Lady Glenys?" Charlotte asked.

"I did. If you wouldn't mind delivering them, I'd appreciate it. I don't dare go near my sister with the ball beginning in less than three hours."

Charlotte took one more peek at the jewels, shut the box with a firm snap, and scurried from the room.

"I know what you're thinking," Haverford said as Charlotte's footsteps faded. "I am a barbarian for not venerating a lot of old documents. I respect what they symbolize, Elizabeth, but they've become one more responsibility. I'd give them to you, except they do require some care and transporting them would incur significant cost."

Elizabeth wrapped her arms around him. "You would give me your family's legacy?"

"There's a catalogue in one of those drawers," he said, gathering her close. "It explains which document is a treaty, which is a charter, which is a royal letter. A royal pardon or two hides among the lot, some marriage lines. Not as exciting as your Milton, whom you should take with you. Take any of the books that catch your fancy with you."

Was Julian ruling in hell, managing debts and responsibilities he'd done nothing to create, or serving in heaven by protecting a legacy he couldn't value personally?

"Are there illuminated manuscripts in this room?"

"Seven, which enjoy the top drawers. As a boy, I liked those because of the artwork, and the glosses. The monks were a humorous lot, writing poetry to their cats and their alewives."

He was making small talk about long-dead monks, offering Elizabeth his treasures, and saying good-bye. Elizabeth wiped a tear from her cheek, which had nothing to do with being in the presence of great documents.

"I thought I could dally, Julian. I'll never dally again. I don't want to leave you."

"Don't say that. Don't—Elizabeth, please don't cry." His thumb brushing across her cheek could not have been more gentle.

"Have you heard from Moreland?"

The slight pause in his breathing, the shift in his posture answered Elizabeth's question.

"What did he say? Uncle Percy can be quite colorful."

Uncle Percy could be utterly pigheaded too. Aunt Esther referred to him as a man of principle. Mama called Uncle Percy set in his ways. Papa referred to his brother as stubborn.

Julian withdrew a note from an inner pocket of his coat. "You should read it. I'm not sure what to make of it, though his disapproval of my request is clear."

Elizabeth took the note over to the light.

Haverford,

While I commend your taste in prospective duchesses, I must remind you: Woman does not live

by books alone. I would disapprove a match for Elizabeth with any man facing insolvency. Attend to
your finances before presuming to woo the fair maid.

Moreland

   PS: My duchess will ruin you *utterly*, et cetera
and so forth.
   PPS: Best of luck.

"This is a maybe, Julian, not a no. He doesn't mention
dueling pistols."

"It's a polite no," Haverford said, taking the note back
and tucking it away. "If you were my niece, I'd have written the same note to a bachelor without means who risked
dragging you into penury. Of all people, a duke knows how
truly useless a title is."

"But it's a maybe," Elizabeth insisted. "It's a conditional yes."

They argued the point by virtue of a kiss, with Haverford offering gentle parting in every caress, and Elizabeth
countering with fierce, stubborn, pigheaded determination.

"Will you save me a dance?" he asked when Elizabeth
left off lecturing him lip-to-lip.

"I will save you all my dances."

"I'd like the good-night waltz," he said. "Thank God the
moon is setting at three, and the ball will break up early as
a result. I'm announcing Glenys and Radnor's engagement
at the supper break."

Announcing his own doom, then, if his theories about
Sherbourne were accurate. "I'll toast their happiness."

Elizabeth stayed in Haverford's arms for long moments,
fortifying herself against the ordeal of the next three days.
By this time on Monday, she'd be many miles away,

trapped in a coach with Aunt Arabella and Charlotte, facing disappointment at home, and more house parties before winter set in.

The document on the wall glinted at her through the glass, a legacy and a millstone. As best she could recall, the whole Runnymede business would have faded into obscurity had not the divine right of kings become an issue with the Stuart line.

Kings did not rule by virtue of a grant from above, that document said, but by a grant from the governed. The notion had a radical air still, suggesting the bargain struck between the crown and the barons was very much a work in progress.

"What would Sherbourne pay for that document?" Elizabeth asked.

"Not a penny," Haverford replied. "He professes himself a student of progress, rather than a slave to the past."

Well, damn. "He's a heathen. It's unfair that he prospers while you face ruin."

Haverford locked the jewel cabinet and opened the door to the corridor. When Elizabeth exited the little room, he retrieved the lamp and locked the vault.

"I face ruin," he said, "but not dishonor. I doubt Sherbourne understands the difference, while to me, it means everything."

Elizabeth loved that about Haverford, loved his fundamental dignity and decency. She would have loved just as much to have found twenty thousand pounds in his vault in place of a lot of dusty old documents and noble sentiments.

Chapter Twenty

Julian opened the dancing with his sister, the highest-ranking lady among all those assembled. Glenys sparkled literally and figuratively, probably happier than anybody to have the final grand entertainment of the house party started. Radnor plucked her from Julian's side before the last strains of the music faded.

Which was as it should be.

"I must admit, Haverford, you have put on an impressive display." Sherbourne sipped a glass of punch and surveyed the dancers assembling for the next set.

"My thanks. I hope you're enjoying yourself." Julian also hoped Sherbourne spilled punch all over his fancy gold and blue waistcoat.

"Must you be so gracious? I've had my arrows literally knocked from the sky, been tittered at, stepped on, condescended to, propositioned, and lectured. Then Haldale made a clumsy attempt to cheat me at whist."

"Poor lad. I assume Lady Pembroke did the lecturing?" Julian did not want to know who had done the propositioning, though how ironic—Sherbourne's list of tribulations somewhat mirrored his own.

"Lady Pembroke exhorted me at length, abetted by the estimable Miss Charlotte."

Charlotte Windham *was* estimable. Julian was about to make that very point when Radnor and Glenys took their positions on the dance floor. Radnor was trying to manufacture a semblance of lordly dignity and failing in all particulars. No couple had ever been more obviously besotted, save for Griffin and Biddy.

"I'll be making an announcement at the supper break, Sherbourne."

"Do tell. You're offering for the elder of the Windhams?"

Must he sound so diffident? The introduction to the dance started, giving Julian a moment to marshal his manners. Glenys had wanted a twelve-piece orchestra, but had settled for a string quartet and pianoforte. The musicians, like the fellow who had chalked a dragon onto the ballroom floor, had demanded to be paid in advance.

Some helpful neighbor had clearly started the rumors of insolvency already. "I cannot afford to offer for Miss Windham, and well you know it."

Sherbourne lifted his wine glass a few inches in Julian's direction. "Poor lad."

Insolent wretch. "Lord Radnor has offered for Lady Glenys. I've given my approval of the match."

Sherbourne sipped his punch in silence, studying one dancer in particular. Charlotte Windham had stood up with Sir Nigel, who was apparently in conversation with the lady's bosom, if his gaze was any indication.

"You might have waited until the house party was concluded, Haverford. I was considering offering for Lady Glenys, and well you know it. Bad form, Your Grace."

"Lady Glenys would not have accepted your suit." Not once Radnor had entered the lists in earnest.

"We'll never know what she might have done, given the settlements I had in mind."

The music started, the dancers moved off, and Radnor held Glenys a shade too closely—or Glenys held Radnor too closely.

"Was my sister's happiness to be a hostage to your vanity?" Julian inquired pleasantly. "Is that your notion of gentlemanly honor?"

Charlotte and Sir Nigel twirled past them. The lady's smile had taken on a lupine quality.

"I will now demonstrate my notion of gentlemanly honor," Sherbourne said, "and change the subject. I have at last developed an understanding of why your sort is perpetually waving their dueling pistols about."

That was a gentlemanly change of subject? Julian couldn't challenge Sherbourne—the man wasn't titled—then he realized Sherbourne was watching Sir Nigel leer at Miss Charlotte.

"She'll put him in his place in about eight measures, if I'm not—"

Miss Charlotte lost her footing, such that her heel came down hard on Sir Nigel's instep. In the process of gaining her footing, she somehow managed to lift her knee in a most unfortunate direction.

"One cannot applaud overtly," Julian said, "but a gracious smirk upon next encountering Sir Nigel would be permissible."

"Ah, gracious, just so. My thanks for your instruction,

as always. Has Lady Glenys set a date for the nuptials?"
Sherbourne's tone was exquisitely bored.

"Not that they've told me."

"And the wedding will be small, family only, no doubt."

"The details have yet to be decided." Though a small
wedding was all Julian could afford for his sister. Thank
God for Hugh St. David's twenty acres of oak.

Sherbourne finished his drink and set the empty glass
on the tray of a passing footman. "I won't call in your note
until after Lady Glenys is safely wed. Wouldn't be sporting."

"One doesn't discuss business at a social function,
Sherbourne."

"Whyever not?"

Julian was angry with Sherbourne, for his presumption,
for his greed, for his insouciance regarding a matter that
would have grave consequences for dozens of families.

He was *furious* with his grandfather and father for not
minding the family finances more responsibly. Beneath the
anger, though, ran a dangerous thread of relief, to have
the years of trying, struggling, and not quite failing almost
over.

"You do not bruit your business affairs about in public,
lest somebody—a guest, prospective wife, or society
gossip—hear you callously announce an intention to ruin a
neighbor of longstanding. *Bad form, Sherbourne.*"

"Not so gracious now, are we, Haverford? Bad form is
getting arse over ears in debt, and being unable to pay even
the interest. I commend you for trying to put right what
your forefathers so cavalierly put wrong, but I'm unwilling
to finance aristocratic insolvency indefinitely."

I am arse over escutcheon in love....

To Julian's surprise, another emotion lay beneath even

the relief of being ruined: determination to keep his gentle-manly honor untarnished. He could withstand the censure of his peers, the disappointment of his tenants and staff, even his family's pity, as long as he never jeopardized Elizabeth Windham's respect for him.

She would expect him to go down fighting for his valley, so fight he would.

"Call in your notes," Julian said. "Render me unable to pay my bills in the ordinary course. Ruin the livelihoods of my staff, my tenants, and the merchants who depend on the castle's custom and the custom of my tenants. Bring the valley to its collective knees—though you don't need my money any more than King George needs another art collection—and I will still oppose your damned mining scheme."

Three yards away, Charlotte had solicitously accompanied a pale, limping Sir Nigel to a bench among the ferns.

"You liken me to that fat, mincing dolt who presumes to the throne of Britain?"

"Please, Sherbourne. George lumbers of late. His mincing days are behind him. You ruin me because you can, not because you must. I have never wronged you, and have shown good faith in fulfilling my obligations. You simply want that coal mine and don't care how many people suffer as long as you get it."

Julian kept his voice down—graciousness was beyond him now—and half-hoped Sherbourne would stalk away in high dudgeon.

"She said as much," Sherbourne muttered, as Charlotte Windham hovered by Sir Nigel, patting his shoulder and generally calling attention to his indignity.

"Argue with me all you like," Julian said, "but I hope you didn't disagree with Miss Charlotte."

"I've had enough of your lectures, Haverford. I'll send you an official notice of the loan's acceleration next week, and you'll have another thirty days—"

Julian held up a gloved hand. "Not here, not now. You've put me in a position where I have nothing left to lose, and I will knock you onto your backside if you utter one more word tonight regarding business."

"I might renegotiate the terms, if you asked me to."

Julian drew off his glove, one finger at a time. "I might have negotiated with you regarding a coal mine—a modest, safe, well-run operation, employing no small children, and paying the miners a decent wage—if you had even once asked me to, but you've been too attached to your imaginary victimhood to attempt good faith negotiations. You will excuse me. I'm promised to Miss Trelawny for the minuet."

Julian could have been promised to Beelzebub's mother-in-law for all he cared, he simply needed to get away from Sherbourne, and endure the rest of the evening without resorting to violence.

* * *

"Well done, my dears," Aunt Arabella said. "We're all but through with this house party, not a whiff of scandal in the air, Lady Glenys's engagement announced, and only the resting and packing yet to go."

Charlotte yawned, hand on the door latch to the sitting room she shared with Elizabeth. "I'll be about the resting part. I vow if I have to use my knee on one more bachelor I'm entering a convent."

"Haldale was my cross to bear this evening," Elizabeth said. "I think he's marshaling his courage to make an offer for me."

"Poor lamb," Charlotte said.

"I'm not a poor lamb," Elizabeth retorted, though she was too tired to argue.

"Not you, him. I'm for bed." Charlotte slipped through the door leaving Elizabeth in the corridor with Aunt Arabella.

"Your sister has shown a sad lack of interest where the bachelors are concerned," Aunt said. "Charlotte wasn't quite reckless, but she'll soon get a reputation among the gentlemen."

Charlotte already had a reputation for not suffering fools and a fine reputation it was. "A reputation for stepping on their feet? Perhaps that's exactly her aim."

Aunt looked thoughtful. "Charlotte Windham usually gets what she aims for. Interesting. I wanted you to know, Elizabeth, Benedict Andover has asked to pay me his addresses."

"He's a fine gentleman." The next part of the platitude, *I'm sure he'll make you very happy*, got unaccountably stuck in Elizabeth's throat.

Aunt Arabella, a happy widow rather than a merry widow, was abandoning the most independent status a British woman could attain short of the monarchy, and doing so with a glowing smile.

"We'll not make an announcement for some time," Aunt said. "Probably not until the little season ends."

Which would allow Aunt to herd her nieces to at least six more house parties. At each one, Charlotte would become a little more acerbic, and Elizabeth a little miserable.

"I won't say anything to Charlotte, Aunt. You've made a fine choice. Julian—Haverford—speaks very highly of Mr. Andover."

The utter stillness of a huge edifice late at night settled

around them. Aunt Arabella was getting married, and the Sir Nigels and Haldales were growing bolder, while Charlotte was courting eccentricity, and Julian owed his neighbor *twenty thousand pounds*.

"Aunt, what am I to do?"

Arabella took Elizabeth in her arms. Older women were supposed to be plump, sweet-smelling, and gentle. Arabella's embrace was fierce and bony, and the more comforting for it.

"When you came here, your highest ambition was to invest in lending libraries and be left in peace with your books. You needed to be shaken free of that ambition, but not at the cost of your happiness. I'm sorry, Bethan."

Elizabeth eased back and withdrew the handkerchief no lady attended a ball without. "Haverford owns a copy of the Magna Carta. Did you know that? The 1297 version. All these centuries, the St. Davids have safeguarded a trove of historic documents, championed the less fortunate, and ensured the valley prospered, and it all comes down to money owed for ice sculptures and doomed canals."

"And I heard something about coal mines," Arabella said, patting Elizabeth's shoulder. "Go to bed, my dear. When we're exhausted everything looks bleak. We still have two days before we must depart."

"Good night, Aunt."

Arabella crossed the corridor to her room, leaving Elizabeth alone at the darkest hour of the night, weary in body and spirit. She considered joining Charlotte, but instead took off in the direction of the nearest hidden stairway.

She was outside the book room moments later, and because she always had the key with her, she let herself in, expecting to find the chamber cold, dark, and deserted but for the books.

Julian sat at the desk, apparently so lost in thought he hadn't heard the latch turn.

"You should be in bed," Elizabeth said.

He rose and turned to reveal a duke in dishabille. His cravat was undone and he'd unbuttoned his waistcoat. The firelight winked on a signet ring on his left hand, and his cuffs hung loosely.

"I should be in bed," he said, prowling across the room. "With you."

* * *

Julian had been listing his grievances against an unjust fate—even a duke was permitted a few private moments of resentment—and at the top of the list was an un-ducally selfish regret.

He'd never made love with Elizabeth in a bed.

Or under the oak.

On a blanket halfway up Tudor Hill.

In the castle's main library, among the books she so loved.

But to have never made love with the lady in a proper bed? That wasn't right.

Elizabeth was still in her evening finery, adorned with just enough jewels to signal her status, nowhere near enough to offend good taste. Her hair was drawn back into a simple knot, save for one thick lock cascading over a pale shoulder.

"Will you come with me?" Julian asked.

"Of course."

He opened the door, scooped her up in his arms, and carried her down the corridor. A footman trimming wicks pretended not to see them. A maid carrying a vase of wilted roses bobbed a curtsy and sent a shower of red petals to the floor.

Julian didn't care. Within the week, he'd be writing glowing characters for them all, sending his staff away with as much severance and goodwill as he could scrape together.

For the next hour, he belonged exclusively to Elizabeth.

He took her straight past his sitting room, directly to his bedchamber. The fire was lit, the covers turned back, and a pot of tea sat swaddled in a towel on his desk, as if this night were no different from any other.

"I'll need help with my dress," Elizabeth said.

"Of course." Julian settled her on the vanity stool. "All evening, I was happy to converse with my guests and neighbors, dance with the wallflowers, and flirt with the dowagers. I'm a duke, and those courtesies are still mine to share. I don't want to be the duke now, Elizabeth. I want to be solely and completely your lover."

She turned her face against his middle. "Yes. Solely and completely."

They'd become nearly domestic with each other in their tower room. Julian had undone her hooks and stays a dozen times, Elizabeth had retied his cravat and secured it with a perfectly centered pin just as often.

Now, Julian had no patience, because their store of moments was almost gone. He undid her hooks and loosened her stays, then stepped back, lest he tear her clothing.

"I leave the rest to you," he said, taking the warm water from the hearth and pouring some into the wash basin behind the screen. "Take your time."

Elizabeth rose, her dress slipping from her shoulders. "Please get out of those clothes, Haverford, and *do not* take your time."

Spoken like a duchess. "Yes, ma'am."

She stepped out of her dress, handed it to him, and swanned off to the dressing screen.

By the time she emerged in Julian's favorite dressing gown, he wore only a pair of silk trousers. Her hair hung in a single tidy braid, while Julian's thoughts ran riot.

"The sheets have been warmed," he managed. "May I pour you a cup of tea?"

"You may join me in the bed, assuming you can find me."

So much for cosseting. His bed was enormous, larger than some families' parlors. "I'll find you. Depend upon it."

He washed what needed washing, used the tooth powder, blew out candles, banked the fire, and all the while, Elizabeth watched him.

"Haverford, sunrise will begin in approximately one hour. Must I abduct you into this bed?"

"I'm savoring the anticipation."

"What's wrong, Julian? Radnor and Glenys will be very happy together, and all parties seemed to wish them well."

He settled at Elizabeth's side on the bed. She'd taken off his dressing gown and sat among the pillows with the sheets tucked under her arms.

"Sherbourne is finished toying with me. When I told him Glenys and Radnor had become engaged, he informed me he'd collect on the notes owed him. I'll get a proper legal notice next week, and the public notices will follow after Glenys and Radnor speak their vows."

"Sherbourne told you this *at your own ball*?"

Elizabeth's indignation was balm to Julian's pride. "I have the sense he's been waiting for me to fire Glenys off, if not in his direction, then to some appropriate party. With the lady of the house no longer an issue, Sherbourne can ruin me with a clear conscience."

Elizabeth brushed Julian's hair back. "He has a very odd conscience, if he thinks Lady Glenys will not mourn your ruin merely because she dwells five miles away."

"Mourn she might, but she'll not suffer directly. Sherbourne hasn't made up his mind whether to impersonate a gentleman or a rogue, though I believe the real man dwells somewhere in between."

"Charlotte said something similar. Come here, Julian."

Elizabeth drew him down, and got him situated beneath the covers, his head on her shoulder. In their tower room, the chaise had been an awkward bed, and rather than risk tumbling Elizabeth onto the floor, Julian had taken the outside position.

The bed allowed him to truly relax with his lover, to sprawl physically and emotionally. Worries tried to intrude: He must explain the impending reversal of fortunes to Griffin, probably twelve times in twelve different ways. He must start writing the character references for a large staff, though perhaps Glenys could aid him as far as the maids and laundresses were concerned. He must resign from his committees in the Lords and from his clubs.

Being honorably ruined involved work. Julian could deal with all of that later, for now he would make love to his Elizabeth, probably for the last time.

Except…Elizabeth had sunk her fingers into his hair, and begun massaging his scalp. She had a firm touch that banished woes and every sort of tension. Within minutes, Julian was fast asleep and dreaming of a ruined castle in which the only source of warmth was a great bonfire of books.

Chapter Twenty-One

Elizabeth woke to physical bliss. Perfect warmth surrounded her, the scent of lavender rose from crisp sheets, and the security of Haverford's embrace conspired to coax her back into dreams. Her imagination dwelled on roses that climbed to the castle parapets, and an oak tree in the courtyard that bore a crop of books among its branches.

Instinct pushed those fantasies aside, for beyond the window, light was filling the eastern horizon.

"Haverford, I must seek my bed."

He nuzzled her neck.

"Julian, wake up. The time has come to part."

His arms tightened around her. "Not yet."

The longer Elizabeth tarried the more difficult the parting would be, and the more likely scandal would join the blot of ruin on the St. David family escutcheon.

"I can't do this alone," Elizabeth said, lips grazing Haverford's forearm. "I don't want to do it at all."

He shifted, and Elizabeth at first thought he was leaving the bed. Then she was blanketed with more than six feet of naked duke.

"One last loving, Elizabeth. We have time."

Julian had never asked anything of her, not that she wait up for him, not that she write to him, not that she pretend their parting would be temporary. He was asking now.

Elizabeth slipped her arms around him and closed her eyes. He showered her with kisses—temples, brows, cheeks, chin, jaw, everywhere. She mapped his back and shoulders with caresses.

This should not be the last time. This should be just another morning in the ducal bed, just another loving in long, long years of loving. Elizabeth's conviction that she and Julian should have decades to share warred with the reality that she was in bed with a ruined man. He'd no more offer for her now than she'd set fire to his libraries.

Instead, she let passion set fire to her heart. Julian was prolonging the preliminaries, but he was aroused, and Elizabeth was determined. Between one kiss and the next, she gloved him in her heat, and held him while he shuddered at the joining.

"You ambushed me."

She kissed him. "We've ambushed each other."

He was inside her, and yet she yearned to be closer. Her passion took on a desperation that brooked neither patience nor self-restraint. Elizabeth wanted Julian with a ferocity bordering on rage, and clung to him with the intensity of grief.

They should not have to part, not tomorrow, not ever. Julian should not be ruined because a fool's greed had slipped the leash of decency. Love should not be defeated by the petty considerations of social standing and coin.

The pleasure was exquisite, beyond anything they'd shared in their tower room. For a few instants, sensation as blindingly bright as the Welsh summer sun filled her. Elizabeth was one with her lover, and no other reality existed.

But the brilliant light faded, and in the wake of satisfaction, sorrow seeped into her soul. Julian slipped from her body, and yet, he remained wrapped in her arms.

"I'd stay," Elizabeth said. "Even if you didn't marry me, I'd stay, if you asked it of me."

Julian raised himself up enough to meet her gaze. "I love you for that, and for so much more, Elizabeth, but give me the consolation of knowing that my ruin was not the cause of your own."

Then he was gone, leaving Elizabeth alone in the bed.

* * *

"Turnbull, I just saw the most astonishing sight." Sherbourne set down the tea tray a haggard scullery maid had put together for him in the kitchen.

Turnbull continued brushing Sherbourne's evening coat in a brisk, regular rhythm. "Sir, what have I told you about intruding into the kitchens?"

"You sniff and make faces, but never actually forbid me from seeking sustenance when I'm in need of same. What's a kitchen for, after all?"

"A kitchen is for the cook to organize as he or she sees fit. If you want something from the kitchen, you ring for it, send a footman, or present yourself in the appropriate parlor at the appropriate hour. The breakfast buffet is doubtless being laid out as we speak."

Turnbull was clearly feeling the effects of inadequate sleep. "I was hungry and the breakfast parlor is halfway down the far wing. I just saw Haverford escorting Miss Elizabeth Windham to her chamber door. She was in evening attire, and he was barely decent. Waistcoat and jacket, but no cravat. He does have fine taste in waistcoats—and women."

The brushing stopped. "Sir, you saw no such thing."

"Did too." Sherbourne poured himself a cup of hot, strong tea, added milk and sugar, and strolled to the window. "The lady was less than tidy and looked quite well pleasured. I declare, my sensibilities were sorely tried."

"Your only concern should have been to ensure the lady's sensibilities were not offended."

The castle gardens would soon be visible below, all geometric and tidy save for the occasional topiary dragon or gargoyle.

"The first thing I'll do when I take over this mausoleum is add some color to those gardens. Green and red; red, white, and green...Some people can't see colors. Perhaps Haverford is one of them."

"The castle and grounds are entailed sir, and part of the dukedom. You cannot buy this castle."

"When you're done with that jacket, take yourself belowstairs and find a place to nap, Turnbull. You are positively gloomy. I'll lease the castle for a pittance."

Grandmama would have loved that notion. Sherbourne wasn't so keen on living someplace he needed a map to navigate, but no matter. The castle would soon be his in all but name.

"My thanks for your solicitude, sir, but when I have finished tending to your evening clothes, I will gather my effects and take my leave of you."

"We're not returning to Sherbourne Hall until Monday. Wouldn't want to miss a moment of this farce, particularly not with Haverford and the fair Miss Windham—"

The wardrobe door closed so firmly as to nearly be slammed.

"One does not bandy a lady's name about, sir. Not ever."

"Haverford didn't see me, and the lady saw only her duke." Would Charlotte Windham ever regard a man with the same devotion? Would she risk her reputation stealing a few hours with him in private?

"Then might I say, I have appreciated the opportunity to work for you, Mr. Sherbourne, and I wish you continued good fortune. I regret that I cannot recommend another to fulfill my position, but His Grace's staff will doubtless be desperate enough to accept any offers you care to make them."

Sherbourne turned slowly, for the disdain in Turnbull's voice was all the more surprising for being laced with disappointment.

"I beg your pardon, Turnbull. What the deuce are you saying?"

"Best of luck, sir." He bowed and, in no hurry whatsoever, walked toward the door.

"Just a damned minute. You work for me, and I have not dismissed you."

"I have resigned my position. I'll tender that resignation in writing by post. Good day."

"Turnbull, what the hell are you going on about? Is this how you ask for an increase in wages?"

"The wages you've paid me are embarrassingly generous."

Sherbourne set his teacup on the windowsill. "Why do I have the sense that the embarrassment should be mine?"

Turnbull's gaze went from the teacup to the tray, a familiar reminder that leaving delicate porcelain all over the premises was not the done thing.

"I have endured this blighted house party in an effort to associate with good company," Sherbourne said, pacing the length of the room. "I have comported myself like a gentleman while Haverford is disporting with a woman he can't afford to marry. I've wished Lady Glenys and her prancing marquess well and nearly meant it, and I've kept my hands and my opinions to myself. And yet, you mutiny. Why now?"

Why now, when Sherbourne had been telling himself that victory was at hand, and the pleasure of finally winning simply hadn't sunk in yet?

For it hadn't. He'd left the ballroom at the first opportunity, and sat in the garden watching the moon drift down to the horizon. His mood had sunk with it, but he'd gone back inside in time to watch Charlotte Windham dance the good-night waltz with a fawning, half-drunk baronet.

"You were overheard early in the evening," Turnbull said, "informing the Duke of Haverford that you intend to call in debts amassed over at least three generations. You did this in His Grace's own ballroom, within the hearing of a footman named Thomas Prior. The Priors have served the St. Davids for time out of mind, gone to war with them, gone to London with them, and stood at their bedsides as they lay at death's door. Prior was in tears before he left the ballroom."

"So I'll give the man a job."

"*Prior was in tears for his duke.* For the way of life that has held this valley together for centuries, for his children and grandchildren who will have no duke to serve, no duke to protect them."

"Protect them from what? All I want to do is open one coal mine, Turnbull. Half the Lords owes its solvency to coal mines, and there are coal mines all over Wales."

"There are coal mines all over Wales, but precious few dukes, and you're ruining the best of them. We won't hold your coal mine in contempt—mining is honest work, and blessed hard—we will hold *you* in contempt."

That was the outside of too much. "Because I want to collect the sums owed me? Because I want to offer men jobs?"

Turnbull studied the cherubs cavorting about in the molding twelve feet overhead. "You'll offer them jobs at starvation wages, while you pay the women and children even less than the men. The farms will go to ruin, the housing you put up will be disgraceful, the merchants will go out of business trying to extend credit to families on the brink of starvation, while you grow richer than you already are."

Turnbull put a hand on the door latch, as if he needed the support. "Haverford," he went on, "kept these people fed at his own expense when the harvest was ruined. He maintains the village and the tenant properties without being dunned for simple repairs. He trusts his neighbors and staff to keep an eye on Lord Griffin. Haverford's integrity is all that has prevented you from turning this valley into a glorified coal yard. His farmers, by contrast, are all putting a bit by, year by year because Haverford brought the best breeding stock he could find into their herds."

"He's a ruddy saint," Sherbourne said, stalking back to the window, "when anybody else would have been thrown in jail for their debt, and I'm the devil incarnate for having financed all his largesse. Be off with you. Leave an address at the posting inn and I'll have the balance of your wages sent to you."

"Thank you, sir, but that won't be necessary. You may donate any wages you owe me to the parish poor box."

Turnbull closed the door softly, and Sherbourne fisted both hands rather than snatch up the teacup and hurl it against the wall.

He'd miscalculated, somehow, somewhere, and badly. Ruining Haverford had seemed necessary to bring even one modest coal mine into a valley stuck in the Dark Ages, but if Turnbull was right, the local people would move to bloody Boston before they accepted work at a Sherbourne mine.

Which was beyond stupid. Haverford had been generous with his staff, tenants, and neighbors. He'd made sound decisions with regard to commercial ventures other than mining, but he'd had the freedom to do so because Sherbourne hadn't accelerated the St. David family debts.

Why should Haverford get the credit, when the coin involved had been, indirectly, from the Shebourne coffers?

"It's the outside of too much," Sherbourne muttered. "Beyond the pale."

And yet, he was certain that if he could only discuss the whole business with Charlotte Windham, she could explain it in terms he'd grasp, and possibly even show him how to salvage one properly managed, modest coal mine out of the mess his ambitions had become.

* * *

Saturday was a tired blur for Elizabeth, much of it spent writing letters to every God's blessed Windham, in-law, and close associate Elizabeth could think of. She stayed in her rooms in part to rest, in part to avoid laying eyes on Sherbourne, lest she treat him to a public recitation of her opinion of him.

Sunday morning was taken up with attending services.

"I cannot tell if you are upset to be leaving Haverford," Charlotte said, as the coach horses plodded back to the castle, "upset at the rumors flying about His Grace's finances, or upset that we must wait until tomorrow to leave for home."

Because yesterday had been rainy and the lanes had yet to dry, all of the guests were in their coaches, and thus progress was slow.

"I am not upset, Charlotte. I am furious."

"With Sherbourne? Miss Trelawny shared a hymnal with him. Perhaps she hasn't yet heard the talk."

The rest of the guests were politely snubbing Sherbourne, which was exactly what he deserved. To a person, they would agree that debts ought to be paid when due, but they would also agree that ruining a duke who was honorably servicing his debts was inexcusable.

The gravest sin of all, however, was to have made that ruin public the same evening Lady Glenys's engagement had been announced. The term *sour grapes* was being muttered almost as frequently as *presuming toad*.

"Miss Trelawny's mother has heard the talk," Elizabeth replied. "She doubtless wanted to make certain Haverford knew he was no longer welcome to offer for her daughter."

Not that Julian would.

"The whispers are awful," Charlotte said as the coach hit a rut. "Ruin for me would be people gossiping because I'd had too much punch. My penance would consist of peace and quiet in rural comfort while an endless procession of family looked in on me. A couple years of that, and I'd be allowed to slink back to Town. If the talk is true, Haverford will be a charity case by the end of the year and his exile from polite society absolute."

Charlotte was incapable of cheering anybody up, bless her. "I thought you liked Sherbourne."

"He's interesting. He reminds me of myself."

"If you ever, ever ruin a good man simply for the sake of amassing more coin that you do not need, I will cut you, Charlotte."

That promise hung in the air, honest, but unfortunate. Charlotte liked so few people, and few people liked Charlotte.

"Then if Sherbourne were to offer for me, I'd have to choose between having a sister and having a husband. Good to know."

"That's not what I said." The coach turned up the drive, and Elizabeth felt as rotten as Charlotte had three weeks earlier. "I'm sorry. I should not have said that. The situation between Sherbourne and Haverford is complicated, and I'm not at my best."

"No more house parties," Charlotte said. "We tried, Bethan. We did our best, but even among the realm's most eligible bachelors, I could not be tempted."

"All we need do is endure this afternoon's walking excursion, and then tomorrow we leave."

"I'm counting the hours," Charlotte muttered.

So was Elizabeth, for entirely different reasons.

This being the Sabbath, the party was consigned to taking the air for entertainment. A few young ladies might play quiet melodies in the drawing room before dinner, but the dancing and card playing were over.

Thank God.

Though so, apparently was the loving, and when Elizabeth considered that, she had all she could do not to cry. Again.

* * *

A ruined man was a free man.

This realization was coming over Julian gradually, hour by hour, and yet, his ruin was not fait accompli. He had to endure the afternoon's excursion with his guests, and see them all on their way tomorrow morning.

And say his farewells to Elizabeth. All the ruin in creation wasn't half so painful to bear as that thought. Even this discussion with Griffin wasn't as awkward as Julian had feared.

"We won't lose the castle," Julian said, as Griffin neatly lifted an egg from under a roosting Princess, "but I might have to rent it out."

"You can live with us," Griffin said, petting the hen. "Biddy and Abner and I talked about it. We have lots of room. We aren't cold in the winter like you are at the castle, and we don't have footmen and maids crowding us. When can I marry Biddy?"

God bless an honest brother. "Glenys and Radnor should be allowed to set a date first, Griffin. Glenys has been waiting to be married longer than Biddy has."

Living with Griffin had an odd appeal. He was a cheerful soul, his farm was well run, and his household lately had borne a constant fragrance of shortbread. If not for the equally pervasive miasma of gleeful romance about the premises, Julian might have considered Griffin's offer.

"I like Radnor," Griffin said. "I told him I want Charity to live here with me and Biddy, but Radnor could always visit her."

Radnor had dropped that issue in Julian's lap on the way to church, along with awkward assurances that any help Julian needed would be forthcoming on the instant.

"I'm sure there will be much visiting back and forth all round, Griffin. I also wanted to discuss this business of a mortgage with you."

Griffin whistled for King Henry, who came bounding into the barn, tongue and tail flapping.

"Biddy says mortgages are bad. Abner agreed. We don't need a mortgage. I have lots of money."

"How much do you have, Griffin?"

He named a surprisingly respectable sum.

"Good for you. I'm proud of you. Don't lend it, and don't borrow from anybody without talking to Biddy and Abner first."

" 'Neither a borrower nor lender be,' " Griffin recited— in English. "Biddy says that. I know what it means."

"You're the first St. David in three generations to figure it out." Which was sweet and ironic. "You never did say who raised the topic of a mortgage with you."

Griffin led the way out of the barn, the dog trotting at his heels. He tossed the egg across the barnyard, and Henry bounded after it.

"Did you break that egg on purpose?" Julian asked, taking a seat at the bench near the pump.

"We have enough eggs," Griffin said, coming down beside Julian, "and they just go bad if they're not eaten. Henry likes them as much as I like shortbread."

Elizabeth loved a piece of fresh, warm shortbread. "About the mortgage?"

"I won't borrow any money, Julian. Never, never, never. Biddy made me promise, and a gentleman keeps his promises."

"That he does. I'd best be returning to my guests." And to Elizabeth. She'd hidden for most of yesterday, while Julian had started on the enormous task of dismantling the dukedom's finances.

Julian wanted to linger at his brother's side, where life's greatest moral dilemma was whether to waste an occasional egg. He brushed his boot over the bed of clover beneath the bench while Griffin watched King Henry devour his treat.

A four-leaf clover caught Julian's eye. He plucked it and passed it to Griffin. "If you're ever tempted to buy Biddy a hair ribbon, do it. If she wants a pineapple to serve on a special occasion, buy her one. The sentiment is worth whatever coin you'd have to pay for the token."

Griffin took the clover. "Thank you. A four-leaf clover is good luck. Hair ribbons cost money."

He sounded as if he were reciting one of those empty facts he tended to collect like dropped acorns—or maybe as if he were quoting his ducal brother.

"But memories are priceless, Griffin, and forever after, Biddy would choose the ribbon you gave her as her favorite. She'd treasure that ribbon, maybe sleep with it under her pillow."

"Papa used to give us books," Griffin said. "I treasure the books in my library. I gave Charity a book, and when she lives with us, I will help her read it. Papa gave you many, many, many books."

The dog came panting back from his feast, a spot of eggshell on his nose. Griffin produced a clean handkerchief and wiped away the eggshell, then gently tugged on Henry's silky ear. The beast endured that consideration as patiently as an obedient child might have.

Griffin would manage. With Biddy at his side, on a farm he understood and loved, Griffin would manage. That thought filled Julian with a peace and relief he hadn't known for years, and Griffin was right—in addition to a mountain of debt, Papa had given Julian a multitude of books.

Julian rose from the bench. "I'll let you know as soon as

Glenys and Radnor set a date, and I'll be by on Tuesday to talk some more about Charity."

Griffin patted King Henry on the head, and the dog loped off. "I love Biddy Bowen, and I love my Charity."

Julian pulled his brother in for a tight hug and slapped him on the back. "I love you, Griffin St. David."

"Say it in English."

Julian did, and Griffin hugged him back, and being ruined became less of problem than Julian had thought it would be. Being heartbroken, however, was more painful by the moment.

He walked back to the castle by way of the lake and Tudor Hill, and sat in the library over the noon hour while Radnor and Glenys presided over luncheon. These were Julian's books, the great legacy of the St. David family, thousands and thousands of titles, each one like a silken ribbon bought for the simple pleasure of adding to the collection.

"I wish I'd bought Elizabeth a hair ribbon."

Papa had been gleeful over the purchase of every title, despite mounting debt, despite one more investment gone awry, despite a bow wave of trouble and scandal building before the prow of the Haverford dukedom. He'd been helpless not to indulge in just one more volume, secure in the knowledge that while his finances floundered, the prestige of his library yet flourished.

The previous duke's portrait hung near the biographies, and of course, he'd been immortalized with a book in his hand—*Gulliver's Travels*, which he'd read to his children times without number.

Elizabeth's words came to mind, about not loving books per se, but loving what a book could do—inform, comfort, entertain, enlighten, educate.

Immortalize.

Elizabeth would have no silken ribbon to remind her of her summer idyll, because Julian's plan had not included a budget for falling in love. No budget for Glenys's pineapples and ice sculptures, no budget for Griffin taking a wife.

Plans failed. Doubtless Papa had seen one plan after another fail—why had Julian never acknowledged this?—and yet Papa's joy and faith in his books hadn't faltered. Julian had regarded the books as his legacy—a burden to be maintained and housed—when in fact, the joy and faith were far more precious.

"Thank you, Papa." Nobody heard those quiet words, and they came with a complicated ache. Papa had tried, in his way, though his plan hadn't been one Julian had grasped. "Thank you for the books too."

Plans failed, unforeseen events arose, and love happened—thank God and Elizabeth Windham.

Julian sat among his treasury of books and considered one more thought: Plans could be revised too.

Chapter Twenty-Two

"Now is your chance," Arabella said, as the guests sorted themselves into groups for the final stroll about the lake. "Please, Benny. Make the daft boy see reason."

To Benedict Andover, one of the pleasures of being old was being ignored. Arabella could make her plea—or issue her orders—without any fear of being overheard.

And Benedict could kiss her cheek without any risk of being chastised for it, even by her. The novelty of that, of having secured permission to court a woman he'd admired for decades, put a spring in his step.

"I'll give it a go, Bella, but you said it yourself. Young people are foolish."

She patted his cheek. "Why should we have all the fun? Be off with you, and I'll expect a complete report when we reach the garden."

Andover quickened his pace and caught up with the only duke in the realm nobody sought to walk with.

"Do you mind keeping an old man company, Haverford? I've been informed my escort is unneeded by the lady I'd most like to share the journey with."

Haverford's gaze as he considered the lake was too peaceful for a duke in the midst of ruin. "I'm glad for the company."

And that seemed to amuse him.

"For three weeks, you've wished the lot of us to perdition, and now you're glad for company? Odd, isn't it, how life serves us these turns. Your father often said life was stranger than any tale ever published in a book."

Haverford's pace was just above a saunter, and exactly matched that of Elizabeth Windham, who'd chosen a place closer to the head of the group.

"I can't believe my father noticed much beyond his books, and Mama, of course."

Benedict's objective was to wheedle permission from the duke to sell off a few of the treasures gathering dust in the castle, which meant he had less than an hour to change the mind of a St. David duke. That Arabella believed he could rather invigorated an old man's blood.

"Why would you think your father noticed only his books?"

"Because that is where he spent his time and our coin—almost all of both."

Two swans glided by several yards from shore, one honking raucously at the other, who ignored the noise. A mated pair, would be Benedict's guess, out having their own Sunday constitutional.

"I've always wondered why such a lovely bird was given such an unattractive voice," Benedict said. "But it's the only voice they have, and they manage with it. Your father was the same way."

"He read a fine fairy tale, regardless of his voice."

That was the reply of a man only half-present to the

conversation. Was Haverford musing on his impending ruin, or on the sway of Elizabeth Windham's skirts?

"I refer not to the late duke's voice, Haverford. I refer to his penchant for books. Things were different in our day. A duke did not own commercial ventures, not if he was a Duke of Haverford. The heathen to the north and east might abandon the land, but the Welsh duke had greater respect for tradition."

Haverford gestured to a bench situated to provide a magnificent view of the castle across the lake.

Benedict felt better than he had in years, but perhaps Haverford was tired. Young people had so little stamina for what mattered.

"A respite to enjoy the view would be welcome," Benedict said, taking a seat. "Your father had no head for business. He had no shipping interests, and he abhorred the mines, mostly because his father abhorred the mines. Alcestus St. David invested in books."

Haverford settled on the bench as other guests strolled by. Rather than try to catch the duke's notice, they spared him furtive glances that ranged from pitying to gloating. Both Haldale and Windstruther offered slight bows, to their credit, and they'd all but cut Sherbourne.

"Books were not an investment for Papa," Haverford said when the last guest had strolled by. "They were a passion, an obsession. They made him blind and deaf to all else, and yet, what can one do with a pile of books? Read them or use them to keep the fires going in winter when one can no longer afford bedamned coal. Fortunately, there's an old peat field on Griffin's farm. The books are safe as long as we can cut peat."

Oh, dear. Oh, damn. Arabella had been right. Benedict suspected she would frequently be right.

"Have you considered selling any of the tinder cluttering up your library shelves?"

Haverford closed his eyes and turned his face to the sun. "The solicitors were very clear that selling the books will unravel all that's remaining of my finances, and besides, who'd want them? Most of the nabobs and cits who buy books by the box dwell closer to Town, and books are heavy. Shipping them costs money. Papa never sold a single volume—not one."

The swans were quiet, tooling about on the lake as if doing their bit to enhance the scenery for the guests on shore.

"Besides," Haverford went on more quietly, "they are all I have of my father and grandfather. When I was tempted to sell off another farm, when I faced yet another season in Town arguing politics that would endear me to no one, I'd go into the library and the books would mock me out of my self-pity. Perhaps ruin is turning me daft."

Good God, what a tangle, equal parts love and disappointment, loyalty and bad advice.

"Being the damned duke has turned you daft, Haverford. I'm sure the solicitors were giving you the best guidance they could, but lawyers and book lovers are two very different species. Fortunately for you, I—a rarity among men—qualify as both. Of the two, you're better off listening to a book lover now."

Haverford checked his watch and muttered something about "twelve hundred minutes."

The first group of hikers were halfway around the lake, and Benedict still hadn't made his point. Arabella would tolerate nothing less than a decisive victory, so he tried again.

"What difference will unraveling your finances make at this point, Haverford? Sherbourne is like your papa. The late duke understood rare and antique books, and thus he invested his time and means in books. Sherbourne understands commerce, and he will have his mine, over your ruined reputation if need be. We can't fault either of them any more than we can fault the swans for their voices."

Haverford hunched forward, elbows braced on his knees, a weary, almost defeated pose.

"Andover, how can a man—any man, much less a duke—not understand that the trades must be paid? The cottages repaired? Glenys must be dowered?"

"Your father understood all of that, and he'd be grateful to you for having taken on the very challenges that bested him. Do you expect Sherbourne to know how to be charitable? Of course not. Nobody's taught him how to go about it, though I suspect he's teachable. You have done an excellent job under very trying circumstances, and your father would be proud of you."

Haverford stared at the castle, at the red dragon pennant flapping from the parapets. The sun had struck the angle that caused the rainbow to blossom over the fountain, and from across the lake, the gryphon appeared to be smiling.

Such a lovely castle, and such a bewildered duke.

"How could my father be proud of a bankrupt?" Haverford asked.

Being old gave one insight *and* the courage to use it. "More to the point, how can a son be proud of the father who wasted the family's resources?"

The swans got into another spat, honking and flapping, then returning to their serene gliding amid the ripples they'd caused. Definitely a married pair.

"How to respect the late duke has been something of a puzzle," Haverford said.

A conundrum that could ruin a man's life more surely than debtor's prison. "The answer to that puzzle is buried in your library, Julian. Your father had no grasp of farming and his stewards were a lazy bunch. His title meant the military, church, and diplomacy were beyond his reach. His own father was dead set against mining. Alcestus had few options and fewer allies. When I say he invested in the books, I use the word advisedly."

Haverford withdrew a small cloth bag from a pocket and tossed some of the contents upon the water. The swans about-faced and paddled at speed toward the bread crusts floating on the lake's surface.

"Do you know what matters to me now?" Haverford said. "Not the budgets and market forecasts, not the estimates or promissory notes. Not my father's mistakes or his father's wrong turns. They did the best they could. I've done the best I could. I don't even care if Sherbourne is made whole because he's earned so much interest off the St. Davids, that he ought to be first in line to prevent my ruin. What matters..."

Haverford's gaze was on Elizabeth Windham, who'd gone far enough along the path to be circling back toward the gardens.

"If she is what matters to you, Haverford, if her good opinion is the first and last chapter of your story, then you need to listen to what I have to say. Despite what a clutch of cork-brained lawyers told you, your father did not leave you penniless."

Haverford threw the rest of the bread to the swans. "She is what matters. She is all that matters, and for that reason, I will listen to whatever insight you care to share."

Bella would be so proud of the boy, and of her intended too. "Let's leave this infernal bench. When you get old, you lose what padding the good Lord imbued you with as a younger man. Benches are the very devil."

Haverford laughed and rose. "When you're young, you lack the sense to enjoy a beautiful view with a lovely woman. Benches are never on hand when you need one."

"Just so," Andover said, springing to his feet, and taking the duke's arm. "Just so. Now about your books. If you give me leave, I'd like to contact a few people I know and make a handful of discreet inquiries..."

Haverford listened, the swans glided, the gardens came closer, and Benedict called upon all of his persuasive powers—both the lawyer's and the book lover's—to convince the duke that the time had come to part with a few treasures.

Among which, Benedict might find a morning gift for his darling bride.

* * *

The walking excursion, a procession around the lake to be followed by tea and cakes in the garden, was progressing at the pace of a dowager with bad knees. Elizabeth daundered along with her aunt, while ahead of them, Radnor walked with Glenys.

Benedict Andover had made the entire journey around the lake at Haverford's side. Was nobody else willing to walk with the duke now that Sherbourne had decided to ruin him?

Elizabeth was unhappy with the other guests; she was furious with Haverford.

She had finally, finally found a man she could esteem, desire, and enjoy, a man she respected deeply, and he was tossing her aside out of some misguided surfeit of honor.

"Shall we share a table?" Charlotte asked, coming up on Elizabeth's right.

"Thank you, Charl, but I don't need a pity escort."

"Perhaps I need a pity escort. You tried to warn me about Sherbourne. He's likely to offer me pleasantries and then I'd have to kill him. For the sake of my self-restraint, you are stuck with me. S-t-u-c-k."

"It isn't necessary to spell, Charlotte. We can restrain each other from doing Mr. Sherbourne an injury."

"At least the house party is over. There's some consolation."

God save me from well-intended sisters. "If that's your idea of consolation, then you might find yourself walking back to Kent tomorrow."

The party had finished its circuit of the lake and was dispersing into the gardens at a tired meander. Aunt Arabella took a bench near the rose trellis, and Mr. Andover gestured in the direction of the buffet.

"You should elope," Charlotte said. "Disappear in the dead of night with the handsome duke, and Lady Glenys's house party will become famous."

"And have our private army of cousins come after the would-be bride, sabers drawn? Thank you, no." The guests were choosing tables, and Elizabeth's belly rebelled at the thought of one more glass of punch, one more slice of cake. "Charlotte, I can't do this."

"You are a Windham in love, Bethan. You are within your rights to ignore both common sense and overwhelming odds. What I don't understand is why you plan to get into the coach tomorrow. So Haverford is ruined. You won't have to throw house parties, bother with the season, or put up with a ceremony at St. George's in Hanover Square. Ruined does not look so very awful to me, if you can share it with the only man to distract you from your infernal books."

"He doesn't see it like that." Elizabeth had spent most of the previous night arguing herself out of another trip to

Julian's bedroom. She would not beg, plead, or exhort him to change his blasted plan.

The Deity himself was probably incapable of inspiring Haverford to abandon his plans.

"His Grace is coming this way," Charlotte said, "and he looks determined."

"Determination has ever been his to command. Perhaps I'll share Mr. Sherbourne's table."

"Your Grace." Charlotte curtsied. "You've arranged lovely weather again, and I neglected to bring my shawl. Elizabeth, perhaps you'll be good enough to retrieve it for me?"

Damn you, Charlotte, and bless you. "Your Grace." Elizabeth dipped at the knees—barely. She was angry with the man she loved, which was a new and difficult experience. No handy quote came to mind, no witty passage from some classic tome. Not the Bard, Mrs. Burney, Mr. Burns, or even Old Scratch ruling over perdition had words adequate for the moment.

"Miss Windham." Haverford bowed and offered his arm. "I'll happily accompany you back to the castle, and perhaps you'll select that book I owe you? If you leave the choice until tomorrow, you might forget."

Elizabeth took his arm, and barely refrained from dragging him along the walk. She held her tongue only until Charlotte had sauntered off in the direction of the cake.

"I will never forget you."

Haverford's hand closed over her fingers. "You sound less than pleased to make that admission. Would you be comforted to know that the condition is mutual?"

How ducal he could be, and yet, Elizabeth knew him, knew his body, and knew that beneath his civil tones, he was vibrating with emotions that would shock the guests watching from every corner of the garden.

They reached the library, and when Haverford would have left the door open, she pushed it shut.

"Elizabeth, this is not wise."

"For us to part is sheer folly, Haverford. I will not find your like again, ever, and you will not find mine. I have waited years—half my life—to meet you, and they have been lonely, trying years. Now your great nobility of soul consigns me to the worse purgatory of knowing that I should be at your side, though you deny me that privilege."

Elizabeth stalked across the library, skirts swishing. "I've been here three weeks, Haverford, and you've shown me literary treasures beyond compare, shelf after shelf, but they are nothing, nothing, next to the wonders we share on a lumpy chaise during a stolen hour."

She rounded a bust of Plato and marched back to the dunderhead who would break her heart. "You can tell me where every item in every collection is, but tell me this instead: Why have I never seen you *reading* these beautiful books, Haverford? The only bound volumes I've seen in your hands are ledgers. The only words you see on pages are in your blasted correspondence. What good are these books if they bring you no joy?"

Haverford stood beneath the portrait over the mantel, his expression as severe as if Elizabeth had ruined him all over again, and yet, she could not stop until she'd made him see the foolishness of giving up.

"I love books, but I love lending libraries more," she went on, snatching a book some careless guest had left on the mantel. "Books that merely sit on the shelf, generation after generation, are like children nobody loves. A tragic waste, a reproach. And yet, you are more concerned with housing and dusting these thousands of unread books than you are with your own happiness."

She used the book to point at him. "I cannot allow that to happen, Haverford."

"You cannot allow—?" he said softly.

"I cannot." Elizabeth dashed the back of her free hand against her cheek. "You'd throw away love, just as your father threw away security. I would throw away every blessed book in this castle before I'd let them come between us, Julian. I don't care about ruin, or penury, or a lot of bloody books. I care about you."

Three weeks ago, Elizabeth could not have spoken the word *bloody* aloud. She could not have cried before another. She could not have ignored thirty thousand bound volumes, though now she was entirely concerned with one man who was too honorable for his own good.

Haverford held out a white handkerchief but came no closer to her. "I've asked Sherbourne to meet me within the hour that we might discuss a modest mining operation, and I'm hopeful, determined even, that renegotiation of the various notes and loans will free me to make an offer that, at this point, I cannot make."

Elizabeth paused between blotting her left eye and her right. "You'd consider a mine in this valley?"

Haverford studied her, which was ungentlemanly when her nose was probably red and her eyes doubtless puffy.

He pivoted on his heel and opened a window. "You reminded me that part of my antipathy toward mining was because Griffin came to harm twenty years ago. That has colored my outlook—and doubtless colored my father's outlook—though the state of Welsh mining districts is also not to be dismissed. Sherbourne is apparently willing to bargain—or he was—and so am I."

Elizabeth did not care one tattered Radcliffe novel for what Sherbourne was willing or unwilling to do.

"What of your plan, Julian? The plan that has run and ruined your life? The plan that says if you live to be eighty-seven years and five months old, you might enjoy seventy-two hours of wedded bliss."

He stood by the window, hands behind his back. "Plans can be modified. A budget, a schedule, a series of estimates are all well and good, but they should serve to support a goal, not dictate every particular. The 'best laid plans' of mice, dukes, presuming neighbors, the lot of us ... can benefit from rethinking. Some plans should be chucked over the castle wall, because they make no provision for love."

Elizabeth balled up the handkerchief and stuffed it in a pocket, for Haverford would never get it back. Plans could be modified, and hearts could change.

"If every one of these books went up in flames, Julian, I would rejoice, provided your burden was lighter. Negotiate with Sherbourne if you must, but I'll follow Charlotte's example in this and knock his arrow from the sky. If he insists on ruining you, then I will see to his ruin as well."

Haverford's smile was unlike any previous versions Elizabeth had seen—all diabolical dash and élan.

"You'd ruin him?" he asked.

"I can and I will. I may appear to be a managing bluestocking firmly on the shelf, but the blood of *duchesses* runs in my veins."

Ducal brows rose, but before Haverford could reply, Elizabeth wrapped her arms around him. She kissed him as a conquering army plunders underdefended countryside, kissed him with all the passion and desire in her, and kissed him with a new and slightly violent sense of hope.

If she ruined Sherbourne, her own reputation would doubtless go up in flames as well, and maybe then, her stubborn, handsome, well-planned duke would propose to her.

Elizabeth patted Haverford's cheek, tossed the volume of poetry at his chest—Mr. Burns, as luck would have it—and would have made a grand exit from the library, except Lucas Sherbourne met her right at the door.

"You," she snapped.

Sherbourne offered her a bow.

He was big, male, and standing in the way of her happiness. Elizabeth walloped him across the cheek, the sound reverberating amid the books.

"His Grace is doing you the courtesy," she said, "of allowing you to apologize for your disgraceful behavior at Friday's ball. Fail to appreciate his generosity, Mr. Sherbourne, and every one of the letters I've written to the various dukes, marquesses, earls, and viscounts to whom I'm connected will be in tomorrow's post. Each epistle describes your rudeness and arrogance in detail, and that is just the first volley from my cannon. Please stand aside."

He scurried to the right like a chastened puppy. Elizabeth curtsied to Haverford with more dignity than a queen would show her king, then swept into the corridor without sparing Sherbourne even a glance.

* * *

"I fancy that look on you," Julian said. "One cheek bright red, your shrewd blue eyes for once dazed and uncertain. Do come in, and please close the door."

Sherbourne cradled his left cheek with his palm. "I believe Miss Windham has taken me into dislike."

"She hates you," Julian said, cheerfully. "While I pity you. Have a seat." What a relief, what a *joy*, to sincerely pity Sherbourne.

He closed the door and took four steps into the room.

"Be seated," Julian said, gesturing with the volume of poetry Elizabeth had pitched at him. "Now, if you please."

Sherbourne flipped out his tails and took the chair by the hearth. "I'm meeting with you as a courtesy, Haverford. Say your bit and then—"

"The courtesy is all mine, Sherbourne. I cannot tell Elizabeth Windham what to do when she's determined that a man is in need of ruining, but I can suggest that one small, local mine, run according to model standards of safety, and employing no small children, might be acceptable to me provided you meet certain conditions."

Sherbourne shot his cuffs and sat back, then turned a signet ring on his left smallest finger. He was fidgeting, rearranging emotions and objectives, and that meant he was listening.

"You are not in a position to dictate, Haverford. I've shown your family years of tolerance on notes long past due. For my pains, I'm the ogre of the valley, while you use my money to endear yourself to every yeoman and goatherd in Wales."

That Sherbourne grasped the extent to which the locals resented him, and that he cared about their opinions, boded well.

"Poor lad," Julian said. "You've made a profit off me that approaches usury, and now you want pity for your misfortune. The plan has changed, Sherbourne, and you either bargain with me in good faith, or suffer my continued opposition regarding your mine."

Sherbourne took out a gold watch, flipped it open, then tucked it away—as if the clock on the mantel or the clock on the sideboard weren't visible to him.

"What of your duchess-to-be? Will she pardon me as well?"

"I cannot speak for Elizabeth, but should you and I come to terms, I'll attempt to intercede on your behalf with her. She is very angry, Sherbourne, and very well connected."

Sherbourne tipped his head back and stared at the strawberry-leaf molding twenty feet overhead. "You are willing to support a mine. This admission had not caused the sky to fall, so please do go on."

"You will incur a loss if you call in my notes," Julian said. "I make every payment to the penny, year after year. Call in the notes, and you will have ruined me, disgraced yourself without any aid from Elizabeth, and lost money as well. Not a sound plan, Sherbourne, which is why I give you an opportunity to revise it."

Sherbourne crossed both his ankles and his arms. "What can Elizabeth Windham do to me?"

"Whatever she jolly well pleases. Her uncle is a duke, one sister married a duke, another married a ducal heir. Among her cousins and cousins-by-marriage I count two marquesses, four earls, a viscount, several—"

Sherbourne yawned behind a manicured hand. "Hardly the circles I travel in."

Julian set the volume of poetry on the mantel. "What do you dream about, Sherbourne? I conclude that, despite all conduct to the contrary, you are simply a man who seeks to be respected by his peers, to make a meaningful contribution, and to raise your children amid peace and plenty with a good woman at your side. Your dreams aren't that different from mine or Griffin's."

Sherbourne rose and picked up the volume of poetry. "Your brilliance will blind me, Haverford, though you forgot the part about how I'd like to enjoy good health for as long as the Creator allows."

"So build a model mine. My willingness to stand aside while you undertake that experiment—for it will be a modest, model mine—will cost you reinstatement of my father's promissory notes on the schedule we've adhered to for years."

Sherbourne ran a finger down the page. "I can build a colliery without any assistance from you, Haverford."

He was holding the book upside down. Julian righted it for him. "You likely can, though you'll tear this valley in two if you try to build that colliery with myself, Radnor, Hugh St. David, and many others standing against it. So far, you've shown an unwillingness to do that."

Sherbourne set the book aside. "I can't build a mine if all you do is remain silently brooding in your castle. Your cronies in the Lords will tut-tut and tsk-tsk and come up with some bill that affects only collieries in this valley, all but sabotaging my works without you lifting a be-ringed finger. I want your support."

He wanted that support badly, and Julian would never have noticed, but for Elizabeth storming the castle. "You'll reinstate my notes and desist from whispering in Griffin's ear about a mortgage."

Sherbourne began a circuit of the room, peering out each window, studying random shelves of books.

"I'd rather not reinstate your notes. You won't have them paid off for nearly a decade, and anything can happen in ten years' time. I can make more money developing a mine than I can waiting for you to dig yourself out of debt."

Sherbourne brushed a gloved palm across Plato's crown. "And I never breathed a word to your brother about a mortgage, though I saw him in close discussion with a worried Radnor last week in the churchyard. My experience of Griffin St. David is that when he wants a word explained, he will not desist until he's satisfied. Stubbornness must be a family trait."

One mystery explained.

But as for others…Julian studied the man wandering around his library. Sherbourne was a fashion plate, but also out of place in genteel surroundings. He was too restless, too blunt, and too ambitious, and yet, he'd made a valid point: The valley had the best herds in Wales because Sherbourne had not called in notes long overdue.

The castle could employ dozens of people in a variety of roles, because Sherbourne had been patient.

The merchants in the village were thriving, in part because Sherbourne was thriving, and had not—until recently—pressed his neighbor for overdue payments.

Something more was needed here, both because Sherbourne had—in his commercially astute heart—been somewhat reasonable, and because Julian was a duke. Dukes looked out for the less fortunate, and any man who lacked the love of a woman such as Elizabeth Windham was a very unfortunate creature, indeed.

Sunshine slanted through the open windows, while Sherbourne peered at the previous duke's portrait over by the biographies. A small bird lit on the sill nearest the fireplace, then flew off into the lovely day.

The wood warbler, one of Papa's favorites.

The something more that was wanted was the courage to go forward with the love Elizabeth Windham had brought to Julian's life.

"You need a charitable endeavor," Julian said. "A project that's visible and genuinely beneficial, not a mere display. Because I am a helpful sort who doesn't carry a grudge, I have a suggestion."

Sherbourne studied the signature in the bottom right corner of Papa's portrait. "Because I am the patient sort, who never tosses out an idea simply because it originated with a long-winded, self-important duke, I will listen."

Julian reshelved the volume of poetry among its companions and said a prayer that Elizabeth was as fond of long-winded, self-important dukes as he hoped she was.

"I'll be selling a few of my more valuable books, probably at auction. Andover will help coordinate the sale."

Sherbourne turned slowly. "You're selling the famed St. David collection?"

"Not the entire collection. I'll offer some of the duplicates, rarities, and more historically significant volumes at an exclusive auction some weeks hence. The majority of the proceeds from that sale will be spent getting you disentangled from my finances."

Sherbourne's cool indifference slipped. "You have *twenty thousand pounds* worth of books and you've wasted years paying me avoidable interest? Haverford, you're daft."

"I had a long talk with Benedict Andover as we walked around the lake. Much to my delight"—much to Julian's utter, elated confoundment—"I have a modest fortune in literary treasures, while he has the connections to find me buyers for the best of the lot. The books don't matter to me half so much as Elizabeth Windham does, nor half so much as I matter to her."

Which was...lovely. That Elizabeth had had to spell this out for Julian was lowering, but he'd make it up to her. He and Sherbourne would make it up to her, rather.

"You're sitting on a fortune in books, and you instead yoked yourself to debts you might have dispensed with years ago. The aristocracy is not right in the brainbox, Haverford. Simply not right. Was the prestige of having all these books gathering dust in your castle worth the burden of debt you carried? I cannot fathom such financial lunacy."

Sherbourne wasn't trying to be rude, he was genuinely bewildered.

"Safeguarding my family's legacy mattered and still does, but back to your charitable endeavor."

Sherbourne resumed his seat by the hearth. "I'm not given to charity, Haverford. You've surely noticed that much."

"You're about to change that lamentably narrow focus, Sherbourne, because the people in this valley do matter to you, because I've been assured you can be taught, and because you've offended my prospective duchess."

He sent Julian an exasperated look. "The lady with the earls, marquesses, dukes, and whatnot aiming their pistols at me?"

"The very one. My business affairs with you will sort themselves out soon enough, but when it comes to redeeming yourself in Elizabeth's eyes, I fear only one thing can save you."

Sherbourne studied his boots, which gleamed with a military shine in the brilliant Welsh sunlight. "I won't like this, will I?"

"I don't like making monthly payments to you. We do what we must to ensure the family name remains unblemished. A charitable endeavor will relieve you of ogre-at-large status, do some honest good, and safeguard you against any stray bullets, political or otherwise, fired by Elizabeth's large and magnificently influential family."

"Lunacy must be contagious, because I am yet in this library listening to a man who kept more than twenty thousand pounds worth of books simply for the pleasure of dusting them."

"Sherbourne, try to focus. Your situation merely calls for a sound plan, and your plan must involve a quantity of lending libraries."

Chapter Twenty-Three

The breeze was a perfect benevolence, the air scented with scythed clover and sea salt, and the only sound was the St. David pennant luffing gently a dozen yards away.

Elizabeth tied the string of the kite around one of the cannon at the corner of the parapets and took the bench where Haverford had embraced her so tenderly days ago.

"Are you saying good-bye?" Haverford stood by the carved door below her, holding two books.

"I am revisiting lovely memories. How did your meeting with Sherbourne go?"

Haverford came up the steps. "Sherbourne isn't an ogre, and he's developed a passion for lending libraries."

Great upheaval could unhinge even the stoutest minds. "Sit with me, and tell me what happened."

Haverford didn't sit. He stood beside the bench, gaze on the verdure stretching out from the castle in all directions.

He set the books on the dip in the crenellations, one thin volume, one very thick.

"May I show you something, Elizabeth?"

Elizabeth had seen the coachmen and grooms readying the vehicles by the carriage house, despite it being the Sabbath. Flocks grazed in their pastures, the occasional sea gull wheeled overhead.

"You could not show me anything lovelier than this view, Haverford. You really are quite right to defend your heritage."

"Stop that. Next you'll be regretting that you knocked sense into Sherbourne. He's building a mine."

The kite swooped by, a red dragon on a green and white field, reminiscent of the flag that had flown over the king's victory at Bosworth.

"I'm sorry," Elizabeth said, rising and slipping her arms around the duke. "You fought long and well, and I'm sorry."

He held her, his chin propped on her crown. "Sherbourne will be sorry soon. I made him agree to a list of conditions as long as my pedigree. No children working below the mine's surface, no women, half days on Saturday and Sundays free. I could have asked him to return the dower house and he would have agreed, he was so surprised to find a reasonable human being where an intransigent title had always stood."

"You're not intransigent." Though Julian was stubborn. Witness, his devotion to a lot of damned books nobody would ever read.

"Look there," he said, turning Elizabeth and pointing toward the sea. "Sherbourne thinks to develop a colliery over the lip of that hill. We won't even be able to see it, and he's assured me no ironworks will be built. I honestly think he's happy."

Elizabeth turned back into Julian's embrace. "Good for him, I suppose, but what of you? What of the debts and loans?"

The dragon swooped by again, then darted up into the sky and hung suspended at the end of its twine.

"Have I told you that I love you, Elizabeth?"

How would she ever, ever leave him? "Julian, you needn't—"

"I love you," he said, "and I respect my family's legacy, but I do not love those books, at least not most of them. I'm speaking to Andover about having an auction, and selling the curiosities, duplicates, and more fragile antiques. You are absolutely correct that books that just sit on the shelf are like unloved children. Glenys and Griffin are both well situated. It's time I found new homes for some of those books."

Julian spoke calmly, and yet, Elizabeth could feel the tension in him, the worry. His heart beat steadily beneath her cheek, and he hadn't asked her permission to sell the books, but her reply would matter to him.

"Of all your many virtues," she said, "your kindness, conscientiousness, graciousness, loyalty to your siblings and staff, your passion"—she kissed him—"I most admire your courage. Courage to hold fast against terrible odds, courage to let go. Courage to protect good traditions, courage to change the ones that no longer serve a purpose. Sell all of the books, Julian, and I will only love you more."

He sighed and the embrace became closer. They stood thus, wrapped in each other's arms, the sun beaming down, the dragon sailing above, until Julian stepped back and took Elizabeth's hand.

"Sherbourne has promised to purchase from me an inventory sufficient to stock a group of lending libraries.

He'll be grateful for your direction regarding how those institutions should be established and maintained."

Elizabeth sank to the bench. "*Sherbourne* is funding lending libraries? Lucas Sherbourne?"

"A dozen or so, though you'll have to guide him in the particulars."

A penniless duke had somehow arranged for the creation of a dozen lending libraries, which would be abundantly stocked from the shelves of one of the finest collections in the realm.

"This is a very devious plan, Haverford. I like it."

He came down beside her. "Thought you might. You never did choose a book from my library, Elizabeth, so I also took the liberty of choosing a pair of books for you."

A parting gift? Elizabeth's emotions were a muddle—she didn't want any blasted lending libraries if she couldn't have the duke who'd made them possible—but truly, Julian had managed the impossible.

"You need not give me anything more," she said. "I have memories, a beloved friend in you, and I'm hopeful that in time, given your rapprochement with Mr. Sherbourne, that our friendship might grow into something—"

He kissed her. "I love you, without limit or condition, but this polite balderdash doesn't become you half so much as hurling thunderbolts and righting the wrongs of the shire. This is my general ledger." He passed her the slim volume.

"I've seen it before."

"I usually keep it hidden under lock and key, but I want you to understand my situation, Elizabeth. I'm not wealthy, though I'll manage well enough. These debts are a large part of who I am."

"I don't care an acorn's worth about your debts, Julian."

She cared very much that forty-two coaches were lined up on the drive, that the Windham coaches were near the head of the queue.

"This is my family Bible—in Welsh, of course," he said, passing over the more substantial volume. "I would like to add your name to the succession of duchesses gracing the front pages. Will you marry me, Elizabeth? Will you live with me and put my castle to rights? Climb the occasional oak with me, and wander up Tudor Hill? Read to our children, call on Biddy and Griffin, drop in on Radnor, and possibly even tolerate Sherbourne at our table on occasion?"

He slid to one knee before her. "I want the good times and the difficult, the challenges and the triumphs. I have no plan for the rest of my life other than to love you, to be loved by you, and to face life together, come what may."

The Bible was a comforting weight in Elizabeth's lap, anchoring her to the bench when her spirits were flying aloft to cavort with the dragon. She put her arms around her duke, and drew him very close.

"Yes," she whispered in his ear. "Yes, I will be your wife, your duchess, your dragoness, and your love. Yes."

They remained on the parapets for much of the afternoon, laughing, loving, and hatching an occasional plan—Charlotte and Sherbourne had seemed to notice one another, after all—while above them, the dragon danced in the sunshine.

Epilogue

The wedding was small, St. George's being a modest edifice capable of holding little more than two hundred people.

Those who didn't attend the Duke of Haverford's nuptials consoled themselves by attending the Duchess of Haverford's library auction. The weather was lovely, Christie's was thronged, and everybody—everybody from royal princesses to academics to society couples looking to enhance their book collections—came to bid.

"One can hardly credit that my darling niece has organized this entire gathering," the Duke of Moreland observed.

Amid polite applause, the auctioneer knocked down an Elizabethan Bible to Lucas Sherbourne, who'd managed to bid enthusiastically but not aggressively.

"Your Grace forgets," Haverford replied. "My duchess has had the benefit of guidance from your duchess."

"Just so, and whomsoever Her Grace of Moreland

guides is bound for success. When did cloth of gold become suitable for the masculine daytime wardrobe?"

Moreland referred to Sherbourne's waistcoat. "Mr. Sherbourne has thrown himself into Elizabeth's lending library scheme with every appearance of good faith. Perhaps his waistcoat will attract others to the same cause."

Or blind them. Charlotte Windham, however, seemed determined to pretend her program fascinated her whenever Sherbourne chanced to look her way.

"His waistcoat could guide ships through dense fog," Moreland said. "Somebody should warn your friend Sherbourne that Her Grace of Quimbey will not accept defeat quietly."

Sherbourne had outbid the duchess on a Shakespeare quarto not thirty minutes ago.

Across the room, Elizabeth was whispering in her aunt's ear. Her Grace of Moreland had ensconced herself beside the Duke of Wellington, and among the bidders were more titles, nabobs, learned professors, and old fortunes than Haverford had ever seen assembled under one roof.

"There is no defeat here today, Moreland," Haverford said, as Hugh St. David and Radnor began brisk bidding for a second Welsh Bible. "There is only great enthusiasm for great literature. I'm finally coming to understand why my duchess is so passionate about her libraries."

"She's a Windham," Moreland scoffed. "Of course she's passionate."

Haverford allowed the older man his pride, in part because Moreland was right. Elizabeth had thrown herself into the management of Haverford Castle. She'd sorted the library collection into a family book treasury, lending library stock, and tomes intended for the auction, and the latter group was larger than the other two put together.

Elizabeth disentangled herself from her aunt and took the place at Haverford's side. "Uncle, you should bid on something."

Moreland set down his glass of punch. "Why don't I give that Sherbourne fellow a run for his money?"

"He has rather a lot of money," Elizabeth said. "I'd appreciate it if you chose one of the smaller items, something more pretty than valuable."

"A gift for a lady, perhaps?"

When Moreland smiled, he was the embodiment of familial benevolence. Sherbourne was about to lose a tidy sum, and that prospect always cheered Julian.

"Exactly," Elizabeth said, patting her uncle's arm. Moreland marched off, taking the seat beside Her Grace of Quimbey.

"Sherbourne's doomed," Haverford said. "Lovely thought. Hugh and Delphine seem besotted, and Radnor and Glenys are bidding on all the romantic poetry." Hugh and Delphine sat nearly in each other's laps, and Radnor and Glenys had exchanged a half-dozen kisses blown across the auction hall.

Romantic devotion apparently inspired the ardor of bibliophiles, for the bidding had galloped along all afternoon.

Elizabeth wound her arm through Haverford's. She did this—touched him frequently and affectionately in public—and the pleasure of that, the soul-deep joy of being openly acknowledged as her spouse—had repaired something in Haverford's heart he still couldn't find words for.

"There's hope for Mr. Sherbourne," she said. "His democratic inclinations seem to be rooted in genuine respect for the common man."

To blazes with Sherbourne. Haverford leaned closer to his wife. "How are you, Elizabeth?"

"I'll be ready for a nap when this is over. One worried."

One should not have. The bidding was enthusiastic and the gathering impressive. "I am ever prepared to join my duchess for a nap. Her health and happiness are my greatest concern."

And what a pleasure that was, to have sorted endless responsibilities and duties into a hierarchy that brought meaning and joy to Haverford's days—and nights. As long as Elizabeth was happy and happy with him, the rest of his ducal tasks and obligations were manageable.

The best plans were, indeed, the simplest, and guided always by love.

Thus far, Elizabeth had seemed very pleased to be his duchess. She'd taken on the challenge of running the castle, dragged her duke about on social calls, found a governess for Charity who could also tutor Griffin in English, and supervised Sherbourne's lending libraries charity.

"Haverford, Uncle Percy is starting a bidding war."

Starting wars was probably Uncle Percy's idea of a hobby, for Moreland provoked two more bidding wars before the afternoon was gone. Haverford could not keep a tally of the sums earned, but he never lost sight of his wife. She was gracious, lovely, good-natured, and brilliant at managing a crowd.

No other duke could possibly be as happy as Haverford, for no other duke had Elizabeth for his duchess.

"Come with me," he said, taking Elizabeth by the hand when the last of the items—a first edition of Mr. Burns's poems—had been knocked down.

"Where are we going?"

"To bed, madam."

"One does delight in your sense of ducal command, Haverford, but our guests—"

"Will be more than adequately congratulated and thanked by your family. Your auction was a triumph, Your Grace, and now you will rest."

He led her not to the street, but to the mews, where his town coach stood waiting.

"Haverford, you will please tell John Coachman to take the long way home."

"My dear, we're three streets over from the townhouse." He didn't need to finish the thought: Marital bliss in a moving coach was all well and good—had been well and good on several occasions—but a ducal bed had its charms as well.

"Very well," Elizabeth said, climbing into the coach. "I bow to your greater sense of comfort, if not your greater restraint."

This time. She'd accost him tomorrow when he was at his ledgers or practicing his guitar. Elizabeth excelled at the art of the conjugal ambush.

"I heard Andover trying to talk you into making this auction an annual event," Haverford said, when he and Elizabeth were settled on the forward-facing seat.

"One cannot think that far ahead," Elizabeth replied, yawning. "Today was successful in significant part because Her Grace of Moreland lent her cachet."

"And because you knew exactly which offerings would draw the book lovers into the bright light of day, coin purses clutched in their shy little fists."

Elizabeth's hand was clutched in Haverford's not-so-little fist. Holding hands had already become a habit, as had kissing each other in greating and parting.

"Her Grace of Moreland has lent her cachet in another direction," Elizabeth said.

Fatigue was stealing over Haverford now that he was

private with his duchess. He'd been worrying about her for weeks in anticipation of this auction, while she'd been worrying about every detail of the undertaking.

"She's a Windham," he said. "Her Grace will find mischief to get up to, but because she's a duchess, we'll call it lending her cachet."

Elizabeth kissed him. "You are such a quick study, but I think you'll approve of Aunt's latest project. I saw her introducing Mr. Sherbourne to no less than a viscount, an earl, and a dowager duchess."

Sherbourne? "*He's* Her Grace's next project?"

"One can't be certain. He was looking a bit dazed, though bearing up under the strain."

"One does, when Her Grace of Moreland is fixed on an objective." And Elizabeth would be just like her aunt, if Haverford were lucky.

"Elizabeth?"

"Hmm?" She already sounded sleepy.

"Thank you. For everything."

"You're welcome. Thank you too, Julian. I am the happiest duchess in the realm."

Haverford devoted the ensuing weeks, months, years, and decades to ensuring she remained ever thus. The task was made easy by the fact that Elizabeth was determined on a reciprocal challenge, and thus Their Graces of Haverford eventually became known by their affectionate friends, family, and even neighbors, as the Duke and Duchess of Happiness.

Keep reading for a peek at
Charlotte's story in

A ROGUE OF HER OWN

Available Spring 2018

Chapter One

"Heed me, Miss Charlotte, for you won't be getting other offers, no matter that your uncle is a duke. I am a viscount, and you shall like being my viscountess very well."

Charlotte Windham had no choice but to *heed* Viscount Neederby, for he was nearly dragging her along Lady Belchamp's wilderness walk by the arm.

"My lord, while I am ever receptive to knowledgeable guidance, this is not the time or the place to make a declaration." Never and nowhere suited Charlotte when it came to proposals from such as Neederby.

He marched onward nonetheless, walking and pontificating at the same time being one of his few accomplishments.

"I must beg to differ, my dear, for receptive to guidance you most assuredly are not. Married to me, your sadly headstrong propensities would be a thing of the past. It will be my duty and pleasure as your devoted spouse to instruct you in all matters."

He sent her a look, one intended to convey tender indulgence or a disturbance of the bowels. Charlotte wasn't sure which.

"Might we circle back toward the buffet, your lordship? All this hiking about has left me with an appetite."

Neederby finally came to a halt, though he'd chosen a spot overlooking the Thames. What imbecile had decided that scenic views were a mandatory improvement on Nature as the Almighty had designed her?

"Were you being arch, Miss Charlotte? I believe you were. I have appetites too, dontcha know."

Neederby fancied himself a Corinthian. Hostesses added him to guest lists because he had a title, and had yet to lose either his hair or his teeth in any quantity. In Charlotte's estimation, his brains had gone missing entirely.

"I haven't an arch bone in my body, your lordship. I am, however, hungry." The occasion was a Venetian breakfast, and Charlotte had intended to do justice to the lavish buffet.

Her belly was roiling, though, at the sound of the water rushing by more than ten yards below the iron balustrade along Lady Belchamp's walkway.

"One hears things," Neederby said, wiggling his eyebrows. "About *certain* people."

Charlotte heard the river roaring below and tried to edge back from the overlook. "I have no interest in gossip, sir, though a plate of Lady Belchamp's buffet offerings has great appeal."

His lordship refused to budge and clamped a gloved hand over Charlotte's fingers. "What about *my* offerings? I'm tireless in the saddle, as they say, and you're in want of a fellow to show you the *bridal* path, as it were."

Equestrian analogies never led anywhere decent. Charlotte

escaped Neederby's grasp by twisting her arm, a move her cousins had shown her more than ten years ago.

"I'm famished, your lordship, though I'd enjoy a morning hack in proper company someday next spring, if you happen to be back in London. At present, we can return to the buffet, or I'll leave you here to admire the view."

Either way, the gossips would add to their store of ammunition. Charlotte had taken too long on this ramble with his lordship, or she'd returned to the party without his escort, both choices unacceptable for a lady.

As the only remaining unmarried Windham, Charlotte had earned the enmity of every wallflower, failed debutante, matchmaker, or fortune hunter in Mayfair. The little season brought the wilted and the wounded out in quantity, while Charlotte—who considered herself neither—longed to retire to the country on the next available coach.

Neederby moved more quickly than he reasoned, and thus Charlotte found herself between him and the railing.

"When anybody's looking," he said, "you're all haughty airs and tidy bows, but I know what you fast girls really want. Married to me, you'd be more than content."

Married to him, Charlotte would be a candidate for Bedlam. "I need breakfast, you buffoon, and I haven't been a girl for years. Get away from me."

Charlotte also needed room to drive her knee into his jewelbox, and she needed to breathe.

Neederby took a step closer, and Charlotte backed up until the railing was all that prevented her from falling into the torrent below. Her vision began to dim at the edges and the roaring in her ears merged with the noise of the river.

Not now. Please, not here, not now, not with the biggest nincompoop in all of nincompoopdom strutting and spouting marital ambitions at my side.

The thought had barely formed when Neederby was abruptly dragged three feet to the right.

"Sherbourne," his lordship squawked. "Devilish bad taste to interrupt a man when he's paying his addresses."

Lucas Sherbourne was tall, blond, solidly built, and at that moment, a pathetically welcome sight.

"If that's your idea of paying your addresses," Sherbourne said, "then I'd like to introduce you to my version of target practice at dawn."

ABOUT THE AUTHOR

Grace Burrowes grew up in central Pennsylvania and is the sixth out of seven children. She discovered romance novels when in junior high (back when there was such a thing), and has been reading them voraciously ever since. Grace has a bachelor's degree in political science, a bachelor of music in music history (both from the Pennsylvania State University); a master's degree in conflict transformation from Eastern Mennonite University; and a juris doctor from the National Law Center at the George Washington University.

Grace writes Georgian, Regency, Scottish Victorian, and contemporary romances in both novella and novel lengths. She's a member of Romance Writers of America, and enjoys giving workshops and speaking at writers' conferences. She also loves to hear from her readers, and can be reached through her website, graceburrowes.com.

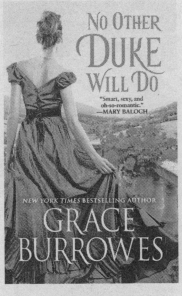

NO OTHER DUKE WILL DO
By Grace Burrowes

From Grace Burrowes comes the next installment in the *New York Times* bestselling Windham Brides series! It's the house party of the decade, and everyone is looking for a spouse—especially Julian St. David, Duke of Haverford. The moment he meets Elizabeth Windham, their attraction is overwhelming, unexpected…and absolutely impossible. With meddling siblings, the threat of financial ruin, and gossips lurking behind every potted palm, will they find true love or true disaster?

Fall in Love with Forever Romance

ALWAYS YOU
By Denise Grover Swank

Matt Osborn had no idea coaching his five-year-old nephew's soccer team would get him so much attention from the mothers—attention he doesn't want now that he's given up on love and having a family of his own. Yep, Matt's the last of his bachelor buddies, and plans on staying that way. That is, until he finds himself face-to-face with the woman who broke his heart. The latest from *USA Today* bestselling author Denise Grover Swank is a winner!

Fall in Love with Forever Romance

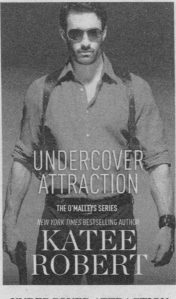

UNDERCOVER ATTRACTION
By Katee Robert

New York Times and *USA Today* bestselling author Katee Robert continues her smoking-hot O'Malleys series. Ex-cop Charlotte Finch used to think there was a clear line between right and wrong. Then her fellow officers betrayed her, and the world is no longer so black and white. Especially when it's Aiden O'Malley, one of the most dangerous men in Boston, who offers her a chance for justice. The only catch: She'll have to pretend to be his fiancée for his plan to work.

Fall in Love with Forever Romance

THE BACHELOR CONTRACT
By Rachel Van Dyken

Brant Wellington could have spent the rest of his life living under the magical spell of alcohol, women, and forgetting his problems. That is, until a certain bachelor auction forces him back on the family payroll and off to assess one of the Wellington resorts. Only no one warned him that his past would be there waiting for him...Don't miss the newest book from #1 *New York Times* bestselling author Rachel Van Dyken!

WICKED INTENTIONS
By Elizabeth Hoyt

Don't miss *Wicked Intentions*, the *New York Times* bestseller that started Elizabeth Hoyt's classic Maiden Lane series!

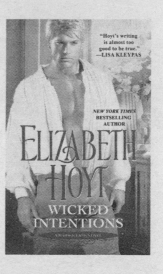